COFFEE TEA THE CHEF & ME

CAROLINE JAMES

RANJAM PUBLISHING COMPANY

COFFEE TEA THE CHEF & ME

By
Caroline James

This book was previously published as
So, You Think You're A Celebrity...Chef?

All Rights Reserved under the Copyright, Designs and Patents Act, 1988.
The moral right of the author has been asserted.

Copyright © Caroline James 2013

No part of this publication may be reproduced, copied, stored in a retrieval system, or transmitted, in any form or by any means, without the prior written consent of the copyright holder, nor be otherwise circulated in any form of binding or cover other than that in which it is published and without a similar condition being imposed on the subsequent purchaser.

Disclaimer

All characters, institutions, organisations and events in this novel, other than those clearly in the public domain, are fictitious and any resemblance to any actual institution, organisation or person, living or dead, is purely coincidental.

Cover Design

Alli Smith

Second Edition Published by Ramjam Publishing 2015
ISBN 978-0-9573782-7-8

A CIP catalogue record for this title is available from the British Library.

DEDICATION

For Jamie, my inspiration

With love

IN THE BEGINNING...

Hilary Hargreaves stared at the dishevelled chef. She removed her tortoiseshell glasses and leaned forward to peer at his face. Was that cocaine on his nose, or had he been snorting icing sugar whilst dusting his fairy cakes that morning? She tapped her pen against the palm of her hand and considered giving him a good spanking, but he'd either like it, or have her up on an abuse charge.

Hilary leaned forward and asked, "So, Chef, you think you're a celebrity?"

The chef began to babble about his dexterity in the kitchen and that all his family and friends thought he'd be wonderful on a TV show. He'd got through to the final round in a baking competition and was convinced that he could go far.

Hilary listened patiently and assured the chef that the agency would consider his application and be in touch in due course. She watched the retreating figure as he left her office then reached into the top drawer of her desk, where the ice-blue glass of a bottle of Bombay Sapphire gin twinkled invitingly. She poured herself a bracer and thought about the chef. Surely she was getting too old for all this? Hilary sighed as the alcohol hit her bloodstream and began to soothe her nerves.

Another day in paradise at Hargreaves Promotions.

1

Hilary slammed the door of the black cab and muttered crossly at the driver. He'd been pleasant when she'd flagged him down in Wardour Street and it was a relief to fall into the back of the taxi to get out of the rain, but when he realised that her destination was only five minutes away, his attitude changed. Hilary closed her purse and buried it deep in a pocket of her Coach Kensington briefcase. He certainly wasn't getting a tip.

It was bucketing down and Hilary tightened the belt on her trench coat then pushed through the bedraggled hordes all heading for sanctuary in the covered markets of Covent Garden. She reached a discreet doorway, where a simple plaque announced the entrance of the legendary Rancher's Restaurant – a theatrical nirvana for serious A-listers and media moguls. She shook the rain off her shoulders and secured a comb in the pleat of hair at the nape of her neck.

The commissionaire, who held the door ajar, admired Hilary's style in her beloved vintage clothing. He smiled as she skipped past and headed down the dimly lit stairway to the restaurant's reception desk.

Joe, the Maître d', greeted her. "Hi, Miss Hargreaves," he said, "sure is wet out there today." Joe hailed from Bromsgrove but led his London life with a strong American accent, and as he took Hilary's coat a cloakroom girl stepped forward and carefully hung it on a padded hanger.

"You can say that again, Joe," Hilary replied and looked around the room – a New York-style interior, with exposed brick and dark wood, plastered with show posters and photographs. There was a buzz of chattering media luvvies, which was periodically broken when new arrivals appeared and bravely took a seat at tables allocated in order of importance.

Joe guided Hilary to a raised centre booth that overlooked the room. "Your usual?" he asked.

"Make it a large one," Hilary said and smiled as she sucked her stomach in and eased into the booth. She reached into her briefcase and pulled out a moleskin note book, fountain pen and ancient ivory spectacle case and placed them on the linen cloth. Her fingers brushed a packet of menthol cigarettes and sighing, Hilary silently cursed the day smoking was banned from all public places.

Joe appeared with her drink on a silver tray and made a display of twirling it, before carefully depositing the drink beside her. Condensation ran down the side of the glass and sparkled invitingly. Hilary took a long swig. Heaven! Bombay Gin with a dash of tonic and a good squeeze of fresh lime over several chunks of ice. The cold alcohol hit her veins and Hilary relaxed.

"Thanks, Joe," she said. Hilary flicked open her spectacle case and pushed a pair of bronze glasses along the bridge of her nose. Pink rhinestones twinkled along the brow line of the aluminium frame. "What's on the special today?"

"Every day's special for you, Miss Hargreaves." Joe fussed around the place settings. Immaculate as ever in a smart waistcoat and black tie, his gold tooth glinted as he beamed at his favourite client, who was an agent to some of the most high profile chefs in the business. He wouldn't need a waiter's pad for Hilary's order – she would ruminate over the menu and ask for the specials board but always chose the same dish: corn-fed chicken breast with roasted vegetable hash.

Hilary glanced at her watch, her client was late.

∽

ZELDA MARTIN FLICKED through her iPhone contacts and found Hilary's number. She tapped out a text apology. If the traffic didn't move soon she was going to be horribly late and her agent would have a fit. The lunch meeting must be important – Zelda was rarely summoned to Rancher's. The only other occasions had been to sign her contract when she joined Hargreaves Promotions and to celebrate a two-book deal a year later.

Zelda flicked her long blonde hair off her shoulders and stared out of the window. They were crossing Chelsea Bridge and would soon be on the North Bank; with any luck she'd make it in twenty minutes. Her animal print Sonia Rykiel jacket was very tight and Zelda stroked the buttons. She'd managed to lose ten pounds in Portugal, thanks to Daddy who'd sent a chef over. The chef had devised a detox diet and Zelda had rigidly adhered to it. Harry, her partner, said she looked marvellous and as slim as the day they met but Zelda knew that wasn't true – she was thirty pounds heavier, but at least she was losing weight. Hilary would scrutinise every inch and God help Zelda if Hilary wasn't happy with what she saw.

∽

"SAME AGAIN?" Joe picked up Hilary's empty glass.

"Yes please, Joe. I'll be back in a couple of minutes." Hilary grabbed her bag and eased herself off the banquette. Her mobile bleeped persistently.

At the top of the stairs, the commissionaire opened the door and Hilary stood in the porch. She pushed a cigarette into a cabriole holder and he produced a lighter from the depths of his pinstriped pockets. Hilary dragged deeply and sighed with satisfaction as the menthol and nicotine hit her veins.

A text from Zelda announced traffic delays in Battersea, ETA –

five minutes. That would be a first! Hilary thought sarcastically; her patience had run very thin with this particular client...

~

Zelda was barely out of university when Hilary had discovered her at an in-store cookery demonstration in Oxford Street, helping a chef who was a household name.

The demo wasn't going well. The chef was slurring over the sushi and looked set to slice his fingers into a fricassee, when Hilary took a call from the hysterical store manager.

"He's as pissed as a fart and about to set the smoke alarms off!" he'd screamed into her ear. "DO something!"

The CEO of the famous store was due to open the new food hall in approximately thirty minutes and the manager was panic-stricken. Hilary listened patiently and gently asked if Chef had an assistant. Having established that he did, she calmly instructed the manager to put the assistant on stage to do the demonstration, get security to remove Chef and she'd be there in a jiffy. Hilary raced out of her office in Soho and grabbed her assistant's bicycle from the stairwell, there was no time for a taxi and pedal power might just save the day. She'd don a pinafore and pitch in if she had to, it wouldn't be the first time!

Hilary took her life in her hands as she flew round Piccadilly and lunged along Regent Street, cutting through the back roads and veering perilously up one-way streets. She hoisted the skirt of her 1950s knitted suit, and as her stocking-tops flashed she ignored the wolf-whistles from a group of builders in New Bond Street. She screeched to a halt at precisely ten minutes after ten and thrust the bike in the foyer of the department store and hurled herself into the food hall, where a pretty blonde creature stood on stage, cooking prawns in a spiced chilli sauce as she chatted to an animated audience of press and shoppers.

She was a natural.

At the front of the crowd the CEO was mesmerised. Hilary closed her eyes and mumbled thanks to the Great Kitchen Creator, or whatever higher deity had saved her day. As the demo ended, Hilary watched the blonde air-kiss the CEO and wave him happily on his way.

The store manager beamed and flung his arms round her. "Hilary, darling, who's the sexy Sloane slaving over the hot stove – says her name is Zelda?" He glanced at Hilary's hair and pulled a face. "Is it windy outside?" Hilary's normally immaculate French pleat had tumbled out of its comb and stood at right angles.

It later transpired that the CEO had schooled at Uppingham with Daddy and Chef knew Mummy, so Zelda had thought it might be jolly fun to assist Chef for a day. In her gap year in Indonesia she'd done a bit of cooking, and on her return Mummy thought a spell at Ballymagee, the famous Irish cookery school for the seriously well-heeled, might teach Zelda a few dinner party tricks and thus entice a double-barrel in the marriage stakes.

Hilary smelt talent and signed her on the spot.

There was a gap in the market for student cooking and Zelda had been able to fill it. The CEO was easily convinced that a range of student starter-packs would sell, and with Zelda's pretty face on the wrapping, they flew off the shelves in home-wares throughout the country. The first book deal, The Only Student Cookbook, became an international bestseller. Upwardly Mobile Meals followed and Zelda appeared at food festivals and events throughout the country. She cooked her way through several guest slots on forgettable TV shows and became a minor celebrity. Hilary was pleased that her hunch had paid off.

Then Zelda met Harry Revill-Mackintosh.

Something-in-the-city-with-Daddy, Harry had a split-parting and a Hugh Grant accent and Zelda was smitten. Cosied up in their love nest in Notting Hill, Zelda let things slip. Her weight ballooned and the camera was no longer kind, she was late on set and always had an excuse.

The work dried up. One had to be reliable in this business and competition was fierce. Hilary was tired of Zelda but conscious of a depleted revenue stream and knew that unless she pulled off something enticing soon, her client would disappear down the aisle and be popping out mini Harrys annually.

Then the script for The Zimmers appeared on Hilary's desk.

It was a proposal for daytime TV – to entertain the baby-boomer fifty-pluses. The Zimmers set out to bridge the generation gap between disaffected teens, who lived on junk food, and old codgers whom no one listened to any more. Taking traditional recipes, a savvy young cook would get youngsters off fast-food and sit them round the table to break bread with an older generation, thus making food from the past "cool". Zelda had auditioned for the role of cook and, to Hilary's astonishment, was offered the position. Zelda and The Zimmers had been commissioned for an hour long, four-part series on prime-time TV. Hilary was sure that having a name like Zelda had clinched the deal; quite how the young Sloane would blend with jellied eels in Peckham and lobby in Liverpool remained to be seen. Today was the day to break the glad tidings, and Hilary hoped that Zelda's sojourn to Daddy's pad in Portugal had done the trick and a considerably reduced Zelda would appear at any moment.

She finished her cigarette and returned to the restaurant.

"Your guest is here, Miss Hargreaves," Joe said and held back a chair. Zelda gushed through the restaurant and threw herself onto the banquette opposite Hilary.

"Zelda, darling!" Hilary said. "You're late, come and sit down." She patted the seat beside her, then removed her glasses and studied her client. Zelda's jacket didn't meet and her face was puffy. "And how was Portugal?"

Zelda batted her eyelashes and set her pretty blue eyes on Hilary. She was a beautiful girl despite her puffy face. She wriggled elegant fingers and Pandora and Tiffany bracelets jingled as she spoke.

"It was super! Daddy's chef is a dream and I've lost weight, I feel rested and happy and ready for a new project."

Zelda smiled at Joe, his gold tooth glinted as he smiled back. He popped the cork on a bottle of champagne.

"Well, that's good to hear. You'll need to be at the top of your game." Hilary handed Zelda a glass and grinned. "I'm delighted to tell you that you've landed The Zimmers!"

Zelda squealed with joy and they chinked glasses. Joe hovered by the table with menus but Hilary waved him away.

"My usual please, Joe, and Zelda will have a tuna salad with no dressing." Hilary downed her drink and smiled at her client. "Cheers," she said, "to Zelda and The Zimmers!"

2

Bob twirled on the ancient office chair; the leather was cracked and his long fingers picked at the edges as he stared out of the sash window. Like his boss, everything was vintage in the office.

He thought about Hilary and sighed as the chair creaked and groaned under his weight, not that his weight was a problem – he'd lost pounds since his trip to Tibet, and his work suits hung off him. He'd found the outrageous Ozwald Boateng get-up, that he sported today, in a charity shop in Chipping Hodbury two days ago. It was bright orange and Bob loved it. The suit's tailored lines fitted his new streamlined physique perfectly and he'd teamed it with a black t-shirt. He was pleased with his appearance, it was essential to keep up with the procession of designer clad talent that frequented the office. He rolled back a cuff and pushed it up his tanned arm, where brown leather bracelets jostled beside a string of prayer beads wound tightly around his wrist.

Bob stroked the smooth droplets and closed his eyes. His mind swam with images as he transported himself back to the magical mountains in Tibet. Colourful and frayed prayer bunting fluttered in the warm Tibetan breeze and he visualised himself kneeling by a pile of smooth stones as he added his own to the top and chanted thanks to his God for bringing him safely to the mountains.

He leaned back and repeated the soothing chants, letting his mind focus on his inner core and with each deep breath, felt calm and safe as he began to drift into the safety of his inner mental sanctum...

∽

HILARY PRESSED a security code onto a keypad. It buzzed and she pushed the front door to her office open and entered, then flicked it closed with her kitten heel pump and climbed the stairs. Her footing was cushioned by the soft red pile of an expensive carpet. Bob had assured her that red was a good feng shui colour – associated with romance, wealth and happiness. Hilary sighed and wondered why she put up with his nonsense.

The foyer of Hargreaves Promotions was deserted and Hilary cursed as she swept past Lottie's cluttered desk. The girl was nowhere to be seen and the switchboard lights flickered like traffic lights as they remained unanswered. A curious sound emanated from Bob's office, the drone was low-pitched and sounded painful. Hilary peered through the frosted glass on the panel door then thrust the door open.

"Good grief, Bob, have you been tangoed?" Hilary planted herself in the doorway and stared at her assistant in his vivid outfit. He was all beads, bangles and Buddha since he'd come back from Tibet and Hilary's patience was wearing thin. "Where in God's name did you get that suit?" she asked. "You look like a space hopper!"

Bob ignored his boss. He kept his eyes closed and fondled the prayer beads. "Go away, Hilary," he said quietly. "It's my lunch break."

"No, it isn't," Hilary said. "It's three o'clock in the afternoon and this place is like the Marie Celeste. Where's Lottie?"

Bob tucked himself under the worn leather top of his mahogany desk and folded his arms. "She's gone to get a panini," he replied.

"We've never stopped all day and I shall faint if I don't get some carbs."

Hilary stared at a book on Bob's desk – My Spiritual Journey, Dalai Lama. He leaned forward and stroked the cover protectively.

"Goolanga," Hilary muttered. "Aren't you a little old for all this Hari Krishna nonsense?"

"Don't knock something you know nothing about," Bob said and gazed fondly at his hero's image.

"I know that my office has ground to a complete standstill the moment I step out for a quick meeting." Hilary tapped her elegant 1950s suede shoe'd foot. "Go and answer the phones please, then make us both an espresso. I want to hear all about the literary festival in the Cotswolds." She turned to leave but called over her shoulder, "When you're quite sure that your chakras are where they should be and you're ready to do some work…"

Bob screwed his eyes up and let out a hiss between clenched teeth as he watched Hilary retreat. He glanced at the clock on the wall – Hilary's "quick meeting" had been the best part of four hours. Bob stroked his beads and breathed through his nose and filled his lungs with air, then exhaled slowly. He'd give Hilary five minutes then brace himself for her interrogation.

He closed his eyes again and thought about the weekend. It had been awash with literary luvvies who'd flocked to the annual festival. Hilary had insisted that he chaperone one of their clients, Prunella Gray, who was appearing at the festival to talk about her recently published autobiography. The festival was set in Chipping Hodbury, a quintessential English town in the heart of affluent middle England. Pretty limestone buildings, adorned with flowering window boxes, lined the high street which led to a double-arched bridge where the River Hod meandered beneath. Chipping Hodbury Theatre was surrounded by tall weeping willows and gracious lawns which swept down to the banks of the river where ducks and geese waddled about, searching for scraps of discarded sandwiches whilst the literary crowd sipped chilled white wine and picnicked in the glorious sunshine.

Bob thought about the dashing compere, Anthony Merryweather, who'd watched their arrival and rushed down the theatre steps to open the door of their courtesy car and greet them. He welcomed them to the festival then swept Prunella away to prepare for her audience. After several drinks backstage, Anthony and Bob exchanged numbers and the weekend suddenly brightened for Bob.

Prunella had given a riveting talk and left the stage to a standing ovation. Enthralled fans hung onto her every word as she embroiled her life story and described the many perils she'd encountered in the kitchens of well-known establishments during her career progression. Prunella was an established household name in the world of food and drink and her warts-and-all autobiography looked set to be a best seller. She had Hilary to thank for her success but "thanks" was a swear word to Prunella Gray and she'd been ruthless in her climb to the top. Bob had strict instructions to stay with her all weekend and Hilary's warnings rung in his ears – Prunella was not to be left alone, especially with journalists!

It had been exhausting as Prunella had a rampant appetite for vodka. She was known as the Poison Dwarf in culinary circles and, in Bob's opinion, was an absolute bitch. He'd seen chefs freeze like snared prey and jack-knife away to avoid her at restaurant openings and media events, where she tracked her victims. Her sweet little face peered out from a heavy dark fringe and reminded Bob of the Bette Davis film What Ever Happened to Baby Jane. Baby Jane was most definitely alive and well and lived in a town house in Queen's Park, where he'd deposited a drunken Prunella in a heap on Sunday evening.

Bob smiled as he remembered that he was meeting Anthony the following evening at a restaurant called Dabbous. He couldn't wait to drop this in to Hilary – there was a long waiting list for a table but Anthony knew the manager and had procured a table for eight o'clock.

A tapping sound startled Bob.

Lottie, the company receptionist, pushed open the door with her pert bottom. Her size three feet, daintily encased in pink pumps, danced into the room. She balanced a plate of prawn filled panini in one hand and a mug of peppermint tea in the other and teetered over to Bob's desk.

"You've got two minutes to eat this. Hilary is on the war-path and wants you in her office pronto." Lottie shook her tousled hair and adjusted a polka-dot bandana. "Prunella's been on the phone," Lottie continued. "She says you abandoned her all weekend and copped off with a compere as camp as Christmas, then left her to her own devices."

Bob spat out several prawns. He gazed at Lottie with saucer-like eyes. "Shite!" he mumbled.

"That's not very Dalai Lama – you'd better say a few chants before you go in." Lottie wandered away to her desk in reception. She slipped a head-set on and began to take calls on the pulsating switchboard.

"Hargreaves Promotions. How may I help you today?"

~

HILARY HEAPED two spoons of sugar into her espresso and stirred the hot brown liquid. There was a pile of paperwork on her desk and the inbox on her email was full. She sipped her coffee and thought about her clients. They were all like egotistical children and the higher they climbed, the more demanding they became. She felt that her role of agent was often confused with therapist, mother, solicitor and bank manager. They thought little of loading her with their problems and she would wave her magic wand and make it all get better, after all wasn't that what they paid her a hefty percentage of their income to do? To make them successful and line the route with a soft cushion of permission, enabling them to behave in just about any manner they chose, secure in the knowledge that good old Hilary would always have their back.

She flipped open a compact and studied her lips in the mirror, then applied a thick layer of waxy red gloss before running her tongue over her teeth and smiling. Good job there's life in the old dog... Hilary thought to herself and snapped the compact closed. She leaned forward and pressed the intercom.

"Lottie, tell Bob to get his backside in here."

She hi-lighted a page on her computer screen and scanned the news. A headline read: POP GOES PRUNELLA! Hilary winced. The red-top screamed the words alongside a photo of an inebriated, Prunella Gray, clutching a bottle of soda as she fell out of the Chipping Hodbury Arms in the early hours on Sunday. Hilary tapped a pencil on the desk and pursed her lips. She looked up as Bob eased himself around the door frame and melted into the chair opposite her desk.

Hilary continued to tap.

"The reviews are very good for Prunella's book..." Bob began.

Hilary's glacial stare pierced Bob's faltering confidence and as he began to sink lower into the ancient leather, a spring caught his left buttock.

"Ouch!" he squirmed. "Are you ever going to get some decent furniture in this decrepit building?" He rubbed his skin and glowered at Hilary.

"Something needs to wake you up! You clearly had an early night on Saturday." She turned the screen towards Bob and watched him colour as he read the article. "I quite specifically gave you the strictest instructions never to leave Prunella's side, even if she was taking a pee or shagging a vicar, and what did you do?" Hilary leaned forward and waved her pencil in Bob's face. "You hot foot it away, with Anthony bleedin' Merryweather – the biggest gossip on the literary circuit. No doubt you're going to tell me that Baby Jane was safely tucked up in bed with a hot water bottle, when you decided to venture into the sleaze halls of Chipping Hodbury?"

Bob raised his eyebrows. He was about to retaliate but realised it was useless: Hilary was on a rant and nothing would stop it. He wouldn't have called Anthony's charming Grade Two listed town house a sleaze hall, but he couldn't get a word in.

"You should have slept across her bedroom door..." Hilary continued. She put her pencil down and knocked back the dregs of her coffee. "Anyway, it hasn't done any harm." Hilary relaxed. "The publishers have just ordered another ten thousand copies – the book is flying off the shelves." She gave Bob a smile. "Prunella is speaking at the Chefs' Forum AGM tomorrow so make sure you're suited and booted and ready to pick her up at six o'clock, preferably not in that suit." Hilary grimaced.

"I can't!" Bob wailed. "I'm having dinner at Dabbous with Anthony!"

Hilary's eyes lit up.

"Dabbous?" she said. "How wonderful – tell Anthony I'll meet him there at eight o'clock, it's time we had a catch up."

Bob sighed. It was no use arguing. He reached for his beads and silently uttered a calming chant.

The door bust open and Lottie flung herself into the room.

"Hilary, Lenny Crispin, that chef from Ireland, is on the phone again and says he simply has to speak to you," Lottie gushed.

"Tell him I'm busy."

"But he phones at least six times a day and says he will turn up on the doorstep if I don't put him through."

"Lottie, do you like working here?" Hilary stared at her receptionist. Lottie had begun to nervously twist the bangle on her wrist.

"You know I do, Hilary, but... well, it's hard to say no – he's so persistent!"

"If I spoke to every caller who thinks that getting through one round of their local bakery competition makes them the next Gordon Ramsey, it would be like a football match in here. Now go and tell him to put his details on an email – to Bob. And I'll have another espresso while you're fannying about." Hilary reached for a folder off the top of the pile of paperwork.

"Do you still need me?" Bob asked.

"We're done," Hilary said.

She didn't look up as Bob rose to his feet. He pulled a face and stuck his tongue out before retreating from her inner sanctum.

3

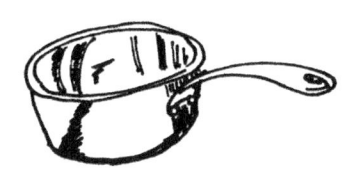

Zelda stood in her Poggenpohl kitchen and stared at the ingredients on the chopping board. Her knife was poised above a large piece of stewing steak and Zelda shuddered as she noted the thick layer of yellowing fat surrounding the meat. She puffed out her lips and sighed heavily, then began to cut the foul looking object into small cubes.

The previous day she had met with the researcher and producer from The Zimmers and although she would have a home economist from the catering facility on the set to prepare the dishes when filming, she'd been encouraged to try the recipes at home, to get "the feel of things."

Zelda felt sick. The cheapest cut of meat she normally handled was prime fillet steak and the components of today's recipe, Scouse, were in her opinion, utterly vile. She placed the meat in an oven dish and scattered a handful of pearl barley over the top. It reminded her of feeding the pigeons in St Mark's Square in Venice when Harry had whisked her off for a romantic weekend; surely people didn't eat these miniature pebbles? She continued to chop carrots and celery and thought about the new series. Filming began in two weeks and the first stop was Liverpool, where she would meet an old couple who lived in a place called Toxteth. They would be joined by a group of teenagers to chat about what they ate and budgets, then they'd all eat a hearty dish of Scouse. Harry told her that she would get along fine with everyone; he said she was a people person and assured her that the folk in the north would love her. After all, he said, look how well she got on with everyone at the Hurlingham Club – all ages and occupations, from city bankers to doctors and designers.

Zelda wasn't so sure. The series was unscripted and although Hilary had assured Zelda that she would be given a very clear brief and told what to say, Zelda was beginning to panic. What if these people lived on a council estate? She'd never been within a fifty mile radius of such place and hadn't a clue what to talk about, at least food would unite them. Surely she couldn't go wrong if she told them about her favourite recipes and maybe cooked a couple, and they could always talk about clothes – there had to be designer shops in Liverpool, didn't everyone like a label?

Feeling considerably cheered, Zelda lifted the dish into the oven, set the timer and poured herself a large glass of scrummy Chablis. She was supposed to be sticking to the Herbalife diet this week but one glass wouldn't make any difference, it was liquid after all. She'd have a lovely bath with some of that new bath foam from Champneys – Distant Shores – it might help her get into her part, Toxteth certainly felt like a very distant shore from where she was standing. She could even have one of those heavenly Harrods chocolates that Daddy had sent over. Zelda smiled and pushed the kitchen debris to one side. Carmalita could sort that all out when she came into clean today.

Zelda flicked her long blonde locks over her shoulder and ambled through to the master bedroom. There, she ran hot water into the huge roll-top bath that stood under a floor-to-ceiling window overlooking the immaculate private gardens beneath. She sighed with satisfaction and popped a chocolate into her mouth.

∼

HILARY LAY in the bath in her Kensington apartment. Hot oily water covered her body and she luxuriated in the scent of pomegranate and Casablanca lily as it infused the air around her.

She was looking forward to dinner that evening and although Anthony Merryweather was an outrageous gossip, he was very entertaining. Hilary was conscious that Anthony clearly had an interest in Bob and was grateful that he was open about it. She was surrounded by closet gays with her clients – what was it about chefs? Must be all that heat in the kitchen, she thought, and sat up to scrub her back with a loofa. It would make things so much easier if certain people accepted who and what they were and lived their lives accordingly. It was tiresome to say the least to keep the press at bay when the handsome French hunk who was a housewives' favourite insisted on beating more than a meringue with the very cute male food stylist from Let's Get Baking… a new weekly series that she'd had to crawl over hot coals to secure for him.

Hilary reached for a towel from the heated rail and rubbed the thick Egyptian cotton vigorously over her body, then stared into a mirror that ran the full width of one wall. Devoid of any make-up, Hilary considered her skin and turned her head to each side to study the lines on her brow. The skin was almost wrinkle-free. Time enough for Botox, she thought, pleased that continuous attention to her beauty routine had enabled her skin to stay firm. She wasn't bad for a forty-something, not that she'd dream of telling anyone her age. Hilary pursed her lips and studied the fine lines surrounding her heart shaped mouth – she really should stop smoking!

She unclipped her hair and let it fall to her shoulders, the soft auburn waves curling over her creamy white skin. The towel slipped and as Hilary began to apply a moisturising lotion to her body, she debated on an outfit for the evening. The red velvet, 1950s swing dress, that she'd last worn at Goodwood Revival, would be fun. Anthony would like to be seen with some arm-candy and the dress made her curves look soft and feminine. What a waste…

Not that Hilary was looking for attention; she'd given up on male company several years earlier. The love of her life – the notorious chef Mickey Lloyd – had gone back to his wife and now lived in Thailand. He'd broken her heart after a summer romance and it was several years before she'd allowed anyone to get close to her again. When Joel came along, she'd been cautious but in time, they got engaged. Hilary was horrified when he disappeared into the sunset with her savings, forwarding address unknown. What a fool she'd been! Several years younger than herself, Joel was a con-man, whom she later learnt preyed on wealthy women. He'd left her penniless and she vowed that she'd never get involved with anyone again. The humiliation had been horrible, as was the climb back into business. But she'd begun again and created an agency that specialised in the representation of clients related to the food industry.

The world of celebrity chefs continued to amaze Hilary. Each year she thought that the bubble would burst, but the public's voracious appetite for all things food related had continued to grow, and her clients became media personalities basking in their new found popularity. Big money was to be made from endorsements and appearances and, as every young catering student dreamed of being the next Jamie Oliver, Hilary found herself swamped with applications for representation. She could afford to be choosy, but it was hard work and often took years of development with a client before any money was made. The last she'd heard of Joel was that he'd married into a property empire and was standing for local election. Typical con! Hilary thought, as she folded the towel neatly and placed it back on the rail. After her relationship with Joel had broken down, she had hardened and it was no wonder everyone thought she was a tough cookie. She knew that her clients called her the Rottweiler behind her back, but they should be grateful that she was so fiercely protective.

Her parents were killed in a car crash when she was a teen and with no siblings and no estate to inherit, she'd been plunged into the working world without any choices, finding waitress work the only thing she was qualified to do. Hilary had worked hard and progressed through the trade, and when she met Joel she owned a successful outside catering business with prestigious London clients, but all that had been lost as he systematically stole from her. It was a chance meeting one Sunday afternoon that set her on the road to recovery.

A friend had tickets to a cookery demonstration and invited Hilary to accompany her to a new school in the West End. Hilary sat and listened to the chef bang on about the qualities of a shiny set of copper-based saucepans which, he said, produced the most sublime sauces and soups. After the demonstration, whilst other members of the audience tasted his concoctions, Hilary asked if the pan manufacturer was paying him to use the saucepans. He'd looked at her with surprise and commented, "No, but if you can get some money out of them you can represent me." Not one to turn her back on a challenge, she set about contacting the company, sold the chef's merits in a neatly packed proposal and soon found herself issuing a lucrative contract for a twelve month sponsorship to a delighted chef. Her agency was born!

In the years that followed Hilary worked harder than ever, always conscious that she could lose everything and having had that happen once, she was determined to never let it happen again. If that meant staying single for the rest of her days, so be it. She'd never trust a man again!

The French ormolu clock on the hall table struck seven and Hilary hurried to her dressing room. Her home in Marchant Gardens was tastefully decorated with antique furniture and Hilary had a rare talent for finding treasures at flea markets, charity shops and auction houses. She used her spare time to indulge herself in a passion that had grown over the years. Her favourite London haunts were Spitalfields Market and Camden Passage in Islington and her flat still had its original fireplace, sash windows, cornices and ceiling roses.

Hilary reached into a mahogany two-door wardrobe and found the velvet dress. She finished dressing and satisfied with her appearance, went through to the lounge where she poured herself a gin and tonic and sat down to wait for her taxi. She took a cigarette from a silver box and looked out of the first-floor window to the road below. As she inhaled, she thought about Zelda Martin. How the hell was the girl going to cope with the harsh realities of working class

Britain? Hilary smiled; that would be the pull of the programme! Posh meets poverty and vice versa. Whether or not tripe and onions would ever reach the world of Zelda, in Kensington and Chelsea, would remain to be seen, but Hilary felt sure that there would be tears and tantrums in abundance and Zelda would make brilliant viewing.

As her taxi pulled up, Hilary downed her drink and smiled to herself, then stubbed out her cigarette and re-applied her lipstick. Dinner at Dabbous! She hoped that Anthony was on form...

4

Lottie hurried up the carpeted stairs and flung her keys on the desk in reception. The persistent bleep of the alarm followed her across the room and she raced to the console to punch in a set of numbers.

Silence, phew!

Lottie eased a rucksack off her back and wriggled her slight frame out of her duffle coat. She wore a short red, sleeveless dress, with green tights and a bright yellow scarf knotted round her tiny waist. Like a set of traffic lights! Lottie could almost hear her boss comment on the outfit, and wished that she'd taken a bit more time to get ready that morning. She reached into her pocket and pulled out an elastic band, then pulled her curly hair into a ponytail and fastened it on one side of her head.

Lottie was hungry. The bacon and egg roll in her rucksack smelt absolutely delicious. She threw herself onto a chair, tore into the packaging, took a bite and closed her eyes. The warm yolk oozed over the crisp bacon and she sighed with pleasure.

"Bit early for an orgasm, isn't it?" Bob bounced into the foyer and removed his cycle helmet. He placed it on Lottie's desk and perched beside her. "Give us a bite, then." Bob reached over to take the warm crusty offering. "Bloody lovely!" he said and licked his lips.

"You're early." Lottie grinned as she watched ketchup run down Bob's chin.

"Haven't bothered going to bed." Bob dabbed at the ketchup. "That wretched woman kept me up half the friggin' night as I trailed after her removing every evil substance known to man from her sticky little paws." He shuddered as he thought about Prunella's speech the previous evening and her insistence on joining The Monday Club – a group of chefs on their day off who careered into several drinking holes around Russell Square in a race to see who could drink, ingest, snort or smoke the most banned substances before they got back to work the next day. "Heaven knows where she ended up." Bob stood up and pulled a jacket from an olive green bicycle shopper. He shook it out and plunged his arms into the sleeves. "Twitter will be hot this morning, or not – if she slept with whom I suspect she slept with…"

Lottie pulled a face and shuddered. "Crikey, Bob," she said, "Hilary will have a fit! Prunella is walking a fine line after Chipping Hodbury… Hilary will kill her." Lottie resumed an attack on her breakfast.

"Not the way book sales are going," he replied. "Baby Jane's little missile is in the top ten today; Hilary will be delighted. Anyway, what she doesn't see won't harm her." Bob grinned and patted the top of Lottie's head, then did a twirl and pointed his smart new Converse trainers and danced across reception to his office. "Mum's the word darling!" Bob called over his shoulder and winked at Lottie, and clutching the long string of prayer beads wound round his neck, he disappeared into his office to begin the working day.

∽

HILARY SAT in the back of a shiny black Mercedes and watched a group of school children queuing along the Cromwell Road. A young teacher appeared anguished as he lunged forward to stop two little boys break out of the line and run towards the steps of the Natural History museum. Mutiny in the ranks, Hilary thought. It must be catching. She wondered how Bob had coped with Prunella the previous night. Several phone calls to him during the evening had set alarm bells ringing, even though he'd assured her that he had everything under control. Hilary balanced her iPad on her knee and sifted through her emails as her driver carefully wound the vehicle through the busy Knightsbridge roads.

An email from Anthony thanked her for her company at dinner. Hilary smiled. They'd had a delightful time and she'd caught up with plenty of gossip from the world of literary festivals and launches. Anthony was very well connected and it was always good for Hilary to have someone on the ground at such events. She hadn't batted an eyelash as she paid the three figure bill. Dabbous had been worth every penny. She'd explained that Bob was otherwise engaged that evening, but she would ensure that he rescheduled their dinner, at the agencies expense, in the very near future. And as she'd left Anthony walking unsteadily along Whitworth Street, she'd heard him hail a taxi to take him to Russell Square.

Hilary scrolled over a long list of emails. She had her weekly meeting with Frances this morning to go over finances. Frances was a brilliant book-keeper and Hilary was delighted that the business was in good shape at the moment, but things could change rapidly in this economy and she needed to keep on top of it.

She checked the company Twitter account to see what Lottie was posting. Hilary loathed Twitter and all social networking, it often caused terrible problems – especially in the early hours when clients were lulled by their fix of choice and made comments that Hilary often had legal battles over as she rectified reputations that were previously squeaky-clean. Sponsors and TV execs did not want their protégées' shenanigans going viral.

Hilary flicked open Lottie's latest tweet.

"Congrats to #FatDick Chef for latest award..." Hilary jumped so suddenly that the iPad on her knee fell to the floor.

"Everything all right, Miss Hargreaves?" the driver asked. He watched Hilary in his rear view mirror, her face was like thunder.

"Fine, thanks!" Hilary snapped as she scrambled to retrieve the iPad and banged out the office number on her mobile.

"Hargreaves Promotions. How may I help you today?" Lottie trilled.

"What the devil have you put on Twitter?" Hilary bellowed.

There was a temporary silence.

"Nothing much," Lottie said. "I just congratulated the Fat Duck Restaurant in Cornwall for their restaurant of the year award…"

"I suggest you grow wings rapidly and fly over the account to see what you've tweeted. I'll be in in ten minutes!" Hilary thrust the phone into her Corde handbag and snapped the Bakelite clasp shut. She closed her eyes and counted to ten. The image of a good slug of Bombay Sapphire gin swirling into a tumbler raced across her subconscious. "Put your foot down," she said to the driver, and felt the car accelerate as they flew through the underpass at Hyde Park corner into Piccadilly and headed to her office beyond.

∼

OVER THE WATER in southern Ireland, Lenny Crispin sat in his rented cottage and nursed a mug of lukewarm coffee as he contemplated a plan of attack. Hargreaves Promotions was the key to his success and he simply had to get on their books.

But Hilary Hargreaves was proving a tough nut to crack.

Lenny could generally charm his way through the most difficult situation but getting past the dippy girl on reception was a challenge.

He stared idly out of the window and watched the yachts in the bay racing over the sparkling waters as they headed to Kindale, the "Gourmet Capital of Ireland", an affluent and pretty coastal town where the race would end and revelries last long into the night. Most nights were party nights in Kindale, with over fifty pubs and fine restaurants serving a population of three thousand, their ranks swelled with visitors who poured into the town to enjoy the eclectic mixture of Irish, British, colonial and Spanish architecture, quirky shops and galleries, and most importantly – superb cuisine. Kindale was a mecca for seafood lovers and some of the finest crustaceans in Europe were fished from the surrounding waters.

Lenny liked the atmosphere in Kindale and the residents were loaded. Predominately Irish, he thought that they were an arty-farty bunch with the odd rock star, writer or actor thrown in. They all seemed to have money to burn, and he intended to capitalise on this as soon as possible!

Lenny planned to set up a cookery school and had ear-marked a property. He'd call it the European World of Cookery and attract clients from far afield. Cork airport was only a few miles from Kindale and he had visions of transporting the mega-rich in fine style to the gracious property he'd selected for his venture.

The property was an old manor house and belonged to a middle-aged pop star from the late 1980s. Long Tom Hendry had lived there as a recluse for the last decade but had found a sudden and unexpected popularity when his record label had taken a risk and re-issued a reggae version of one of his hit albums. It had gone global. Promoters wanted him to go to the Caribbean and cash in on his new-found fame in warmer climes, and Long Tom's manager had encouraged him to rent out his Irish property.

All Lenny needed to secure his idea of the European World of Cookery was finance, and lots of it.

Lenny knew that if he could just raise his profile and get a few serious gigs as a celebrity chef, he'd have the sponsors falling over backwards to set him up and then, who knows… He'd take the money and run! Cookery schools sounded like bloody hard work and Lenny wasn't overly keen on anything more taxing than unwrapping a packet of puff pastry and swirling a jar of Loyd Grossman's tomato and basil sauce over the top, claiming it to be a secret recipe from a fictitious, third generation, Italian grandmamma. It wouldn't be the first time he'd pulled off a scam. Why work when you could con money out of unsuspecting punters? He'd never done an honest day's work in his life.

Lenny sighed and eased his considerable frame forward. The yachts were nearly out of sight and he should head down to Kindale and mix with the exuberant land-lovers who would be waiting quayside with bottles of Dom Perignon. You never knew who you could con a couple of euros out of and Lenny intended to do exactly that, only with several noughts on the end. He was going to make a shed-load of dosh!

He stood up and reached for the phone. First, he had to nail that agent... He dialled the London number.

"Hargreaves Promotions. How may I help you today?"

Lenny smiled and began his plan of attack.

5

Hilary stood by the open window in her office and took a long drag on her cigarette, then blew the smoke out over the street below. She held a phone to her ear and looked thoughtful as she considered the options being presented to her by production for The Zimmers. The "look" they'd suggested for Zelda Martin was that of street fashion, whereby Zelda would turn up at unsuspecting homes, fresh from a market or organic butcher, in leggings, t-shirt and a denim jacket.

Hilary begged to differ.

"Let her choose her own clothes," Hilary told Ailsa Craig, the fiery little pocket rocket, in charge of wardrobe, from Mile Seven Productions.

"We canna be lettin' her do that!" Ailsa yelled back in broad Glaswegian.

"She'll be more comfortable working in familiar garb," Hilary said. "Don't worry, she'll get it right, I'll have a word with her." Ailsa continued to rant but Hilary assured her that all would be well and disconnected the call. She stubbed her cigarette out and placed the ashtray in her desk drawer.

"Such a horrible habit," Bob said as he walked into the room and scowled at Hilary. "You'll stunt your growth." He flung himself onto a chair.

"I can think of worse," Hilary replied and sat down. She wore jet black Cats Eye glasses and peered over the top of the frames.

"All roads led to Russell Square, I hear?" Hilary asked as she watched Bob run a hand over his smooth bald head.

"I can't image what you mean." Bob wasn't taking the bait.

"I don't want to see a hotel bill for a double room going through your expense account." Sixth sense told Hilary that Bob had met up with Anthony, when he should have been tailing Prunella. "Frances says the business is in good shape, let's keep it that way." Hilary picked up a silver fountain pen and studied the basket weave engraving.

"Time I asked for a pay rise then." Bob wasn't backing down. Hilary could taunt him till the cows came home; he knew his worth and she'd be hard pressed to find a more dedicated assistant. If he had the odd little fling along the way, it was all very subtle. Just because Hilary never got laid it didn't mean her staff had to stay celibate.

"Personally, Bob, I couldn't give a rosy rat's arse who you bonk in your spare time, but if I find it was on Prunella's time and you're getting paid double to shadow her, I won't be best pleased."

Bob was silent. He held Hilary's gaze and gave her a haughty look, but his heart lurched and he reached for his prayer beads and silently uttered, "Ohm Sa," as he visualised calm waters from the Ganges washing over his soul.

"You'll break your pacifier if you don't calm down." Hilary looked away and began to write.

Bob stopped fondling his beads and made a mental note to remove the hotel invoice from his expense file, but the night with Anthony had been worth it! He just prayed that Prunella hadn't ended up in the middle of a gang bang and, if she had, that the participants had consumed enough illegal contraband to erase all memory. Baby Jane, in flagrante, was a hideous thought.

Hilary's telephone rang.

"Lenny Crispin on line three for you," Lottie announced.

"Tell him I'm busy," Hilary snapped.

"I'm surprised you don't talk to him," Bob interjected. "You know he's living in Mickey Lloyd's cottage in County Cork?"

Hilary dropped her pen. It rolled across the desk. Bob reached out to catch it. As he leaned down, he glanced at Hilary's startled expression. Bingo! he thought, and smiled to himself. So it was true – Hilary still held a torch for the notorious Mickey Lloyd! Bob placed the pen carefully beside Hilary's hand and watched as she picked it up. She seemed flummoxed.

He sat back in his chair and thought about the gossip he'd heard recently. Bob knew that, in another life, a very long time ago, Hilary had had a serious fling with Mickey. Some said he'd been the love of her life. Hilary had been the caterer for the crew on a TV show that Mickey was filming in Devon. Mickey loved to drink and party and rumour had it that they'd had a raunchy and passionate time during those long summer weeks. Mickey lived in the Far East now, having hot footed it out of the country when years of unpaid taxes caught up with him.

"The government took the pub off him," Bob said idly. "Mickey lost his property in Spain to his wife, but I hear he hung on to Fool's Landing, the cottage in Ireland. He rents it out." Bob played with his beads and watched Hilary's reaction.

For once he blessed Prunella, who'd been in a drunken state when she'd gossiped the news, reminiscing about old times as she told Bob all about Hilary's fling. Prunella had set sail with Mickey many moons ago, to interview him for an article in a glossy foodie magazine. Mickey was filming a TV series, and Prunella had caught up with him on the set in Devon. She clearly remembered Mickey's relationship with Hilary and took great pleasure in recounting the intimate details for Bob and how the affair had come to an abrupt end when the current Mrs Lloyd turned up on the set and threatened to divorce Mickey and make Hilary walk the plank and hang her off the end.

Bob grinned as he imagined the scene, but he was soon brought out of his daydream as Hilary barked into the phone.

"Put Mr Crispin through!"

Within two minutes Hilary had instructed Lenny to be on the next flight to London, and told him that she'd meet him in Ranchers the following day.

"Kissed the Blarney stone?" Bob grinned. "You were actually nice to him; have you started early today?"

"Bog-off, Bob," Hilary replied. "Go and find out what happened to Prunella and start covering your tracks. If she's still out cold under a dead weight of chefs you'll have some explaining to do."

"Yes, boss!" Bob stood and gave Hilary a wink.

Hilary watched Bob retreat. He was worth his weight in gold and she knew that he was perfect partner material, should she ever decide to take things a bit easier.

She reached into her desk to pour a shot of gin and equalled the measure with tonic. She'd had a shock – she hadn't thought of Mickey in ages, but the very mention of his name was unsettling and brought back memories and feelings that she'd tried so often to forget.

He'd been the love of her life.

Hilary took a sip of her drink and thought back to a warm summer in Devon when a man with the bluest of eyes and softest brown curls had charmed his way into her bedroom. Hilary smiled as she nostalgically remembered her time with Mickey. It was actually a grotty old caravan and had been her accommodation on the set of Around the Coast with Mickey Lloyd. Mickey had completely taken hold of her heart and she'd gone headlong into their romance, instantly falling for his wit and charisma and whispered words of passion in his sexy Irish brogue.

They'd spent long steamy sessions, night after night, partying until they both had to be up and ready for another day's filming. Mickey had been her first and only true love and when he promised to take her to his cottage in southern Ireland, Hilary had been ecstatic.

She clutched her drink and stared blankly out through the open window, wondering what the cottage was like these days. Mickey had painted such a quaint picture of Fool's Landing and as they'd watched the sun set over the sea in Devon, he'd told her that it was a very special place, in a most beautiful part of Ireland, and his heart had always belonged there. He'd wanted to share it with her.

None of that had happened and he'd turned out to be a complete shit, like most of the men she'd ever been involved with. Hilary sighed and finished her drink, shook her head and cleared her thoughts then flicked the intercom.

"Lottie, get me a table at Ranchers for two tomorrow. Mr Crispin will be joining me."

Hilary pushed her glass to one side and picked up her pen. It was no good thinking about Mickey. After all, it was unlikely that she'd ever see him again.

~

Lenny Crispin stood by the window in the lounge of the cottage at Fool's Landing and stared out at the water in the estuary. It meandered gently along the coast, where, in the distance, he could see the buildings of the town of Kindale. Tall graceful trees surrounded the cottage and their russet coloured leaves rustled gently as they swayed in a warm autumnal breeze. Below the cottage, by the boat house at the end of a wooden pier, a cabin cruiser was moored. It bobbed in the waters lapping the shore.

Lenny watched the idyllic scene and grinned. Hilary Hargreaves would be like putty in his hands and he was certain he'd be gracing the demonstration stage at a major food show soon, or even be seen on screen for a Saturday morning cookery programme.

He wondered what had changed her mind. It must be his charm offensive with that daft receptionist – the chocolates from William Curley in Belgravia had obviously worked, seriously expensive but worth every penny. He'd better start packing!

Lenny thought about what to wear to Ranchers. He wandered

through to one of the two bedrooms in the cottage and found an overnight bag. A pretty quilted counterpane covered the mattress and Lenny flung the bag on the bed and reached into the wardrobe where he found two Paul Smith shirts, Valentino jeans and a smart jacket. The shirts were a bit tight over his paunch but Lenny knew the jacket would cover it.

He reached for the phone and dialed Aer Lingus.

∽

Zelda sat on the train and stared out at the countryside whizzing by; London felt a long way away.

She was miffed.

The production company had reserved her seats in second class and Zelda was uncomfortable. Two young men, drinking lager from cans, shared her table and played a boisterous game of cards. She'd have to have a word with Hilary, there were certain lines to be drawn and second class travel was one of them!

Zelda looked anxiously towards her Louis Vuitton cases. Carmelita had packed them previous day and they were piled high on the luggage rack; Zelda prayed that everything was safe. She gripped her Hermes tote and reached for her iPhone, she'd send Harry a text – at least he would be sympathetic. The call sheet for The Zimmers lay on the table before her and Zelda could see that a car had been booked to meet her at Liverpool Lime Street. Thank God. She hoped it would be something comfortable, like a Merc, after all, she'd told them she'd got lots of luggage.

∽

Bob and Lottie sat in Bob's office and gossiped about Mickey Lloyd. They ate warm chicken wraps from the local deli.

"I can feel a trip to Ireland coming on," Bob said and grinned as he swivelled in his chair.

"I didn't think Hilary had any boyfriends." Lottie had finished her wrap and picked up the box of chocolates which Lenny had sent. She chose a smooth truffle from the luxurious gold and black box.

Bob pushed his plate to one side and wiped his mouth with a paper napkin. He tossed it in the bin and reached for the chocolates. "Oh, our boss has sailed many a sea, she's no Virgin Mary. Prunella said Mickey Lloyd couldn't keep his hands off her when she was catering on the set of Around the Coast with Mickey Lloyd."

"Bet he got plenty of second helpings," Lottie giggled.

"Pass me a salt caramel and keep your voice down; she'll skin us alive if she finds out we know."

"Where did Prunella end up the other night?" Lottie stood up and shook crumbs off her mini skirt, then tugged at lime green tights and began to dance, pirouetting gracefully in her pixie boots.

Bob sucked on the soft salty caramel and watched her antics. "Don't know and don't care," he replied. "Prunella is a liability." He stood and took Lottie's hands then swung her into a salsa. They swooped and dived round the room until they fell back, into their chairs, exhausted.

"Exercise over, time to get back to work." Bob sat at his desk and cracked his knuckles. "I've a client list as long as your legs to get through. Man the phones, my beauty, let the mayhem begin!"

6

Hilary sat on the banquette and looked around the room. It was, as usual, packed in Ranchers and she nodded as several people waved in her direction or tried to catch her eye.

She wore a brightly coloured, diamond-patterned Versace knit and a long pencil skirt. The top was tight across her chest, as was the skirt on her hips, and Hilary wished she'd walked past the tray of cakes in reception that morning. She couldn't resist Patisserie Valerie, and Lottie had arranged a selection of pastries and cakes alongside freshly brewed coffee, ready for a casting session for Rock Chef, a ten-part competition soon to be screened.

As she strode through to her office, Hilary had been horrified by the array of pierced and tattooed talent lining the walls. Bob, assisted by, Heidi, an agent who worked for Hilary from home and came into the office when needed, certainly had their worked cut out that morning.

Hilary scrolled down her iPad and saw ten emails and texts from Zelda. Liverpool was obviously not to her liking. Hilary made a note to call Zelda, she clearly needed to smooth her ruffled feathers, she couldn't afford tears and tantrums or at the very worst Zelda storming off set. She wondered what had happened now, having overcome the dress code yesterday when Zelda turned up in Toxteth in her latest Prada jacket and Rag & Bone skinny jeans. Ailsa had insisted Zelda would be more convincing in a Primark outfit, but after Zelda's mild hysterics and much foot stomping, Hilary had spoken to the producer and Zelda got her way. Hilary winced as she thought of the skinny jeans: two pork sausages with a light Lycra coating came to mind. She raised her glass and summoned Joe for a refill.

"Is business good, Miss Hargreaves?" Joe asked as he hovered over the table and brushed the linen cloth with a small bristle brush.

"Not bad, Joe. I'd like a share in this place though." Hilary nodded at the heaving tables.

"Ah, they heard you were in." Joe smiled and picked up the empty glass. "I'll see to this." He grinned fondly at Hilary and backed away from the table.

Across the room, Hilary noticed quite a commotion as a tall, lean man in a leather jacket wandered through the diners. People whispered and stared as he passed. He wore a cowboy hat, white t-shirt and jeans and his thick hair was scraped back into a ponytail. A group stood up as he arrived at their table and there was much back slapping and shaking of hands as he sat down.

Joe appeared with Hilary's gin and placed it beside her. He saw Hilary watching the performance across the room.

"Long Tom Hendry," Joe said. "Do you remember him?"

"Vaguely," Hilary replied and returned her attention to her drink.

"Made a mint in the 1980s, mostly known for his hit No More War, about the Vietnam War." Joe held his tray to his chest and looked across the room. "Gone and reinvented himself with a new record contract. His label has brought out a reggae version of his best-selling album and he's shot to number one in the Caribbean."

"Lucky for some," Hilary said.

"I hear he's moving out of Ireland for a while." Joe moved a dish of green olives closer to Hilary.

Hilary perked up. "Ireland?"

"Been holed up there for years it seems, bit of a recluse." Joe spun round. "I think your guest has arrived…" He shot across the room to reception.

Hilary picked up an olive. The flesh was plump, soft and cold. She took a sip of gin and contemplated the rock star. Spooky! All roads lead to Ireland! Was someone trying to tell her something? Was Bob's karma rubbing off on her? Her meeting with Lenny should be interesting.

"Miss Hargreaves, your guest, Mr Crispin." Joe pulled the table out to allow Hilary's guest to sit on the opposite side.

"Hello, darlin'." Lenny Crispin eased his considerable frame onto the banquette.

Hilary's eyes were wide. She dropped the remains of the olive and studied her guest.

"Mr Crispin," Hilary replied curtly, and shook his outstretched hand.

"Call me Lenny, why don't yah. Everyone else does." He clicked his fingers at Joe. "Bottle of your finest champagne, my son, me and the little lady here have got some celebrating to do."

Hilary fell back in her seat aghast! Did this man have no manners?

"I'm not tracing an Irish accent here, Lenny," she began.

"Nah, babe, I'm from Essex – born and bred. Done all me cookin' in the pubs and clubs and some very fancy joints, I can tell you."

Joe appeared with champagne and raised an eyebrow in Hilary's direction. He poured two glasses and handed out menus as he began to explain the daily specials but Hilary waved him away. Joe bowed and retreated quickly.

"Cheers!" Lenny raised his glass. "Here's to a long and fruitful relationship!"

Hilary picked up her gin and drained the glass, then reached for her champagne. "So, Lenny, tell me all about yourself and your new project."

"Well, darlin', I've got this cookery school I'm creating the European World of Cookery. It's going to be one of a kind." He topped his glass up and began to tell her all about his plans, how he'd got hold of an old manor near Kindale, the Gourmet Capital of Ireland – just south of Cork, which was waist-high in money.

"The owner's moving out," he told her, "and happy for me to do my own thing, within reason. Planning welcomed the change-of-use application as it will create employment and bring trade to the area. Sponsors are falling over to provide equipment such as china, appliances and technology and the school will host celebrity chefs to run courses in the stunning surroundings." Lenny explained that his accountant and lawyers were drawing up all the paperwork and name dropped two high-profile London offices.

Hilary was impressed when she heard the names and was about to ask more, but Lenny didn't pause for breath as he went on to explain how he was organising an open weekend for everyone involved, to view the site and get a feel of the scale of the venture.

"The weekend coincides with the Gourmet Food Festival in Kindale; it's a three-day extravaganza. This will allow them all to experience the fantastic produce, restaurants and hospitality available in the area."

"So, what do you want from me?" Hilary asked. She sat back and gazed at the portly little character; he didn't seem to know when to apply the edit button. She looked him in the eye and wondered what recreational drug he was taking.

"Demmin' gigs at the major shows and TV darlin' – let's spread the word!" Lenny raised his glass. "Raise my profile and you and I will make a fortune. You can be my agent and broker all my deals, you'll also supply the celebrity chefs and get a cut of profits."

"Can you cook?" she asked.

Lenny clutched his chest. He appeared horrified and closed his eyes.

"Can I cook?" he whispered. "She asks if I can cook..."

"And?" Hilary drummed her fingers impatiently on the table.

"Lenny is wounded, dear lady, wounded through to his core." He opened his eyes and continued. "I learnt to cook at my mother's knee, and have been a slave to the stove ever since. Wait till you try my signature dishes and specialities, never mind your Michael Roux –

this boy knows his business... Garçon!" he shouted. "Another bottle!" Lenny clicked his fingers.

Joe, who was one table away, ignored him.

"So are you in?" Lenny asked. "Are you going to take this once in a lifetime opportunity to work with my humble self and step aboard my culinary train to foodie heaven for the ride of your life?" Lenny finally stopped talking.

Hilary caught Joe's eye. He held up a second bottle of champagne but she shook her head then turned back to Lenny.

"Well," she began, "your proposal is certainly very interesting and I would consider a trip to Ireland to look at the possibilities. But before I even begin to consider representing you, there are formalities that we have to undertake." She took a sip of water and looked him in the eye. "Firstly, I will need you to fill out some forms so that we can do a background check, employment history – that sort of thing, references too, of course. Then I need a screen test, to see what you look like on camera," Hilary stared at his paunch, "which can often be cruel and you may find a healthy diet and exercise regime would help." She watched Lenny sit up straight, breathe in and attempt to button his jacket. "And of course," she continued, "we need to experience your wonderful cooking."

"No problem, darlin'," Lenny responded and waved his empty glass at Joe. "You let me have the paperwork and I'll get all that sorted. Just get yourself to Stansted a week on Thursday, I'll sort the flight. Bring who you like." Lenny inched himself out from the table. "Excuse me a mo', babe, just seen someone I know."

Hilary watched him follow Long Tom Hendry into the Gents. Joe placed a fresh gin and tonic beside her and she sipped it as she waited for Lenny to come back. The minutes ticked by and Hilary began to get impatient. She drummed her fingers on the table and glared as she watched Lenny return, with Long Tom at his side.

"Darlin'!" Lenny greeted her. "I want you to meet my mate, Long Tom Hendry, who you must know, probably remember his hit No More War. Long Tom, meet my agent..."

Long Tom held out his hand and raised his hat an inch or so. "Pleasure's all mine," he said.

Hilary was seething and glared at Lenny.

"We're still in discussions, Lenny," she said through gritted teeth and nodded at Long Tom, who seemed to have quite a sparkle in his eye.

"I knew the two of you would get on." Lenny slapped Long Tom on the back. "Bet old Hilary here was right up your protest street and going without her bra back in the days when you'd only to open your mouth and another platinum disc hit the wall of fame in your guest carsey." Lenny guffawed, oblivious to Hilary's glacial expression.

"I'm sure the lady never needed a bra." Long Tom stared at Hilary's chest. "She has a great pair of—"

"Menus, Miss Hargreaves?" Joe swooped in and removed the glass from Hilary's white knuckled grip.

"Long Tom's letting me use his Irish crib for the cookery school," Lenny said. "A few alterations and we'll be rockin' and rollin' all the way to the bank." Lenny sniffed as he shook his head and smiled. "Expect the two of you will hook up when Hilary hits Ireland. We'll show her some good old Irish hospitality."

Hilary watched Lenny walk Long Tom back to his table. How dare this jumped up little man talk to her in such a familiar fashion? And as for that ageing pop star... She took a large swig from the replenished glass that Joe had placed beside her.

"Gawd, I'm hungry." Lenny had returned and squeezed his frame back on the banquette. He picked up a menu. "What would you recommend, darlin'?"

Joe stood by the table and held an order pad, his pen poised.

"My usual please, Joe," Hilary said, "and Lenny will have a tuna salad with no dressing."

∽

"THAT MAN IS INSUFFERABLE!" Hilary stormed through the door of

Bob's office and flung her Mappin & Webb lizard skin clutch bag across his desk.

Heidi stared at the bag with longing as she watched it skim across a stack of Rock Chef application forms. Hilary's accessories were to die for.

"Can we take it that Mr Crispin won't be benefitting from our representation?" Bob stood up and guided Hilary into his chair.

"I didn't say that," Hilary snarled. "I'm just totally gobsmacked by his arrogance and complete and utter confidence that everyone he has on his wish list will jump up and fall into line wherever he wants them to."

"Has he any talent?" Bob asked. He stood behind Hilary and began to massage her shoulders.

"He's got the gift of the gab and a bloody good idea." Hilary closed her eyes and began to relax as Bob's soothing fingers worked their magic through her tense muscles.

"Over qualified by our usual standards then…" Bob caught Heidi's eye and winked.

"Do you fancy four days in Ireland?" Hilary gently moved her head from side to side as Bob manipulated her neck.

"Moi?" Bob was startled. He stepped up his massage, magic was happening!

"I think we should go and have a look at Lenny's plans," Hilary said. "I could do with getting away from the office and there's a food festival that coincides with the trip – you could eye up any new talent."

Bob let out a sigh of pleasure. He was more than happy to eye up new talent.

"I'm talking chefs." Hilary opened her eyes and pushed Bob's hands away. "Now, have you found any Rock Chefs while I've been hard at it?" She started to rifle through the paperwork on Bob's desk.

"There's a couple that could rock around a rolling pin if push came to shove." Bob clicked his fingers and Heidi, who was gazing at Hilary's rhinestone lorgnettes with admiration, snapped to attention and handed him a folder.

"Very good, get on with it then." Hilary ignored the folder and reached for her bag. She rose to her feet and headed for the door, bumping into Lottie, who'd entered the room carrying an espresso.

"I'll have that at my desk, Lottie," Hilary called as she sailed past. "Get an application pack out to Lenny Crispin this afternoon, and I want it back pronto!"

7

The sky look formidably overcast and stormy as Hilary and Bob's courtesy car pulled off the perimeter road at Stansted airport and headed for a security gate.

"Have you got your passport ready?" Hilary asked Bob. She stared out at the metal fencing and watched a guard speak to their driver, then wave the limousine through.

"Doesn't look like we'll need it," Bob said. He sat forward and watched their vehicle get in line behind three others. The procession stopped and various occupants disembarked and were shown into a private hospitality suite, alongside a runway. Their uniformed driver raced round to Hilary's door and helped her climb out of the luxurious vehicle.

"Bloody hell, this is posh!" Bob whispered. He tucked Hilary's arm into his own and guided her into the building.

"Darlin'!" Lenny's voice boomed out as he raced forward to greet them. "Lookin' as glamorous as ever!" He lunged forward and kissed Hilary on both cheeks. "This your old man?" Lenny asked Hilary as he pumped Bob's hand and slapped him heartily on the shoulder. "You're a lucky fella!"

"Lenny, meet my assistant Bob," Hilary said. "Bob, this is Lenny Crispin – you've heard me talk about him."

"Oh, indeed I have…" Bob winced; his shoulder felt as though it was dislocated.

"Come and meet the rest of the gang," Lenny said.

"You need to get him on a diet," Bob whispered to Hilary as he watched Lenny waddle ahead of them.

Hilary swept into the room and looked around as they made their entrance. She wore a black fur coat and Christian Dior sunglasses with a scarlet Bulgari silk headscarf. Several men, all suited and booted, turned and stared.

"No, it's not Jackie O," Lenny shouted out. "Everyone, meet my agent – the lovely Hilary Hargreaves, and her assistant Bob."

"Sounds like a circus act!" Hilary hissed.

"Agent?" Lenny looked quizzically at Bob. "He's jumping the gun a bit, isn't he?"

"He'll have a gun rammed firmly up his backside if he says it again," Hilary whispered, and forced a grin as she greeted everyone.

A dark-haired man in a smart black suit spoke to Lenny. He wore a badge on his lapel which read Jet Set Air, Operations Manager, beneath a gold winged crest. Bob walked over to a table that was covered with a white linen cloth and picked up two glasses of pink champagne. He moved slowly as he passed the men and tried to overhear their conversation.

Hilary was making small talk with a turkey farmer from Essex whom, it transpired, had recently been contacted by Lenny in the hope that Lenny could do for Romney's Gold Turkeys what Marco Pierre White had done for Bernard Mathews, which wasn't a lot in Hilary's professional opinion. Roger Romney had inherited a turkey farm from his father and had turned it into a multi-million pound business. Lenny smelled money and using his Essex connection had lured Roger onto the trip.

Roger excused himself as Bob returned. He needed to find "the little boys' room" before the flight.

"You'll never guess..." Bob thrust the champagne into Hilary's outstretched hand.

"Lenny is a secret millionaire and we're all part of a reality TV programme?" Hilary replied sarcastically before she sipped her drink.

"Don't take the piss." Bob felt excited. "Lenny hasn't paid for the plane. Apparently there's a Lear jet on the tarmac that won't be going anywhere unless he flashes a black American Express card before it clears for take-off."

"Bloody hell!" Hilary gasped. "There won't be any change out of forty grand if he's chartered it."

They moved forward and watched in fascination as the operations manager protested with Lenny. Lenny turned away and spoke to a man in a camel cashmere trench coat. The man nodded and walked over to the operations manager. They spoke for several moments then shook hands.

"The man in the coat is David Hugo, a partner at Pillings law firm in the city," Hilary told Bob. "He's known as Mr Can-Do, represents a lot of footballers."

"He'll be used to getting his clients out of the shit then," Bob replied, fascinated by the scene unfolding before them.

"I reckon he's just okay'd the flight. He's told them our man is good for the money," Hilary said, emptying her glass.

A voice rang out over from a tannoy. "Ladies and gentlemen, if you would like to make your way to the tarmac, your Jet Set Air flight for Cork is preparing for departure."

"Fuck a duck!" Bob cried and grabbed another drink as they lined up near the exit door.

"Or a turkey!" Roger Romney cried out as he joined them.

Hilary removed her sunglasses and looked around the room. The atmosphere was jolly as the well-heeled crowd, about sixteen in number, prepared to board. She smiled as she took Bob's arm; she had a feeling she was going to enjoy this trip!

THE FLIGHT from Stansted was bumpy but the guests hardly felt a thing. Cushioned on soft leather couches and bucket chairs, everyone began to bond as a pretty hostess handed round canapés and vast quantities of champagne. Solicitors and accountants rubbed well-tailored shoulders with the MDs from a technology company, a major kitchen appliance brand, a French vineyard owner, and an upmarket holiday company.

The jet was luxurious and had a fully stocked bar with every drink imaginable. Lenny stood behind it and made them all a cocktail.

"A Legally Legless for you, me old mate," Lenny cried and handed David Hugo a tall glass. A rainbow of liqueurs blended together over several chunks of ice.

"It's a Wild Turkey for you, Roger the Dodger!" Kenny said, and placed a Kentucky bourbon whisky beside Roger.

"Christ, I shall be legless," Hilary said as she sat with Roger and watched the antics.

"No change there then," Bob muttered from across the aisle and raised his glass. He was drinking Lenny's version of a Red Hot Screw, and was already on his second.

"And here's something special for Lady H," Lenny announced, "The 007!"

"I think you've got the wrong sort of agent, Lenny," Hilary said as she stared suspiciously at the orange creation in her hand. Two coloured straws and a paper parasol, with a cherry impaled on the stick, topped the drink.

"You'll always be a special agent to me, darlin'," Lenny leered and disappeared into the gold-plated bathroom at the rear of the plane.

Hilary sipped the drink and offered the glass to Roger. "It tastes surprisingly nice."

Roger smelt it suspiciously then took a slug. "Bloody marvellous!" he agreed. "Here, let's liven it up a bit." He tipped some of his bourbon into the glass and gave it a swirl, then offered Hilary a straw. She sucked greedily.

"Don't mind if I chew your cherry do you?" Roger grinned as he picked up the parasol.

"Be my guest." Hilary smiled back and drained the glass.

Bob rolled his eyes and shook his head. He signalled to Lenny, who'd appeared from the bathroom, rubbing his nose.

"Another round over here, Chef!" Bob called out and waved his empty glass.

"Can he cook?" Roger whispered to Hilary and nodded towards Lenny, who was making his way down the plane.

"Can't boil an egg," Hilary replied. "Well, I'd be surprised if he could do much more, but looking at this lot, I'm not sure it matters."

The journey seemed to be over as quickly as it had begun and before the guests drank themselves into comas, the hostess asked them to buckle up and prepare for landing.

The flight landed smoothly on the runway in Cork and an airport official boarded and asked the occupants for their travel documents. He took a cursory glance as passports fluttered in outstretched hands and thanked Lenny for the invitation to join them all in Kindale later, then disappeared down the steps, where a fleet of cars waited. The party soon had their luggage loaded, and after being made comfortable, they were whisked off the tarmac toward the road leading south.

Cork to Kindale is a pretty journey and a distance of no more than twenty miles, but with various pit stops at local hostelries, the journey took four hours. The cars eventually pulled onto the long private avenue leading to Flatterley Manor. From the first view, the gracious property looked like a perfectly proportioned Palladian doll's house.

The manor was built on the lands of Flatterley Friary, a monastery of the Franciscan order, whose slender mediaeval church tower could be seen from the avenue. In the 1980s, the house had been abandoned and the farmland divided. Long Tom Hendry had rescued it from advanced dereliction and although it needed a great deal of money spent to keep in in good repair, he'd partly restored it in keeping with its historic character. Long Tom had lived there for years, but never ventured far and was only occasionally seen in the local community when he wanted a pint of milk or a paper.

Until now.

The sudden success of Long Tom's album in a new reggae format had given his career a massive lift. The executives at his record label, delighted that they were managing to prise him out of his dusty old manor, had arranged a couple of concerts in the Caribbean to launch his come-back.

Lenny assembled the guests by the front door. James, the butler at Flatterley Manor, stood beside him with a large bunch of keys.

"Ladies and gentlemen," Lenny began, "welcome to the European World of Cookery! We're going to have a walk round so you can all get a feel for the place."

"Should be interesting, most of us can hardly stand..." Bob whispered.

The party teetered off.

The Georgian house was filled with an abundance of antique furniture, china and interesting objects. There were old books and pictures everywhere. Hilary ran her finger along a shelf in the panelled library and created a deep channel in the layer of dust. She raised an eyebrow. "Long Tom's not big on housework," she commented.

"Not the sort of style you'd expect of a rock star." Bob looked puzzled as he wandered round the faded old furniture, stepping on tired rugs as he twitched ancient drapes.

"The punters will love it," Hilary said. "Think of Mr and Mrs Nouveau Riche from Ohio, Texas. They'll imagine they are Lord and Lady Flatterley, and while she's enamoured by the performance in the pantry, with whichever celebrity chef is dish of the day, he'll be out in the country fly fishing, foxhunting or enjoying a round of golf. It's genius! Lenny will make a fortune."

The tour continued and Lenny took them to a large brick and glass orangery at the side of the main kitchen in the house.

"This will be the cookery school," Lenny announced. His excitement showed as he flew around the room explaining where the work stations and demonstration area would go. Craig Kelly, MD of Kelly's Kitchen Supplies, began to take photos and write notes.

After the orangery, they were taken back into the house and escorted up a grand curving staircase to the first floor. Lenny led them down a long corridor.

"There are just a few suites in the house for guests with serious dosh, but most will stay in Kindale – give the locals a slice of the pie." Lenny was sweating as he raced up and down, opening doors to bedrooms beyond. "We'll move them about in our fleet vehicles," he continued. "But this is what I want you all to see…"

He thrust open a pair of double doors at the end of the corridor and beckoned for everyone to follow. The guests were plunged into a massive room, as black as ink.

"Hang on folks!" Lenny cried, and within moments the room came to life. A large disco ball in the centre began to spin and coloured lasers bounced off the walls.

"Blimey, it's Saturday Night Fever, circa 1970s, my favourite era!" Bob said, and began to cut some shapes as the Bee Gees boomed out over massive speakers.

"This is a bit more up your average rock star's street," Roger yelled into Hilary's ear, then grabbed her hands and pulled her onto the dance floor.

Far from the maddening crowd in London, the pressures of work and six hours of heavy alcohol consumption had loosened more than just tongues as everyone took to the floor and let themselves go with their own interpretation of moves to Night Fever. David Hugo shed his coat and began a fine impression of John Travolta. Hilary was having a marvellous time, and as long forgotten steps came easily, she danced around the floor.

"You should be dancing, YEAH!"

Hilary turned as she heard Bob sing. The guests had formed a circle and Bob was strutting his stuff in the middle.

But something made Hilary look up. There, on a balcony,

watching the antics, stood Long Tom Hendry. He leaned on a rail and raised his hat.

Their eyes met and Hilary froze.

A long-forgotten feeling boomeranged in her tummy and she felt as though she was stark naked under his penetrating gaze. Long Tom smiled and gave her a wink. His deep brown eyes were like magnets and Hilary found it difficult to tear her gaze away. Flustered, she turned, just as Bob, who had flung himself on his knees with his arms outstretched, slid across the floor to a grand finale as the song ended.

"YEAH!" Bob cried, and came to an abrupt halt at Hilary's feet. The guests gave him a thunderous round of applause.

"Look out, Bob! You nearly knocked me over…" Hilary felt goosebumps on the back of her neck and her heart was doing strange bunny hops. "Get up!" she said, and reaching for Bob's hand, pulled him to his feet. She turned to look back at the balcony but Lenny had put the main lights on and flooded the room with light.

Long Tom was nowhere to be seen.

Hilary wondered if she'd been dreaming as she followed the others out into the corridor and down the stairs to the waiting vehicles.

"OH MY GOD!"

Hilary heard Bob cry out and followed his line of vision. Bob held his hands to his face and stared at his knees. His trousers were torn and bloody grazes peeped out of the ragged fabric.

"I've got sodding splinters from that dance floor," he wailed. "You'd think Long Tom would at least keep it polished and smooth!"

"That'll teach you to think you're Mr Dance-Off 1978," Hilary said.

They settled into the back of their car and she dabbed at his knees with a tissue. "Now, pull out your prayer beads and say a few Ohm Sas. We'll soon have you comfortably ensconced in our hotel, where, I have no doubt that you'll find plenty more trousers in the multitude of suitcases you brought for three nights."

"These were my favourites!" Bob said, sulking.

Their car set off and travelled gently through the countryside. After a while, it slowed down to maneuver a long bend, where a pretty little cottage, set back from the road, overlooked a wide estuary.

"Oh look!" Bob was suddenly animated. "That's Fool's Landing. Isn't that Mickey Lloyd's property?" He knew damn well that this was the home of Hilary's ex – Bob had done his homework in the days before there trip. "It's quite deceiving; the property's hidden by all those trees." A long, low, whitewashed building nestled under a shroud of trees and bushes, and wooden decking ran alongside. The cottage had a magnificent view of the water and rolling hills beyond.

Hilary spun round and leaned over Bob to look out of the window, but the cottage was now in the distance.

"Shall I tell the driver to stop?" Bob asked eagerly.

"Don't be so stupid. Why on earth should we do that?" Hilary said.

Peeved by her response, Bob rubbed his knees and sulked again.

Hilary stared out of the window as the green and lush pastures whizzed by. How she longed to stop and have a tramp round the cottage, even if it was only to peer through the windows. Damn Mickey Lloyd! – still in her head after all these years. Hilary remembered his delicious blue eyes, dancing brown curls and sing-song Irish lilt. "Be Jesus, Hilary, you're breaking my heart…" he'd whispered to her as he ran nimble fingers through her hair and held her in his strong, muscular arms.

She closed her eyes and could almost smell his warm tanned skin and feel the soft rub of his cashmere sweater. Mickey loved the finest clothes and thought little of blowing his money on bespoke outfits from his tailor in Savile Row.

Christ! What was she doing? Hilary shook her head. Mickey Lloyd was history and that was where she intended to keep him. She suddenly felt very sober and thought back to the incident in the ballroom with Long Tom. Long Tom was at least a hundred years old. What cheek! But he, too, had delicious eyes and a suggestive smile. She was going to have to watch herself – too much Irish hospitality wasn't good for her health. Or her heart!

She sat up and rummaged through her Coach bag, found her

iPad and pulled on a window blind to obliterate the fields and lanes beyond. Hilary reached for her glasses and sighed as the device sprang to life. She told herself that she needed to work and focusing on Hargreaves Promotions, wondered how they were coping in her absence.

8

Heidi sat in a first class compartment on the early morning train from London to Liverpool and tucked into a full English breakfast. She was looking forward to her trip, even though Hilary had warned her of difficulties with Zelda Martin.

A steward topped Heidi's coffee up and asked if she would like more toast. She nodded and swallowed a mouthful of bacon. She was fuelling up on food, not knowing where the next meal would be, although catering on set was generally plentiful. Hilary had warned her to steer Zelda away from the mobile kitchen where, it seemed, Zelda was spending most of her free time. Heidi buttered her toast and ate it with gusto – she didn't have a weight problem and despite a voracious appetite, never gained a pound. Her lithe, size ten figure was as perfect at thirty as it had been at sixteen. She wondered if it would stay that way once she had children. Heidi secretly longed for a baby and hoped that her body clock wasn't ticking too fast. Her partner, Stewie, would make a wonderful dad, and they'd planned a family since the first day they'd met, but so far, without success.

Her day had begun early. She'd crept out of her flat in Muswell Hill just after six o'clock and had managed to sneak to her waiting taxi without waking Stewie or Bonky, her cat, who was curled up in a soft, slumbering ball in the crook of Stewie's legs. She'd packed the night before, so had only to shower and grab her bag before scrawling a note on the back of an old envelope, to remind Stewie to do some grocery shopping. She'd propped the note against an Emma Bridgewater teapot on the kitchen table.

The steward fussed around the table as he cleared the breakfast debris. Heidi reached for her bag. She began to apply make-up to her flawless complexion and as she carefully brushed eye shadow over her oval shaped lids, she thought about her boss. Always get your war paint on! A Hilary-Hargreaves Golden-Rule...

Heidi smiled as she remembered one of the first things Hilary had taught her. Ignore what anyone else was doing – a good outfit and well made-up face gave you the cutting edge, never mind all the luvvies who bounced around in jeans and trainers all day. Hilary insisted on well-dressed staff representing Hargreaves Promotions, and a generous salary enabled them to maintain her standards.

Heidi loved working for Hilary.

Hilary had head-hunted her from Storming PR, sensing agent potential when Heidi successfully ran a marketing campaign for a leading supermarket chain. Hilary had supplied a chef and together they worked on the campaign. Chef had his face beamed across billboards around the country, on TV, in national magazines and become a household name. Everyone was delighted with the results. It had been easy for Heidi to leave Storming PR. Hilary had promised her a client list of her own and within two years she was working with some of the most well-known chefs in the industry. No two days were the same.

Heidi worked from home, with occasional catch-up days with the team in the office, but she was generally out on the road at food festivals, openings and events – anywhere where her clients need a chaperone, she ensured that she maximised their public profile and kept everyone happy.

Heidi finished applying her make-up and was running her fingers through her short, cropped blonde hair as the steward passed down the aisle.

"Gooseable!" he whispered, and slipped her a few packets of complimentary biscuits.

Heidi smiled. She was going to have to get used to the Scouse accent over the next couple of days!

∽

Zelda sat up in her king sized bed and stretched her arms out wide. A button popped off the front of her silk pyjamas and flew across the room.

"Rats!" she cursed. She ambled out of bed to retrieve it and placed the button safely in her toiletry bag, where Carmelita could find it.

The phone rang.

"Morning, Miss Martin. This is to remind you that your car will be leaving in an hour."

Zelda thanked the receptionist and asked if her breakfast was on the way. Assured that it would be with her in five minutes, Zelda pulled her long hair into a protective cap and stepped into the shower. She rubbed Molton Brown gel vigorously into her skin and pulled a face – her tummy seemed to be getting rounder, not flatter as Hilary would wish. Zelda sighed. The constant struggle with her weight was an ongoing battle; if only she could resist the heavenly catering when they were filming. The gorgeous chap from Bon Appetit! had made her chocolate brownies yesterday afternoon. They were so scrumptious that she'd eaten all six in one sitting and brought a box back to her hotel to have after supper. Zelda stepped out of the shower and wrapped a fluffy towelling robe round her body; it felt tight and barely met. What on earth was she to do?

She could hear her mobile ringing and lumbered through to the bedroom, where a waitress had let herself in and was setting a breakfast table up by the window.

"Hello?" Zelda spoke into the phone.

"Morning, Zelda," Heidi spoke cheerfully. "I'm on my way up – see you in a jiffy…"

"Bugger!" Zelda swore again and stared longingly at the laden table. Heidi would have a fit if she saw it. No doubt, the Rottweiler had given strict instructions for Heidi to calculate every calorie that passed Zelda's lips. Zelda silently cursed Hilary and her hourglass figure and reached for a linen napkin. She threw it over the breakfast then opened the window to let the mouth-watering smell of sausage and bacon drift out to the street below.

There was a gentle tap on the door

"It's open," Zelda called out.

Heidi bounced into the room like a chic golden goddess and Zelda's heart sank. She forced a smile and leaned forward to air kiss Heidi's cheeks.

"Darling, you look marvellous!" Zelda smiled. "Come in and make yourself comfortable. I'm just getting dressed."

Heidi walked over to the table and peeped under the napkin.

"Oh, how kind, Zelda," Heidi said. "I'm starving. Barely ate on the train. You're such a sweetie to have ordered breakfast for me." Heidi sat down and began to tuck in.

"Help yourself." Zelda gritted her teeth and ignored her rumbling stomach as she rummaged in the wardrobe. "Had mine earlier, before my run..." She stared at the row of hangers and wondered what outfit she might squeeze into today.

An hour later, Heidi helped Zelda into their car and they were driven away to the location for the day's filming. Heidi held the call sheet and script and began to go through the format. It was the final day at Mr and Mrs Lobley's terrace house in Toxteth, and teenagers Terry Towels and Mandy Riley were joining the Lobleys to savour the delights of Lobley's Lobby, otherwise known as Scouse – a dish that Zelda had practiced at home in London.

"It's perfectly vile," Zelda complained to Heidi. "I can't imagine how anyone could like it; the meat is as tough as boots."

Heidi glanced at Zelda's soft suede Fratelli Rosetti boots and wondered what it was like to live on Planet Zelda.

"Yesterday we had to endure a rubbery takeaway pizza and something called a Whopper – a horrid burger in an inedible bread bun."

Zelda's stomach growled, she was grumpy and yearned for her breakfast.

Heidi had read through the script a couple of days ago. Terry and Mandy (known off-set as Tugger Towles and Randy Mandy – two out-of-work teens who spent their job seekers allowance on fast food and fags) had shared their lunch with the Lobleys, and today it was the turn of the Lobleys to provide the meal. By the end of the day Zelda would have knocked up her interpretation of both meals, working to a strict budget with nutrition as a priority.

Heidi wondered what the participants would think of Zelda's Toxteth Tartlets – a dish Zelda had dreamed up to replace the soggy burgers. It consisted of a nutty bread dough infused with sun-ripe tomatoes and filled with organic root vegetables. Lobley's Lobby had the Zelda twist too, and was now Scrummy Scouse, replacing stewing steak with free-range chicken. Heidi felt anxious. A free-range chicken was more than a day's job seeker allowance or pension credit and she hadn't noticed any organic vegetables stores on their journey through Toxteth. Hilary must know what she was doing?

Which way would the participants vote? Heidi prayed that Scrummy Scouse would tickle their taste buds, and remembered Hilary's comments that this would make riveting TV!

～

AILSA CRAIG SAT on a wall and munched a muesli biscuit. She took a sip of strong dark tea and sighed. It was overcast again in Liverpool and she longed to be back in Glasgow. With luck, she'd be heading home that evening. This was the third and final day in Toxteth; next week they'd locate to Stoke-on-Trent. Ailsa wondered what dazzling little outfits Zelda would have packed in the Louis Vuitton to entertain the troops in Tunstall – wherever that was.

Ailsa finished her biscuit and gave Gary from Bon Appetit! a thumbs up. He'd excelled himself with the home-made fruity breakfast bar; it was sweet and substantial – a bit like Gary. Ailsa wouldn't mind half an hour in the back of his catering van, he could plump her fruit up any time. Gary was gorgeous! Ailsa smiled as she recalled teatime on set the previous day. Gary had produced the most delicious warm brownies and carefully presented them to Zelda. He'd later confided to Ailsa that he thought Zelda was lovely – like a young Nigella, curves and catering were such a turn on!

Ailsa sighed, she'd never been blessed with curves and her flat chest and tiny hips were more suited to the catwalk than the bedroom, but her height let her down. She stood five foot two in her stockinged feet and had known at an early age that the nearest she'd get to a glamour model was dressing it. Over the years she'd built up a successful business as a freelance stylist. Her work was varied, from fashion to pop groups, but she'd never styled a female chef before and was struggling with Zelda Martin. Zelda's agent insisted that Zelda be allowed to wear her own clothes. Ailsa couldn't for the life of her see how clothing better suited to Sloane Street and Belgravia would work for filming on Zelda and The Zimmers. The Lobleys had gasped yesterday when Zelda flashed her diamond-set Chanel watch as she bit into Tugger Towles's burger and declared it unfit for human consumption. Tugger's eyes had lit up as he stared at the watch and Ailsa hoped that Zelda wouldn't be squealing later that her jewellery was missing.

A car pulled up and Ailsa hopped off the wall and went to meet it.

"Morning, Ailsa," Zelda said and introduced Heidi. "You two will get on well." Zelda looked them both up and down; she yearned to have their sylph-like physiques.

"Let's run through your wardrobe and sort out your make-up," Ailsa said as she led Zelda and Heidi through to the Lobleys' front room, which was being improvised as Zelda's dressing room.

"How quaint," Zelda muttered as she eyed Mrs Lobley's collection of porcelain dolls proudly displayed in a glass fronted cabinet. A fierce-faced creature in flounces and lace stared out from under a tight fitting bonnet, her rouged cheeks reminded Zelda of pools of blood and shuddered.

Ailsa checked Zelda's outfit. She was wearing a white Dolce &

Gabbana Active Body T-Shirt, over leggings which were tucked into boots. Ailsa walked around Zelda and nodded her head in approval.

"I'm liking it," Ailsa said, and whipped out a denim overshirt from Primark. She'd cut the label out earlier and smiled as Zelda screwed her eyes up to try and see the make.

"Vivienne doesn'a like her wee labels on show," Ailsa whispered confidingly to Zelda, who beamed as she slipped her arms into the shirt. Ailsa turned back the cuffs and raised the collar under Zelda's flowing hair. She looked great, the t-shirt skimmed pounds off her!

"Ready for you, darling!" Frank the assistant producer called through the door and, with Heidi and Ailsa trailing in her wake, Zelda sailed onto the set.

9

Hilary stood by the window in her second floor executive suite and opened the curtains. The heavy gold drapes fell softly to one side to reveal the marina below. She squinted at the view.

Fishing boats returning with the morning's catch headed for the harbour, where flocks of birds gathered, as nets were shaken over the backwash. Hilary could hear their cries and watched the greedy gulls scavenge for morsels. The sky was as blue as a robin's egg and sunshine peeped out of fluffy white clouds, promising a warm day. She looked down at tourists who meandered along a wooden boardwalk, they stopped occasionally to sit at a bench and enjoy the weather, while the world of Kindale went about its business at a leisurely pace.

Hilary ran her fingers through her hair and felt her head. Everything was intact but she had one hell of hangover. Fragments of the night before flashed like splinters slicing into her memory. Wincing as she groped for the nearest chair, she lowered herself onto the soft comfortable upholstery. A door opened in the vestibule and Hilary turned slowly.

Bob staggered into the room. He was as white as his towelling robe and clutched the furniture as he made his way unsteadily across to the window and fell into a chair beside Hilary.

"Close the curtains," Bob wailed and covered his eyes with his hands.

"Who let you in?" Hilary asked. She was concerned that she'd left the door unlocked.

"Housekeeping. I didn't think you'd appreciate being knocked-up, though from the way you were behaving last night, I expect I'm too late…" Bob groaned and fell forward to rest his head on his knees.

Hilary sat up. What was Bob implying? She vaguely remembered being rounded up by Lenny and taken to Fishy Wishy, a popular restaurant on the quayside. Lenny had organised a meal for his guests, courtesy of Sheamus O'Shaunessy, the proprietor and chef whom, Lenny had assured, would be raking it in once the cookery school was open.

"I never want to see another Fishy Wishy Pie as long as I live." Bob was the colour of putty and Hilary wondered if she should help him to the bathroom.

"Was it off?" she asked.

"No, it was delicious. But Lenny insisted that it could only be eaten with pints of Black Velvet, and I lost count at six."

"But you don't drink Guinness!"

"Neither do you." Bob sat up.

"Christ!" they both said, and stared out at the sea as memories of the never-ending supply of Guinness and champagne flooded back.

"Did Roger…?" Hilary tentatively began.

"Yes, I made sure he got back to his room," Bob snapped. "It's a wonder, though. I never thought I'd live to see the day that you'd do an impersonation of a turkey. Thank God the table was strong enough to support you." Bob glared at Hilary. "I've never seen a man so turned on, especially when you began to gobble!"

"Gobble?" Hilary was aghast.

"Oh yes, you can gobble with the best of them – you had the whole restaurant doing it. Sheamus is thinking of changing his menu…"

Hilary reached for her bag and took out her sunglasses. She put them on and closed her eyes. The darkness was soothing.

"I've ordered breakfast. Orange juice, toast and black coffee. At least we've got the day to recover before the festival dinner tonight." Bob tugged on his robe and frowned at the grazes on his knees.

The Kindale Gourmet Food Festival officially began that day and was launching with a cook-off in the town centre. Kindale was twinned with Porthampton, a hamlet on the east end of Long Island, New York, and chefs from Kindale and Porthampton annually exchanged bases and travelled to compete in food based festivities. The Porthampton chefs had arrived earlier in the week and were already up and sharpening their knives in preparation for the cook-off. Later in the day, a black-tie ball would be held to open the festival. Tomorrow, an event called The Mad Hatter's Taste of Kindale would take place, followed by Fruits De Mer, a seafood extravaganza, on the final day.

A loud knock heralded the arrival of breakfast. Hilary moved a pile of magazines to one side, while a pleasant waiter placed a tray down on the table and asked Hilary to sign the check. He handed her a pen and winked as he placed the signed copy in the bill folder.

"Bloody cheek!" Hilary said as she watched him depart.

"Probably heard that you do a good gobble," Bob replied and reached for a glass of freshly squeezed orange juice.

"I do hope you're not going to bang on about that all weekend," Hilary said as she spread a slice of toast with thick creamy butter and cut it into quarters.

"Bang?" Bob raised his eyebrows. "I don't think it's me who'll be doing any banging. I suggest you lay off the Black Velvet and I'll do the same." He leaned over and took a piece of toast. "Mmm... lovely and salty, I'm beginning to feel a bit brighter already."

The soda bread was working its magic. Hilary removed her sunglasses and sat forward to butter another slice.

"I think I'll have a swim and maybe a massage then perhaps wander into town to have a look at the cook-off," she said.

"I think I might just join you, Miss Hargreaves," Bob replied and chinked glasses with his boss.

The sun flooded through the window and bathed them both in a warm golden light as they sat eating their breakfast contentedly and Hilary contemplated the day. Kindale was turning out to be quite a pleasant place after all!

~

Lenny sat at the kitchen table and looked out at the little cabin cruiser heading back to the shores of Fool's Landing. He watched the lone occupant pull alongside the jetty, tie up the boat then hop onto the landing stage. Lenny rubbed his hands together and rose to put the kettle on. Breakfast had just arrived!

Lenny placed a large skillet on the Aga and tossed a chunk of butter into the pan. He chopped up onion and mushrooms and began to sauté them in the hot fat. He was thinking about recipes and what to perfect as a signature dish, Hilary was bound to get him some demonstrations and hopefully a TV slot after this weekend. He needed to be ready.

His repertoire certainly needed some work.

He could grill a steak, deep-fry chips and knock up a decent enough breakfast but the intricacies of fine dining were sadly lacking in his culinary cupboard. Not that Lenny was worried. He'd bluffed his way out of far worse situations in the past, a little bit of cooking wasn't going to daunt him. He stirred the mushrooms and thought about the last couple of days. Thank God that the Gourmet Food Festival had coincided with the promo trip to the proposed cookery school. Everyone was now settled into a comfortable hotel in Kindale, with passes to all the events, and all at their own expense! Who could resist the temptations of the festival? There was a great weekend lined up and it would be madness not to stay over and see what Kindale had to offer.

Lenny sighed. He'd got to get the sponsors on board soon; he could do with some chunks of cash injected into his bank account. He needed cash, and fast. Long Tom's letting agent wanted a security deposit and twelve months up front to secure the property, and as soon as he made the commitment, Lenny would have to be seen to employ builders, to get the orangery knocked into shape ready for the appliances that he hoped would be on order from Kelly's Kitchen Supplies by the end of the weekend.

Last night, Craig Kelly had verbally agreed to supply all the kit. He'd assured Lenny that he could have anything he wanted, but Craig was under the influence of eight pints of Black Velvet at the time. Lenny hoped that Craig would remember his promise. Craig was loaded, and if he wanted his branding all over the school he'd have to dig deeper. At least David Hugo's presence added clout and David Hugo was clearly impressed that the likes of Hilary, Roger and Craig were part of the recipe.

There had been that sticky moment at the airport too, when the operations manager from Jet Set Air refused to let the plane take off without payment in full. Lenny had claimed that his bank was at fault as the transfer had been made, thankfully David Hugo had stepped in and said that Lenny was good for his word and that Pillings would authorise a line of credit. Lenny smiled. This was easier than he'd expected! His little plan was coming to the boil nicely!

The kitchen door flew open.

"I hope that pan is as hot as a tart's backside!" Mickey Lloyd walked over to the stone sink and thrust half a dozen mackerel onto the wooden draining board. He wore a white t-shirt, faded jeans and espadrilles. His tan was as golden as the leather brogues sitting neatly by the kitchen door, where he'd carefully placed them last night. Mickey took a sharp knife from a rack above the Aga and turned the cold water tap on. The firm-muscled fish gazed up with lifeless eyes from greenish blue bodies as he began to gut the fish.

"Breakfast, dear boy," Mickey said. "One of the greatest pleasures in life." He reached for an egg from a dish on the table and broke it into onto a plate with his right hand, then beat it thoroughly with a fork. With his left hand he deftly dredged some flour onto a plate and seasoned it. He dunked the filleted fish into the egg, coated it with flour and threw it into the hot pan.

He pushed the mushrooms and onions to one side and watched the mackerel sizzle. When the fish had turned a golden brown on each side, Mickey repeated the process, then plated the meal and sat opposite Lenny at the large pine table. He poured two glasses of Drombeg liqueur and thrust one into Lenny's hand.

They raised their glasses and stared at the dark brown contents.

"Made locally with only the finest spring water. Smooth, subtle and with a distinctive smoky flavor." Mickey knocked his drink back and banged the glass down. "Perfect with mackerel. Tuck in!"

Lenny tore a piece of potato farl and dipped it into the sautéed mushrooms. The bread was fried in the mackerel juices and the salty flavour made Lenny smack his lips together.

"Lovely jubbly," Lenny said and reached for a bottle of tomato sauce. He proceeded to smother his breakfast in the vinegary substance.

"Sacrilege!" Mickey cried out, and poured them both another drink.

Mickey had turned up in the early hours of the morning. He'd let himself into his cottage and turned on all the lights, startling Lenny, who woke from a deep sleep to the brilliant glare of the overhead light.

"WHO'S THERE?" Lenny had cried out.

"Sorry to disturb you, old man," Mickey said as he put his head round the bedroom door. "Let me introduce myself." He'd crossed the room and held out his hand.

"Gawd, you 'ad me worried," Lenny said as he sat up. He was shaking as he gripped Mickey's hand. "Thought I was somewhere else for a moment..." He was white and perspiration had broken out across his forehead.

Mickey told Lenny that he looked like he needed a bracer and they'd settled themselves in the lounge, where Lenny poked the fire into life and Mickey opened a bottle of red wine. Mickey explained that he'd recently been sitting at a bar in Bali, watching diners tuck into plates of seafood at the restaurant that bore his name over the door, when he'd heard an Irish accent from a table of holidaymakers nearby.

Suddenly, he'd longed for home.

"So I called the airport straight away to make a reservation and told the restaurant owners that I was taking off for a while. In no time at all I found myself on the next flight to Heathrow. I remembered that the Gourmet Food Festival was due to take place, and having not missed one in the last thirty years, am delighted to land in Cork in plenty of time for the festivities. I'm sorry I gave you a bit of a jolt," Mickey apologised. "The letting agent had mentioned that there was a tenant at Fool's Landing, and seeing as you were was on your own, I didn't think you'd mind a bit of company."

Mind? Bunking up with the Mickey Lloyd!

Lenny was over the moon. He couldn't be happier, and as they drank the wine and opened another, he told Mickey of his plans for Flatterley Manor. Mickey thought the cookery school was a splendid idea and offered to run some courses.

"I've VIP guests staying in Kindale," Lenny told Mickey. "They've flown over to view the property and get a feel for the proposal. My agent, Hilary Hargreaves, is in town too."

"Hilary, you say?" Mickey eyes misted over. "I used to know a Hilary many years ago; a lovely lass with long auburn hair and eyes as green as emeralds."

"Well, this one's a stunner," Lenny said. "You should 'ave seen her tripping the light fandango last night. I nearly jumped on the table and joined her."

They'd bade each other goodnight some time later and as Lenny fell onto the quilted counterpane on his bed, he reminded himself to get Mickey to teach him a signature dish, then fell into a deep and relaxing sleep.

∼

HILARY WAS ENJOYING her hot stone massage. The warm pebbles were comforting on her spine and she felt herself falling into a relaxed state, as soothing sounds of the sea echoed gently from discreetly placed speakers in the comfortable spa room at the Kindale House Hotel.

Bob was pounding up and down the pool as a penance for losing sight of his spirituality over the last twenty-four hours. He refused to surface until he'd done a hundred lengths, followed by meditation. He needed to restore his karma.

He'll have it back in a jiffy, with the first pint of Black Velvet, Hilary thought cynically. Nothing like the hair of the dog to sort all that out! She rolled over as the pretty little red-haired masseur rubbed and kneaded the muscles and joints around her shoulders.

It was pure heaven to be away from the office and constant phones and problems. Lottie was under strict instruction not to divert calls and Heidi would deal with any emergencies. Hilary wondered how Heidi was coping with Zelda and reminded herself to call after her massage. She'd several missed calls on her phone, more than likely all from Heidi.

"Will there be anything else I can get for you, Miss Hargreaves?"

"Just a glass of water please," Hilary replied. "I'll have it by the pool." Hilary secured her robe tightly and stepping into soft towelling slippers, went to find Bob.

Bob lay sprawled across a wooden steamer chair with his eyes closed. He fondled the long length of prayer beads around his neck.

"Cracked your karma yet?" Hilary asked, as she sipped her water and laid a fluffy white towel on the chair alongside. She picked up a magazine.

"Aum Nama Shiva…" Bob repeated three times, ignoring Hilary as she made herself comfortable.

"When your wisdom from within is fully restored, would you like to join me for a coffee?" Hilary flicked through the pages of The Opinion, west Cork's monthly magazine.

"Don't mock my mantras," Bob said and sat up. He looked around and noticed a stag party from east London heading for the Jacuzzi. Bob felt grateful that he'd finished his exercise for the day and stretched his arms out. He held his hands high over his head and flexed his fingers.

"Waving at anyone I know?" Hilary asked without looking up.

"I hardly think you're in a position to mock," Bob replied, referring to Hilary's antics the night before. Hilary silently agreed and decided to change the subject.

"Well, it's good to know that the new sewer pipes in the south of Cork are finally going to be laid." She yawned as she skimmed the local news. The drainage report was detailed in full, alongside local events and the dates-for-your-diary section.

Hilary suddenly sat up and pushed her Liberty glasses further up her nose.

"Kindale's very own rock resident to set sail for Caribbean gigs…" she read out loud from the magazine. "Catch him for a final farewell at the closing night of the Gourmet Festival, where Long Tom Hendry will be performing an intimate session, before he departs for warmer climes…"

"Intimate session?" Bob leaned over to see the article. "Oh, how exciting! We'll be able to join in the fun."

The gig was on the last night of the festival. Hilary hadn't heard Long Tom play in years and wondered if his voice was a good as it used to be. Jools Holland had once described Long Tom as a white man who sings like a black man, with the throatiest gravel this side of the Atlantic. She made a mental note to ask Lenny about tickets and put the magazine to one side.

"Well, I suppose we should get dressed, have a quick coffee and go and have a look at this cook-off?"

Bob was on his feet. He rolled his towel neatly and tucked it under his arm. His body was still tanned from his time in Tibet and Hilary thought he looked dashing in his speedos. She suddenly felt quite warm towards him, he was great company after all, and as loyal as anyone she'd ever known. She gathered her things and searched for her slippers.

"Are you looking for these?" Bob held up the towelling slip-ons.

Hilary slipped her arm through his and gave him a peck on the cheek.

Bob looked startled. "Blimey, the Irish air is certainly thawing you!" he said and squeezed her arm to his chest as they walked to the changing rooms.

"See you soon, Cinderella!" Bob gave a little wave.

Hilary watched him disappear. She clutched her robe and smiled, then hurried to prepare herself for the day.

10

Lottie applied a coat of bright green varnish to her nails and wondered if she should dress up as a leprechaun to welcome Hilary and Bob back from Ireland on Monday. Bob would appreciate her efforts, but Hilary probably wouldn't notice. Perhaps she'd just keep the green nails as a gesture and get a loaf of soda bread in for lunch.

The office was quiet for a Friday and Lottie felt a sense of responsibility with Hilary and Bob away, but Heidi and Frances would be in soon. Lottie was longing to hear all about Heidi's time in Toxteth with Zelda Martin.

Lottie liked Heidi. She seemed to appreciate Lottie's dress sense and was always good for a gossip and, most importantly, Heidi generally turned up with a bag full of freebies from clients and sponsors.

The phone rang on Hilary's direct line and Lottie picked it up.

"Hilary, darling, thank God I've got hold of you," Prunella Gray began.

"Good morning, Prunella, I'm afraid Hilary isn't in today." Lottie said.

"WHAT!" Prunella screamed. "Where the hell is she? I've been trying her mobile all morning."

"She's in southern Ireland for a couple of days and has probably turned her mobile off."

"OFF?" Prunella yelled. "But I have to speak to her!" she demanded. "Tell her to call me back. NOW!" Prunella hung up and Lottie made a face as she wrote the call on a message pad. Prunella was so rude! Lottie felt like ignoring the call and letting her stew, but she'd noted in the diary that Prunella had a photo shoot at her home today. Her anguish was probably justified. Lottie left a message on Hilary's phone and hoped that her boss would get back to her soon.

She stared at her nails, another coat and they'd be perfect.

∼

HEIDI JUMPED on the tube at Highgate and jostled for space in an aisle. It was standing room only at this time of day on the Northern line and she was glad that she wasn't office based; the journey would be unbearable on a daily basis. Not that it took her long to get into the West End. Unlike Stewie, who'd earlier battled his way across the rush hour traffic, to get to a location shoot in Queen's Park. He had a full load in his car, with various camera and lighting equipment. Stewie was a food photographer and, on Hilary's recommendation, was working with Prunella Gray today. Prunella had created a series of recipes for a sponsor to use in a new campaign, to promote a pineapple health drink called PAP. Heidi couldn't imagine why any sponsor would want to use Prunella in such a campaign, but the success of her autobiography was projecting Prunella into the limelight and she was much in demand. Hilary had even mentioned talk of a TV drama based on the book. The sponsor was using Prunella's recipes on their website and Heidi knew that Prunella was getting paid handsomely for the work.

Heidi felt sorry for Stewie. He had a long day ahead of him and she hoped that Prunella was in a good mood. At least Hilary had booked a home economist and a food stylist to be there for the day. All Prunella had to do was pose with the finished dishes alongside a bottle of PAP and smile nicely for the camera.

The tube pulled into Tottenham Court Road station and Heidi jumped off. She made her way through the crowd of early shoppers on Oxford Street, then turned into Wardour Street and strolled down the road towards the offices of Hargreaves Promotions. She hoped that she'd have time to do some shopping; there was an Agent Provocateur round the corner and she felt like a treating herself to some new undies. Another month had gone by and still no sign of the patter of tiny feet; Heidi thought that she may as well splash out. She might pick up some of Stewie's favourite chocolates too and then have a bite to eat in the the Pig and Whistle, with Lottie and Frances. Heidi looked forward to her day.

She stopped to pick up a couple of cappuccinos from an Italian deli. Lottie loved the frothy coffee and Heidi always treated her when she had a day in the office.

"Anyone home?" Heidi called out as she ran up the stairs and pushed the door to reception gently with her foot.

"Cappuccino! How lovely," Lottie exclaimed and took the cardboard cups from Heidi's hands.

"Nice nails," Heidi commented as she took off her coat and hung it on a stand. "Come and talk to me while I settle in."

Heidi had a desk in the corner of Bob's office. She flicked on a lamp and sat down, then reached for her laptop. Lottie put the drinks on the desk and wheeled Bob's ancient chair across the room so she could sit opposite Heidi while they sipped their coffee. Chocolate-stained froth clung to Lottie's pink lips.

Heidi handed her a box of brownies. "Try these, they're divine. Gary, the caterer on The Zimmers, made them."

Lottie bit into a thick chocolate chunk and closed her eyes. "Ecstasy!" she murmured.

"Any word from Ireland?" Heidi asked.

"No, it's all gone quiet." Lottie looked thoughtful. "I wish Hilary would call, I've left her a couple of messages." She dipped a brownie into her coffee, the gooey chocolate oozed and Lottie sighed with contentment.

"Well, the most surprising thing happened yesterday," Heidi said, as her laptop sprung into life and she searched for emails. "Zelda was a hit in Liverpool!"

"Are you sure?" Lottie looked puzzled. "Bob said it was a recipe for disaster. He thought she'd flop horribly amongst the working class."

"Flop? No, they bloody loved her!" Heidi shook her head in amazement and remembered the reaction of the Lobleys as they tucked into a hearty slice of Zelda's Toxteth Tartlet and a bowl of Scrummy Scouse. Everyone had declared her recipes a cut above their daily fare and with a few adjustments to bring the ingredients into a cost effective budget, the filming would be carefully edited to show Zelda winning the participants over. Even Tugger Towles had taken a slice of tart home to his pregnant partner, and Randy Mandy was last seen racing out of the Lobleys with Zelda's "designer" shirt on her back. She had Zelda's blessing of course; Zelda was keen to bring haute couture to the masses.

"Well I never." Lottie drained her coffee. "Does Hilary know?"

"Can't get hold of her," Heidi replied. "I'm sending her an email." Heidi's mobile rang and she reached into her bag.

It was Stewie.

"Sweetheart," Stewie began, "has anyone spoken to Prunella today?"

"I'm not sure," Heidi replied cautiously. Stewie never called her when he was working.

"Well, it might be an idea to get Hilary to call her," Stewie said. "The Vice President of PAP turned up today and started to throw his weight around. He's American and not used to the likes of Prunella."

"Why? What on earth has she done?"

"She made an appearance about an hour late, which isn't a normally problem, but demanded to know who 'the seedy little tosser in the cheap suit,' was…"

Heidi closed her eyes as she listened to Stewie describe Prunella's actions. Dressed in a lace housecoat that had seen far better days, and with traces of the previous night's face powder and lipstick forming crater-like cracks in her heavily Botoxed face, Prunella had demanded that the Vice President leave the house until she was well and truly ready for him, at which point he stormed off, muttering something about speaking to his lawyers.

Heidi visualised the contract going up in smoke. Hilary would have a fit!

"Carry on with the shoot and I'll deal with Prunella. I'll be over as soon as I can." Heidi hung up.

"Problems?" Lottie asked.

"You bet," Heidi replied, reaching for her coat.

Lottie pushed Bob's chair back and pulled a sulky face; she'd been looking forward to a gossip with Heidi. "I wondered why Prunella was so steamed up earlier."

"You mean, she called and you didn't tell me?" Heidi asked, incredulous.

Lottie pouted. "She's a vile woman."

"She may be vile but she's brings in a shed-load of commission." Heidi grabbed her bag and headed for the door. "When Hilary calls, tell her I'm on my way to Prunella's." Heidi pecked Lottie on the cheek and brushed a brownie crumb off her chin. "Catch you later." She rushed down the stairs, off in search of a taxi.

∾

THE MAIN SQUARE in Kindale was buzzing. A crowd had gathered around a makeshift stage, where two cooking stations were assembled under a tarpaulin canopy. Several chefs, smartly attired in freshly laundered monogramed jackets, stood beside the worktops and prepared the ingredients for their dishes. They talked amongst themselves and threw friendly banter across the stoves – the Irish on one side and the Americans on the other.

Master of Ceremonies for the festival was a popular TV presenter. A rotund and red-faced man, Dougie Davies loved to dine and drink and this event was his favourite. He stood at the front of the stage and tapped gently on a microphone.

"Now if I can just get a word in edgeways..." Dougie began. The chefs stopped talking and stood to attention. "We're gathered on this fine day to welcome our overseas friends from Porthampton, once more, to the shores of Kindale." There was a polite round of applause as the American chefs grinned and waved at the crowd. Dougie introduced the Irish chefs and everyone went wild, loud cheers echoed round the square.

"For those unfamiliar with the event, there will be several head-to-head cook-offs with the crowd voting for the most popular dishes." Dougie then fired off a couple of jokes and made innuendos about the amount of alcohol the Americans had consumed the previous evening, before declaring the proceedings officially underway.

Bob and Hilary stood at the back of the crowd but Bob wanted to get closer to the stage and gently edged Hilary forward. Everyone was very accommodating, and on learning that it was Bob and Hilary's first time at the festival soon made space for them at the side of the stage. Delicious aromas permeated the crisp autumn air as the chefs tossed well-seasoned scallops in bubbling hot butter and placed them on slithers of pesto croutons. Assistants offered them to the audience.

"Oh my," Bob exclaimed as he bit into a soft fleshy scallop. "Absolute heaven."

Hilary yearned for a cigarette but didn't feel it appropriate to light up in public. She shook her head when offered a scallop, she must watch her weight this weekend – there was food wherever they went. She turned up the leopard print fur on the collar of her La Riviera swing coat and suppressed a yawn, while the chefs continued their demonstration and Bob grazed happily on each delicious offering. Hilary stamped her feet, the air was cold and she was glad that she was wearing woollen palazzo pants and a cashmere sweater.

Dougie Davies was coming to the end of his repertoire but as the final dishes were handed out, there was a stirring in the crowd. Several cheers went up and people moved to one side to allow the newcomers to approach the stage.

Hilary tugged on Bob's sleeve, she'd seen enough and wanted to retreat to the warmth of the Joe Edwards Bar, which looked cosy and inviting. She stood on tip-toe and looked through the window where a fire crackled brightly in a wood-burning stove.

"Be Jesus, as I live and breathe!" Dougie cried out and sent a piercing shrill through the sound system as he cheered into his microphone.

Startled, Hilary turned.

Dressed in a three-piece maroon corduroy suit, suede brogues and a green bow tie, Mickey Lloyd leapt onto the stage.

The crowd went mad.

Hilary gasped and gripped Bob's arm. Trailing in his wake, Lenny attempted to jump onto the stage too, but he was nowhere near as athletic as Mickey and stumbled back, to be encompassed by the crowd that had surged forward.

Hilary couldn't believe her eyes. Her heart was doing an Irish jig and threatened a solo performance of River Dance as it pounded under her jumper. She couldn't take her eyes off Mickey. He was as handsome as ever and the pain of their separation, all those years ago, ripped through Hilary's chest like a knife. She clutched onto Bob and watched the performance on stage.

Dougie and Mickey were back-slapping and shaking hands, as Dougie introduced Mickey to the chefs and told the crowd that they were in for a treat: their home-town boy had returned to the fold and was just in time for an impromptu cook-off.

Lenny appeared at the back of the stage, his hair was ruffled and he brushed dust off his trousers but, unperturbed, he inched forward and stood beside Mickey. Mickey introduced him and in no time Dougie announced that the next challenge would be Anglo-Irish, between Lenny and Mickey.

"This should be interesting…" Bob commented, placing his arm protectively around Hilary's shoulders.

Encouraged by the crowd, Mickey and Lenny selected raw fish from an ice box and took their positions. Dougie instructed the crowd to count down and they were off!

Mickey had chosen sole and with a rapier-like finesse began to fillet, bone and roll the delicate fish. Lenny had chosen a more commonly eaten fish, and as he seasoned a mackerel and coated it in egg and flour, he felt his confidence rising. In no time at all Dougie had the crowd counting down again as Mickey and Lenny finished their dishes and leapt back from the table to tumultuous applause.

"Well I never!" Bob exclaimed. "It seems our Lenny can cook…"

But Hilary was oblivious to the shenanigans on stage. She stared at Mickey as if seeing a ghost from the past. In all the years that had followed their affair, she'd never expected their paths to cross again. She'd buried the hurt and humiliation that he'd inflicted, deep within her memory, vowing never to let it resurface. But here he was, standing before her and looking as attractive as he did on the day they parted. Her legs began to tremble and she felt weak as she watched his smiling face and laughing eyes tease and entertain the crowd. The man was more gorgeous than ever! He'd aged well, despite a hint of grey in his thick hair, a healthy tan enhanced it and his sparkling blue eyes were like deep tropical pools. Hilary wanted to dive in; the years had been kind to Mickey Lloyd.

"You need a drink." Bob gripped Hilary and steered her away from the stage. She seemed to be in a trance as he maneuvered her into the Joe Edwards Bar and found a seat in an alcove by the fire.

"Back in a jiffy," Bob said, and hurried to the bar.

Hilary felt cold despite the warmth in the room. She stared into the flames and remembered a fire in another life time – the last time she'd seen Mickey…

They'd spent a wonderful summer, filming in Devon. Around the Coast with Mickey Lloyd was a roaring success. It was his fifth series and following Spain, Ireland, Scotland and northern England, Mickey was based in glorious Devon and sailed the southern coasts, cooking his way around hamlets and shorelines, meeting a wealth of interesting characters along the way. Hilary had an outside catering company in those days and her mobile unit stayed on set for the duration of filming. She acted as home economist for the programme and also made food for the crew.

Romance with Mickey had sparked on the first night. The crew had dispersed to their accommodation at the end of day's filming, and as the sun set over the sea, Mickey had ambled over to her unit and watched her pack up. He produced a bottle of wine and lit a fire with driftwood. They sat on the warm sand staring into the flames and soon were holding hands.

Hilary had instantly fallen in love.

He was like no other man, before or since, and as the weeks went by he assured her that their love was forever and he'd never leave her side.

Until the day his wife turned up.

Filming was over and a wrap party took place on the beach with locals, family and friends of the crew. The party was in full flow and with gallons of wine and cider consumed and a local band pounding out popular tunes, a good time was being had by all. Mickey and Hilary danced by the fire, under a blood-red sunset, oblivious to the storm brewing on the boardwalk as Mrs Lotitia Lloyd stepped out of her Land Cruiser and glared at her husband.

Lotitia had snared Mickey when he was filming in Spain and he was a valuable commodity, but Lotitia had no prenuptial arrangement and wasn't prepared to give him up so early in their marriage. She'd thundered across the sand and wrenched him away, before directing a tirade of abuse on Hilary.

Hilary thought about her last memory of Mickey. She'd watched him climb into the Land Cruiser beside Lotitia and disappear in a cloud of sand as they roared away from the beach. He'd never even turned to say goodbye.

"Get this down you." Bob thrust a gin and tonic into Hilary's hand. He stood beside the fire and stared out of the window. The crowd had dispersed and the chefs had packed up their utensils. Dougie, Mickey and Lenny were nowhere to be seen.

"Fancy a stroll down to the marina?" Bob asked as Hilary drained her glass. "Fresh air might do you good?" he added hesitantly.

Hilary was as quiet as the grave and had turned very pale. "I won't be a moment," she said, and disappeared into the Ladies room.

Bob drummed his fingers on the bar and looked at his watch. He hoped Hilary wasn't booking a flight back to London; he'd been looking forward to the weekend's festivities. Damn Mickey Lloyd!

There was a commotion by the door and Bob groaned as he saw Dougie, Mickey and Lenny enter the bar. They were laughing and joking and arguing about who would get the first round in.

"The Three Musketeers..." Bob muttered, and gritted his teeth. He looked across the room. Hilary was heading towards them! Bob reached for his prayer beads and began to murmur a chant.

"Darlin'!" Lenny yelled as he spotted Hilary. He bumbled forward and grabbed her arm, then turned to introduce her to Dougie and Mickey.

Hilary nodded at Dougie and glared at Mickey.

"We've met," she said coldly.

Mickey's jaw dropped open. He was lost for words and stared at Hilary in disbelief.

"Blindin', darlin'," Lenny said. "What's your poison, lads? Hilary here is partial to a Black Velvet or two... Landlord!" Lenny turned to the bar.

In a flash, Mickey had regained his composure and with a smile that would ignite an Olympic torch, reached for Hilary's hand.

"Of all the gin joints, in all the towns, in all the world, she walks into mine," Mickey whispered. "How are you, Hilary?"

He leaned forward to kiss her cheek and Hilary felt his warm lips brush her skin, a familiar masculine smell threatened to buckle her legs.

"She's extremely well but incredibly busy, thank you!" Bob had no time for Mickey's Irish charm and Humphrey Bogart impersonation and placed himself between the long-lost lovers like a wall. "Nice to see you all but Hilary has calls to make and things to do..." He put his arm around her and giving a bemused Mickey an icy glare, guided Hilary out of the bar.

They stepped into the square. It was deserted. Everyone had retreated from the chill to revive themselves in the many surrounding hostelries. Bob walked Hilary briskly through the town.

"Any more skeletons in the closet you haven't told me about? I'm not sure if my heart can take all this smouldering passion."

"Don't be such a drama queen," Hilary replied. She'd had a severe shock seeing Mickey again but was determined not to show Bob how deeply it had affected her. Fighting to regain her composure, she pointed to a pub that overlooked the marina.

"The Trident Arms looks very inviting," she said. "Let's go and have a drink, we've plenty of time and I've got calls to make."

Bob breathed a sigh of relief. He looked at the boats on the water where end-of-season holidaymakers milled about by the shore. Hilary was back to normal and as long as the Trident had a good supply of Bombay Sapphire, things should be all right. He smiled as they strolled over to the pub and wondered what would happen next.

11

Zelda was enjoying herself. She sat in the fifth floor café at Harvey Nichols and sipped a glass of champagne, happy to be back on her own stomping ground.

"Tell me all about it." Madeleine, Zelda's mother, sat opposite her daughter in the plush restaurant, noting that Zelda seemed very cheerful since she'd returned from Liverpool.

"Oh, it was pretty ghastly, but I managed to survive," Zelda said and looked around the busy room. Their table overlooked the roof tops of Knightsbridge, where earlier that morning Zelda had indulged her love of labels and gone to town with Madeleine's American Express card. Thank goodness Martin, Zelda's father, still paid Madeleine a hefty alimony.

Martin Arnold Martin was loaded.

Zelda was saving her fee from The Zimmers. She fancied a holiday when filming was over and the hefty lump sum she'd receive, when everything was in the can, would go a long way towards some new clothes.

"Did you make any new friends?" Madeleine asked, as she picked at a warm leaf salad and pushed tiny pieces of chorizo to one side.

She had her eye on an Elin Kling shirt in the designer room downstairs, but there was only a size eight on the rail. She pushed the remaining salad to one side.

Zelda, meanwhile, tucked into a plate of creamy cannelloni, smothered in finely grated parmesan cheese. She thought about the Marcus Lupfer merino wool jumper she'd purchased earlier. Thank goodness the designer went up to a size sixteen, it would look fab teamed with the J Brand stretchy jeans she'd found in Harrods. Aisla had told her to dress down for her appearance in Stoke the following week. Zelda was thrilled that she'd achieved "the look", but still kept to her labels.

"How are you getting on with the crew?" Madeleine stared at her daughter's plate. Zelda had the appetite of a horse; takes after her father! Madeleine thought bitterly as she envisaged her ex with Brigitta, his curvaceous new wife – a high flying Swedish beauty who worked alongside Martin in his city law firm.

"Oh, they're all quite a jolly lot," Zelda replied. "There's a really dishy chap who does all the catering, he's always slipping me little treats. He was so sweet to me last week and always seemed to pop up with a plate of scrummy nibbles whenever I had a break." Her eyes twinkled as she thought about Gary.

Gary was terribly handsome and even though he cooked all day, he had the body of an athlete, with lovely strong arms and huge muscles that rippled from the rolled-up sleeves of his crisp white shirt. Zelda thought about Harry's arms, which were quite puny in comparison. Harry used to row for Cambridge and had once looked quite fit, but his working life in the city seemed to curtail any exercise and the only action his muscles got now were to lift a pink gin with his cronies, after work.

"Darling, don't you think you should be a little more careful about what you eat?" Madeleine frowned. Her face puckered into tiny creases and reminded Zelda of the mock-croc clutch bag that she'd looked at earlier.

"Not everyone wants to be rake thin like you, Mother," Zelda snapped. "Daddy clearly prefers the fuller figure." Zelda looked away as her mother winced and gulped her champagne.

"Brigitta is like a beanpole," Madeleine hissed. She thought of Martin's new wife, the tall and beautiful bitch had a very shapely body and carried it magnificently on her Swedish frame. She glanced at her Cartier watch. There was still time to go and get the shirt. The credit card was burning a hole in her leather tote, Martin would pay dearly for divorcing her!

Madeleine signalled for the bill.

"I want a dessert." Zelda pouted and glared at her mother who was so difficult these days. Divorce didn't suit Madeleine.

"You're dining with your father tomorrow and I'm quite sure the multi-talented Brigitta will have knocked up an old Gustafson family recipe and you'll have wall-to-wall desserts covering his weekend retreat," Madeleine growled.

Harry was driving Zelda to Martin's Cotswold home the next day; he wanted to give his new Porsche a spin and said the journey would be fun. Brigitta had promised to show Zelda her pancake recipe, something she might be able to use in Stoke. Zelda thought Brigitta was really rather nice. She was a super cook and Zelda loved all her Swedish recipes – they had a great deal in common.

Zelda drained her glass and scraped her chair back, relieved that she'd moved in with Harry; life in Madeleine's Chelsea household was considerably strained since Martin had re-married. Mummy could be so difficult sometimes. She smiled sweetly at her mother and thought about the credit card, she'd no doubt manage to get Madeleine to pay for some lovely Elemis products downstairs; they usually lingered in the beauty department before they left the store and Madeleine always spent a bomb on marine cream for her face. Heaven knows she needs it! Zelda thought as she led her mother out of the café and headed for the lift.

∽

HEIDI HAD ARRIVED in fashionable Queen's Park in record time and ran up the steps of Prunella's chic town house.

She could hear raised voices.

Heidi closed her eyes and crossed her fingers as she knocked on the stained glass of the imposing front door and waited patiently. It was eventually opened by a frazzled Stewie.

"Prunella is upstairs having a hissy fit and won't come down," Stewie said as he let Heidi into the hallway and led her past a spacious sitting room and light and airy dining area. "We've done the shoot and I just need her to pose with the finished dishes, then we can get out of this hell hole." He ushered Heidi into an open plan kitchen, where his cameras were set up. The home economist and food stylist were pacing nervously in the garden at the back of the house.

"If that's that American arsehole, you can tell him to stick his pineapples…" Prunella yelled over the first floor banister.

"Good luck!" Stewie said, as Heidi tentatively began to climb the stairs.

Prunella stood on the landing. She still wore her dressing gown and carried a tumbler of vodka. She glared at Heidi.

"Where's Hilary?" Prunella yelled.

Heidi braced herself.

"Hilary is working in Ireland, Prunella, dear," Heidi began. "Why don't you come with me and we'll find you something nice to wear…"

"Don't you patronise me, you jumped up excuse for an agent. I want Hilary here this instant, and don't try and fob me off with that limp handed wimp in an orange suit, either." Prunella drained her glass and thrust it down on a side table.

Heidi ignored Prunella's retort about Bob and took a step forward.

"Sorry, Prunella, but you'll just have to put up with me." Heidi could feel herself getting angry and silently counted to ten. "Now, I know that you've fallen out with the Vice President of PAP, but if we can just finish the photos, I'm sure that Hilary will ensure that your contract is safe. She'll win him round once he's sees how fabulous your recipes are."

Prunella leaned on the frame of her bedroom door and stared at Heidi as she reached up and ran her fingers through her unkempt hair and teased the jet black fringe over one heavily made-up eye. She tugged playfully at the cord on her gown and ran her tongue suggestively over crimson stained lips.

"Very well, little one," Prunella cooed, suddenly softening as she batted false eyelashes and pushed the door open. "Why don't you come and help me…"

Heidi glanced down the stairs at Stewie, who crossed his fingers, then signed a thumbs-up as he nodded encouragement.

Heidi took a deep breath and followed Prunella into the depths of her boudoir.

∼

The fire in Fool's Landing crackled in the open grate. It gave heat and heart to the cosy lounge, where Mickey and Lenny sat on a sofa and worked their way down a bottle of Chateauneuf du Pape.

Mickey topped Lenny's glass up. "Looking forward to the ball, dear boy?"

"Not half," Lenny replied. He stared into the fire, deep in thought. It was time for him to crank his plan up a gear, and with his guests firmly entrenched around a dining table later that evening, he intended to start getting financial commitments from them all.

Lenny decided to begin with Mickey.

"So, how do you feel about putting a few layers of dosh down and getting some shares in the cookery school?" he asked.

"Me, old chap?" Mickey held his glass up to the fire and swirled the ruby red contents.

"You could do a few courses from time to time," Lenny said, "getting paid of course," he added. "A reasonable investment for a number of shares, with handsome annual dividends. Got to be worth a butcher's?" Lenny glanced sideways at Mickey. "You don't have to be here very much. I'm supposed to move up to the manor but I could keep this cottage on and look after it for you, perhaps do a contra deal and you get rid of the letting agent?"

Mickey took a slurp of his wine. The bottle was almost empty and he stood up eager to find a replacement.

"Give it some thought..." Lenny called out as Mickey disappeared into the kitchen.

Mickey walked over to the larder and browsed the shelves. He took his time and let Lenny's words sink in as he carefully chose another bottle. Lenny was a pushy character and seemed intent on getting an investment out of him.

But Mickey wasn't so sure.

As much as he liked the whole idea of the European World of Cookery, he had niggling doubts about Lenny. There was something about the man that simply didn't resonate and he certainly couldn't cook! Mickey was fully aware that Lenny watched his every move, no doubt making notes behind his back, as he absorbed every little detail that Mickey applied to the art of cooking.

"Found one!" Mickey said as he returned to the lounge and opened the bottle with finesse. "I'll certainly consider your idea," Mickey said, topping up their glasses. He walked over to the window and stared out at the estuary, while Lenny continued to ramble on about his plans for the cookery school.

But Mickey wasn't listening. His gaze followed the water along the coast until it came to the marina at Kindale. He looked at the silhouettes of the numerous hotels surrounding the bay and wondered which one Hilary was staying in.

He'd had quite a jolt when he'd seen her in the pub the previous day. Never, in all the years that had passed, had he expected to see her again. Time had been kind and she was as ravishing as she was that summer in Devon, more so in fact – maturity suited her. Mickey felt himself stir as he thought about her glorious creamy skin and the abundance of auburn hair nestling on slim shoulders that carried her shapely figure with style.

What a bloody fool he'd been! His wife at the time – what was she called? ... Lotitia? Mickey could barely remember, but she'd been hell bent on fleecing him of every last penny if he ever mentioned Hilary's name again. He'd been forced to stay by her Spanish side for a few miserable years before she ran off with a bullfighter from Pamplona, who was gored to death at the annual festival, obviously not running as fast as he had when he first ran into Lotitia.

Mickey sighed. He'd made some stupid mistakes in his time but losing Hilary was the worst. There's wasn't a fiddler's hope that he could win her back again, he'd felt real hostility in her eyes when confronted in the pub. What a fool! She was successful and competent and drop-dead gorgeous, sex-on-legs ... if only he'd stayed with her, how different his life might have been.

Instead he'd blown his money on stupid investments, had problems with his tax, and had to travel to Thailand to finally knuckle down and make some money again. Thank goodness for his TV success, although faded now, he was still a celebrity in some culinary circles and had traded on it ever since. Not that it would matter one jot to Hilary, who was used to celebrity chefs and not fazed in the slightest by the so-called charm of the successful world they moved around in.

"You might want to have some branded products in your own name; we'll have a gift shop..."

Mickey could hear Lenny droning on about the merits of investing in his radical idea. He turned from the window and drained his glass.

"Well, I suggest we pull out all the stops, dear boy, and see how interested the other possible investors are."

Lenny wrenched his portly frame unsteadily off the sofa. Mickey slapped him on the back.

"A shower, shave and dash of cologne should set us up for the evening's festivities," he said, and raced ahead of Lenny towards the bathroom. He wanted to ensure he got first shout on the hot water from the cottage's ancient boiler and shut the door firmly behind him. As he pushed the latch across, Mickey smiled and thought about the evening ahead. "Operation Hilary" was about to begin!

HILARY TWISTED an art deco bracelet onto her wrist. The carved celluloid was shaped like a serpent and had tiny jewelled eyes that stared menacingly.

"Love the rags!" Bob said. He stood in the middle of Hilary's suite and nodded approvingly as Hilary strolled over to the mini bar and poured them both a drink. She wore a black fringed, flapper-style cocktail dress with a long, 1920s lamp glass bead necklace.

"I've ordered hats today," Bob said as he took a drink from Hilary's outstretched hand. "It seems that the event tomorrow involves headgear and everyone has to wear something creative. There's a prize for the best."

Hilary raised her eyebrows. Hats? She hadn't worn a hat since Ascot. She'd no idea what Bob was rambling on about.

"It's called the Mad Hatter's Taste of Kindale, and you wear a hat as you go round the town in groups, tasting lots of delicious food, which is laid on by all the participating restaurants."

Hilary nodded and sipped her drink. Bob would no doubt organise something tasteful. Hats were the least of her worries right now. She'd been trying to get hold of the Vice President of PAP all evening and he wasn't returning her calls. Prunella had really put her size three in it this time. No doubt the poor man was lying on a therapist's couch, somewhere deep in Harley Street, in an attempt to have all memory of an inebriated Prunella, falling out of her nightwear, firmly erased from his memory. Hilary had spoken to Heidi, who seemed quite traumatised by the whole experience but had eventually succeeded in getting Prunella to finish the shoot, and with Stewie's talent for touching up even the most challenging photos – the results that were now on Hilary's iPad were superb. Prunella looked radiant, and the PAP recipes were excellent.

"Poor old Heidi's had a tough day," Bob commented.

"Did you speak to her too?" Hilary asked.

"I told her to grab a handful of tranquilisers out of my top drawer."

"I thought she seemed a bit distant," Hilary said. "What actually happened?"

"Baby Jane laid a trap and lured our Heidi into her lair. The poor cow found herself neck-deep in broderie anglaise on Prunella's four-poster, with the evil one making it clear that she wanted far more than styling advice before she'd put a toe back in the kitchen..."

"Oh Christ!" Hilary closed her eyes. "Prunella came on to Heidi?"

"With all guns blazing, it seems." Bob smiled and twirled his glass. "Good job our Heidi's tough. It took her the best part of an hour to convince Baby Jane that she wasn't a lipstick lesbian."

Hilary shook her head. Prunella was a liability! If she wasn't such a high earner, she'd find herself in breach of contract and looking for a new agent. Being pissed whilst working was gross misconduct and Hilary wasn't quite sure what clause covered "sexual advances to staff members" or any other members Prunella could get her sticky little paws on.

"Send Heidi a bouquet and a bottle of Bolly, she deserves a medal..." Hilary said.

"On it like sonic!" Bob tapped a note onto his iPad. "But we must get to the ball, Cinderella." He smoothed the sleeves of his dark suit and held out his arm.

Hilary reached for a black beaded purse. She wasn't looking forward to the evening. Mickey Lloyd's appearance earlier that day had unsettled her far more than she was willing to let on and she was dreading being in any room where he was likely to be present. He could go to hell and back for all she was concerned and she would avoid his Irish charm at all costs. Hilary told herself that she didn't give a toss for his attentions. Mickey Lloyd was firmly in her past.

"Beautiful!" Bob cried as Hilary took his arm. "Let's see what the so-called Gourmet Capital of Ireland has to offer!"

He closed the door gently behind them as he led Hilary off to the ball.

12

Long Tom Hendry sat on a piano stool by a large bay window in the music room at Flatterley Manor. He ran his fingers over a beautiful Steinway grand piano, the smooth polished wood felt familiar and warm to his touch. In the garden outside, two peacocks strutted across a neatly mowed lawn. As they ambled towards a waterfall feature, they fanned their magnificent blue, green and gold tail feathers, the reflection caught the late afternoon light and sent sparkling shadows dancing across the water.

But the atmosphere in the music room was far from sparkling. Tension bit at the air around Long Tom and his breathing was laboured as he stared at the keyboard and felt the first signs of a panic attack. His heart raced and hands trembled as they hovered. He took a deep breath and flexed his fingers, but a hidden force was at work and weighed heavily; it wouldn't allow them to rest on the keys.

He groaned and closed his eyes.

Long Tom remembered his excitement when the piano had first been delivered. Elton had told him that there was no finer instrument in the universe and Long Tom had waited a year for the manufacturer to build the piano to his specification. They'd refused to hurry it and the carefully selected woods that made up the rims, top and sound-boards had been cured for months in specialist kilns and conditioning rooms, the hard rock maple and mahogany and finest acoustic-quality spruce assured the full, rich Steinway sound. The piano was Long Tom's passion, his love and inspiration, and many moons ago he'd spent hours upon hours and days upon days, composing some of his sweetest songs on this very keyboard.

But Long Tom hadn't touched the piano in three years.

He opened his eyes and took a deep breath. Could he play again? His heart was pounding and he felt a cold sweat break out on the back of his neck. It trickled slowly through the long tendrils of thick hair that flowed over his shoulders, untethered from his usual distinguishing ponytail. He pushed his fingers into his furrowed temples and harshly rubbed the skin. If only he could get some clarity… if only the notes would come back!

Long Tom had stopped playing the piano on the day he'd stopped drinking. His manager, Pete, had found him hunched in an inert state over his most treasured possession, in the gallery of Long Tom's London town house in Chester Square. The town house had been bought on the proceeds of his best-selling album No More War, My Friends. Pete had received a call from yet another passing girlfriend, who warned of the state she'd left the rock star in. Long Tom's relationships crumbled as fast as his decline into alcoholism; he'd already wrecked his two marriages and had little interest in commitment.

His only commitment was to the bottle.

Pete had no idea how long his client had been slumped over the piano. Long Tom was in a drunken stupor, amongst stale vomit that encrusted the pearly white keys, staining them a pale sickly yellow. As sickly as Long Tom's pallid complexion and the filthy clothes he wore.

Pete feared for Long Tom's life – had he finally gone too far? He'd leaned over to take stock of the damage and heard Long Tom mumble a faint whisper. Pete bent down even further and strained to listen to the words he never thought he'd hear…

"I want to get sober…"

Pete could hardly believe his ears. He'd found Long Tom in this state so many times and was used to picking up the pieces, but this was the first time he'd ever heard those words.

Taking swift action, Pete picked up the phone and dialled.

That same day, Pete found a place at The Abbey, and before nightfall, Long Tom was admitted to the clinic. And so began the torturous journey of drying-out and detoxifying Long Tom's body of the years of alcohol abuse that had led him to a complete breakdown, in both mind and body.

It was a long and difficult road for Long Tom in the year that followed his desperate plea. The Abbey had been a stepping stone and after the first month he was moved to a centre in the north east of England. Pete told the media that Long Tom had retired to Ireland – to Flatterley Manor, a property that Long Tom had never used and wanted to get to know, while he took some time out to write new music. The paparazzi eventually got tired of staking out the grounds of the Irish home – clearly Long Tom had become a recluse; they never saw him and the residents of Kindale put up a brick wall of silence. Many were related to staff at the manor, whom Pete had made sure had decent salaries coming in while their boss was in recovery. Their signed confidentiality contracts were safely tucked away with Long Tom's lawyers, and with other scandalous news from the world of rock more pressing, the press left the story alone.

In truth, Pete had whisked Long Tom off to a rehab centre called Hope House, in Whitby: a bracing seaside town where no one raised an eyebrow that a rock legend was amidst their carefully monitored existence. Hope House had helped a friend of Pete's in his early days in the music industry and Pete hoped that it would help Long Tom. It ran on charity and local authority funding and took addicts from all walks of life, mostly the seedy side, where drugs and booze were an escape from the drudgery of the real world and the poverty or difficult environments they'd found themselves in. Pete felt that Long Tom needed a reality check to shake him out of his addiction and unlike the comforts of the numbingly expensive Abbey Clinic, where residents so often returned, the harshness of the Whitby weather and reality of life in Hope House might, in time, blow away his demons and give Long Tom back his life.

Long Tom lived his day-to-day life in recovery as Tom Broad, a mixed up fellow who'd fallen into hell and wanted to find a way out of it, but in Hope House his fellow inmates and therapists knew the truth. There's was no hiding place in recovery sessions. Intimate disclosures and laying the soul bare were all part of the healing process. To his room-mates, Tom Broad was just an ordinary man with problems. He had to deal with the same daily fears that they all had and they were unfazed by his previous life. A rock star was no of more importance than the addicted drug dealer who'd wrecked the lives of hundreds and now wanted to repent; or the back street kid hooked on online gaming and crack cocaine, who'd persistently beaten and robbed his own mother to get money for a fix. As they studied, absorbed, and worked through the programme, all were all sworn to secrecy concerning their personal and past lives. Hope House had a veiled wall of trust and Pete managed to keep Long Tom's uncomfortable secret away from the media.

Very slowly, he healed.

The year passed and Long Tom worked hard to face his great creator or whatever higher deity was giving him a second chance. It was a tough road to travel and there were times when he simply wanted to walk away and find the nearest bar. Life in rehab hurt, but not as much as life as a drunk.

On a cold spring morning, Long Tom said goodbye to his friends in Whitby and thanked his therapists and the people who'd helped him heal and had given him faith again.

He returned to his life and headed to Flatterley Manor.

Not long afterwards, Hope House received an anonymous donation that would keep them going for many years. Little did the Trust know that it was sent by one of rock's most infamous hell-raisers, as a "thank you" for saving his life.

A gentle tap on the heavy oak door of the music room startled Long Tom. He slammed the cover over the keyboard and spun round as James, his butler, walked across a faded Aubusson carpet. He held a silver tray.

"Your tea, sir."

"Thanks," Long Tom said. He watched James position a side table, then reach for a mat and carefully place a mug of steaming black tea beside a jug of fresh milk. The manor, though jaded, had an air of dignity but Long Tom preferred basic comforts and tea came in his favourite old china mug, much to the concern of James, his carer-come-man servant. James had been with Long Tom since he'd moved to Flatterley Manor and would have preferred to serve tea with a silver pot and fine bone china.

Long Tom crossed to the table and poured a good slug of milk into the strong tea and looked around the room. He knew that the manor needed female warmth and attention to bring it to life, but he was as scared of starting a new relationship as he was of composing a song. In his mind, any chink in his defence mechanism might lead him back to the bottle and so he deliberately chose a solitary existence, interspersed with visits from Pete.

"Will you require the car this evening, sir?" James asked.

Long Tom sighed and thought about the night ahead. He'd been invited to the ball in Kindale and was reluctant to go, but he knew he should make the effort. His tour began soon and Pete thought it would be good for him to begin socialising. He'd been shut away for too long. He'd agreed to do a gig at the festival on Sunday night, just an hour or so in an informal setting at the Trident Arms and Long Tom knew it would be packed, the locals were delighted that their rock star recluse was making his come-back in their very own town.

"Yes, I'm going out later," Long Tom told James.

"Very good, sir," James said and quietly padded out of the room.

Long Tom wished that James wasn't so formal but it wasn't a criticism, James was a god-send and looked after him with the greatest care. Schooled in the old ways, James worked alongside a cook, a housekeeper and discreet security guards and did his best to ensure that Long Tom's solitary life was comfortable. The staff would stay on when Long Tom went on tour, they'd supervise the cookery school opening and maintain the manor.

Long Tom sighed. He wasn't sure if he was doing the right thing in allowing the cookery school. He certainly didn't need the money, but the manor needed life, it had lost its pulse and so would Long Tom if he continued to fester away in the large, gloomy building. He had to go forth and get his life back. He'd thought he'd be able to compose again within these walls but during the time since he came out of rehab he'd done little more that read, walk and pamper his peacocks. He longed to compose again and tunes danced teasingly in his head, but he couldn't get them down and his fingers refused to return to the keyboard. Long Tom knew that he had to stimulate his creativity but he didn't know how.

It had been a stroke of luck that his record label had brought out his old album with a reggae twist and he'd never thought that it would work. Pete, however, had been adamant and even though Long Tom refused to go to London to record, the record company re-mastered his old hits and the results had been amazing. Radio stations in the Caribbean were playing his songs all day and night and slowly the rest of the world was waking up to the reincarnation of Long Tom Hendry. It was time to get back on the wheel of fortune. Long Tom wasn't sure if he could take the pressure again – would he start drinking? Would the devil and temptation rear its ugly head?

There was only one way to find out and it began this weekend.

He had a gig to do and Lenny was pressing to finalise plans for the cookery school. It was time for Long Tom to go back into the real world, to take the dust sheets off his London town house, go on tour and find out if his talent would return.

And maybe he needed to get laid.

That, too, was a distant memory. Sex without alcohol was like tea without milk and Long Tom wasn't sure that he could face either. He sipped his tea and stared at the piano. The ominous dark shape looked threatening and hostile and Long Tom felt a ripple of fear course through his body again. He stared at his hand as he held the mug. It used to shake, at least that had stopped, but even now he longed for a proper drink. He glared at the piano; it seemed to taunt him. He longed to fling the mug across the room and smash it against the smooth dark wood.

Long Tom placed the mug on the table and with a troubled sigh went to prepare for the evening ahead.

13

The streets of Kindale were packed with people who'd flocked into the town for the gourmet festival. Lively bars, cosy pubs and busy restaurants overflowed as Mickey Lloyd hurried along the road, heading to Kindale House Hotel where the ball was about to begin.

He welcomed a few moments away from Lenny, who seemed glued to his side at every available opportunity. That evening, diners had eaten at the many restaurants participating in the festival, and now everyone headed to the ballroom, where a champagne reception was laid on and a band tuned up in readiness for a night of drinking and dancing.

Mickey stepped up his pace and kept his head down in an attempt to avoid the well-wishers who were thrilled to have him back. There would be designated tables at the ball and Mickey was determined to get a place next to Hilary. Lenny hadn't been able to co-ordinate his party and Mickey and Lenny had ended up dining in Fishy Wishy with Dougie Davies and the chefs from Porthampton. Dougie held court and chatted animatedly as the chefs asked him questions about his television career. He'd joked that the first six months were fun, but the following thirty-five years had been hard work. Mickey smiled throughout the meal; he made an entertaining dinner guest but as each course was served, he wondered where Hilary was. He was furious that he'd not caught up with her.

The organisers had arranged a novelty taxi to ferry guests around Kindale over the weekend. It took the form of a train, with an engine and driver at the front pulling eight little carriages, and as the train headed along the crowded road, Mickey heard a horn blast loudly to warn revellers. He turned sharply to avoid a collision, and came face to face with a carriage full of guests, all heading to the ball. Bob leaned out of the window and blew on a paper trumpet.

"Peep peep!" Bob laughed.

"Gobble gobble!" Roger Romney yelled.

Mickey peered into the carriage and searched frantically for Hilary, but the train had gathered pace and went past in a flash. He cursed as he pushed through the crowds, and with a renewed determination headed for the hotel.

HILARY SAT BACK in her seat on the train. She'd seen Mickey search amongst the faces of the occupants of the carriage and was grateful to Bob and Roger for unintentionally obscuring his view. She intended to avoid Mickey for as long as possible – completely if she could. The thought of being in close proximity to Mickey again made alarm bells pound in her head. Their relationship was well and truly in the past and she intended to keep it that way. It would be so easy to fall for his charms again, only to be left devastated when he moved onto pastures new. As he surely would. Men like Mickey were eternal philanderers and Hilary knew that he'd never change.

Earlier, with Bob by her side, they'd met with Roger Romney, Craig Kelly and David Hugo. They all stood in the foyer of the hotel and waited for Lenny to arrive and take them to a restaurant for dinner. Fortified by a round of drinks and seeing the novelty train approach, they had decided to hop on and play hooky from Lenny's vigorous demands, at least for the first part of the evening. They'd been dropped off at the Joe Edwards Bar, and found a table in the fine-dining restaurant, where Hilary had eaten the best fish chowder she'd ever tasted. Conscious of mountains of food to come the next day at The Mad Hatter's Taste of Kindale, she declined dessert and kept her hand over her glass each time their waiter attempted to replenish it.

"You're very controlled this evening," Bob commented. He scraped the last traces of Irish coffee cake from his plate and sighed contentedly.

Roger called the table to order.

"Our train is about to depart," he began. "No doubt our host Lenny is having palpitations caused by our absence and will be wondering where we all are," Roger smiled, "and our cheque books!"

Everyone headed for the train. As they began to board, Roger helped Hilary into a carriage and whispered into her ear, "I'm looking forward to seeing you dance again!"

"I shall be having an early night," Hilary replied primly. She'd no intention of repeating her performance from the previous evening and had deliberately maintained sobriety to avoid a further episode of the "gobble dance".

Bob smiled and winked at Roger and together they leaned out of the window as the train sped along the narrow streets of Kindale.

～

The ballroom at Kindale House Hotel was packed. The band, smart in evening attire, was in full swing and a ginger haired MC held a fiddle and loosened his shoe-string tie. He encouraged guests to their feet, to dance to a rendition of popular Irish hits.

An anxious Lenny met them at the doorway.

"Gawd, I thought I'd lost you all!" Lenny said with relief, and maneuvered the party to a large circular table he'd reserved by the dance floor. Bottles of the festival sponsor's champagne sat in buckets of ice on the centre of the table. "Come on, fill your boots!" Lenny yelled and began to hand out drinks as everyone took their places.

They were joined on the table by Dougie Davies and members of the organising committee. The American chefs and a party named the Porthampton Friends of Kindale, who'd also made the trip to Ireland, sat on tables either side.

"Cheers!" Lenny cried and knocked back his drink with gusto. "Are you 'aving a Guinness in that, darlin'?" he yelled over to Hilary. "Got a nice sturdy table for you to dance on!"

Hilary sipped her champagne and glared at him. The man was so uncouth, although she knew she deserved his comments after her behaviour the previous evening.

Lenny was oblivious to her reaction and waddled over to the adjoining tables – he'd smelt money from the American visitors and began his charm offensive as he invited them to listen to his plans for the cookery school.

Hilary looked around the packed room, the place was buzzing and the band had certainly got everyone in a party mood. She declined invitations to dance from Bob and Roger and watched as they found partners from the choice of attractive females, all dressed to the nines in their colourful party frocks.

The band played a medley of Van Morrison songs and there was a cheer as Brown Eyed Girl began. Hilary smiled; it was one of her favourites. She was completely absorbed in the music and didn't notice that someone had crept up behind her and pulled out a chair.

"Hey, where did you go...?" Mickey sang softly into Hilary's ear.

"What the hell!" Hilary gasped as Mickey sat down beside her and placed his arm along the back of her chair. He was inches away and she could smell his aftershave and feel his warmth against her naked shoulders.

"Do you mind!" Hilary reached for her bag. As she grabbed the beaded purse it knocked her flute of champagne and the contents spilt onto her knees.

Mickey rushed forward and placed his hand on her legs. His firm, warm fingers sent probes, like currents of high voltage electricity, shooting through Hilary's flesh as he slowly and sensuously rubbed the liquid away. His blue eyes bored into her and the corners of his mouth teased upwards in a knowing smile. Hilary felt blood rush to her neck and pound over her face and temples. Long forgotten waves of sexual excitement flooded over her.

"You're my... brown-eyed girl," Mickey whispered into her ear. Hilary closed her eyes and thought that she would quite simply melt away, as his lips lightly brushed her neck and made their way down her shoulder.

"Yoo-hoo!" Bob flung himself down on a vacant chair and whipping a handkerchief from his top pocket, wiped the perspiration from his over-heated brow. "You two seem to know each other," he said. He couldn't help but notice the sexual tension beside him.

Hilary jerked away. Mickey leaned forward to retrieve her glass and filled it with more champagne, then poured a glass for Bob and one for himself.

"You haven't introduced me." Mickey smiled and placed his arm back on Hilary's chair.

"Bob, this is Mickey Lloyd," Hilary snapped, absolutely furious with herself for allowing Mickey to touch nerves that had long lain dormant. She took a large swig of her drink.

Bob grinned. "Obviously. I understand you two have a history?" He raised his eyebrows.

"We had more than that..." Mickey replied, and began to caress Hilary's shoulder again.

"We worked together a long time ago," Hilary retorted and sat forward. His fingers were like electrodes and she wasn't sure that she could resist the magnetism of their touch much longer.

"Is everyone getting along nicely?" Lenny appeared with an arm around Dougie Davies as Roger pulled his dance partner over to the table for a glass of champagne.

"Gee, Bob! They're playing our song!" A large lady in a red taffeta dress, a member of the Porthampton Friends of Kindale, pulled Bob to his feet. Mickey spoke to Dougie as Craig and David joined the party and they all laughed heartily as Dougie began to tell a joke.

Hilary sensed an opportunity to escape. She carefully picked up her bag and, sliding off her seat and with speed that surprised her, ran from the room.

The foyer was packed as Hilary pushed through the throng, then moved quickly through the entrance. She needed fresh air and time to catch her breath. Damn Mickey Lloyd! He'd completely unnerved her. Her hands shook as she reached into her bag and found a pack of cigarettes. She was adamant that she wasn't going to get involved with him again – it would only end in heartbreak and she knew full well that it would be her heart that got broken. Hilary tapped a cigarette out of the box and placed it in a tortoiseshell holder and then rummaged around in her bag for a light.

"Bad habit – can be addictive…"

Long Tom Hendry flicked a lighter and the gold casing sparkled as he held the flame out. He studied Hilary carefully, his eyes bright with amusement.

Hilary jerked backwards in surprise and wondered where the hell Long Tom had come from? As he leaned forward, she looked at his face. It was shadowed slightly by a large Stetson. The flame illuminated the world-weary smile of a man who has been everywhere and seen everything. Accepting the light, she looked anxiously around, fearful that Mickey might have followed her, before dragging deeply on the menthol and nicotine.

"You seem a little flustered?" Long Tom said and tucked the lighter into the back pocket of his jeans. He wore a tuxedo jacket and open-necked shirt with his cowboy hat and boots and raised an eyebrow as he stared at Hilary and waited for an answer.

"Erm, it was very hot in there," she began.

"I noticed," Long Tom said, and reached out and touched Hilary's arm. "But you're cold." It was a statement and before Hilary could reply, he'd shrugged off his jacket and placed it around her shoulders.

"You seem to attract quite a lot of attention." Long Tom eyes slowly followed the length of her body, from the delicate heels of her Vivier designed, Christian Dior 1950s pumps, to her curves in the closely fitted fringed dress.

"None of it welcome, I can assure you." Hilary watched him. Long

Tom was calm and quite unconcerned by the people milling around them, all keen to catch his eye. He courteously signed a couple of autographs.

Hilary dropped her cigarette in a metal box on the wall and placed the holder back in her bag. Suddenly, she felt anxious to get away from the frenzy.

"Are you going back in?" Long Tom asked.

"I don't think so; I've sort of had enough of it all for today."

Hilary suddenly felt tired. She couldn't handle any more pressure from Lenny and the thought of facing Mickey again made her feel quite weak; she really should have poured a drink over his head but instead, had nearly melted into his arms in total surrender. Damn the man! She'd been so determined not to fall under his spell again!

A sleek dark car with tinted windows drew silently alongside them. The passenger window glided open.

"Ready, sir?" the driver spoke to Long Tom.

Long Tom turned to Hilary.

"Oh, sorry," Hilary said, "you want your jacket."

Long Tom was silent. He was keen to get away from the ball, people had been crowding round and thrusting drinks at him all night and although he'd managed to resist the alcohol, he wasn't sure that he could trust himself much longer. He needed to get back to the sanctity of Flatterley Manor. But the rambling old place was empty and lonely and Long Tom yearned for some company, if only to listen to some music and watch the peacocks in the moonlight.

"Come with me," he said.

"What?" Hilary was bemused, had she heard him correctly? Did this ageing rock singer whom she hardly knew, really think that she was about to jump into his limo and speed off into the night?

"There's no strings, babe," Long Tom said quietly. "I just don't want to be alone."

Suddenly Hilary felt defenseless. She didn't want to be alone either. A crowd was moving towards them and she saw Mickey looking anxiously down the road. He was looking for her!

Long Tom moved forward and held out his hand and Hilary

turned and looked at him. His dark brown eyes looked warm and kind, skin crinkled at the corners as he raised his eyebrows.

"Coming?" he asked softly.

Mickey seemed to be getting closer. He would see her at any moment! Hilary took a deep breath and closed her eyes. When she opened them, she found herself reaching out and taking Long Tom's hand.

It felt warm, strong and safe.

Hilary stepped forward and let Long Tom guide her into the dark and inviting interior of the limo and they gently sped away into the night.

14

It was a perfect autumnal day for the middle of October. The rolling hills and tree-lined lanes of the sunny Cotswold countryside welcomed the many late-season visitors who milled around happily. They found themselves bathed in an unexpected golden sunshine as they took afternoon refreshments in quaint teashops, or strolled through the charming lanes where rich russet and burnt orange leaves swirled gently along the pavements in the warm breeze.

On the road to Chipping Hodbury, Zelda and Harry made their way to Martin Martin's country residence. They sat side-by-side and sped past the spectacular backdrop of ancient limestone villages, tasteful country homes and well-kept gardens. Zelda pushed her designer sunglasses onto the bridge of her nose and knotted a Hermes scarf under her chin. Harry had insisted on having the top down on the Porsche and as much as Zelda pretended to enjoy the experience of wind whooshing around her ear lobes, it was playing havoc with her hair. She'd had it blow-dried into a sleek style at Charles Worthington earlier that morning, but from the way Harry was driving, Zelda feared that she would arrive at Daddy's looking as though she'd been plugged into an electric socket for the duration of the journey.

"Harry, darling, could you possibly slow down a tad!" she called out as she gripped the edge of her seat with one hand and held the scarf in place with the other.

"Got to see what the little lady can do, sweetie!" Harry yelled back happily. He'd had a beam from ear to ear ever since he'd collected the Porsche from a dealership in Mayfair earlier in the week. Harry adjusted his Burberry driving cap to sit at a jaunty angle and then patted Zelda's knee. "Good job we've plenty of ballast on the bends!" he said, staring at Zelda's thighs as he pushed his foot firmly against the accelerator pedal.

Zelda braced herself and glared straight ahead. Harry's reference to her weight was irritating and she wondered if she should comment on the flat cap. Harry thought it made him look preppy but Zelda thought he looked a complete prick. He was quite irksome at the moment and Zelda wasn't sure if he was being spiteful because she'd been away all week, or if his new found arrogance was built on complacency. She had a feeling that he was going to have a word with Daddy today and was certain that the small, square, box-like shape that bulged in the breast pocket of his Harris Tweed jacket contained an engagement ring. Zelda was puzzled that she wasn't experiencing a ripple of excitement. Surely she should be ecstatic at the thought of pending nuptials? After all, wasn't that what she'd hoped for since the day she'd met Harry?

"Nearly there, old bean!" Harry called out and thrust the car through the gates of a private estate.

"Slow down!" Zelda shouted. She'd had quite enough of this show of male bravado. The scarf had given up during the last five miles and her eyes and nose were streaming. She wasn't the slightest bit impressed with the sporty performance of the Porsche and longed for the solidity of Daddy's Range Rover. To cap it all, Harry had the audacity to poke her in the ribs as he slowed down and swerved the car across the gravel, then came to an abrupt halt at the entrance of Martin Martin's Cotswold home.

"Chill out, old gal!" Harry said. He climbed out of the car and hurried round to the passenger side to help Zelda.

"If you poke me again, I shall slap you," Zelda snapped and pushed Harry's outstretched hand away.

"Surprised you felt it, enough padding there these days…" Harry mumbled peevishly.

The front door opened and a large black Labrador bounded across the gravel towards Zelda. It was followed by Martin and Brigitta.

"Oh, Rupie Woopy! Mommy wommy's missed you!" Zelda cried out and embraced the delighted dog, who proceeded to lick Zelda's hands and face as his thick tail thumped with joy. She tickled the dog's ears and showered him with kisses.

"Lucky for some…" Harry said grumpily as he watched Zelda greet, Rupert, the family pet. Harry couldn't remember the last time she'd shown him that much affection, but at least that would be remedied today! The ring was burning a hole in his pocket and he was keen to get Martin on one side as soon as possible.

"Harry, my good man!" Martin shook Harry's hand enthusiastically and Brigitta air kissed both Harry's cheeks.

"Put Rupert down, Zelda darling, and come and tell us all your news." Martin embraced his daughter. "What on earth have you done to your hair?" Martin stared wide-eyed at the normally sleek blonde tresses that stood at right angles to Zelda's head.

Zelda glowered in Harry's direction.

Brigitta, sensing the tension, took Zelda's arm. She assured Zelda that her hair was utterly charming and led her into the house.

~

IN THE COMFORT of the luxuriously appointed Edwardian-style kitchen, Brigitta busied herself with preparations for a substantial brunch. She moved between the antique-style yellow and cream cabinets as she assembled a variety of vegetables, cold meats, cheese and savouries, then reached for a board on the granite topped work surface and began to chop, while Zelda perched on a tall stool alongside and pulled her dishevelled hair into a ponytail. Brigitta was interested in Zelda's filming schedule and wanted to hear all about Zelda and The Zimmers.

"Well, it's quite a hoot so far," Zelda said. "The first week is in the can and next week I'm going to somewhere called the Potteries, to a place called Tunstall, which is somewhere ghastly in the Midlands. I'm taking an early train to Stoke-on-Trent on Monday morning." Zelda sighed and wondered where she'd be staying; she couldn't imagine any five star hotels in any place that called itself the Potteries.

As they chatted about suitable recipes for the forthcoming week, Brigitta wanted to know what food Zelda was preparing and who she'd be working with. Zelda told her that a staple part of the diet in Stoke was something called an oatcake – a floppy object made from oats and water, which, the researchers had disclosed, was eaten with just about everything.

"They probably roll it round chips," Zelda muttered and picked at fat green olives in an earthenware dish. "I'm going to have to be very creative…" She reached for a cookery book from the extensive collection on the shelves beneath the counter and began to flick through the pages.

Brigitta promised to show Zelda how to make Swedish pancakes, a light and healthy version, with lots of different fillings that would be sure to impress the Tunstall team and give Zelda another high score.

Zelda yawned. Her sugar level must be dropping and she was hungry, she wouldn't mind a drink too.

"Where are our fine fillies?" Harry called out as he entered the kitchen. He held a glass of whisky and his cheeks were rosy. Zelda assumed that the drink wasn't his first. He seemed very jolly and she felt sure that Harry must have had a word with Daddy and got the all clear to ask for his daughter's hand. Harry looked horribly red and sweaty and Zelda didn't think that it suited him at all. It was a good job they were staying tonight; Harry seemed intent on a serious drinking session with Daddy, who also held a glass of whisky and was giving Harry a hearty slap on the back as he joined them in the kitchen.

The doorbell chimed and Martin turned to answer it. "By the way, I've invited a few friends over," he said as he disappeared into the hallway.

Brigitta placed a plate of canapés on the counter and Zelda leaned over to help herself to the warm cheesy pastries. They were delicious. She licked her lips and took a couple more.

"Steady on, Zelda." Harry wrapped her knuckles with a spoon. "Save some for the rest of us."

Martin returned and began to fill a silver bucket with ice. "Everyone's in the lounge, come and join us?" he said. "Bring the canapés and olives will you, Zelda?"

"If there's any left!" Harry chuckled as he strode out of the kitchen.

Zelda resisted the urge to hurl a hot canapé at the back of Harry's head. She hopped off her stool and smoothed her cashmere sweater over her ample hips, then picked up the nibbles and followed her soon-to-be fiancé.

∽

THE DELICIOUS BRUNCH went on for several hours. Brigitta had prepared a Smorgasbord of multiple dishes and laid them out, buffet style, in the dining room for everyone to help themselves. Joined by a dozen or so friends from Chipping Hodbury, they all sat around a vast mahogany table and savoured the delights before them. Martin and Brigitta were perfect hosts and kept their guests supplied with wine and drinks to accompany the Swedish feast. After the meal, everyone retired to the lounge and relaxed on comfortable sofas and chairs by a roaring log fire that crackled in an inglenook fireplace.

Zelda curled up with Rupert on a leather couch and wrapped a cashmere blanket over her knees. Anthony Merryweather sat beside her. She'd been introduced to Anthony earlier and instantly liked him. He'd been a friend of Martin's since Martin and Brigitta had bought their weekend retreat in Chipping Hodbury, and Zelda listened with interest as Anthony told her stories of the various celebrities and actors who came to the theatre and their escapades off-stage. Rupert nuzzled his head on Zelda's lap and lazily stretched his back legs over Anthony's knees.

They stroked the dog lovingly.

"I believe we have a certain lady in common," Anthony whispered to Zelda. He was feeling very mellow, Martin's brunches were an absolute must and Brigitta's cooking was to die for. He made a mental note to send them some complementary tickets for the next event at the theatre.

Zelda rubbed Rupert's ears and looked puzzled.

"Hilary Hargreaves?" Anthony said and raised his eyebrows.

"Oh gosh, you mean my agent?" Zelda looked surprised.

"Absolutely. Known her for years. Quite a woman, wouldn't you say?" Anthony smiled and watched the firelight sparkle against the pale amber of the brandy that he nursed in a cut-glass goblet.

"I don't have a great deal to do with her," Zelda replied. "I just get summoned when something important is about to happen." She thought about her book deals and the TV series and the lunches she shared with Hilary at Ranchers, hardly a place for intimate conversation and Hilary never disclosed anything about her private life.

"Have you met her assistant, Bob?" Anthony eyes glazed over and he smiled as he rubbed Rupert's soft paws and stared into the fire.

"Oh yes," Zelda said. "Bob always helps me out and warns me when Hilary's on the war path. He's fabulous."

"Hmm... I think so too." Anthony looked dreamy.

Harry suddenly interrupted their conversation. He rattled a spoon on the side of a glass and called for everyone's attention.

"I say, everyone, could I have a moment please?"

Harry walked over to Zelda and stopped in front of her. Zelda gathered herself into a sitting position and eased Rupert's head off her knee. She tried to look surprised as Harry dropped to one knee and deftly produced a small leather box from his trouser pocket.

Anthony gasped and quickly moved himself into an upright position.

"Zelda, darling, I wonder if you would do me the greatest honour of becoming my wife?" Harry said and fumbled with the box.

Zelda heard an excited murmur as the guests realised what was happening. She leaned forward and stared at the two-carat diamond ring in a platinum setting. Harry was trying to get it on her finger, he looked anxious as he willed her to reply. Zelda stared at his eager face, he was hot and sweaty again and his hair, normally foppish and reasonably groomed was sticking to his head. She could sense her father urging her to accept. Harry was quite a catch after all, with his country seat, double-barrel and first in line to his family's property empire, she'd be mad not to say yes.

But Zelda was very tired. She'd eaten far too much and her stomach felt heavy as Rupert nudged her arm away from Harry's outstretched hand.

The ring glinted, the box said Asprey's of London.

"Oh, I suppose so..."

"Oh, darling, you've made me so happy!" Harry fumbled with her finger. The ring wouldn't go past the knuckle.

"Oh really, Harry," Zelda snapped and grabbed the ring, "you could have got the right size!" She tried to push it on, but the ring wouldn't fit no matter how hard Zelda pushed.

"Well, it's not my fault if you've put on weight; even your fingers are fat!" Harry looked crestfallen and slid the ring back into the box.

Brigitta sensed the tension and, realising that Zelda was about to burst into tears as she rubbed frantically at her finger, began to clap her hands. As everyone joined in, Brigitta told Harry that it was just the heat in the room and the ring would fit perfectly in the morning. Harry seemed to cheer up and beamed as he shook the many outstretched hands. Martin appeared with a magnum of champagne and popped the cork over the newly engaged couple, which startled Rupert and he made a dash to retrieve the cork, stamping over Harry in the process. Everyone cheered and wished Harry and Zelda well.

Zelda wondered if she should call her mother. She winced as she thought about Madeleine's reaction. There was no doubt that she'd be pleased that Harry had finally popped the question, but

Madeleine would be inconsolable that he'd done it under the roof of the Swedish One. Zelda sighed. She'd have it in the neck for weeks. Oh well, at least she was filming and wouldn't be around to take the backlash from Madeleine.

Zelda watched Harry as he shook everyone's hand. She supposed he'd make her go on a diet now! He wouldn't want her waddling down the aisle. She sighed and struggled to her feet, forcing a smile as she was warmly congratulated and champagne thrust into her hand. Zelda gulped her drink down and wondered why she didn't feel a sense of euphoria and happiness that must surely follow a marriage proposal?

Suddenly, Stoke-on-Trent didn't seem such a bad place after all…

15

Lenny stood in the kitchen at Fool's Landing and smacked his lips together. He picked up a fork and turned three slices of thick Irish bacon in a cast iron skillet. The smell of sizzling fat was delicious and Lenny's mouth watered as he cut thick pieces of soda bread and spread them with creamy yellow butter. He reached for a bottle of tomato sauce from a shelf above the stove and squirted red liquid all over the bread.

"Lovely jubbly..." Lenny said to himself as he stirred three spoons of sugar into a mug of strong tea. He took a large slurp and smiled smugly. Things were starting to go to plan.

Lenny sat at the kitchen table and as he began to eat his breakfast, he thought about the night before. Finally, he'd managed to get a commitment from Roger Romney and a cheque for fifty thousand pounds nestled in Lenny's trouser pocket. David Hugo had stumped up a similar amount and would be arranging a bank draft that morning, as would Craig Kelly, who also fancied his company's name all over the branding for the European World of Cookery. Lenny sighed with pleasure. His scheme was at last coming to fruition! If he could get a few more backers like Roger, Craig and David in the bag he'd be laughing all the way to the bank. He needed to work a bit harder on Hilary though. A TV appearance or a high profile demonstration would give him greater credibility. Just a one-off slot would do, on a prime-time show – something like that would double the amount he was asking from investors.

But Lenny had absolutely no intention of opening a cookery school.

He wiped a crust of bread in the sauce on his plate and chewed thoughtfully. He reckoned he'd got six weeks at most to pull his scam off, time enough to launder the money through an off-shore account. At this rate he reckoned he'd have half a million tucked away nicely by Christmas and he could hole up in Spain till the heat died down.

Lenny wiped his mouth on the back of his hand then threw his plate on top of a pile of dirty china in the stone sink and thought about his latest shenanigan. People were so gullible. Promise them the bright lights and an involvement with fame, fortune and TV and they followed like sheep, all you had to do was find the right investors. Once one fell to his charms, they all went over like a pack of cards – no one wanted to miss out on his "deal of the decade... you'll never have another chance!"

Having Mickey Lloyd on board was an unexpected bonus. Lenny couldn't believe his luck that Mickey had returned so conveniently and already, just the mention of his name had celebrity chefs pounding the pathway to Lenny's door with requests for guest appearances. Lenny was dropping names like confetti and the investors loved it! Even the Americans were starting to take an interest and he'd be very surprised if several multi-dollar cheques weren't burning a hole in his wallet by Sunday evening. Lenny rubbed his hands together. If he could just hold off from putting a deposit down on Flatterley Manor – no need to waste any of the money that had started to pour in. Long Tom Hendry's people didn't seem to be pushing and Long Tom was off on tour next week, if Lenny could keep the fantasy going just long enough to hit a few more investors, he'd be home and dry and supping a sangria with

Santa on the Costa Del Sol, where, he felt sure, there was ample opportunity for another scam.

Lenny stretched his shoulders and yawned as he stared out of the windows to the estuary below. The earlier rain had cleared and weak sunshine pushed through the clouds where a rainbow curved over the water and faded into the mist shrouding the streets of Kindale. Lenny traced the end of the rainbow with a chubby finger and grinned. That's where my pot of gold lies! he thought, smiling. It was The Mad Hatter's Taste of Kindale event today – another opportunity for everyone to get completely blotto and susceptible to his charms.

With a satisfied sigh, Lenny maneuvered his hefty frame past the furniture in the untidy lounge and hurried to get changed, in readiness for the day to come.

∼

Mickey's head was pounding. He squeezed his eyelids together in an attempt to shut out the pain as sunlight streamed into the bedroom.

He was losing the battle.

Mickey could hear a shower running and a waft of perfume drifted from the direction of the bathroom. He slowly opened his eyes and groaned. Discarded clothes were strewn around the room and an empty bottle of whisky sat beside two sticky glasses on a table by the window.

"I wish I was in Dixie…"

A female was singing and Mickey could hear splashing sounds as the events of the previous evening came flooding back. He carefully lifted the cotton sheet and slid out of the bed, where his clothes lay on the floor alongside several articles of feminine clothing. Mickey shook his head, he must have been legless last night – he couldn't remember the last time he'd failed to fold his clothes neatly. He stifled a groan as a wave of pain struck his sore head and with haste, he dressed and gathered his property.

"Mickey, dahlin', I'm ready for you!" a voice rang out.

Mickey swiftly picked up his shoes and reached for the lock on the door. Steam poured into the room from the bathroom and he heard the shower click off. Taking a deep breath, he flicked the lock back and thrust himself through the bedroom door. He let out a sigh of relief as he found himself safely on the other side.

"Be Jesus! Would that be the walk of shame you're doing there…" Dougie Davies closed an adjacent bedroom door and slapped Mickey on the back as they both stepped out into the corridor.

"I'd be moving along if I was you," Dougie said. They could hear a female voice calling Mickey's name, the American twang sounded angry. He guided Mickey hastily towards the lift.

Mickey thrust his feet into patent shoes and flung his dinner jacket over his shoulder. A housekeeping trolley was stationed in the hallway and as he went past, he picked up a bottle of water and two packets of shortbread biscuits.

"You've been doing your bit for Irish and American goodwill, no doubt." Dougie smiled as he pressed the button for the ground floor. "Good man!" He stepped to one side to allow Mickey to go ahead into the foyer of the Kindale House Hotel.

Mickey bit into a shortbread and shook his head. The secretary from the Porthampton Friends of Kindale had been a large lady and Mickey felt as if he'd spent a night in a boxing ring with Mike Tyson. He unscrewed the cap off the water bottle and took a long swig.

"Hair of the dog?" Dougie asked and nodded towards the bar.

"Jesus, no," Mickey replied. He wanted nothing more taxing than a comfortable ride back to Fool's Landing and a couple of hours kip.

"Be seeing you later then. Don't forget your hat!" Dougie said and disappeared into the bar.

Mickey yawned and scratched his head. It was the Mad Hatter's event today. He wasn't sure if he was up to it but he didn't want to miss a chance to spend time with Hilary – she would be leaving on Monday and time was running out. He stepped into the sunshine and hailed a cab, the light was painful on his eyes and Mickey wished he'd got his sunglasses. A car pulled up alongside and he leaned in to give the driver directions and as he turned to climb into the back of the vehicle, he noticed a limo cruise to a halt by the door. A chauffeur jumped out and ran round to open the back door. Mickey jumped into his cab and took a biscuit from his pocket. His stomach was growling, the sooner he had a plate of carbohydrate the better. As they sped away, he hoped that Lenny hadn't eaten all the soda bread and bacon.

∼

Hilary waited until the taxi was in the distance. The last thing she wanted was for Mickey to see her getting out of Long Tom's limo.

As Mickey's taxi rounded the corner of the hotel grounds, Hilary nodded to the driver and climbed out. She reached for her sunglasses and hurried across the foyer to the lift; she was still wearing last night's clothes and prayed that she didn't bump into anyone she knew. The lift seemed to take an eternity to arrive at her floor and as she stepped out into the corridor she noticed a housekeeping trolley. Hilary smiled at a chambermaid and asked if she might have a bottle of water. The maid grinned happily as Hilary thrust a ten-euro note into her hand.

Safely in her suite, Hilary stepped out of her clothes and ran a bath. She poured a generous amount of bath oil into the steaming water then slid gratefully in and sighed with pleasure as the luxuriously scented suds caressed her body.

How she'd longed to have her body caressed the night before.

Hilary was astounded that she'd let Long Tom lead her into his limo, it was completely out of character and she couldn't remember a time when she'd been so reckless. It was years since she'd thrown caution to the wind, but as Mickey had descended on her and was moments away from pouncing, Hilary felt herself propelled into no man's land and had taken the opportunity Long Tom offered. She'd no idea what was about to happen and had gratefully gone along for the ride.

They'd arrived at Flatterley Manor in no time at all and as the limo crept stealthily over the gravel drive, James appeared on the steps. Long Tom thanked his butler and driver and assured them that he had no further need of their services. He took Hilary's hand and walked her to the lawns that led down to a large lake. Several peacocks suddenly appeared and made their way over. Silhouetted in the moonlight, the large birds glided over the damp grass until they reached Long Tom. He began to talk to them and told Hilary of his fondness for the birds, that they were not only beautiful but extremely intelligent and even though they were generally to be found on the ground, they often slept in trees or other elevated roosting spots. Two dull brown birds shuffled across the lawn and one of the colourful birds raised and fanned its feathers, then began to prance and strut, showing off the striking plumage.

"He's proud of how he looks to the ladies," Long Tom said as they watched the display.

"As vain as a peacock..." Hilary said.

"The brown birds are female, peahens, they don't compare to the males," Long Tom explained as the males turned their back to the females and wagged their short tail feathers, hidden underneath the long ones, quickly back and forth. The sound of rustling feathers added to their dance.

"The girls really like that." Long Tom smiled. "If only the human species was as easily pleased."

"I'm sure you've shaken many a tail feather in your time," Hilary replied.

"They make good watch dogs too," Long Tom said, ignoring Hilary's comment. "They've scared off many a journalist." He smiled thoughtfully. "Their call is shrill and repetitive, like a scream, sounds a bit like a woman..." Long Tom seemed distant.

They wandered around the garden in the moonlight, followed by the peacocks. Hilary thought it all felt very surreal as she listened to Long Tom talk about the manor. He explained that he was leaving it next week and going on a short tour, and when that was finished, he intended living in London again.

"Are you looking forward to the tour?" Hilary asked as they stopped by a fountain surrounded by a pool of clear water.

Long Tom threw a stone and as it landed, they watched the inky dark water ripple out. "It has to be done, babe," he stated, and threw in another stone. "I've become a recluse, I've no confidence." He turned and looked Hilary in the eye. "Not something a lady like you would ever worry about."

"What do you mean?" Hilary was curious.

"You're successful and you look wonderful, people must fall at your feet."

Hilary sighed and wondered if Long Tom was on any medication, he couldn't be further from the truth.

"It takes quite a lot of doing," she replied. "I never seem to be able to take my finger off the pulse. I'm scared of it all falling apart... again."

"And I'm scared of it beginning... again." Long Tom moved forward and took Hilary in his arms. He unclipped the comb on the back of her hair and buried his face in the tresses as they poured over her shoulders.

His hat fell to the ground.

Hilary felt his hot breath on her neck and closed her eyes. This was surely the most romantic place ever to be standing in the warm embrace of a complete stranger. Long Tom was nuzzling her neck and kissed it gently. As he raised his head, he murmured that she was beautiful. Hilary opened her eyes. His face looked haunted and sad and she longed to wipe the pain away. She reached up and touched his cheek to caress his face.

Long Tom sighed. "Let's go into the house," he whispered and taking her hand again, they walked slowly through the garden, past the orangery and entered the house by the kitchen door.

"Want a drink?" he asked as he filled a kettle.

"I wouldn't mind a cup of tea," Hilary replied. She actually longed for a gin but knew that it wouldn't be appropriate to ask for one.

"Ginger, fruit, breakfast or Earl Grey?" Long Tom asked as he opened the cupboard door of an old Irish pine dresser. "I'm partial to peppermint at this time of night."

"That will be fine," Hilary said as she wandered around the homely kitchen. At the far end of the large room she saw two curved rocking chairs by a wood burning stove. Long Tom walked ahead and placed the steaming tea beside the chairs. He leaned down and opened the stove, then threw a couple of logs onto the fire and watched the flames leap into life. He straightened up and indicated to Hilary to take a seat. The chairs were upholstered in patchwork and Long Tom carefully placed a matching rug round Hilary's shoulders.

They sipped their tea and stared into the flames.

For the next few hours they talked about their lives. The sanctity of the warm kitchen and quiet of the night seemed to create an atmosphere of trust and they confided openly to each other.

Hilary told him that her parents had died and how she'd struggled to get started in business. She told him all about Mickey Lloyd and how she'd been avoiding him earlier. Then she spoke of her ex-boyfriend, Joel, and how he'd fleeced her and left her to start over, how difficult it had been to get back on her feet, and that she was scared of losing it again.

Long Tom told Hilary that he was an alcoholic. He spoke quietly as he explained that his life before rehab was a blur, and he described the agonies he'd been through to get sober.

"I'm scared too," Long Tom admitted, "scared of the temptations and worst of all, I'm no longer able to play the piano or compose a song. I'd always been drunk when I'd written and played, I know that the two were interlinked. It was the same with relationships, that's why I become a recluse."

"But you've started to go out again, and you're going on tour?"

"Got no choice, babe. It's wither away here till I'm six feet under, or give it one last shout." Long Tom sighed. "Pete will be with me, he'll form a steel wall, but once an addict always an addict, so they say..."

"You'll be okay." Hilary sat forward. "You're very brave, it will come right. I'm sure you'll be composing again, by Christmas I bet!" She tried to bring some optimism to the conversation.

Long Tom laughed and scraped back his chair as he stood. "I think my composing days are over." The kitchen was light, sun streamed through double doors that opened to the vegetable garden.

"I'll be happy if I can stand in front of a crowd tomorrow night and sing – that's all I've got to do. Remembering the words would be helpful too." He smiled.

Hilary knew that he was trying to reassure himself that he wasn't nervous about his future. "Well, I'll make sure I'm there tomorrow to cheer you along, I love your music and know the words of all your songs." Hilary got to her feet. "You have an amazing voice."

"I'm an old man now," Long Tom said. "The vocal chords ain't what they used to be."

"Nonsense, you're as old as you feel, and you'll be fine, I promise," Hilary whispered.

Long Tom reached out and as Hilary gazed into his dark eyes, she felt him draw her into an embrace. His warm lips brushed hers and she felt herself respond as she melted into his arms. They kissed with longing.

"Wow…" Long Tom whispered and stared into her eyes.

Hilary felt weak, she ached for him. He seemed hesitant to take things further and his confidence was clearly in need of a boost. Would it be inappropriate for her to ask if they could go to his bedroom? She was about to make the suggestion when the kitchen door opened and James bustled in.

Long Tom and Hilary flew apart and as they spun round, James rolled up his sleeves and headed towards the sink.

"Morning, James," Long Tom called out.

"Oh, sir!" James was clearly startled. "I am so sorry, I didn't see you there…"

"Could you arrange the car please, Hilary is going back to Kindale."

"Right away, sir!" James disappeared.

They walked in silence to the hallway.

"Are you in Kindale today?" Hilary asked.

"No, I need to go over my songs." Long Tom smiled. "I'll see you tomorrow… if you decide to go."

"Of course I'll go. I wouldn't miss your performance for the world."

Long Tom shook his head and helped Hilary into the car. "Be careful of those chefs, they've got their knives out," he said. "Lenny will try to tap you up for money; he's working hard on me."

"But my knives are sharper," Hilary replied and waved as the car pulled away.

Long Tom stood on the steps of Flatterley Manor, his hands deep in his pockets as he watched the car retreat. Two peacocks wandered over the gravel towards him and began to spread their tail feathers. He clicked his fingers and spoke to the birds, then turned and disappeared into the house.

16

Bob was ecstatic. He'd received an early morning call from Anthony and they'd chatted for over an hour. Things seemed to be going well between them and they'd arranged to meet next week, when Bob was back in London. He was going to cook dinner for Anthony.

As he showered and dressed, Bob planned a menu.

He'd make a special Tibetan meal and impress Anthony with his knowledge of Tibetan food, perhaps they'd start with Guthuk soup with noodles and vegetables, followed by Momos – dumplings filled with meat. Bob chanted happily to himself as he contemplated the meal and thought about what to wear for the Mad Hatter's Taste of Kindale today, something not to formal, he decided. Bob selected a casual shirt and smart trousers, it felt quite warm this morning but he chose a jacket too, just in case. He glanced across his bedroom to a table by the window, where two hats sat side by side. He hoped Hilary wouldn't have a fit when she saw them.

There was a knock on the door and Bob bounded across the room to see who was there.

"Are you ready?" Hilary stepped into the room and walked straight past Bob. She sat on the bed and yawned.

"Dear heart, you look exhausted! I thought you'd be as fresh as a daisy after your early night."

"Early night?" Hilary raised her eyebrows.

"You disappeared so suddenly," Bob replied. "I presumed you were trying to get away from Mickey Lloyd?"

Hilary sighed. She smoothed the skirt of her shantung silk dress and yawned again. "I'd better come clean," she said, "put the kettle on."

Bob was beside himself with concern. He fussed round Hilary and made her a cup of strong black coffee, then pulled up a chair and leaning forward, stroked her arm and told her to take her time.

"Nothing happened," Hilary explained, and replayed the events of the previous evening. "I know more about bloody peacocks that I ever want to. Did you know they eat cat food and raisins as snacks but mostly enjoy cracked corn and grubs?"

"No, sweetie, I didn't," Bob said calmly, wishing she'd get to the point.

"Do you know what a group of peacocks are called?" Hilary went on.

"No, darling, can't say I do."

"Parties. Parties, would you believe?" Hilary was aghast. "The only party that occurred last night was the wretched party in the park with the peacocks…"

"Erm, are you saying that you didn't…" Bob hesitated.

Hilary was silent.

"Oh, for goodness' sake!" Bob snapped, and jumped up from the chair, the tension too much for him. "Did you get your leg over or what?"

Hilary looked up. Bob was red-faced and fit to bust. She burst out laughing.

"If only, Bob! We spent the night swapping life stories with a cosy cup of tea by the fire. Long Tom has really got issues."

"Oh dear." Bob slumped down on the bed beside Hilary. "I'd rather hoped…"

"Yes, well never mind about that. What happened after I left? Has

Lenny signed the whole of Kindale up for shares in his cookery school?"

Bob pulled a face, he stared at his nails and pushed a cuticle. "Mickey was pretty pissed and the last I saw of him, he was wrapped round a large amount of red taffeta with an enormous cleavage, singing The Star Spangled Banner."

Hilary shook her head. That would explain Mickey's early morning exit from the hotel. He'd obviously not changed his ways and she was grateful that she'd managed to get away from him.

"But you'll never guess..." Bob continued, "I had a call from Anthony and guess who's got engaged?"

"You haven't!" Hilary gasped.

"No, no, not me." Bob playfully hit Hilary's arm. "Go on, who do you think?"

"I haven't a clue and left my crystal ball at home. Come on, tell me, who?" Hilary urged.

"Our little Zelda!" Bob announced.

"Hardly little," Hilary replied, and visualised Harry stumbling over the threshold, buried beneath mountains of a duchesse satin-covered Zelda in her couture wedding gown. "Do we have a date?"

"Sometime in the spring, by all accounts. They're checking out churches in Chelsea as we speak."

Hilary stood up, she ought to call Zelda and congratulate her. Inevitably, there would be an engagement party. She needed to track down the Vice President from PAP too, and call Heidi to make sure the office was sorted for the forthcoming week. She glanced at her watch. Bob was preening himself in front of a mirror.

"Are you ready? We better get this silly event over with," Hilary said.

"Silly? I can't wait," Bob replied. "It's the highlight of the weekend! Delicious food and drink all day in different venues and dancing and hundreds of people having fun..." He turned and picked up Hilary's hat. "Ta Dah!"

Bob held out an object that resembled a cheeseboard.

"What on earth..." Hilary stepped forward and stared at the hat. It was indeed a cheeseboard. A thin layer of board, resembling wood, was glued to a large hair clip. On the board, miniature pieces of coloured cheese sat beside a bunch of grapes and three biscuits.

"Are you mad?" Hilary glanced down at her dress. It was cut in a deep V at the front, the fabric a soft lilac which shimmered with a grey hue as she moved. A 1950s' style hooped petticoat gave the skirt fullness. "I'll look ridiculous!"

"You and everyone else in Kindale." Bob wasn't taking no for an answer, he'd gone to great lengths to have the hats made. He reached over and put the hat on Hilary's head and clipped it in place. "You look wonderful!" he said, as he tilted the hat to a jaunty angle.

Hilary saw her reflection in the mirror. Surprisingly, the hat looked great! She moved her face from side to side and smiled. What the hell... it was only for a few hours!

"Cheese and wine!" Bob announced and then held up his own hat, a similar contraption that held a miniature bottle of wine and a goblet, glued firmly in place. He fixed the hat into position on his bald head and secured it with thin elastic under his chin. The milliner had assured him that it would stay in place, whatever the weather. He looked out of the window to the scene below.

"It's a perfect day! We'll be able to walk to each venue," Bob exclaimed as he watched folk, in a variety of headgear, gather at the front of the hotel. A piper in full uniform began a welcoming tune; his kilt swung as he squeezed his bagpipes and marched ahead. "There's a champagne reception in the ballroom, where the hats will be judged, and then we're put into groups to go round the town."

"Sounds marvellous," Hilary said sarcastically.

"Oh look!" Bob cried excitedly. "I can see the White Rabbit and the Dormouse! I wonder who'll we'll be with?"

"It has to be the Mad Hatter." Hilary stared at Bob's headgear, then picked up her bag and with a final glance in the mirror, took Bob's arm and they headed off to the ballroom.

MICKEY'S TAXI pulled into the side of the road at Fool's Landing. He paid the driver then stepped onto wooden decking at the back of the cottage and wandered past the solid stone walls. He felt weary as he lifted the latch on the stable door and walked into the kitchen.

The room smelt stale and fusty.

Greasy pots, soiled utensils and plates with congealed cooking fat were stacked high in the stone sink. Mickey shook his head in disgust as he opened a window. Fresh air instantly billowed into the room. He sighed as he squirted washing-up liquid and ran the hot tap. Lenny was such a slob! Mickey didn't think that Lenny would ever make a chef, even though he claimed to be one. Mickey set to work and began to tidy the kitchen; he couldn't bear to be amongst clutter and mess.

A little while later he sat down at a well-scrubbed kitchen table and tucked into toasted soda bread, fried mackerel and poached eggs. Lenny had eaten all the bacon but Mickey wasn't really bothered, the freezer was well stocked with fish, even though he'd no doubt that Lenny was working his way through that too.

Mickey yawned and glanced at his watch. He'd grab a few hours' sleep, then wander down to Kindale and see how the Mad Hatters were getting along. With any luck they'd all be well down several bottles of the festival sponsor's wine and Hilary might be in a good mood after her early night. He'd searched everywhere for her last night but she'd obviously gone to bed.

He pushed his empty plate away and rubbed his hands together, life was slowly returning to his battered body, the carbs had hit the spot. Mickey took his plate to the sink, then carefully washed and dried it and placed it in an oak cupboard. He wandered into the lounge and shook his head as he noticed the fireplace overflowing with ashes and cushions scattered all over the floor. Dirty mugs and sticky glasses sat beside an empty beer bottle on the coffee table. He wasn't sure if he could take much more of Lenny and his horrible habits, he was sure that there'd been traces of cocaine on the marble topped wash-stand in the bathroom yesterday. Mickey didn't give a rat's behind what Lenny stuck up his nose; he just didn't want him doing it at Fool's Landing.

But Mickey was the guest, not Lenny. Lenny had rented the cottage and by rights Mickey shouldn't be there at all. Still, Mickey thought as he placed the crockery in the kitchen sink, it wasn't for long, Lenny only had a couple more weeks on the tenancy and then he planned to move to the manor.

Mickey yearned to come back to Kindale. Thailand had lost its appeal. He had some money in the bank and if he could spend more time back here he felt sure that work would flow with the cookery school and a few guest appearances on local TV. There might even be another TV series out there. But he needed to get on the right side of Hilary, she had her finger on the button and one click of her well-manicured fingers could have lucrative work pouring in. She knew the game and could make or break a chef. Mickey felt like mixing business with pleasure and Hilary could satisfy both. Yes, it was definitely time to come home.

Mickey began to collect cushions and placed them on the sofa. He lay down and pulled a thick wool rug over his tired body. Forty winks and he'd be as good as new!

∽

HILARY FELT as though she had stepped into a parallel universe. The ballroom at Kindale House Hotel was packed with animated revellers, all wearing an outrageous display of headgear, from Roman Emperors, pirates and cowboys, to a party of ladies with tiers of cupcakes sprouting off their carefully styled coiffeurs. The room was buzzing.

Hilary had never seen anything like it.

"Gobble, gobble!" Roger Romney cried and lunged forward through the crowd to greet Bob and Hilary. He wore a polystyrene turkey on his head and golden brown drumsticks bounced over his ears.

"I hope you took the giblets out before you stuffed your head up the turkey's bottom," Hilary commented to him as she took a glass of champagne from a passing waiter.

"Do you think I'm in with a chance of winning first prize?" Roger grabbed a drumstick and waved it at her.

"The trophy has your name on it, Roger," Hilary replied, and turned to see Craig Kelly balancing a set of foam kitchen scales on his head, whilst David Hugo had somehow secured an iPad to a bowler hat, it played a YouTube re-run of Around the Coast with Mickey Lloyd. Hilary jumped back. The episode was set in Devon.

"Thought I'd get into the spirit of things." David rolled his eyes upwards and gesticulated towards the screen. "The home-town boy is back, so to speak..."

Hilary glanced towards the stage, where Dougie Davies was giving an interview for a local TV station. Lenny stood next to him and beamed at the camera.

"Good job he's not being asked to cook," Bob whispered to Hilary as they watched Dougie introduce Lenny, who was busy explaining that a fabulous new international cookery school was coming to the area.

After several rounds of drinks, a bell was heard and the room became silent. Dougie announced the winner of the hat contest – a group of girls dressed as space cadets, complete with Perspex helmets and air tubes. He then introduced the hosts for the day: the Mad Hatter, the Dormouse and Alice. Each carried a large sign with their designated name and wore clothing appropriate to their character. The room was split into three groups and Lenny's guests were all assigned to the Mad Hatter.

Hilary was feeling quite mellow and giggled as the Mad Hatter bounced off the stage and gathered them into an orderly line.

"Forward!" he cried and led them out of the ballroom and onto the streets of Kindale to the first venue. He wore an enormous hat with a wide brim and a sign, tucked into the band, read "10/6d". He'd made up his face with theatrical white paint and blackened his eyes, and his large round mouth was tinted deep red.

"Bloody scary..." Bob mumbled as they hurried to keep up. The

Mad Hatter ambled ahead, his red blazer and wide baggy trousers billowing in the breeze.

"I think this is fun," Hilary replied.

They arrived at the Trident Arms, where two dozen trestle tables were laden with a sumptuous display of seafood and delicacies, lovingly prepared by the local restaurants.

Hilary took a crab cake and bit into it.

"Good?" Bob asked as he tipped his head back and slid an oyster down his throat.

"Utterly divine," Hilary replied.

They moved around the room and nibbled at the offerings, which showcased the culinary skills of the chefs of Kindale. Hilary sipped a glass of chardonnay as Bob tried a local whisky.

"Not dancing today?" Asked Sheamus from Fishy Wishy and proceeded to flap his arms and make gobbling sounds.

"Maybe later." Hilary smiled and forked a scallop from a skillet on the Fishy Wishy table. The soft white flesh dripped with warm garlic butter.

When everyone had satisfied themselves, the Mad Hatter gathered them all together and off they set again, to another venue on the trail. The weather was kind and the streets of Kindale were filled with hundreds of laughing and jovial festival goers, all wearing a bizarre assortment of headgear, and as they passed each other, on their way from one venue to another, they called out and made ribald remarks. By early evening, everyone gathered back at Kindale House Hotel, where music and entertainment had begun in the ballroom.

"I'm not sure that I can manage a night of Irish jigging," Hilary admitted to Bob as they climbed out of the courtesy train and wandered into the foyer. "I feel absolutely whacked."

"Well, you did stop up all night," Bob said as he tapped his feet to loud accordion music and studied the progression of inebriated guests heading for the ballroom. He was looking forward to a dance.

"I might go and have a coffee in the bar. Save me a seat," Hilary said, and wandered away to sit down on a low settee in a dimly lit corner. She picked up a menu and ordered an espresso.

Mickey suddenly appeared and leaned over the back of the mock velvet settee and whispered in Hilary's ear, "You're drowning in Draylon, I hardly recognised you there."

Hilary spun round and accidently brushed the side of his face. "Christ, Mickey, do you have to creep up on me!" she hissed. She sat back as he reached for an arm rest and nimbly slid himself next to her.

"Do you always walk round with a stinking bishop on your head?" Mickey asked, poking at Hilary's hat.

"It's a local Irish cheese," Hilary snapped, then unclipped the hat and placed it on the table.

Her hair fell to her shoulders.

Mickey gathered a lock in his fingers and rubbed softly. "Still gorgeous, after all these years," he said with a sigh.

Hilary remembered seeing him earlier that morning dressed in his evening suit as he crawled out of the hotel. She snatched her hair away.

The waiter placed Hilary's coffee on the table and Mickey studied the wine list. She watched as he chose a red wine and asked for two glasses. He wore a pale grey cashmere suit with a silk waistcoat and a burgundy bow tie with navy spots sat neatly at the neck of his crisp white cotton shirt.

"What do you want, Mickey?" Hilary asked. She felt tired and vulnerable, the night with Long Tom had disturbed her – she'd felt emotions stir that had long lain dormant, and Mickey's kiss yesterday had also unsettled her. There must be something in the Irish air, she thought as she sipped her coffee.

"I want you of course," Mickey replied and reached out to touch her arm.

"Well you had your chance all those years ago and you blew it." Hilary moved her arm out of his reach. "You disappeared into a Spanish sunset and I never heard another word. You were absolutely despicable!"

"We were young, too much pain to wade through. It's different now." Mickey leaned forward and tried to take Hilary's hand.

"The only pain was your wretched wife catching you out. You could at least have mentioned her to me, I thought she was ancient history when you took up with me. I never expected you to walk back into the marital home without so much as a backward glance."

The waiter placed the wine and glasses on the table, then poured a small amount for Mickey to taste. Mickey waved the waiter away and reached again for Hilary's hand.

"I was a bloody fool, I should never have let you go," he gripped her hand tightly and continued, "but the past is gone and I can't make it better. It's the future I care about, and we could have a great future together. I'd come back to the UK if you said you wanted to be with me."

Hilary was aghast. After all these years he thought a couple of smooth words and a kiss and she would drop everything and melt into his arms. Was he mad?

Or was she?

Hilary stared at his heavenly blue eyes, his hand was warm and as his fingers caressed her skin gently, she imagined them drifting over her arm and across her neck then sliding into the bodice of her dress…

What was she doing! Mickey was a complete shit with a reputation to match. Hilary pulled away. She needed to get a grip, after her night with Long Tom and now Mickey inches away from beating a path to her bedroom, her defences were down and she needed to pull them back up again!

Hilary abruptly rose to her feet. She brushed against the bottle on the table and almost knocked the red wine over.

"Watch your dress!" Mickey grabbed the bottle.

"Watch your attitude!" Hilary retorted and without a backward glance, stomped out of the lounge. As she crossed the foyer, she bumped headlong into Lenny.

"Darlin'!" Lenny beamed. "What's your poison? I'm in the chair…" He pulled a roll of banknotes out of his trouser pocket.

"Sponsors obviously falling over each other…" Hilary said as she stared at the money. There must be at least a thousand euros in Lenny's podgy hand.

"Can't complain," Lenny replied, "it's coming together nicely. The Porthampton people love the concept too."

"Well, isn't that great," Hilary said sweetly and smiled. "Mickey's in the bar, he was asking where you were – he's got a bottle of wine and a delicious cheeseboard waiting for you."

Lenny's eyes lit up. He bundled the money back into his pocket as a large blonde bounced across the foyer and grabbed his arm. She had white greasepaint smeared across her mouth and flushed cheeks.

"Lenny, sweetheart," she drawled, "you promised you'd help me find that naughty Mickey…" The secretary from the Porthampton Friends of Kindale gave a teasing pout as she cuddled up to Lenny. Lenny stared longingly at her deep cleavage.

Hilary made her exit.

"If you see Bob, tell him I'm having an early night," Hilary said and blew Lenny a kiss. She nodded at the secretary and told them to have fun, then hurried to the lift where she pressed the button and watched the panel indicate that the lift was on the way. The music from the ballroom was loud and the floor vibrated with two hundred pounding feet. A Daniel O'Donnell impersonator had broken into a rousing version of Tipperary Girl. Hilary heard the accordion music and the chorus of the song: "Hair of gold, eyes of blue, prettiest girl I ever knew…'

The lift doors opened abruptly and Hilary stood back. A shape fell forward and as it straightened itself, Hilary recognised the remnants of the Mad Hatter. The greasepaint on his white face was smudged and grotesque, the rouged lips emphasised stained teeth and his black eyes looked wild. His red wig had come askew and as he doffed his hat, he waved an object that resembled an American flag. He stopped and listened to the music, then sang out with the chorus, "She was my Tipperary Girl!" As he leapt past Hilary, he grinned with a sinister leer and Hilary realised that the flag he was waving was, in fact, a pair of ladies knickers. She shook her head and stepped into the lift. In the middle of the floor, a polystyrene turkey drumstick lay squashed into the carpet. Hilary stared at it and wondered where the rest of the carcass had ended up. She felt as if she'd fallen through the Looking Glass...

The lift stopped at her floor and kicking the drumstick to one side, Hilary stepped out. "Gobble, gobble!" she muttered and, with a yawn, headed for her room.

17

Heidi and Stewie were propped up against large downy pillows in their comfortable sleigh bed at home in Muswell Hill. The Sunday papers lay strewn all over the counterpane as they read their way through them and enjoyed a leisurely continental breakfast.

"It says here that Mickey Lloyd was seen boarding a flight to Cork last week," Stewie said, and bit into a buttery croissant. The crumbs fell softly over his naked chest.

"I'll call Bob in a bit and find out what's going on," Heidi replied. "I'm sure Mickey had a thing with Hilary once." She licked apricot jam off her fingers and picked up the Mail on Sunday. "Holy Smoke! Have you seen this?" Heidi sat up straight and blinked as she read out the headline, "'PAP Goes Prunella!' Oh heck, Hilary is going to have a heart attack." Heidi winced as she scanned a photo of an inebriated Prunella leaving a London night club wearing a pineapple on her head. The words underneath read,

"Celebrity Chef Prunella Gray takes one for the team as she mixes a sponsor's fruit drink with a cocktail of alcohol at Annabel's last night…"

It went on to say that Prunella had arrived earlier that evening with a party of young males. A close friend, who didn't want to be named, confided that Prunella had holed up in a private room and entertained her guests with, amongst other things, PAP Potion – a cocktail she'd created using equal measure of PAP and a well-known vodka brand.

Heidi put the paper down and picked up her orange juice. "The PAP account is on life support after the photo shoot and the Vice President hasn't been seen since. He'll go ape when he sees this." Heidi drank the juice. "I wonder if Hilary has seen it."

Stewie wiped his mouth with a napkin and pushed the papers to one side. He reached over and took the glass from Heidi's hand and placed it on the bedside table.

"Well, little one, it's Sunday morning and you're off all day." Stewie snuggled against Heidi and slipped his hand inside her pyjamas. "Why don't you show me again, only this time in more detail, exactly what Prunella wanted to do to you..." He thrust his head under the duvet and Heidi giggled loudly then flung her paper across the room and dived down to join him.

∽

ZELDA SAT in a wicker chair in the garden annexe at her mother's Chelsea home and watched Madeleine light her third consecutive cigarette. Zelda hadn't smoked since her university days but she suddenly had the urge to grab the packet and join in. Instead, she reached for the cut-glass biscuit barrel and took the last of the double-choc-chip biscuits and dunked it in her frothy coffee.

"I cannot believe that he proposed under her roof!" Madeleine yelled as she stormed around the room, her thin face apoplectic with rage. "Despite all his breeding, Harry never gave me a second thought! How could he humiliate me so badly? The Swedish bitch must be rubbing her hands together – she's certainly pulled one over me this time!" Madeleine ranted.

Zelda sighed and tried to block out her mother's fury as Madeleine stormed around the room. Zelda contemplated a trip to the kitchen to see if there was anything to eat, but she knew she'd be followed and given a ticking off for scoffing all the biscuits, they were reserved for guests. Madeleine's cupboards made Old Mother Hubbard's look like the food hall in Harrods and Zelda wondered how the hell her mother survived, she never seemed to eat. At least Zelda had eaten an early lunch, Carmelita had made her favourite – Eggs Benedict. Carmelita was thrilled to hear news of the forthcoming nuptials and served Zelda a double helping of hollandaise sauce on her muffin. Earlier that morning, Zelda had grabbed a bite at her father's, before she'd driven a hung-over-Harry back to London, but Brigitta's portion of healthy muesli had hardly hit the spot.

"And the idiot didn't even get the size right!" Madeleine grabbed Zelda's finger. "Where is this rock that Brigitta no doubt helped Harry to choose? She screwed that up!" Madeleine yelled.

Zelda stood up. She'd had enough. Her mother was impossible and nothing that Zelda could say would calm her down. Zelda needed to go home and get ready for work the next day, Carmelita would want to know what to pack for Stoke-on-Trent and Harry would be slowly coming back to life after his heavy drinking session with Daddy last night. He'd soon sober up when he realised that Zelda had the Porsche.

Zelda pulled on her leather DKNY car coat and turned the sheepskin collar snugly round her neck. It was a man's coat but Zelda didn't care, it was possibly the only thing in her wardrobe that fitted her comfortably. A silk scarf trailed from the pocket and Zelda tucked it back in, not a chance that she'd need it, the roof was well and truly up on the Porsche and would be staying that way while she had a spin round town on her own. There was a nice new deli in East Dulwich that she wanted to try.

Madeleine was still yelling as Zelda waved goodbye and moved through the house. As she stepped out onto the driveway she heard her mother's parting shot.

"And you look like a fat lesbian in that coat! You won't keep a double-barrel for long in that get-up..."

∽

LONG TOM HENDRY paced around the music studio at Flatterley Manor. He heard his voice through the headphones he was wearing and sang along to the track.

This wasn't working.

He remembered the words but his voice was letting him down. He knew that it didn't really matter for the gig tonight; the crowd would be delighted that he was there, that he'd actually turned up and was on a stage in their home town. They'd probably drown him out with their own rendition of his songs.

But it mattered to Long Tom.

He hadn't sung live in years and felt a flutter of fear in his chest. Was he going to have a panic attack? In times gone by he'd quell the fear with a stiff drink and a handful of tablets then keep drinking till the gig was over, before partying long into the night. Now his only comfort was a cup of peppermint tea, and he felt like pouring that in the many plants that adorned the room.

What could he do to calm himself? He paced up and down and tried to remember all the lessons he'd learnt in rehab. But nothing seemed to work.

If only he could get the thought of booze out of his head, either that or get laid, and he couldn't seem to do that anymore either. He wished that he'd overcome his fear the other night when Hilary was with him. He thought about their kiss and knew that she had wanted him to take her to his bedroom, but Long Tom had panicked and there wasn't a cat in hell's chance of him being able to perform. If only he could get over that issue too! Sex would be like a sedative, and sex with Hilary would be like a trip to the moon. She was a gorgeous woman. Long Tom's days of brash young models and groupies gathered round his dressing room door were long over, he didn't want a young female – he wanted comfort and love, someone to walk through the garden, hand-in-hand with him, someone to feed the peacocks with. Sex would be a bonus, but one he doubted he'd experience again. Maybe he should see a doctor? Long Tom shook his head. Viagra was a stimulant but those days, along with the booze, were over and he had to make sure that it stayed that way.

He picked up his music and stood very still. It was his first test on the road back, but this time the journey would be different. This time he would be sober.

Long Tom opened his mouth and began to sing.

∾

BOB PAUSED at Hilary's bedroom door. He held a stack of newspapers in his arm and hesitated as he re-read the headline and stared at the photo. Prunella was completely pie-eyed and a carton of PAP was clearly visible in the tote bag she'd slung over her shoulder.

Hilary was going to have a fit.

Bob raised his hand to knock but the door was flung open.

"Come in!" Hilary barked, and he tentatively followed her retreating back, into the suite.

Hilary stood by the open window and blew smoke out over Kindale marina. She dragged heavily and tapped her nails on the sill.

"I take it you've seen the paper..." Bob began and waited for Hilary to finish her cigarette. She closed the window and turned back to the room.

"It's genius!" Hilary announced.

Bob dropped the papers, flabbergasted. He sat down on Hilary's bed and watched her pace around the room, her silk gown fluttering as she moved, the soft lines draped seductively over her naked flesh. Bob said a silent thank you to his God of Temptation. It paid to be gay sometimes.

"Sales of PAP will go through the roof over the next few days," Hilary said as she raced ahead of Bob with her plans. "Get Stewie to do another shoot tomorrow, with cocktail glasses and jug of PAP Potion. Make sure you get a bottle of vodka in the shot, I've already got a sponsorship from the vodka company. Get the paperwork over, I've emailed you the contact." Hilary barely paused for breath. "Get photos of upwardly-mobile young things drinking it in every social situation you can think of," she continued.

Bob reached into his jacket and pulled out a notebook, then began to make notes.

"Find a few pensioners and get Stewie to shoot them drinking it..." Hilary went on.

"Literally?" Bob asked as he envisaged a massacre scene of prostrate pensioners covered in bloody pineapples.

Hilary ignored him.

"Get a video on YouTube – 'The Three 'Ps': Prunella's PAP Potion, it will go viral. I want the recipe online by lunchtime and every food blogger you can muster to be tweeting it out. Pull in favours – say I'm asking."

"But the Vice President isn't speaking to you and he's teetotal," Bob protested. "He'll go bonkers if you add this into the campaign."

"He won't when he sees the sales figures. Give me seventy-two hours..."

Hilary disappeared into the bathroom and Bob began to make calls. He had some difficulty getting hold of Heidi and Stewie but on his third attempt, they picked up.

"She's not put out a contract on Prunella?" Heidi asked incredulously.

"Quite the opposite," Bob replied, and left them with strict instructions to pull in whatever man power they needed to carry out Hilary's instructions.

"Plan Prunella activated," Bob said as Hilary appeared, dressed and ready for the Fruits de Mer luncheon. "Shall I get Prunella on the phone for you?"

"No, leave her," Hilary replied. "She won't have sobered up yet." She picked up an ivory hair comb and pushed it into a pleat at the back of her hair. The comb had a panel of pretty enamel roses weaving through lace filigree, which matched the fine lace of her cream, Dior slip dress. "You don't need to call anyone else, we're on holiday, remember?"

~

Mickey had managed to commandeer the shower and took his time as he began his ablutions in the bathroom. He languished under the piping hot water, smiling in the knowledge that Lenny would be lucky to get a dribble of warmth by the time Mickey had finished.

What a palaver it had been last night! Lenny was ecstatic to see him in the bar and determined that the secretary from the Porthampton Friends of Kindale came along for the ride. Little did Lenny know that she'd already been ridden, several times! Mickey had made his excuses and managed to extricate himself, leaving Lenny and the secretary to their own devices. With little intention of doing a routine with the Daniel O'Donnell act, Mickey steered clear of the ballroom and ended up in the Trident Arms with Dougie Davies and an all-night game of poker. To his delight he'd cleaned up. The game ended as dawn crept up over the sea and with his pockets full of cash, Mickey had grabbed a ride back to Fool's Landing to get some sleep.

He began to sing as he showered. Poker always brought him luck and today was his last chance to make an impression on Hilary. She could make or break his move back to the UK, and with a little subtle persuasion he had no doubt that he would make his way into her bed. After all, anything could happen in Kindale!

~

Lenny thought he was dying. He lay on his bed and wondered which part of his body he should attempt to move first. His arms felt as though they'd been ripped out of their sockets and his legs seem to be suffering from severe paralysis. That left his aching body which, he was convinced, would be a mass of bruises. His head he could mend and he reached for a small plastic bag of white powder from the dressing table drawer.

A few moments later, feeling considerably revived, Lenny stood in his robe by the bathroom door. Above the rattle of the decrepit old shower, he could hear Mickey singing,

"'Urry up, mate!" Lenny called out. "We're running late for the lunch and I want to get the best table." Lenny hopped about from one foot to the other and leapt back as Mickey flung the door open.

"Blinding night, eh?" Lenny said as Mickey marched past. "That American gal certainly knows how to party!" Lenny closed the bathroom door and eased himself into the shower. He contemplated a trip to America sometime in the future, and if last night's sex was anything to go by, he could be spending a considerable time out there, state-to-state-sex with American crumpet! Lenny rubbed his hands together and chuckled. And she'd pledged a lump sum of the Porthampton Friends of Kindale committee funds, for the cookery school. "We'll do international links with the Porthampton chefs and your cute ol' country manor!" the secretary had whispered, as she'd pounced on Lenny's prostrate body for the umpteenth time. Lenny smiled and turned the shower to the hot setting. The only "international link" she was going to be involved in was transferring dollars to Lenny's online account! He grabbed a bar of soap and a loofa and began to shower under a trickle of lukewarm water.

∼

THE FRUIT DE MER luncheon was held in the ballroom at Kindale House Hotel and this, the final banquet of the weekend, was certainly a show stopper. Chefs from the town had worked alongside the Porthampton chefs all morning, in preparation for the event and now, dressed in tall hats and freshly laundered jackets, they stood with uniformed staff and waited for the guests to arrive.

Lenny led his party to a table by the stage and ushered everyone to their seats. Hilary and Bob settled themselves into their chairs and admired the large circular table, which was dressed with a magnificent central flower arrangement and a collection of seashells scattered over the linen cloth. They nibbled on fresh salmon pate and bread sticks as waiters poured chilled white wine.

Dougie Davies leapt onto the stage with the secretary of the Porthampton Friends of Kindale, and welcomed the diners to the luncheon. He thanked them in anticipation of their participation in the auction to follow and told them that the proceeds would go to a local charity.

The first course arrived.

Mickey sat opposite Hilary and as she cracked open a lobster claw, he tried to catch her eye, but Hilary ignored Mickey and engaged herself in a stimulating conversation with Roger, who sat next to her, as they discussed the merits of artificial insemination and the future of British turkey farmers. Lenny ensured that his guests were all happy, and between courses, he moved around the room in his networking quest.

The highlight of the meal was the main course. Tiers of seafood were placed on each table and everyone gasped as they reached for cameras to capture images of the stunning displays. Crustaceans of every description were layered together – crab, lobster, oysters, mussels, clams and prawns – and as the guests happily devoured their way through the feast, staff hovered with silver buckets to remove the discarded shells and replenish the tiers.

As coffee was served, Mickey excused himself and left the room. Hilary sat back at last and looked around. It had been a sumptuous meal, one she would never forget. The surrounding seas of Kindale had given up their finest fruits and the pot pourri of dishes that they'd tasted would remain with her for a long time. She contemplated the weekend and realised that she'd enjoyed herself. How good it had been to get away from the office. Despite Prunella's shenanigans, Hilary had managed to switch off. She was frustrated with Mickey but flattered too, she couldn't remember the last time she was aware of male attention and it had given her a reality check, that perhaps life shouldn't be all work and no play.

She thought about Long Tom and wondered how he was feeling. It was silly really, that his manager insisted that Long Tom's alcoholism be kept a secret, although perhaps Pete was right – the public and press could be ruthless and negativity could put Long Tom back in rehab.

The band began to play a waltz and diners pushed back their chairs and took to the floor.

Bob appeared beside Hilary.

"May I have this dance, madam?" He bowed slightly and held out his arm.

"With pleasure," Hilary replied and with a smile, she joined Bob and walked out onto the floor.

18

Long Tom sat in the back of the limo and closed his eyes as the lush green countryside rolled by, but Long Tom was oblivious to its charm. As the vehicle moved smoothly through the streets of Kindale, he felt light palpitations across his chest. His doctor had assured him that it was normal, nothing more than anxiety, which was to be expected when he was due to make a public appearance. In years gone by he'd have reached for a drink to steady his nerves but now Long Tom focused on the breathing techniques he'd learnt in rehab.

The car pulled onto the pub car park and the organisers leapt out of the shadows to escort Long Tom. He tilted his hat to cover his eyes and keeping his head down, allowed himself to be led to a backstage room where a local band waited to rehearse the set.

The band, who'd been playing at the festival all weekend, couldn't believe their luck. A living legend was about to perform for the first time in years and they were supporting him! They'd been rehearsing the numbers for weeks and knew every possible version that Long Tom might need. It was a complete contrast from their usual rendition of Tipperary Girl and other Irish favourites.

Long Tom braced himself as he approached the room. The last time he'd performed live was at the Nuremburg Arena, where thousands of fans had screamed their appreciation when he stumbled onto the stage. He took a deep breath, straightened his shoulders and holding his head high, strode into the room.

∼

LENNY MARSHALLED his party together and ushered them into a private minibus. He wasn't relying on the courtesy train, the world and his wife would be trying to get into the gig tonight and Lenny knew that places were strictly limited. He'd met with the organisers earlier and after parting with a hefty back-hander, had guaranteed that they had places near the front of the stage.

Mickey rushed forward to try and sit next to Hilary but she'd squeezed onto the back seat between Roger and Bob.

"Now, Roger," Hilary said firmly, "I don't want you to gobble once this evening, gobbling is forbidden; we're here to listen to some great music."

"You must be all gobbled out," Bob said and patted Roger's knee.

The minibus pulled up at the pub, where crowds were attempting to storm the main door. Fortunately, security was in abundance and escorted Lenny's group through the throng. Hilary would have liked to slip backstage and wish Long Tom luck, but she didn't feel that it was appropriate, he probably wouldn't welcome well-wishers. She noticed James making his way to the side of the room. The butler was casually dressed and waved when he recognised Hilary.

It was standing room only at the front, but Lenny had organised drinks and the mood was animated as background songs played and everyone felt the excitement build. Eventually the band came out on stage and began to tune up.

Dougie Davies nudged Hilary. "Do you think he's still got it?"

"I'm sure he never lost it," Hilary replied curtly as the audience applauded the band. It was hard to be heard and as Hilary turned away from Dougie, she came face-to-face with Mickey.

"Looking as sexy as ever!" Mickey yelled and slid his hand over Hilary's bottom.

"Bugger off, Mickey!" Hilary yelled back, but she was powerless to prevent his wandering hand and looked around anxiously for Bob. He was a row behind and oblivious to Hilary's predicament as he clinked glasses with Roger, Craig, David and a group from the Porthampton Friends of Kindale.

Hilary was wedged between Dougie and Mickey, and as the tension rose in the room and the noise built into a crescendo, she realised that she was stuck.

The presenter had come out onto the stage and was trying to be heard over cries of "We want Long Tom! We want Long Tom!" The crowd yelled and stamped their feet and, realising that his mission was pointless, the presenter waved to the animated crowd and ran off the stage.

The band started a slow drum roll and as it built, the stage went black.

When the lights came on again, Long Tom stood under a single spotlight. The crowd gasped and became silent as they stared at the solitary figure.

"Hello," he spoke softly into the microphone, "my name's Long Tom Hendry."

The band began to play No More War, and Long Tom stared out into the audience as the recognisable music filled the room.

He began to sing.

Hilary crossed her fingers and closed her eyes.

The rich gravelly drawl began slowly and as he headed towards the chorus, it roared out and ricocheted off the walls. His voice was magnificent.

The crowd went wild.

Everyone joined in. Mickey, Hilary and Dougie swayed together and the tempo in the room built with heat and excitement. It was clear to all – Long Tom Hendry was back!

Long Tom finished the song and thanked his audience. He seemed happy on the stage, and as he continued with a medley of some of his old hits, he visibly relaxed. The crowd cheered and sang along to the familiar and much-loved tunes; everyone was having a tremendous night.

"He must be pushing his late fifties!" Mickey shouted into Hilary's ear.

"You'll not see fifty again!" Hilary shouted back.

"But look how well I've worn," Mickey said with a grin and ran his hand up and down her back.

Hilary was boiling, the heat in the room had reached furnace level and Mickey's clammy hand was playing a tune on her spine. The feeling wasn't unpleasant.

"Be Jesus, but it's dry in here!" Dougie called out and looked around for Lenny, who was making his way along the front of the stage with armfuls of water in plastic bottles. As Lenny squeezed through the crowd, he threw a bottle up to Long John, who caught it and without pause in the song, tipped his hat in acknowledgment. Lenny then passed the bottles along the row to Mickey, Hilary and Dougie.

Dougie unscrewed the cap on his bottle and let out a sigh. "Ah, that's more like it..." he said, and drank greedily.

Hilary removed the top on her bottle and took a sip, the heat was unbearable and she was thirsty. As the liquid hit her tongue, Hilary's eyes widened and she stared at the bottle with horror – Lenny had laced the water with vodka! The nearly neat alcohol burned like fire in her mouth. She looked around frantically and saw Mickey and Dougie tip their bottles back, and as they steadily drank, they both winked at her.

Hilary spun round and stared at the stage. The song had ended and Long Tom was wiping perspiration off his face with a towel. He put the towel down and picked up water bottle, then began to unscrew the top...

∼

"Wake up, Sweetheart, everything's fine, you're quite safe."

Hilary felt someone stroking her arm, her head felt muzzy and she had a painful throbbing sensation in her temple. She half opened her eyes and blinked as stark white walls came into focus under the dim glow of a curved light. She wondered where on earth she was.

"I'm here," Bob's voice whispered. "You've just had a little bump."

Hilary realised that she was in a bed and felt Bob's hands fussing around the covers as he tucked a sheet snugly round her legs. She turned her head and looked at him.

"Oh, thank God!" Bob exclaimed. "You're awake." He reached for the prayer beads round his neck, then closed his eyes and whispered a prayer.

"What happened?" Hilary asked.

"Erm…" Bob didn't know where to begin. "Can you remember anything?"

"I remember being in a pub." Hilary looked confused, "Long Tom was singing, I think…" She looked at Bob and searched his face for an explanation.

Bob tucked his beads back into his shirt and took Hilary's hand. He ought to tell her – at some point she'd have to give the event insurers an explanation. Bob took a deep breath and thought carefully about what he was going to say, he couldn't for the life of him understand what Hilary had done. She'd somehow managed to elevate her body from the close proximity of Mickey and Dougie and had flung herself onto the stage, where she dragged a bottle of water out of Long Tom's hands. She'd proceeded to pour the contents all over the floor, but as two security guards leapt to Long Tom's rescue, they'd grabbed Hilary from behind and the water spilt over an amplifier, which fused all the lights. In the tussle that ensued in semi-darkness, Hilary had fallen onto the corner of a large speaker and as she went down, she badly gashed her buttock before knocking herself unconscious.

"Can you remember the ambulance?" Bob asked. He rubbed her hand in an attempt to bring back clarity as he thought about her fall and her blood-stained dress, which was ripped and clearly ruined. The emergency generators had eventually kicked in and as light was restored to the event, the extent of Hilary's injuries became apparent.

Bob had battled for his life to reach the stage and it was no mean feat pushing Mickey and Long Tom out of the way to reach his boss. Bob preened as he thought about the scene, he was quite proud of himself; if anyone was going to take care of Hilary, it was Bob!

"It's starting to come back…" Hilary said quietly.

A nurse came into the room and fussed around Hilary's bed. She checked the drip that was attached to Hilary's arm, and took a reading from the monitor. "Miss Hargreaves needs rest," she said to Bob.

"I'd like a drink of water," Hilary said as she watched the nurse move around the room.

"I'll get you one," Bob said and patted Hilary's hand. "Back in a jiffy."

The nurse followed Bob out of the room and Hilary leaned back on the pillows and closed her eyes. Her head was beginning to pound and there was a pain in her left buttock. She heard the door open and footsteps click across the floor towards the bed.

"Can I sign you up for the tour?" Long Tom whispered. "I need a good minder…"

Hilary opened her eyes and gasped when she saw Long Tom. He sat down on the side of her bed.

"James told me what was in the bottle." Long Tom smiled and took Hilary's hand.

"He did?" Hilary said.

Long Tom explained that in the confusion that followed Hilary's departure by ambulance, James, who'd witnessed the whole thing, had found the bottle and tasted the few drops of vodka that remained in the bottom.

"I owe you one, madam." Long Tom tilted his head on one side and grinned. "You look lovely, despite the war wound."

Hilary reached up and felt a lump, the size of an egg, on the side of her temple.

"How's your arse?" Long Tom asked.

Hilary looked confused.

"You've a cut that's taken twelve stitches," he said.

"Oh, never mind that," Hilary sat forward, "what about your gig? I buggered that up, it will cost thousands."

"Nah, the audience loved it." Long Tom said. "I paid everyone's bar bill and kept the drinks flowing then sang acappella for a bit, before signing autographs. I've covered all costs to the pub."

"You can't do that!" Hilary was horrified by the mayhem she'd caused.

Long Tom dismissed her concern.

"It was worth it," he said. "You should see where I got to sign autographs!" Long Tom put his head back and laughed. "There was this large blonde chick with an American accent…"

The nurse came back into the room, followed by Bob. He held a plastic cup of water.

"We really must let Miss Hargreaves rest!" the nurse said crossly, glaring at Bob and Long Tom.

Long Tom stood up and nodded. "We really must," he mimicked, and with a wink, tipped his hat at Hilary then turned and left the room.

"Bloody hell…" Bob mumbled as he watched Long Tom stride away.

"I'll take that," the nurse said. She reached for the cup and having relieved Bob of the water, shooed him away.

"I'll see you in the morning, sweetheart!" Bob called out as he left the room. "Shout if you want me!" He threw the nurse an angry glance and flounced out of the room.

In truth, he was glad to be on his way and back to the comfort of his hotel room. It had been an agonizingly stressful evening, but now that he knew that Hilary would be all right, he looked forward to sinking into the warm comfort of his duck-down duvet. He wondered if Anthony was still awake. Bob glanced at his watch. Just enough time to make a call!

∼

The breakfast room at Kindale House Hotel was half empty. Festival goers were heading home today and most had disappeared to pack up their belongings and settle their bills.

Lenny had assembled his party in one corner of the room and was trying to bring an air of joviality to the subdued atmosphere that hung over them. The excesses of the weekend had taken their toll and they were all concerned about Hilary.

"Now then, fellas," Lenny began, "it's been a blindin' weekend and I want to thank you all for your support with the cookery school." He handed out printed forms. "If I haven't already had your cheques, could you fill in your bank details so that we can start the ball rolling on the endorsements."

Roger and David pushed the forms away; Lenny had already received their cheques and they watched Craig begin to fill in his bank details.

They looked up as Mickey walked across the room and called out to them, "Does anyone know where Hilary is?" Mickey wore a pale blue linen shirt and jeans with deck shoes and looked like he'd just stepped off his boat.

"She's in Cork hospital," Roger snapped, astonished that Mickey would ask such a stupid question. They'd all called last night to see how Hilary was and had been told that she'd make a full recovery, she just needed rest.

"No, she isn't," Mickey replied. "They said she discharged herself last night."

Bob bounced into the room and noticed the concerned and questioning faces. "Don't be worrying yourselves about our Hilary," he said and sat himself on a banquette. "She's perfectly well and making her own way home. I'm travelling with you lot and I'd like to be leaving soon." He picked up a croissant and nibbled the edge.

Lenny grabbed Craig's form and buried it in a folder. "Our minibus for the airport will be here shortly," he announced. The flight from Cork to London departed late morning and Lenny sighed with relief. He'd secured some decent investments and would soon have this lot off his hands. They were flying back with Air Lingus but

Lenny chose not to mention it. He turned to Mickey and slapped him on the back. "See you back at the ranch, mate!"

Mickey gritted his teeth and forced a smile. He couldn't understand what was going on. He needed Lenny's company like a dose of the clap. Where the hell was Hilary?

"Bob, where is she?" Mickey sat down on the banquette.

"I can't tell you, but she's perfectly all right and in good hands, don't you worry yourself." Bob patted Mickey's knee.

Mickey folded his arms, thinking Hilary was probably in a private clinic in Cork, which would no doubt be the best place for her to recuperate. He wondered which way to play his cards, as he'd reached stalemate. He decided to work on Bob, who was clearly the best route to Hilary and Mickey wanted to get on the agencies books.

"I've got a lot of enquiries for work coming in," Mickey began. Bob raised his eyebrows and gave Mickey his full attention. "Yes. TV, a book – that sort of thing," Mickey lied. "I really could do with a UK based agent to handle stuff for me and I wondered if you'd be interested in taking me on?"

Bob smiled. Mickey might think he was subtle but Bob understood exactly what he wanted – work and a direct route to Hilary's bedroom. Bob feigned indifference and told Mickey to give him a call in the next couple of days and he'd see what he could do. Bob handed Mickey his business card. After all, Bob thought, Mickey was a household name, he just needed a little guidance and a few strings pulling and he could be back on the ladder of success. Bob thought that Hilary needed to consider this from a business point of view – it could be very lucrative.

Bob poured himself a coffee and spread jam on his croissant. He couldn't wait to get back to London to tell Heidi and Lottie all about the weekend and he needed to go shopping, he'd a meal to prepare for Anthony!

Lenny announced the arrival of the minibus and helped everyone gather their cases and settle themselves comfortably. He climbed on board and sat on a seat at the front.

Mickey shook hands with the departing guests and assured them that he'd see them at the cookery school soon.

Dougie Davies appeared from the bar to wave them all off. A broad grin spread across his ruddy face as he called out effusive messages. "Missing you already!" he cried. He had a glass of whisky in one hand and a large bubbling blonde in the other.

"Oh gee, you're all heading off to little ol' London, see you guys next year!" the blonde cried and waved enthusiastically as the engine started and the minibus began to pull away. "Don't forget to come and cook for us in Porthampton!" she called out to Mickey, then gripped Dougie's hand and led him towards the lift.

Mickey stood in the deserted foyer. It wasn't quite how he'd imagined the weekend to end, but all was not lost. He felt Bob's business card in the pocket of his jeans and rubbed it thoughtfully as he remembered Bob patting his knee. Bob would snap him up in a heartbeat and thus soften Hilary in the process. She wouldn't be able to resist an opportunity to make some decent money off the back of Mickey and with his feet firmly under the table, he would enjoy beating the path to her bedroom. He just had to add the right ingredients, simmer them all gently then bring quickly to the boil – it was a recipe for success! Mickey rubbed his hands together with anticipation and sighed happily. He'd go and have some time on his boat before bracing himself for another night with Lenny, but first he felt in need of a livener and headed for the bar.

19

Hilary lay perfectly still. She felt drowsy from all the painkillers she'd been given at the hospital but it wasn't an unpleasant feeling, in fact, quite the opposite. Even the weird cry of the peacocks from beneath her window – a cross between a pneumatic drill and a donkey braying, didn't disturb her relaxed state. She yawned and snuggled into the soft folds of warm Egyptian cotton.

A little while later, she heard a gentle tap on the bedroom door and James appeared with a tray of breakfast tea.

"Good morning, Miss Hargreaves." He smiled as he fussed about with a silver pot and hot water jug. He held a metal strainer over a porcelain cup. "How do you take your tea?"

Hilary sat up. "White, no sugar, please."

"I hope the peacocks haven't disturbed you," James said as he carefully poured. "They make the devil of a noise at this time of day." He placed the tea on the cabinet beside Hilary and walked over to the bay window, then gently drew the heavy gold drapes back and hooked them over brass arms on the oak panelled wall. Light poured in and highlighted years of polish on the sturdy antique furniture.

Hilary surveyed her comfortable surroundings.

Long Tom had insisted that she be taken to Flatterley Manor to recuperate in comfort. He'd been firm with the bossy nurse at the hospital and told the doctor that he'd take full responsibility for Hilary's recovery; his own doctor was on standby and would check on Hilary in the morning. Hilary felt no desire to resist. It was stark, cold and noisy in the hospital room. Flatterley Manor seemed like a heavenly refuge and she was quite compliant as Long Tom and James wrapped her in a thick blanket and whisked her away to the warmth of the limo. Her cases had been collected from the hotel, where Bob had them packed and ready.

"Is my minder conscious?" Long Tom stuck his head round the door.

Hilary wished she'd brushed her hair and hastily tried to finger comb the unruly locks. She reached for her tea as Long Tom ambled across the room and sat down beside her.

"How are you today?" he asked. He was dressed in pale blue jeans and a white t-shirt and his hair was pulled back in a neat ponytail. He wore a gold stud in one ear. She thought he looked ten years younger without his hat.

"I feel fine," Hilary replied. "You really don't have to fuss around me." She felt embarrassed by Long Tom's scrutiny. He pushed hair back from her brow and studied her bruises; his fingers warm on her skin.

"Find some arnica please, and see that it's applied frequently," Long Tom said over his shoulder to James, "that will help the bruising. The doc will be here soon, make sure you have anything he recommends or Hilary needs."

"Very good, sir." James leaned forward and replenished Hilary's cup. "Would you care for a cup of tea, sir?"

Long Tom glanced at the pale liquid and shook his head then raised an eyebrow and glanced at the covers surrounding Hilary's lower body. "How's your arse?" he asked.

Hilary felt herself blush. Her bottom was beginning to feel sore and the stitches pulled. The painkillers were wearing off.

"It's perfectly fine, thank you."

"Bed rest for you, babe, no arguments." Long Tom stood up and turned his head towards the window. "Soothing, eh?" He nodded towards the peacocks on the lawn below. Hilary thought they were as soothing as a siren scrawling in a motorway pile-up, but didn't think it appropriate to comment.

"Lovely," she replied.

"We thought you'd be comfortable in here, overlooking the garden where the birds can keep an eye on you." Long Tom smiled again and it seemed to light the room up. James raised his eyebrows and shook his head as he followed Long Tom's gaze into the garden.

"I'll see you later, when the doc's been. Things to do…" Long Tom wandered towards the door. As he reached it, he turned back and winked at Hilary then blew her a kiss, before closing the door and disappearing into the corridor.

Hilary stared at the door and reached up, as if to catch the kiss. The man was driving her mad; she may be battered and bruised and her bum felt like it had fallen in a cheese grater, but her heart had a strange flutter that wouldn't go away. It had begun the night before when Long Tom wrapped his arm around her in the limo and she'd laid her head on his comforting shoulder. His warm skin and musky aftershave seemed familiar and inviting and Hilary longed to look up and kiss him. His hair was loose. It tangled with her own and she'd had the urge to plait it all together as the car moved silently through the night. Hilary wished that Long Tom had stayed a while; she wanted him near and longed to talk to him about his gig and how he felt. She wondered how soon he'd be going away.

James coughed lightly and woke Hilary from her daydream. "Shall I ask cook to prepare some breakfast?" he asked.

"No thanks, James. I think I'll rest a bit longer, I feel quite tired." Hilary yawned while James gently fussed round the bed and folded the sheet neatly, as Hilary turned on her side.

"Not peacock feathers in here by any chance?" she asked and gathered the enormous feather pillow around her head.

"Oh my lord, no." James rolled his eyes back and as Hilary settled herself, she got the impression that James wasn't over fond of the peacocks...

∽

BOB THRUST A TWENTY-POUND note towards the taxi driver and told him to keep the change. He gathered his bags and flung himself on the intercom at the offices of Hargreaves Promotions.

"It's me!" he yelled. "I need a hand!" Bob turned his key in the lock and pushed the door open and was greeted by Lottie pounding down the stairs. She wore a bright green mini dress with green and white striped tights.

"I was going to wear a shamrock hat to welcome you back," Lottie said, "but seeing as Hilary's indisposed—"

"You thought you'd keep it simple," Bob finished her sentence and stared at the bright outfit. "You look divine, darling!" He threw his arms around her gave her a hug. "What a weekend we've had!"

They lugged Bob's luggage up the stairs and deposited it in the foyer. Heidi had prepared a tray of coffee with a big box of macaroons from Patisserie Valerie. She gave Bob a hug too, and as he made himself comfortable in his old leather chair, the girls perched either side of his desk and demanded to hear all about the Irish jaunt.

Bob took his time. The soft macaroons were delicious and as he dunked one into his milky coffee he remembered the weekend. Bob thought it had all gone extremely well and they'd soon have two new signings – Mickey and Lenny; and a base in Ireland – for events. Bob envisaged a TV series and could already picture Mickey wandering in the sunny herb garden at Flatterley Manor with a freshly picked bunch of dill, to go with the delicious seafood he'd caught earlier, from the estuary – where his boat bobbed about, as a crew filmed him boiling a lobster, with a large glass of wine in his hand – ready for his regular "slurp".

"But what's the news on Hilary?" Heidi pushed Bob's chair with her foot. "When is she back? How is she?"

"Oh, you know the Rottweiler, she'll be back before the bruises have faded and the stitches out. I've no doubt the phone will be ringing tomorrow and madam will be issuing her orders." Bob sipped his coffee.

"Who's this Long Johns?" Lottie asked. She pushed a spotty headband into her blonde curls.

"Long TOM," Bob and Heidi corrected.

"He's a recovering alcoholic and an ageing rocker with a penchant for peacocks and not at all interested in Hilary." Bob thought about the night Hilary had spent in Long Tom's kitchen. "She seems to have saved him from the demon drink," Bob explained, "hence the episode at the gig which led to her injuries. In his effort to repay her, he's holed her up at the manor – in some comfort I might add, to recuperate." Bob visualised Hilary propped up in bed, being waited on hand and foot. "Where the real drama comes into play," Bob continued, "is with the rampant Mickey Lloyd, who can't keep his hands off her and is looking for far more than a signed contract to re-launch his career."

"Oh, how exciting!" Heidi rubbed her hands. "And Zelda's got engaged! Romance isn't dead… How's your love-life, Bob?"

Bob put his feet on the desk and leaned back in his chair, he studied his immaculate nails. "I'm cooking dinner for Anthony tomorrow," he said with a smile.

"DON'T DO TIBETAN!" Heidi and Lottie yelled. Vivid memories of Bob's soggy meatballs and vile soup came flooding back to them both.

Bob felt piqued. He pushed his chair back and stood. "I'll never cook for either of you again!" he retorted. "Now bugger off and get some work done, this place needs to run like a well-oiled machine while madam is away. Pack up and piss off and leave me a macaroon…" he reached out for the box, "or I'll give Prunella your mobile number!" he called after Heidi as he shooed the girls away, then sat back in his chair and began to read his messages. Bob contemplated his menu for dinner with Anthony – he needed to make some changes!

ZELDA STEPPED off the train in Stoke-on-Trent and wondered where the hell she'd landed. The air was damp and as grey as the mass of vacant travellers scurrying along the platform to connecting trains and taxis. She looked around for someone to help with her cases as students with huge rucksacks, like shells on their backs, pushed past on their way to the college she'd seen from the train. Zelda sighed. Presumably someone would be waiting outside? She saw an exit sign and began to struggle down the platform, then followed the crowd into an underpass.

Zelda was tired. The weekend had been draining and instead of feeling the euphoria she'd expected in returning to the set as a "newly engaged", she felt nothing but apathy. Her mother had continued to rant all day yesterday and Zelda had ended up unplugging the phone and turning her mobile off.

Harry had been grumpy too. His hangover was horrid and he'd made it ten times worse by having a hair-of-the-dog at teatime, which seemed to revive him in the most unattractive manner. Zelda had point blank refused to do it doggy-fashion in the dining room, much to Harry's frustration. A slobbering and drunken Harry was more than Zelda could stand. He'd hurled insults about her weight and repeated that the ring didn't fit and how did she think that made a chap feel? She didn't give a damn how a chap felt as long as he wasn't feeling her, and they'd parted company that morning in a stony silence. Zelda had picked up the snack box that Carmelita had carefully prepared, while Harry had munched moodily on his cornflakes. He didn't respond when Zelda called out that she was leaving and slammed the front door.

Zelda emerged from the underpass and dragged her Louis Vuitton cases up grubby stone steps. She was close to tears and wished she hadn't had the full English breakfast on the train; the soggy fried bread was heavy in her stomach. She looked around anxiously, wondering who the hell they'd send to meet her this time.

"Zelda! Over here!" a voice called out.

She spun round and saw Gary, the caterer, running across the entrance hall. He was out of breath and gasped as he stopped abruptly in front of her.

"Made it!" Gary said with a smile. He reached down to relieve Zelda of her cases. "There's all hell let loose on the set and they forgot to book a car for you. I was twiddling my thumbs, so volunteered to do a taxi run. Did you have a good journey?"

Zelda was speechless. The last person she'd expected to see was Gary. Bemused, she nodded as he led her out into the damp air and helped her into his catering truck.

"Sorry about the transport," Gary said. "Not really fitting for the star of the show."

Zelda thought it was all rather jolly as she sat upright in the front and strapped herself in. A delicious smell of baking permeated the cabin.

"Please, help yourself to a cupcake." He pointed towards a plastic box on the dashboard. "It's a new recipe using chocolate and a dash of chilli. I'd value your opinion," he said shyly, and turned the ignition.

Zelda opened the box and helped herself. "Scrummy!" she announced.

Gary smiled. "Have another."

"Don't mind if I do." Zelda dived into the box and took two. She handed one to Gary. He took a bite of the cake and then pulled out to join the busy traffic.

Gary chatted constantly as they travelled through the towns that formed part of the five towns of Stoke-on-Trent, which, he explained, was famous for the pottery industry; no doubt Zelda had a Wedgewood dinner service at home? They saw strange cone-like buildings, built of brick with tall narrow chimneys. Gary told her that they were pot banks – kilns for the pottery which, sadly, was an industry in deep decline and few factories remained now as work had mostly moved out to the Far East.

He drove down a steep bank and as they headed towards Burslem, Gary pointed towards the town hall. A large sculpture of a golden angel sat on top of the building.

"See that angel?" Gary asked. Zelda looked up at the murky sky where the stunning gold object shone brightly, it seemed to survey the panorama of the potteries below. "They say it inspired Robbie Williams to write his famous song Angels. He grew up a few streets away and went to school locally."

Zelda was fascinated. Far from the humdrum of affluent life in Kensington and Chelsea, she found herself interested in the dreary streets of the communities they passed through. Nationalities from every country seemed to be scurrying to and fro as they went about their business. Rain began to fall, with a hint of sleet lashing on the windscreen.

Gary told her that they were heading to Tunstall, to a house in a street that had, until yesterday, enjoyed a quiet location at the end of a row of terraces – former homes for pottery workers. That morning, bulldozers had moved in to a neighbouring street and had begun to demolish a disused factory. The noise and dust made it impossible for filming and the series producer was having a nervous breakdown.

"Brace yourself!" Gary laughed as he drove the van towards the set.

"It can't possibly be as bad as the atmosphere I've come away from..."

Zelda turned to Gary and smiled back. He really was the most handsome fellow! She loved how his face lit up when he smiled, his eyes seemed to twinkle and his whole body language suggested fun.

Zelda waved when she saw Aisla, who leant on a wall and dragged heavily on a cigarette. As Gary helped her out of the van, Zelda looked around at the damp street and felt happier than she had in days. The rain had stopped and a weak ray of sunshine was trying to force its way through the cloud overhead.

Gary assembled an awning on the side of the van and then handed Zelda and Aisla a steaming cup of coffee. Perhaps Stoke wouldn't be so bad after all, Zelda thought, as she met Gary's eyes over the china mug and began to sip the refreshing drink. All thoughts of Harry and her manic mother were completely forgotten as Zelda reached for her script and began to focus on the day.

20

Long Tom's dressing room at Flatterley Manor was covered in suitcases. The walk-in closets were open and a large selection of shirts, trousers and jackets hung on a separate rail. Boots and shoes of every description were stacked neatly in a separate unit, where James stood amidst the mayhem and silently worked through his check-list of things to pack for the forthcoming tour.

There were big gaps.

James studied the list and came to the conclusion that Long Tom hadn't bought any new items for years and the current offerings of rows upon rows of colour-coded clothes, racked in the closets and stacked neatly on shelves, weren't at all suitable. He stared at dozens of bright Versace shirts, all labelled, from a tour in South America many years ago. Scores of plain black Prada shirts hung neatly alongside. James decided these must be from Long Tom's dark days and closed the closet quickly. Pete had booked a top stylist and she was working feverishly to have the required wardrobe ready for Long Tom, who was flying to his London house later for final preparations, before departing for Barbados.

On opening a drawer in a tall slim unit, James shook his head. There were dozens of pairs of sunglasses in the unit and he began to pack a selection. He'd do the best he could from this end and hoped that the stylist would get it right in London.

~

Long Tom wandered round the garden. He held a bag of grain and a tub of dried grubs and as he walked, he threw the food for his beloved peacocks. He sighed, he didn't want to leave them. He wasn't sure when he would be back at the manor, and if Lenny and the team were installed and cooking up a storm, he knew it could be an awful long time, if ever. He stared at the mixture of mature deciduous trees bunched around the walled garden, which would soon be freshly dug over to produce vegetables and herbs for the cookery school. Perhaps he'd relocate to the Home Counties, buy a place with plenty of grounds and trees and water, where he could create the perfect paradise for the peacocks. He made a mental note to ask Pete to make tentative enquiries about properties for sale.

He walked on and stood by the fountain and gazed across the ornamental lake, which had been dug by hand in the 19th century. Long Tom stared at the water and the untidy banks on the far side and thought that it would be perfect for trout fishing. Had he planned to stay, he thought he might have restored it.

Long Tom scratched his head. The demons were dancing around in his head again and he asked himself if he was making the right decision? It had been an amazing feeling to sing in Kindale, but it was only a pub – facing a crowd of two thousand or more at a stadium in Barbados was an entirely different gig. He was looking forward to meeting up with his old band members and some new recruits, brought in by Pete. They had a week's rehearsals in London to do before the tour and he'd need to knuckle down.

He stared up at the house. The drapes in the large bay window on the first floor were drawn back. Hilary must be awake. Long Tom thrust his hands in his pockets and watched the light fall in shadows on the building as clouds passed overhead. What to do about Hilary? He'd been mortified when she'd hurt herself and was overwhelmed that she'd reacted so passionately when she thought that he was in danger. God knows what would have happened had he swigged the vodka. He shuddered at the thought. Lenny was an idiot but he couldn't blame him, no one had known about Long Tom's problem. The very least Long Tom could do was ensure that Hilary was comfortable and able to recuperate somewhere quiet with twenty-four hour care. He remembered her sitting up in the four-poster bed that morning, her magnificent hair flowing over the pillows, like some 18th century mistress waiting for her king to come. He sighed heavily. He didn't think he'd ever come again. How he'd longed to lift the sheets and climb in beside her, then bury himself in her warm comforting body and resurrect his past life. The frustration was killing him. His demons told him to drink and lose all his inhibitions to enable his manhood to start working again, but his head knew that just one drop would spell disaster and ultimately kill him. It was a sacrifice he had to make. Long Tom felt his pent up anger, it raged constantly – no wonder he couldn't write a song or play the piano. His demons were certainly testing him. He looked down and smiled at the peacocks; they'd followed him to the water and wandered round his legs. Long Tom shrugged, he had a tour to do and that, at the moment, was his priority.

∽

LENNY LAY in the roll-top bath at Fool's Landing and smiled smugly to himself. He could hardly believe that the weekend had been so lucrative. Never in his wildest dreams had he expected so much sponsorship to pour into his offshore account in such a short space of time. At this rate, he thought as he eased his bulk forward and twiddled the hot tap, he was bang on target for a disappearing act before Christmas. He'd need to go through the motions at Flatterley Manor and with Long Tom off on tour, that wouldn't be difficult. He could put back the completion date on the lease, make some excuse to the estate agent, but still use it for show-rounds and generate a few thousand euros more to add to his ever increasing stash.

His main aim now was to get on TV. The vain side of Lenny knew that he'd never have another chance to showcase his cooking to a wide audience, it was a risk. He'd no intention of hanging around, but he thought of the DVD he'd have for years to come: cooking on prime time TV! The highlight of his biggest scam to date! No one would find him in southern Spain and he fancied that trip to America.

But first he had to crack Hilary. He didn't expect her to cough up sponsorship but she could pull the relevant strings to get him on a cookery show. The show, Saturday Cook Shop, would work. It had the best ratings of any cookery show on TV. He'd stand alongside the host, an A-lister in the culinary world, and dazzle with his dish – something with seafood, a recipe that he could pinch from Mickey. Water had reached the top of the bath and as Lenny lay back, it splashed over the top, flooding the wooden floor. Lenny didn't notice, he'd closed his eyes and was dreaming of life on a lounger on a terrace in Spain. The warm water was like sunshine caressing his body, and in minutes Lenny had fallen in a deep and satisfied sleep.

∼

MICKEY TIED up the cabin cruiser and hurled a net of mackerel onto the pier. He hopped over the side of the boat and retrieved his catch, then strode purposefully up the path to the cottage. The fishing trip had done him good, although he wished he'd netted something more interesting than mackerel, but as Lenny ate anything and everything, Mickey didn't really care. He flicked the latch on the kitchen door and let himself in. The usual mess confronted him and he moved dirty pots to one side in the sink and placed the fish on the wooden drainer.

The cottage was quiet. Where the hell was Lenny? He'd obviously been here, if the carnage was anything to go by. Mickey reached for the kettle, it was still warm.

"Lenny?" Mickey called. Lenny's bedroom door was open and clothes spilled over the furniture, the bed covers lay in a crumpled heap on the floor.

"Lenny!" Mickey stood in the hallway and stared at the wooden floor where water trickling from under the bathroom door was forming a pool. "LENNY! For God's sake man, get your fat arse out of the bath, you're flooding the house!"

Mickey retreated into the kitchen, where he reached into a cupboard and poured himself a large glass of whisky. He was livid; he was at the end of his tether with Lenny!

The alcohol soon soothed his nerves.

Mickey wandered into the lounge and ignoring the debris, stood by the window and stared out at the estuary. So Hilary had holed up at Flatterley Manor last night! Mickey had called her office earlier and with a thick layer of Irish charm, managed to extract Hilary's whereabouts from a dizzy sounding girl. Hilary's whereabouts were no surprise to Mickey, who now knew that Long Tom was a washed up drunk – it was the least the ageing singer could do. There wasn't a chance that Hilary would give Long Tom so much as a glance and Mickey could hardly have brought her back here, Lenny would never have left them alone. But would she have come to the cottage? Mickey doubted it. He knew he'd got a lot of work to do and intended to crack on without delay. It was time to head to London; Bob should be back in the office now and as Mickey turned from the window, he felt Bob's card in his pocket. No time like the present, he thought, and reached for his mobile phone.

∽

HILARY HAD ENJOYED her late breakfast. Lightly poached eggs on crisp granary bread with a coating of salty Irish butter. Delicious! She was feeling quite revived and didn't think it necessary for the doctor to come and check her over. He arrived mid-morning and after a thorough examination, told her that she needed a few day's rest and time for the stitches to heal, before she would be well enough to travel.

She looked around the room and began to drum her fingers on the bed covers. In the bay window, the curtains were pulled back and as she looked out at clouds passing overhead, light fell in shadows over the room. The house seemed very quiet and she wondered what Long Tom was doing.

She heard a gentle knock on the door.

"Was everything satisfactory with your breakfast, Miss Hargreaves?" James moved gracefully across the room.

"Just what I needed, James, thank you," Hilary replied. "Is anyone else about?"

"Mr Hendry is preparing to depart and will be flying to London shortly," James replied.

Long Tom was flying to London? That meant she'd be left at the manor with just the staff. Hilary sat upright as the realisation hit her. Tom's tour was due to start, of course he would be travelling to London! Hilary imagined all the things he'd have to do in preparation.

"Is he booked on a flight at a specific time?" Hilary asked as she watched James gather the breakfast china onto a silver tray.

"Just his usual flight," James replied. "His manager always charters a jet from Jet Set Air."

Hilary's mind raced. What on earth was she doing lying around in bed when she had an office to run? After all, she admitted to herself, the only reason she'd agreed to come to Flatterley Manor was to snatch a few hours with Long Tom, but if he was hot-footing it off to London there was little point in her hanging around here. She threw the covers back and swung her legs over the side of the bed. Her stitches pulled and she winced.

"Be an absolute darling, James, and see if you can grab me a seat on the flight," Hilary said as she stood up.

"Is that wise, madam?" James asked with some concern as Hilary moved tentatively across the room.

"Wise or not, James, I'm going," Hilary replied. "I've got a business to run…" She disappeared into the bathroom.

James lifted the tray and smiled to himself, he had inkling that there was more to Hilary's agenda than met the eye. He thought that this was something to be encouraged and hurried out of the room to arrange her seat on the flight.

Hilary stepped out of her silky nightgown and pulled a plastic cap over her hair then walked into a tiled area in the bathroom. She turned the shower on and stepped under soft jets of water which burst from the walls. They felt marvellous on her skin. She held a hand-towel over her stitches in an attempt to keep the wound dry and wondered if the rest of Lenny's party had arrived back in London, no doubt they would be in touch in due course to discuss the cookery school and their involvement. Hilary didn't want to add Lenny to the agency's portfolio, she didn't trust him and certainly didn't like him, and it went against all her instincts to sign him up. But he could add value. She hoped that Lottie had managed to check Lenny's references and that the details were on Hilary's desk. Information on his past would help her decision.

Hilary stepped out of the shower and reached for an enormous fluffy towel on the heated rail, then wrapped it round her body.

She wondered what Mickey was doing.

They hadn't had a chance to say goodbye and despite the fact that she'd sworn to herself that she'd never get romantically involved with him again, she had to give him credit for trying. It wouldn't be difficult to succumb.

Hilary rubbed briskly at her skin. The charms of Ireland were getting to her! She really needed to get back to reality and make sure that her business was running smoothly. She hurried into the bedroom and opened the wardrobe door. James had hung her clothes neatly on padded hangers. The lace dress had been laundered and Hilary shook her head in disbelief – the rip caused by her fall had been repaired and the dress was ready to wear again. James was a miracle worker! She selected the woollen palazzo pants and cashmere sweater and began to dress. Hilary longed for a cigarette and time to reflect on the weekend but she heard a car pull up on the gravel below her window and hurried across the room to look out. It was Long Tom's driver, preparing their departure for the airport. She must hurry – she'd no intention of missing the flight!

21

Madeleine Martin sat in her sunny garden annexe and picked at the leather on the arm of a luxurious sofa from Darlings of Chelsea. Her manicured nails dug rhythmically into the soft hide and as she surveyed the damage, she imagined she was prodding Brigitta's tanned face.

"I don't know what's got into her..." Harry said, seated opposite Madeleine. He stared at the glass surface on the coffee table between them. His reflection was pensive as he looked thoughtfully at a bowl of garden roses. The soft pastel petals were past their best and spilled out, some had tumbled to the floor. A bit like his relationship... Harry thought, looking at the jaded petals as he considered his spiralling romance with Zelda. He picked up a cup of coffee and took a sip. "I mean, it's not as though she has to do this damned filming business," Harry moaned. "We're hardly short and my folks are giving us the flat as a wedding present."

Madeleine listened to her future son-in-law drone on about the problems he was experiencing with her wayward daughter and was tempted to agree. Zelda certainly seemed to have an attitude problem these days, the filming must be going to her head – the food was certainly going to her hips! Madeleine reached for a cigarette. She thought she'd be furious with Harry, after all, he'd proposed under Martin's roof, with that Swedish bitch alongside, basking in the engagement glory. But Harry looked so glum and as he was the best catch her daughter was ever likely to find, Madeleine softened her voice.

"I wish you'd told me first," Madeleine said, and placed the cigarette on her lips. "You can't imagine how painful it was hearing the news second hand." She looked up as Harry leapt to his feet and proffered a light.

"Devilishly sorry, old thing," Harry said and took a cigarette for himself. "Never gave it a thought. Naturally inclined to ask for Martin's permission before popping the question." He dragged deeply and paced around the room. "Would have helped if Zelda had shown a tad more enthusiasm…" Harry remembered Zelda's expression as she stared at the ring and her look of horror as it refused to get past her podgy knuckle.

"She'll come round as soon as that rock gleams on her finger and people start to comment," Madeleine said, "but she needs to go on a diet." She stubbed her cigarette out in a silver ashtray then poured herself a strong black coffee. Her hand shook as she placed the cafetière back down on a lacquered tray. She couldn't remember the last time she'd eaten, her head felt woozy as she sipped the bitter liquid and felt a surge as the caffeine rushed through her blood. She put her cup on the tray and ran her hand over her hip, the bone was prominent. Madeleine smiled smugly to herself.

"I don't mind a couple of extra pounds," Harry said, "but Zelda does seem to be ballooning."

"We'll have to roll her down the aisle," Madeleine muttered as she sat back in the sofa and drummed her fingers over the damaged leather. She'd order a new sofa at Martin's expense and blame the damage on the cat.

"I mean, after all, she's got you as an example and with your immaculate taste and stunning figure, you'd think she'd control her eating." Harry poured oil over Madeleine's troubled waters and watched as she preened herself; flattery would get him everywhere.

"I'm going to find a personal trainer for her and when she gets back," Madeleine stood up, "I might just join her in between my tennis and yoga sessions. Have you set a date for the wedding?"

"Sometime in spring," Harry replied.

"That will be perfect," Madeleine mused. "The blossom is out and will make a wonderful theme."

"Gives her six months to shed a couple of stone. Is that long enough for you to plan the wedding?"

"I've already begun," Madeleine replied and reached for a large notebook. "You're having a church service in Chelsea, the reception at Claridges, and your honeymoon in the Maldives."

"I say, that's the ticket!" Harry smiled. He'd need to get his parents hooked up with Zelda's as soon as, but he wasn't relishing the thought of their meeting. Madeleine and Brigitta in the same room was sure to cause fireworks. Still, it wasn't his problem. Harry glanced at his Rolex, he needed to get a spin on or he'd be very late for work.

"I'll be in touch," Madeleine said as she pecked Harry's cheeks, "just leave everything to me." She smiled sweetly and watched Harry retreat through the open doors and disappear beyond the garden gate. The wedding will be lavish, Madeleine thought. She intended to roll the red carpet out and Martin would have to pick up the cost, right down to the very last designer detail. Brigitta would be surviving on crispbreads, for the foreseeable future, if Madeleine had her way. She sighed, revenge was a dish best eaten cold and, at that very moment, her dish was positively icy!

~

HILARY'S CAR wound its way through early morning commuter traffic. The traffic was heavy and as the driver carefully negotiated the busy flow round Hyde Park Corner, Hilary stared out at Constitution Arch.

The monument stood proud, topped with the magnificent statue of the Angel of Peace, which towered over the major intersection and surveyed the surrounding historic routes of London. Hilary didn't think that there would be much peace in the office today – they thought she was still in Ireland and weren't expecting her. She made a mental list of all things she had to do.

The car headed along Piccadilly, past street artists setting up for the day, their colourful paintings depicted London scenes and littered the footpaths and railings. Tourists stared at the lavish displays in the windows of Fortnum & Mason, and a crowd of Japanese students headed towards the Royal Academy of Arts.

Hilary thought of the previous day, and of the very different journey she'd made with Long Tom through the quiet country roads to Cork airport, as his car glided past farmlands and green pastures, so different to the busy streets of London.

The journey had been tense. Long Tom had at first shown annoyance with her. He couldn't understand why she'd insisted on travelling back to London or why she wouldn't spend more time at Flatterley Manor to recuperate, but Hilary had ignored his protests. Eventually he'd given in, his attention distracted by a mobile phone that vibrated persistently on the console between them.

"Why don't you answer it?" Hilary asked.

"I don't do mobiles, babe," Long Tom replied and gazed out of the window.

Hilary had been aware that he was about to step back into a life he'd left some time ago and his phone would now ring constantly, as news of his come-back broke and the media invasion began. They'd arrived at the airport and were swiftly taken to the jet and, in what seemed like no time at all, arrived back in London.

"Will you let me know how your tour goes?" Hilary asked as the car slowed in heavy traffic. Long Tom's driver had instructions to drop Hilary at her flat in Kensington then continue to Long Tom's town house in Chester Square.

Long Tom was silent and Hilary wondered if she'd dreamt their brief time together over the last few days, the sharing of confidences and the warm lingering kiss in his kitchen – it all seemed light years away.

"You know how I am with phones, babe." He'd nodded towards the mobile. He sat in one corner of the car and as Hilary watched him from the opposite side, she wondered why he was so distant. She longed to reach out and take his hand. But Long Tom hardly spoke to her and she felt a distinct chill in their relationship.

They'd arrived at Hilary's Kensington home and the driver hurried to open her door and gather the luggage. Long Tom stepped out of the vehicle and stood awkwardly on the pavement. He glanced up at the building.

"Nice pad," Long Tom said as he stared up at the period conversion.

"Want to come in for a coffee?" Hilary replied. She felt herself blush, she wasn't used to humbling herself before a man, but the atmosphere between them was tense and Hilary felt that if she walked away now, she'd never hear from him again.

"No, babe, I'll be on my way." Long Tom tipped his hat and smiled. He'd seemed to linger for a split second, then nodded politely and climbed back into the car. Hilary felt foolish as she stood on the pavement and forced herself to turn and head for the steps as the driver followed with her luggage.

"Make sure you get your arse looked at!"

Hilary heard Long Tom call out and as she put her key in the lock, she turned. He'd sat forward and opened a window.

Their eyes met.

Hilary's heart leapt and she felt an invisible magnet pull her towards the car as she stared into his delicious dark brown eyes. Long Tom stared back and time seemed suspended between them. She yearned to run back to the car and melt into his arms, but she saw him shake his head then sit back and disappear beyond the tinted windows. Her hand had trembled as she forced herself to turn the key and open the door.

Hilary wondered if she would ever see him again and tears pricked at the corners of her eyes as she remembered her last glimpse of Long Tom. When his car had pulled away she'd seen him lean forward and, despite the darkened glass, she knew that he was watching her, but it was short lived, as his vehicle turned onto the main road and accelerated out of sight. Hilary sighed, she must pull herself together!

Her car was approaching Wardour Street and she had much to do. What on earth did she think she was doing, allowing her heart to rule her head! She gathered her Coach bag and applied a fresh coat of lipstick and told herself that she had a business to run. But as Hilary climbed out of the car she felt the stitches tweak on her buttock and she winced. Bloody men! she thought angrily and thanking the driver, hurried into her office.

∼

Long Tom Hendry thrust his hands into the pockets of his jeans and paced around the drawing room of his London town house. He was due at the studio in half an hour and Pete would be arriving to collect him at any moment.

Despite his nerves, Long Tom was looking forward to the day. Members of his old band had been in touch, equally excited by the reunion and, despite a few new faces, Long Tom felt that he had a great team to go on tour with. Pete had no doubt drilled them all with clear instructions on how to handle Long Tom's abstinence, and the coming weeks would be filled with very different activities off-stage to those in days gone by. Pete had told Long Tom that he was taking golf clubs and tennis racquets on tour. Long Tom shook his head at the thought of hours on a golf course in contrast to endless hours in a bar.

He walked over to the French doors and undid the latch, then stepped out onto a wrought iron balcony. London was busy and he could hear a steady hum of traffic beyond the square below. The private gardens were surrounded by a variety of trees that had begun to shed their leaves and the autumn sunshine highlighted the rich shades of gold, red and brown.

Long Tom was reminded of Hilary's tumbling hair.

How he longed to feel the tresses in his hand, to bury his face in the thick perfumed locks. What an idiot he was! Whatever did she think of him? If he'd ever considered himself in with a chance, he could forget it now, he'd treated her appallingly yesterday and had hardly spoken a word during their journey from Ireland. She'd tried her hardest to engage him in conversation, but he'd stalled all her efforts and when they stood outside her home, he could feel her desperation to part on good terms, with a chance of meeting again, or at least the promise of a phone call.

But in truth, he was terrified.

Hilary had touched nerves he'd long forgotten and reawakened a broken heart. Admittedly, he'd broken it with his own excesses, but he'd felt a fear far greater than the thought of going on tour. Going headlong into a relationship scared the life out of Long Tom and he felt his demons dance on his shoulders, telling him that he wasn't worthy and it would never work, after all – he couldn't even get an erection these days, so what woman in her right mind would want him?

Especially someone as special as Hilary.

Long Tom rubbed his hand over his chin and thoughtfully stared ahead. He was grateful that he was sober and intended to stay that way, but if a genie were to pop out of those trees right now and grant him three wishes, he'd wish to compose a new song, to play his piano again and, most of all, to be with Hilary. Pigs might fly! Long Tom thought and looked around the square.

"A penny for your thoughts?" a voice rang out.

Startled, Long Tom turned to see where it had come from and heard a succession of clicks from a camera. A journalist was squatting in the bushes below and aimed a zoom lens up at the balcony. Long Tom smiled. At least it wasn't a genie! He raised his hand and waved, then moved back into the drawing room. He'd better start getting used to it again, if the tour was a success there'll be more than just a solitary journalist camping outside his house.

He heard the doorbell ring, Pete had arrived. Long Tom fastened the doors securely and paused as he locked the windows. He made a decision to turn the lock on his heart too, after all, his band was waiting and the tour was all set, he'd got a lot of work to do. He heard Pete call out, and with fresh determination, Long Tom turned to begin his day.

22

Zelda was up at the crack of dawn. She smiled as she silenced her alarm and climbed out of bed in the Quality Hotel in Stoke, then stretched and bounced across the room to the bathroom, where she hurriedly washed her face and scrubbed her pearly white teeth.

Zelda yawned as she made herself a mug of instant coffee and winced as she added a capsule of UHT milk to the gruesome looking liquid. She reached for a packet of custard creams and hastily ripped it open, then dunked the yellow squares into her drink. The sweetness was pleasing and Zelda munched all four biscuits as she crossed the room to double-glazed windows and pulled the thin drapes aside. She tweaked a net curtain and stared out through the grimy glass. The sun was shining and with hardly a soul in sight, the streets of Stoke looked quite inviting.

Zelda grinned. Gary was meeting her shortly and they were going to go for a jog together. She began to hum as she took a Juicy Couture track suit out of the wardrobe and found a sports bra and vest top. Zelda dressed carefully, then laced a pair of Nike trainers over running socks and pulled her hair into a ponytail. Her mobile phone rang and she glanced at the display.

It was Harry.

Zelda wondered what on earth he was doing up at this time of day – Harry usually had a hangover and rarely raised his head before eight o'clock, when Carmelita arrived to make breakfast. She ignored the call and turning the phone to silent, zipped it into a pocket and hurried to meet Gary. They'd arranged to meet in the foyer.

"Wow, you look fresh faced and bushy tailed," Gary beamed as Zelda approached. He was dressed in running gear too and his white t-shirt showed off his tan and glossy black hair. Zelda thought he looked terribly handsome.

"Oh, hardly," she replied. "It's still the middle of the night!"

They headed out of the double doors and onto the street, then set off on a brisk walk, chatting amiably as Gary guided her through the roads that led to the canal basin and tow paths.

It had been Ailsa's idea for them to go running together. The previous day she'd listened to Gary as he described his run that morning and how great he felt after it. Zelda had been complaining about the lack of lycra in the top Ailsa had chosen and Ailsa had suggested that she might benefit from some exercise, why didn't Zelda go running in the morning with Gary? Neither had taken much persuading.

"Are you ready for a gentle jog?" Gary asked.

"Let's give it a go!" Zelda called out and quickened her pace.

Zelda felt extraordinarily happy. In twenty-four hours, her mood had lifted from one of near despair to that of joy. The pressures in London seemed a long way away and from the moment Gary had met her yesterday, she'd breezed through the filming and been nice to everyone on the set. There'd been a last minute location change, as the noise from the factory demolition created havoc with the sound equipment, which meant that they'd had to work until eleven o'clock, by which time everyone was fraught and tired.

Zelda had been given the challenge of changing a Stoke staple – oatcakes, piled high with cheese and grilled with streaky bacon and thick sausages which had been presented by a young pottery worker named Paul. Paul had rolled the oatcake and its calorie laden contents into his version of a pie and told Zelda that he normally took it to work for his lunch. Zelda had politely complimented Paul on his culinary skills and after off-set consultations with Gary, who'd prepared her recipe in advance, produced her version of Paul's dish – Potter's Pie, a wrap filled with healthy stir-fried vegetables and strips of lean ham. Paul would vote on this tomorrow, after Zelda had cooked with Mr and Mrs Singh, an elderly couple who ran a corner shop and had a very large family. The Singhs had relocated from northern India and had settled in Stoke in the 1970s. Mrs Singh prepared traditional Indian food for her family, cooked in ghee with rich sauces containing nuts, milk and yoghurt.

"You've got a challenge on today!" Gary called out as they jogged past pretty painted canal boats moored in neat rows.

"We'll do curry without calories!" Zelda called back. She'd been practicing at home and had perfected a recipe for Keema Matar, a green pea curry with traditional spices. Zelda had omitted fats from the cooking process and the results produced a delicious, low-calorie dish. The Singhs would cook a traditional meal, to be judged alongside Paul's pie and Zelda's Potters Pie and Keema Matar. Young and old would dine today on all the dishes and Zelda wanted to win; she'd had success in Liverpool and was keen to repeat it in Stoke.

They approached a set of canal locks and the path began to incline. Zelda felt her lungs tighten and slowed her pace.

"Let's walk along this bit," Gary suggested. He'd noticed Zelda struggling.

"How do the locks work?" Zelda asked. She'd never been beside a canal before and was intrigued by the system of locks that stretched out ahead.

"They're staircase locks," Gary said, following Zelda's gaze, "built to enable boats to get from one level to the next. The canal was built by Josiah Wedgewood, who had a factory nearby and wanted a safe transport system to move his goods."

They stopped by a lock and watched a boat glide into the narrow opening, navigated by a ruddy faced man who acknowledged them with a wave. Gary waved back and explained that the lock was used to raise or lower the water level. When a narrow boat went upstream, the bottom gate would be opened to allow the boat to enter. He pointed to paddles on the gate, situated on both sides of the lock. The paddles were shut. When the gate was closed the paddles would be opened and water channelled through a tunnel into the lower lock. Zelda was fascinated as they watched the boat rise and the lock filled. When the water was level, the man opened the upper gate then nimbly hopped back on the boat to continue his journey.

Zelda turned to Gary and asked in wonder, "How do you know so much about everything? Not only do you have knowledge of local history and things, like how a canal works, but you're as fit as a fiddle and can cook like a connoisseur…"

"I spend a lot of time travelling with my job," Gary replied. "I like to get to know the local area – running round it helps."

Zelda was thoughtful. "I suppose if I ran I wouldn't have such a weight problem." She prodded her stomach.

"You're not big," Gary said. "It makes a change to see someone carrying a few extra pounds; most of the people I work with are neurotic about their size."

"They'd get on well with my mother," Zelda said with a scowl, "and my fiancé," she added.

"Fiancé?"

Zelda frowned. "Oh hell, I wasn't going to say anything."

"You're not wearing a ring…"

"It won't fit, my finger is too plump." Zelda held up her hand and stared at her creamy white skin.

"Why don't you want to tell anyone?" Gary asked.

Zelda leaned on a wooden bench beside the lock and sighed. She bit on her lip and felt all the frustrations she'd faced at the weekend well up in her chest. A hot, salty tear dripped onto her cheek.

"Hey, what's up?" Concerned, Gary put his arm around Zelda's shoulder. "Come and sit down."

Zelda allowed him to guide her onto the bench and unable to help herself, she burst into tears and buried her head in his chest.

"Tell me what's wrong," Gary implored, as he rocked her gently and waited for the tears to subside. He reached into a pocket for a tissue and held it out.

"Oh Lord, I was so gloriously happy a moment ago and now look at me!" Zelda took the tissue and wiped her eyes. "I'm really sorry, Gary."

"Don't be sorry. Maybe I can help?"

"It's just that I feel so pressurised," Zelda began. "Harry is quite a catch and my parents are thrilled that he's proposed, it sort of sets me up, if you can understand?" She sniffed, then continued, "Mummy is furious with Daddy for remarrying; she hates his new wife, who he'd had an affair with and left Mummy. Brigitta is gorgeous and much younger and has a great figure. Mummy's like a stick insect and never eats, and tells me that I'm as huge as a house and need to lose weight. She's got Harry on the warpath over my weight too. I know that I've put a few pounds on but I just can't seem to help it. I love my food and love cooking, but I seem to eat without knowing I'm eating and it's just getting all out of hand." Her words tumbled out. "Harry said my finger was too fat for the ring and made a scene, but I'm sure he got the size wrong, he's a bit stupid at times, but blames me and is quite beastly, and I'm not sure that I like him when he's like that." Zelda sniffed. "I suppose I thought that if I didn't tell anyone here that I was engaged, then, in my head, I wouldn't be…"

"Do you want to marry Harry?" Gary asked.

Zelda giggled. "'Marry, Harry?' Gary." She smiled.

"But do you?" Gary was insistent. He still had his arm around Zelda's shoulder and gave her a gentle squeeze.

She sighed. "Oh, I don't know." Zelda crumpled the tissue and looked down at her hands. "I used to think he was the dog's do dahs and all that, with his double-barrel and city job, but since we've lived together I've noticed that he drinks quite a lot, and I don't really like that side of him at all." She wanted to tell Gary that Harry was terrible in bed but as she'd nothing to really compare Harry with, other than a few fumbles and hazy one-night stands at university, she wasn't really in a position to judge.

"But what about your career?" Gary asked.

"I love it," Zelda replied. "Hilary has done so much for me and I love being out on the road filming. I didn't think I would, but I do."

"Would you carry on if you got married?"

Zelda fell silent. She hadn't really thought about the future but knew that Harry wanted to start a family as soon as possible – he'd already said that she'd have to give up work. Harry wanted a son first and they'd need to get him on the school list for Uppingham. Would she be able to carry on working once the demands of family life began? Zelda sighed. She'd have a nanny to oversee as well as Carmelita and they'd have to find a house, the flat wouldn't be at all suitable. The house would no doubt need renovation and she'd have to find an interior designer. The thought of nurseries and school runs made Zelda quite dizzy.

Work suddenly felt like a safe option.

Zelda nestled into Gary's arm. She felt very comfortable and realised that Harry would have a fit if he knew that she was sitting here, in the arms of another man, and let's face it, she thought, she'd never have been here at all had she not landed The Zimmers role. She also realised that The Zimmers would allow her to be independent. With money from the series and her increased profile, if ratings were good, would ensure higher earnings. Did she really need Harry's wealth and so-called status?

Zelda suddenly felt as though she'd experienced an epiphany and with wide eyes turned to Gary.

"You have to be sure, Zelda," Gary said, and reached out with his free hand to touch her face. "Do you love him?"

Zelda felt as though she was in a dream and with Gary's warm hand on her skin, her stomach did a bunny hop and an unfamiliar feeling crept into her groin, making her squirm uncomfortably.

Their eyes met and Zelda thought that she heard Robbie Williams singing Angels, accompanied by a full orchestra, as Gary suddenly pulled her into his arms and began to kiss her passionately. She closed her eyes and responded with equal fervour, while his hands played a symphony on her back and his tongue headed tantalisingly for her tonsils.

"Oh my..." Zelda gasped as they broke away from each other.

"God, I'm so sorry!" Gary exclaimed. "I couldn't help myself, you're just so sweet and so beautiful and—"

He didn't finish his sentence. Zelda grabbed him and wrapped her arms around his muscular body. She kissed him all over as though a clock was on countdown and their time together running out.

"Oh Gary..." she mumbled as he twined his fingers in her hair and pulled her mouth onto his own.

"Wow!" they both exclaimed when they finally parted.

Gary smiled. "I've wanted you since the moment I saw your Scouse."

"Your cupcakes are divine..."

"Your Potter's Pie is historic..."

They kissed again.

Their jog back to the hotel became a run and they held hands as they hurried along the pavements and into the foyer.

"Do you fancy some breakfast?" Zelda asked, as Gary propelled her to the lift.

"Not just yet," Gary replied and glanced at his watch. The lift was taking some time.

They turned to each other.

"What's your room number?" Gary whispered.

"Come and find out..." Zelda whispered back and giggling with delight, they raced up the stairs and ran through the corridors to Zelda's bedroom.

23

Hilary sat at her desk and studied a list of incoming emails on her computer screen. She ploughed through them ruthlessly and made a list on a notepad, prioritising the more urgent demands.

Lottie hovered nearby. She'd placed an espresso next to Hilary, and stood chewing thoughtfully on the end of a ballpoint pen as she watched her boss sip the strong coffee. Lottie wondered how anyone could drink something so vile, and pulled a face.

"The wind will change and your expression will get stuck," Hilary said without looking up. "And stop chewing; you've got ink on your teeth." Hilary pushed the cup to one side. "Have you got Lenny Crispin's references?" she asked for the umpteenth time and drummed her fingers on the desk. The stitches on her wound were hurting today, the skin had bonded together and the gash was healing, but the pain was annoying Hilary and she felt her temper rise as she stared at Lottie and waited for an answer.

"I'm having a bit of trouble with them," Lottie replied, pouting. Her words were an understatement. She'd got absolutely nowhere with any responses to her letters and calls whilst researching Lenny's background. Most of the previous employers that Lenny had provided had never heard of him.

"Trouble?" Hilary raised her eyebrows.

"I'll do another ring round and update you again this morning." Lottie crossed her fingers behind her back and wondered whether she should fabricate a few replies. Hilary's face was like thunder. Lottie decided to speak to Bob and see what he thought about it all.

"I need you to get them, it's urgent!" Hilary waved her hand in dismissal; Lenny's references were high on her list. His scheme seemed to be coming to fruition, despite Hilary's doubts, and if she was going to arrange endorsements, sponsors and chefs to run courses, she had to be confident that the loathsome Lenny was all he was cracked up to be.

Hilary's phone rang.

"The operations manager from Jet Set Air wants to speak to you," Lottie announced.

"Put him through," Hilary said.

"Miss Hargreaves, I'm very concerned about your client, Lenny Crispin," the manager began. He sounded anxious.

"He's not my client," Hilary corrected.

"Well, he's not paid for the flight to Ireland and I'm under some pressure to resolve the issue."

"Have you spoken to David Hugo?" Hilary asked.

"I've tried to get hold of him and left messages, as I have for Mr Crispin." The manager sighed. "Neither of them returns my calls."

"Well, I'm sorry, I can't help you," Hilary said. "I will speak to Mr Crispin though; I'm sure we'll be getting a visit from him soon."

The manager thanked Hilary profusely and she realised that his job was probably on the line. It was unheard of to allow such credit, even if Lenny had David Hugo and Pilling's law firm backing him up.

Hilary heard a knock on her door and looked up as Bob raced into the room.

"I can't believe we flew back on Air Cunnilingus!" Bob moaned. "No doubt you came back in style…" Bob bristled as he flounced around the room. "What on earth are you doing here?" he said crossly. "You're supposed to be in bed – an Irish one if I remember, luxuriating in the lap of luxury while you recover…"

Hilary adjusted her pink Liberty glasses and stared at Bob over the brow-line frame. She was about to snap at him but softened when she saw his look of concern.

"I'm far better keeping busy and the cut is healing nicely, thank you," she said.

"At least you're wearing something sensible," Bob replied, as he moved round the side of Hilary's desk and tucked a cushion carefully alongside the billowy folds of her sateen tea dress. "You don't want anything tight over those stitches…"

"Don't fuss, Bob." Hilary pushed his hand away. "Sit down." She waved in the direction of a comfortable chair. "What's your diary like today?"

"Why?" Bob asked with concern, he was cooking for Anthony later and needed to shop, he couldn't be late leaving the office.

"We've got a table booked at Ranchers, courtesy of the Vice President of PAP. Sales have already shot up and distributors are struggling to keep up with demand." Hilary leaned back in her chair and smiled.

"No wonder you look so smug!" Bob shook his head, Hilary had played a blinder.

"One teeny drawback though," Hilary began.

Bob sat forward, his forehead furrowed with concern. "I have a horrible feeling that I know what's coming…" He gripped the side of his chair.

"Yes, well, the lunch would hardly be complete without Prunella, would it?"

"And you want me to unearth her, embalm the body formerly known as Prunella Gray and present her all perked up and packaged nicely for the Vice President of PAP?"

"The table's booked for one thirty…"

"Give me a gay moment!" Bob shook his head.

"You've got a couple of hours," Hilary replied.

Bob sighed, it was a monumental task. Prunella hardly every

stepped out in daylight and it took a combined team of stylist, make-up and hairdresser at least half a day to drag her out of her current hangover and into whatever "look" they felt was appropriate. The lunch meeting today would require her to be as fresh and healthy as possible. Bob prayed that Prunella hadn't been pouring vodka on her cornflakes.

"I sent the team in first thing," Hilary continued. "You've only to get her in a cab and turn up on time."

"But I'll have to sit next to her and monitor her every move and word." Bob felt like a ventriloquist when he chaperoned Prunella, and always had to be one step ahead as he jumped in and cut her off or changed the subject before she could offend her audience.

"Piece of cake." Hilary smiled and reached into a drawer for a cigarette. She placed a menthol tip in a holder and stood up. Bob watched her walk to the window, open it and then flick a lighter. She dragged deeply and blew smoke over the noisy traffic below.

Bob wrinkled his nose in distaste. "I'd hoped you'd given that up; you hardly smoked in Ireland."

"I suddenly feel like one." Hilary dragged again and looked thoughtful as she stared out over the hustle and bustle of Wardour Street.

Bob glanced at his watch. He'd arranged to meet Mickey this afternoon. "I've got a meeting this afternoon…" he tentatively began.

"Cancel it."

Hilary didn't move. She was watching a young girl on a bicycle weave through the traffic. Her skirt was high on her thigh and a taxi driver wolf whistled through the open window of his cab.

"Erm… I think that might be difficult. The party in question is already in transit." Bob reached for his prayer beads and held his breath.

"Not Mickey Lloyd!" Hilary spun round.

"Now, don't be so hasty. You don't need to deal with him, he can be my client."

"Bloody hell, Bob!" Hilary stubbed her cigarette out and reached into the drawer again. She found two glasses and poured gin and a splash of tonic into both then pushed a glass towards Bob.

It was a good sign. Bob visibly relaxed and stroked his beads. As he sipped his drink, he silently repeated "thank you", five times.

Hilary sat down and stared thoughtfully at Bob. She could see his point: Mickey was marketable. Look what had happened to Paul Hollywood? He'd resurrected his career and risen to stardom faster than his bread dough; there was definitely a market for the older man. The mature Mickey would look wonderful on screen and have a whole new generation of foodie fans clamouring for more. Festivals would be packed if he put in an appearance and his fees would go through the roof. She envisaged a host of lucrative endorsements. It was time he wrote an autobiography too; it could be packaged into at least three books and royalties would roll in for years. Lenny's cookery school would make a great location for a TV series, and Hilary was confident that she could resurrect the old team at the production company that had made the previous programmes, and with several commissioning editors owing her favours, it was only a matter of time before he became a household name again. She nursed her drink and knew that she'd be foolish to turn this down.

"All right, he's your client, do what you need to do but keep him away from me." Hilary's voice was steely.

"That might not be so easy," Bob said.

"It's non-negotiable," Hilary replied. "And cancel him this afternoon... Don't be too keen." She slugged her drink back and stood up as her phone began to ring.

"Mr Crispin on line one," Lottie said.

"Tell him I'm in a meeting, and get those wretched references on my desk," Hilary snapped. She glanced at her watch and turned to Bob. "Get over to Prunella's and work your magic; I intend to get a five-year extension to the PAP deal secured today."

"Strike while the PAP is hot!" Bob grinned and stood up. The gin had mellowed him and he almost felt warm towards Prunella as he contemplated the lunch meeting. If fees continued to pour into the office accounts he would ask Hilary for a partnership in the business.

She paid him well but it would be wonderful to have his name over the door – Hargreaves & Puddicombe Promotions... Bob smiled as he daydreamed.

"Don't start getting ahead of yourself!" Hilary had read Bob's mind and her comment brought him down to earth. "Mickey wouldn't step foot in here if it wasn't for me." She sat down and turned to her computer. Bob watched her fingers fly over the keyboard, and he pulled a childish face.

"As I told Lottie earlier, the wind will change and you'll get stuck..." Hilary didn't look up.

"I'll see you at Ranchers," Bob snapped and marched out of the office.

"Don't be late!" Hilary called out and smiled as she watched Bob retreat.

~

Ranchers restaurant was packed with an animated lunchtime crowd, who hogged tables and conversed noisily, while busy staff hurried between kitchen and bar to satisfy the demands of the affluent diners. A queue had formed on the pavement outside and snaked around the corner towards Covent Garden, where Mickey and Lenny jumped out of a taxi at the end of the street.

Mickey strode away, leaving Lenny to pay the fare.

They'd flown over from Cork that morning and booked into a hotel together to keep costs down. Mickey was meeting with Bob the next day and Lenny intended to pursue sponsors for the cookery school. Unbeknown to each other, they both planned to pin Hilary down – Lenny was determined to get a TV slot and Mickey had more than work on his mind, he was confident that he could rekindle their romance if he continued to pursue her. Bob had told him that she was back in London and Mickey had a suspicion that Bob was dining at Ranchers with Hilary that day; he'd indicated that it was the reason for postponing their meeting. Lenny hurried to keep up with Mickey and as he looked at the crowd, he complained in despair.

"Bleedin' 'ell, mate, we're in a pickle 'ere." Lenny mumbled. He was sure there wasn't a prayer of finding a table without a reservation. Mickey ignored him and walked straight to the front of the queue, where he shook hands with the doorman and placed a ten-pound note discreetly in his hand.

"Nice to see you back, Mr Lloyd," the doorman said and ushered Mickey into the restaurant.

Joe met them at the foot of the stairs.

"Mr Lloyd, it's been a long time," Joe said. "Do you have a reservation?"

Mickey smiled at Joe, then looked over his head and studied the room. His eyes rested on a table by the far wall and he raised his hand and waved. A tall, striking blonde stood up and beckoned him over to her table.

"Mickey Lloyd, I don't believe it!" she exclaimed and leaned forward to kiss him on both cheeks. "When did you get back? Why don't you join us?"

Mickey beamed. "Louella, so good to see you. "Erm…" he hesitated. "We were going to sit…" he gesticulated to the other tables, "but as it's been so long…" Mickey stood back as his old acquaintance instructed Joe to create two more places at her table.

Lenny was wide-eyed as he watched Mickey in action and marvelled at the ease in which Mickey had managed to con a table out of nowhere. Lenny liked his style and grinned happily as he squeezed himself beside Louella and her friend, who was listening to Louella explain that she had been a producer on Mickey's series of Around the Coast with Mickey Lloyd.

Drinks were ordered and conversation became animated as Louella recalled old times and gushed with joy that Mickey was back in the UK. The girls were introduced to Lenny and wanted to know all about the cookery school plans. Lenny was on cloud nine as he probed them both for contacts.

Mickey smiled and made all the right noises but, in truth, he couldn't give a toss for the conversation and listened half-heartedly as he watched the door. He was sure that Hilary would arrive at any moment. Her table was empty but he noticed that champagne was waiting and Joe kept fussing over the cloth and place settings. Mickey was annoyed that Bob had cancelled their meeting today, despite rescheduling for tomorrow. Mickey wanted to see Hilary and was confident that a reunion would have her eating out of his hand; he was anxious to put it in place as soon as possible. He'd a niggling fear that Hilary hadn't been in a clinic and that Long Tom Hendry might have scored an advantage ahead of him.

There was a flurry of activity and Joe rushed past their table. Mickey felt Lenny dig him in the ribs and everyone's eyes were drawn towards the party entering the room. Joe walked ahead of Prunella Grey, who glided across the room like a magnificent swan. Behind her followed Hilary, Bob and the Vice President of PAP. Prunella was wrapped in a white fur and held her neck aloft as Joe guided them to Hilary's reserved table. The diners stared in silence as Prunella floated into her seat, flicked her coal black fringe to one side and licked her deep red lips. She glanced at the champagne and shook her head.

"Surely Ranchers is serving my PAP Potion!" Prunella announced in a voice that carried across the room.

"Prunella, honey, you can have whatever your lil' ol' heart desires!" the Vice President said, beaming as they took their seats.

Hilary nodded towards Joe. The champagne was whisked away and a large jug of a sinister looking yellow liquid appeared.

"PAP Potion for all!" the Vice President called out and instructed Joe to send a complimentary jug to every table, at PAP's expense.

"We'll be rat-arsed," Bob whispered to Hilary, as Joe poured.

"Cheers!" the Vice President said and raised his glass.

Hilary looked across the room. She'd felt Mickey's steely blue eyes bore into her from the moment she'd arrived. He was immaculate as ever, dressed in designer jeans, white cotton shirt and dark blue silk cravat. His hair was brushed back and slightly gelled, it suited his tan. Mickey held a glass in one hand and as a waiter topped it up with PAP Potion, he raised the glass in a toast and winked at Hilary.

She quickly looked away. The wretched man had the ability to unravel her in seconds and she had a business meeting to get through. Prunella was halfway down her second glass and becoming livelier by the second and the Vice President was sitting back on the banquette, his eyes as wide as saucers as he watched Prunella hold court with an adjacent table of young men from a media company. Hilary kicked Bob and made a face that suggested he should be monitoring the conversation more carefully. She'd noticed that Lenny was with Mickey and a couple of blondes from Fenums TV, Hilary recognised Louella Kidd, Head of Development.

Hilary guessed that it was only a matter of time before Lenny would lunge over to her table and crash their meeting. She turned to the Vice President and with an endearing smile, removed a revised contract from a folder. Five minutes later, she returned the contract to the folder and placed it securely in her bag. The ink had barely dried as Hilary winked at Bob and asked Joe for the menus.

Bob smiled back at his boss, she was shit-hot! A few days ago Prunella was in serious breach of contract and the account was teetering on the brink of collapse, now they were signed up for a further five years at a considerable sum and Prunella was set for life. The agency's commission would be huge. He turned his attention back to Prunella, who was regaling the Vice President with tales of her earlier life, which had started on the stage. Her voice got louder with each sentence and the media men on the next table were hanging off her every word as she gossiped wickedly about several well-known actors and their sexual persuasions. Bob was engrossed, he'd no idea that a particular leading lady swung both ways, but he soon curtailed the conversation as he felt Hilary kick his shin again

Hilary was trying to divert the conversation and looked to Bob for support. The Vice President, who only drank fruit juice, seemed oblivious to Prunella's rants. Hilary realised that he was well into his second glass of PAP Potion, which looked exactly like the jug of non-alcoholic PAP pineapple juice in the centre of the table. No wonder he'd signed without a murmur! Hilary began to relax. She'd done her job here and the Vice President would probably slither down the banquette by the time they got to desserts. She drained her glass and excused herself from the table.

Mickey noticed Hilary leave the table and in a flash he'd crossed the floor and followed her to the Ladies room.

Hilary stopped by the cloakroom to chat to the attendant and was in mid-sentence when Mickey suddenly appeared beside her. Stunned, she didn't notice him push a ten-pound note into the attendant's hand and indicate that she should vacate her post. He grabbed Hilary and pulled her into a dark corner of the room. They were surrounded by wool, cashmere and coats of every description, and as hard as Hilary tried to resist, she was drawn into the excitement of the moment.

"You're absolutely reckless!" Hilary scolded and half-heartedly tried to pull away. Mickey had wrapped his arms around her and nuzzled his lips into the soft skin on the curve of her neck.

"Mmm... delicious, Chanel No.5..." Mickey mumbled in Hilary's ear and began to edge his hand under her skirt.

Mickey felt divine and Hilary succumbed to his strong and confident embrace. He was a forbidden fruit and she longed to take a very large bite as she felt his fingers brush past her stocking tops on their gradual ascent. Her knees began to buckle as he continued to whisper endearments in her ear and Hilary felt herself melting in his arms as they were enveloped in the warm dark cocoon of the cloakroom. Mickey's fingers climbed higher and cupped her buttock...

"Ouch!" Hilary screamed. Mickey leapt back. He'd snagged the dressing on her stitches and it pulled sharply.

"Oh Christ, I didn't realise," he blurted out. "I'm sorry, come here..."

Hilary had pulled away and as if waking from a dream, shook her head and pushed him away. He staggered into a rail of outerwear which collapsed, covering him in raincoats.

"I must be insane," Hilary hissed, as she straightened the sateen on the skirt of her dress. "For goodness' sake, Mickey!"

The attendant peeped around the rails and caught Hilary's eye.

"Mr Lloyd can't find his coat!" Hilary snapped and pointed to the moving bundle of gabardine. With a ramrod straight back, she walked haughtily away from the cloakroom and lunged into a cubicle in the Ladies room. There was no guarantee that the ever persistent Mickey would follow her so Hilary hastily locked the door. I must be mad... she thought to herself as her heart hammered. Was she losing her marbles? She'd very nearly committed a cardinal sin – sex in a workplace environment with Mickey Lloyd? And he was a future client!

Hilary tentatively opened the door, then washed her hands and attempted to fix her hair where strands had fallen from the filigree comb at the nape of her neck. She looked at her face in the mirror and touched her forehead, where the egg-shaped lump had been, the swelling had gone and only a faint bruise reminded her of her fall. She dotted concealer on her brow and stared at her reflection. She was forty-something and just about holding up emotionally, her business was a success, after sustained efforts, but her love-life was non-existent. Long Tom had touched areas of her heart that she'd forgotten existed and she yearned to be with him and make his life well, but he'd turned his back on her. Mickey was pure lust. Feelings and emotions that were too close to call, bounced around her body like fire and if she could take a cold shower, she'd leap into it right now. Hilary finished fixing her hair. Would it be so wrong to get involved with Mickey again? Yes, of course it would! she told herself; he was a client and a scum-bag when it came to love, and she really should know better.

Hilary shook her head and closed her eyes, as if to shake Mickey out of her mind but as she looked up she saw Louella Kidd standing beside her. The attractive blonde wore an unmistakably heady, spicy perfume and smiled as she recognised Hilary. The perfume was cloying and Hilary pulled back then nodded a greeting, as she applied a thick coat of lipstick, before hurrying back to her table.

Prunella's shrill cackle rang out as Hilary returned. The table seemed to be overflowing with diners and she stared in horror. Mickey and Lenny were seated comfortably alongside Hilary's guests and chinked glasses with the Vice President. She wanted to bolt but she glanced at Bob's anxious face and braced herself as she sat down.

Bob leaned over and whispered in her ear. "Where the hell have you been?" he hissed. "Mickey says you've invited them to the table to celebrate his new signing and Lenny is about to hook the VP into a cookery school endorsement…"

Hilary looked round at the smiling faces. Her gaze fell on Mickey, who winked and raised his glass. She was astonished by his audacity to gatecrash the lunch. Prunella was edging closer to Mickey and had begun to run her fingers over his cuff, telling him that he seemed like an awfully nice fellow and did he have a female friend? The Vice President, slurring his words, told Lenny that he was to name his price; he wanted PAP all over the branding for the school and where was he to sign? Bob had one hand on Mickey's knee and assured him that they would finalise his contract the next day.

Joe hovered beside Hilary with menus and attempted to take an order. Hilary hadn't a clue what everyone wanted and at this stage, didn't care. Joe placed a drink beside her and Hilary gratefully picked it up. The deliciously cold gin slid down her throat. Thank goodness some things never change, Hilary thought, and nodded her thanks to the every faithful Maître d'.

Joe's gold tooth glinted in the subdued lighting as he studied Hilary's guests and smiled. "Your usual, Miss Hargreaves?" he asked.

"That would be perfect, Joe, thank you," Hilary replied.

24

Anthony Merryweather tucked a serviette into the collar of his lamb's wool sweater and stared at the large white dish before him. It was from a collection by Villeroy and Boch that had been used on a photo shoot and found its way into Bob's kitchen. The bowl was deep with a wide rim and contained a substance that reminded Anthony of thick, gluey wallpaper paste.

"Enjoy!" Bob said cheerfully and sat down opposite Anthony at the wooden dining table, covered in a bright orange and red cloth.

"Erm, looks delicious." Anthony hesitated. "What is it?"

"Drothuk." Bob picked his spoon up and plunged it into the grey looking concoction. "Beef porridge," he explained.

Bob was proud of his skill in mastering the traditional Tibetan dish, and had rushed home in time to prepare dinner for Anthony and hoped that the meal would impress. He pushed a bread basket forward. "Have a slice of Amdo Balep, it's traditional Tibetan bread, I batch freeze it. Do try a slice."

Anthony was hesitant, but encouraged by Bob's smiling face, he took a piece of the warm, yeasty loaf. It was considerably better than the porridge. Anthony pushed the vile, lumpy mass around his plate and felt sure that he would gag if he ate it.

Anthony had arrived at the flat punctually and was greeted warmly by Bob, who wore baggy cotton trousers and leather sandals. He'd rolled the cuffs back on his simple, round collared linen shirt and Anthony noticed the varied collection of beads and bangles on Bob's sinewy forearms and wrists. Anthony liked Bob's casual, bohemian attire and thought that it rather suited him. Bob had produced a strange tasting tea, which, he explained, was called Po Cha. It tasted hot and salty with a slight buttery tinge and wasn't at all unpleasant.

Anthony had wandered around the spacious room and admired the wall hangings that had quotes from the Dalai Lama. A collection of carved, Mani stones lay on a low table and Bob had explained that they were used for prayer. They'd discussed Bob's trip to Tibet, and Anthony did his best to appreciate the influences and long lasting impressions that had stayed with Bob, elements which he'd incorporated into his day-to-day life and were clearly in evidence in his home – all very different from Anthony's strict Catholic upbringing and Victorian-style town house.

"Don't fill up on the starter." Bob laughed and whipped the plates away. He had a feeling that the Drothuk hadn't quite hit the spot as anticipated and remembering Heidi and Lottie's words, hurried to the kitchen, where he put the finishing touches to the main course.

"Thukpa Bhatuk!" Bob proudly announced and placed a steaming dish of vegetables and strips of anaemic looking chicken before Anthony.

"Nice plates," Anthony said. He wasn't at all sure about the food and felt he had to compliment Bob on something. "How was your day?"

"Oh, you'd never believe it..." Bob began and proceeded to tell Anthony all about the lunch. He'd left Ranchers at four o'clock and somehow managed to steer Prunella into a taxi. She was hell bent on getting a ride with the Vice President, who'd offered her a lift, but Bob didn't think the VP would appreciate the kind of ride Prunella had in mind. Spurned by Mickey, who only had eyes for Hilary, Prunella had guzzled several jugs of PAP Potion and, determined not to leave the party without scoring a home run, she scattered her business cards to the media men on the adjacent table – like a fluttering of confetti over their surf 'n' turf specials. Bob had winced. He'd promised Hilary that he'd take Prunella back to Queen's Park and secure her safely in her home, but he'd hot-footed out of the cab at Kilburn Lane and headed to his flat in Mozart Street, where he'd had just enough time for some last minute shopping and dinner preparation.

"Like it?" Bob placed a piece of chicken in his mouth and chewed heartily.

"Very different," Anthony replied as he sucked on an inedible lump of pasta. "Any news of Zelda's forthcoming nuptials, have they set the date?"

Bob shook his head. "Oh my, where do I begin?" He'd had a catch up with Heidi by speaker phone, as he was preparing dinner, and had hardly been able to contain himself when she relayed the recent gossip from the set of The Zimmers.

"It seems our little, well, not so little, Sloane Ranger is heading for danger in deepest darkest Stoke – she's only shagging the chef from Bon Appetite!"

"No!" Anthony's pasta shot out of his mouth. He grabbed a napkin and concealed it. "I can't believe it! What on earth will daddy say?" He thought of Martin and visualised the proud parent back-slapping his future son-in-law, Harry, the previous Sunday.

"I don't think it's daddy we need worry about," Bob replied. "Imagine what Mummy Madeleine will make of it – she's going to hit the roof. If she finds out…" he added with a leer. "Heidi says no one is supposed to know. Zelda and Gary are trying to keep it hushed up, but Aisla found a condom in the pocket of Zelda's jacket and put two and two together."

"Well, I never." Anthony shook his head and followed Bob to a futon draped in colourful throws.

"There's never a dull moment…" Bob grinned and snuggling close to Anthony, placed a hand on his knee.

THE BOEING 747 soared through the night sky on its eight-hour journey from Gatwick to Barbados. The flight was full. It was high season in the Caribbean and there was an animated and excited atmosphere throughout the cabins. Passengers had begun to relax after their evening meal and, as hostesses handed out blankets in economy, those fortunate to be in Upper Class, flipped their leather seats into comfortable full-length beds and settled down to enjoy the in-flight entertainment or doze for a few hours.

Long Tom stretched out on his chair and stared through the window. The sky was inky but a vivid streak of red and gold shot like flames and caressed the soft, plump, darkened cloud beneath. It was a beautiful sight and one that Long Tom wished he could put into words, words that might end up in a song.

Pete, seated next to Long Tom, looked up from his laptop to admire the view, and said. "You don't need a million pounds to appreciate a sight like that..."

Long Tom nodded thoughtfully as Pete returned to the screen and went through their itinerary for the umpteenth time.

You don't need a million pounds... Long Tom thought about the phrase. He wouldn't need more than a handful of pounds if Hilary was sitting beside him, right now, right here. He'd have everything that he'd need. He picked up a leather-bound notebook. It had arrived at his home that morning by courier, gift-wrapped by Smythson of Bond Street. A card, tucked inside the first page, read: Somewhere for your songs, Hilary x.

Long Tom picked up a pencil and began to doodle on a blank page. Night time plays tricks with your mind, he thought. For a moment he'd heard the strains of a song in his head – a new song with new chords that gently repeated as he said the words. Right now, right here – with me. He wrote the words down and doodled idly then sketched the letter H, and made scrolls around it. Hilary Hargreaves. Hilary Hendry. Hilary Hargreaves-Hendry. Long Tom smiled, he was like a teenager anticipating a wife and how her name might sound once joined to his.

He looked out at the silver and white clouds below, they appeared soft and puffy and Long Tom imagined that they were a bed – pillows of eternity to fall onto, to wake up early with your love and leave your problems far below.

We wake up early in the morning, I smile and you smile back at me...

Long Tom wrote the words down.

"Sir, could I trouble you?"

Long Tom looked up from his notebook. A pretty hostess in a smart red skirt and bibbed apron leaned over and whispered politely, "Would you mind closing the window blind?" she asked. "Passengers are sleeping and the light is distracting."

"Oh, sure." Long Tom sat up. He turned and reached for the blind, then slowly pulled it down and watched the rainbow of night colours disappear,

"Thank you, sir," the hostess said and moved away. Pete hadn't looked up.

Long Tom sighed and stretched again. He felt quite tired and reclining his seat into a bed, reached for a blanket, then turned the overhead light off and settled a pillow round his head as he snuggled onto his side to snatch a few hours' sleep. They had a busy day tomorrow.

The notebook fell to the floor but Long Tom hadn't noticed and closing his eyes, began to drift off.

~

LENNY WAS DRIVING MICKEY CRAZY. In fact, at that very moment, Mickey felt like ramming Lenny's fat little face into the wall of their hotel room.

Mickey couldn't believe that he'd agreed to share a room with Lenny at the Molton Hotel in Soho, and even though the hotel classed the room as a junior suite, there didn't seem enough room to swing a cat round, although Mickey felt sure that he could easily swing Lenny round and was sorely tempted. However, he'd halved his costs and with any luck, someone else would pick up his tab for London stays in the future.

Mickey contemplated tomorrow's meeting with Bob.

"That Louella is a cracker," Lenny called out. "'Er mate was hot totty too…"

Lenny lay propped on the pillows of a twin bed and fiddled with a remote control and began to flick through numerous channel stations on the immense flat screen TV attached to the opposite wall. He'd recently stepped out of the shower and wore a white toweling robe with the hotel logo embroidered on a breast pocket. His hair was wet and stuck to his hot red face as he absentmindedly pulled at the belt on the robe, which strained to fasten around his bulging stomach, and scratched his nether region.

Mickey ignored him and reached into the mini-bar. He poured himself a scotch.

"Chuck us a bag of nuts, mate," Lenny said, and ducked as a missile shot across the room. "Honey roast, my favourite!" Lenny ripped the packet open and poured half the contents into his mouth.

Mickey sat down on a chair, as far from Lenny as possible and sipped his drink. He needed a shower but after Lenny's hour-long occupancy, Mickey was giving the bathroom a wide berth while the extraction fan went to work.

Mickey had arranged to meet Louella, later that evening.

"Old Bob's all right, ain't he?" Lenny attempted conversation. "Even if he does bat for the other side…"

Earlier in the day, Lenny had spent a considerable amount of time during lunch, trying to get Bob to get a good word in for him with Hilary. Lenny was determined to get some sort of TV slot before he sloped off into a Spanish sunset; his ego demanded it.

"Says he'll get me a gig at the Good Food Show, demming on stage…" Lenny poured the remaining peanuts into his mouth and threw the empty packet on the floor. He was miffed that Hilary had hardly spoken to him; she'd warned Lenny that she wouldn't lift a finger until his references were returned. Bob, however, was a different animal. Lenny had promised him and a partner a complimentary stay in Ireland if Bob could help with contacts and Bob had taken the bait. The Good Food Show would be knee-deep with all the right people, and Lenny was convinced that if he could blag his way into the VIP room backstage, he'd be on camera faster than the rise of a celebrity chef's soufflé.

"Whatever," Mickey mumbled and drained his glass. He was furious with Hilary for leaving him in the cloakroom earlier, like some half-wit. The attendant had made it ten times worse by calling for security, worried that Mickey was rifling pockets as he battled his way out from under half a ton of all-weather clothing. He stood up and went to the wardrobe – Louella would no doubt want to go to a club – and Mickey placed an outfit for the evening to one side. She needn't think they were dancing till dawn though. He'd take her back to her flat and enjoy a few home comforts until it was time get up, he wanted to be ready for his meeting with Bob. With any luck, Hilary would be in the office and he could continue his plan of attack. He might even take her some flowers.

"Off out?" Lenny sat up. He didn't want to miss anything.

"Just having a shower, then I'll get us a takeaway," Mickey lied. The last thing he wanted was Lenny tagging along.

"Lovely jubbly!" Lenny fell back on the bed and began to scratch again. "I'll have a chow mein, mate," he said and resumed his channel search. "I'll crank us up a bit of porn for later." Lenny chuckled.

Mickey rolled his eyes heavenward and turning his back on Lenny, braced himself and stepped into the bathroom.

~

ZELDA WAS ECSTATIC. They'd started filming her recipes as soon as she'd arrived on set and the results went beyond her expectations. The Singh family, alongside Paul and fellow workmates, had voted Zelda's Keema Matar curry and Potter's Pie a resounding success, and they'd all loved the low calorie versions of their favourite meals. As soon as the director indicated that it was a wrap for the day, Zelda had bounded over to Gary and they'd embraced.

"I told you the recipes would work," Gary said. "That's two out of two – success in Liverpool and Stoke!"

"You canna be certain it'll work in Leeds..." Aisla cut in sharply. Zelda had spilt curry sauce on a Givenchy gathered poplin top and the white fabric appeared to be ruined by the vivid orange stain. Aisla cursed under her breath as she set to work with a dry-cleaning fluid and vowed to shop in Primark for the rest of the shoot. Damn Zelda for buggering up her budget!

"Oh, but you were so helpful." Zelda batted her eyelashes at Gary and stroked his arm. "I couldn't have managed without all your careful preparation and encouragement." She took a sip of cappuccino and giggled when Gary gently wiped the froth from her lip. He handed her a brownie and smiled as Zelda bit into it and closed her eyes and then moaned as the soft warm chocolate slid down her throat. "It's heavenly..." Zelda said and licked her lips suggestively, "like you," she added.

"It's nauseating!" Aisla snapped, and grabbing a brownie for herself, stomped off to pack up for the day.

Zelda and Gary watched Aisla retreat.

"Darling, do you think we should be a little more careful?" Zelda asked as she dunked a second brownie into her drink.

After their early morning run, they'd continued their exertions in the comfort of Zelda's bed and Zelda felt as though she had new blood coursing through her body. Gary's love-making had exhilarated her. He was quite an athlete and Zelda had found herself in unfamiliar positions, moving and grinding muscles that hadn't had a proper work-out for years, if ever! Satisfied and delirious with joy as she experienced one orgasm after another, Zelda didn't miss a beat when Gary told her that he had a girlfriend back home in Manchester. She was a model and they'd been together for two years, but the relationship had been in difficulty for some time as she relied heavily on Gary to get her through bouts of depression, food addictions and the constant ego boosting that her job demanded.

"My relationship back home has been on life support for some time," Gary told Zelda.

"Oh, you poor darling," Zelda had whispered as she snuggled into Gary's delicious body. "Your brownies must be wasted on her..." Zelda had thought about Gary's cooking; she couldn't imagine how anyone could resist his tempting offerings. She'd sighed with pleasure as he'd wrapped his strong arms round her curves, oblivious to the complications of their new found relationship.

"Let's spend as much time together as possible, snatching hours at night while we're away, and then see how we feel about each other when filming is finished," Gary said.

Zelda agreed. "I still have feelings for Harry and it would devastate my family if we were to break up." It was all new territory to Zelda, but so was an orgasm, and Harry certainly had some explaining to do when she returned to London...

25

It was a cold November morning and a pale mist floated above frosty fields either side of the busy motorway as Hilary's car made its way steadily north to Birmingham. She was visiting the Good Food Show today and sat comfortably in the back of a Mercedes, her stitches had been taken out and the wound had healed well. There was only a faint scar to remind her of her fall.

Hilary worked diligently as the miles passed by.

Mickey was now under contract to Hargreaves Promotions and Hilary had agreed a fee for a pilot show with Fenums TV. The pilot was to be shot over the coming months and would follow Mickey as he resumed his career in the UK. A film crew would accompany him to demonstrations and also back home in Ireland, where they would take engaging footage of him out on his cabin cruiser, fishing in the Kindale estuary before bringing the catch home for an alfresco meal on the deck at Fool's Landing. The cookery school at Flatterley Manor would be used too, with lazy, hazy shots of a laid-back Mickey in the gardens, where he'd pick vegetables for an impromptu meal. Lilting Irish music would play in the background and be interspersed with Mickey's voice-over of amusing anecdotes, told in his rich deep tones, giving a hint of the fun to be had if you followed him in his new series. The pilot was to launch him back in front of the public and, if successful, Hilary was confident of a six-part series on prime time TV.

The first series was planned for the Far East, where Mickey still had a consultancy with a restaurant. Mickey's Far Eastern Odyssey would explore the diverse food cultures and Hilary was sure that it would lead to many more series in several countries and continents, as the Mickey Lloyd brand went global and his profile shot through the roof.

The car turned off at the junction for the National Exhibition Centre and Hilary pondered on appropriate sponsorships and endorsements to compliment Mickey's return to fame. She intended to let Bob and his team work on the day-to-day management of Mickey Lloyd, but knew that to manipulate the very best deals, she must be razor-sharp and heavily involved in all negotiations.

Hilary glanced up as the traffic slowed. They were approaching the exhibition halls and crowds of people were making their way inside. She hadn't been to a show like this for some time and under normal circumstances, she'd leave it to Bob and Heidi and whoever they brought in to assist, but the show was busy for her agency and Hilary felt that she should spend a day there. Mickey was filming today and would be in the Super Theatre, and Zelda was making an appearance on the main stage, followed by a book signing.

Other chefs from Hilary's agency would be working hard too. The show was huge, with many cookery theatres and stands where appliance companies hosted their own demonstrations. PAP had a stand and Prunella was appearing intermittently. Hilary prayed that Bob had monitored things closely; the home economists backstage on the PAP stand had been primed and cautioned to test every suspicious bottle within arm's reach of Prunella, but the show was a seething mass of alcohol suppliers and, without caging Prunella, it would be difficult to stop her.

Hilary closed her notebook and placed it into her new Birkin bag, there'd been a long waiting list for this particular edition of the famous bag and Hilary smiled as she caressed the soft leather then rummaged around for a compact. She flicked the enamelled lid open to study her make-up and thought about Lenny, who'd also be at the show. She was furious that his references were still proving elusive and she'd taken the precaution of asking an old friend, who ran Discreet Investigations, to do some background checks.

The chalet company that he'd claimed to work for during several ski seasons had never heard of him, and the contract caterers, where he claimed to be executive head chef for a number of years, had changed hands and were still trawling through their records, promising to dig out some details, but it was taking forever. Nor had they been able to find his name on a credit check, and previous addresses seemed fabricated. Lenny had convinced a number of high rollers to invest in him and money, it seemed, had already changed hands in considerable sums.

Hilary was in tricky situation and sighed as she repaired her lipstick and pouted in front of the small bevelled mirror. So far, she had not agreed to represent Lenny, but the clock was ticking. If his plan to open the European World of Cookery came off, she'd be foolish not to be on board – there were great opportunities for her chefs and sponsors and it was a wonderful location for a festival and filming. Lenny was becoming frustrated with her lethargy and if he were genuine, Hilary knew that loyalties counted for nothing and he would be on another agent's books in no time.

But what if he wasn't genuine? Hilary thought. What if her hunches proved right and he was running a scam? It could ruin her reputation overnight if she associated with him or was seen to be supporting him in any way. She had no intention of going back to basics and beginning again; she'd done that once before after being duped by Joel and it had been a hard climb back.

Hilary closed the compact and returned it to her bag. With any luck, Discreet Investigations would have some news before much longer and she would know exactly which direction to take.

Lenny was demonstrating today. Bob had blagged him a spot on an appliance stand and Lenny had forty minutes to work some magic into the crowd and keep them glued to their seats. It should be interesting! A live audience could make mincemeat of a chef in seconds and it might be like feeding Lenny to the lions. It would certainly give an insight to his cooking capabilities, which, so far, had seemed very thin on the ground.

Hilary's phone rang and she reached into her bag.

"Where are you?" Bob shouted above the noise in the exhibition hall. Hilary could hardly hear him.

"Just arrived. I'll meet you backstage in ten minutes," she shouted back and pulled a fur shrug over her satin brocade suit. It was nipped in at the waist, with a velvet collar and cuffs and as she stepped out of the car, she straightened the pencil skirt and reached for her VIP pass.

˜

BOB WAS BUZZING. He loved being at a show and the novelty never seemed to wear off. This one was the best on the annual circuit and a great opportunity to meet up with everyone in the industry. It was a chance to circulate and mix and remind clients just how hard the agency worked for them.

He sat backstage behind the Super Theatre, in the private VIP lounge, and enjoyed a coffee and cake. The Saturday newspapers were piled on the table. Bob studied the front page of a tabloid where the headline screamed: Hennesey's Kitchen Nightmare! It went on to detail revelations, by the lover of a high profile married chef, who claimed she'd been having an affair with him for the past seven years. The details were gory and included the chef's love of a sexual act which, the newspaper claimed, was too intimate to print in a family newspaper.

"I always thought he was a dark horse!" Heidi said as she pointed to the photograph of the chef. She'd just arrived and threw her bag on a chair beside Bob. They pored over the print and giggled as they read the revelations.

"I'd heard he liked a threesome," Bob replied, "but didn't realise he was into all this…"

"I wonder what poor Mrs Hennesey makes of it all?" Heidi continued to read the story out loud.

"You can ask her yourself!" Bob hissed and dug Heidi in the ribs.

Chef Hennesey and his wife had appeared and noting the pile of newspapers, gave Bob and Heidi a thunderous look.

"Morning darlings!" a voice rang out.

Hilary appeared and swept up to Chef Hennesey. "Must be a slow press day," she said, with a nod towards the headlines as the chef kissed Hilary's cheeks. "It'll boost your ratings though." Hilary smiled sweetly and greeted the chef's wife. "Mrs Hennesey, you look adorable. I hope the younger Henneseys were all faring well?"

Considerably cheered, the Henneseys moved along.

"Daft bugger…" Hilary whispered to their retreating backs and unbuttoned her shrug as Bob held out a seat. "He'd never have been in that mess if he'd let me look after him." She'd seen the headlines earlier and imagined the flurry of activity over at Team Hennesey, where his people were no doubt frantically trying to silence the press.

"You look very glamorous," Bob said, taking Hilary's shrug.

Heidi stared at Hilary's new bag with envy.

Hilary looked around the room. She recognised most of the faces and smiled as several people waved.

"Where's Mickey?" she asked.

"He's at the hotel but about to leave. He's not demming till ten." Bob poured Hilary a coffee and glanced at his Blackberry. "The crew's filming him as he arrives. I'm meeting them here, before he goes on stage."

Hilary sipped her drink and thought about Mickey. He'd sent her an enormous bouquet of pink lilies on the day he'd met with Bob and signed his contract. Hilary knew that she should have taken him out for dinner, to celebrate, but after Mickey gatecrashed her table at Ranchers and their experience in the cloakroom, she'd kept her distance.

The room was filling up. Hilary heard a squeal and turned to see

Zelda as she embraced Heidi. Heidi pulled out a chair and indicated that Zelda should join them.

"You look wonderful," Hilary said as she greeted Zelda. The rumours were obviously true, Zelda was positively glowing! Hilary raised an eyebrow as Bob winked behind Zelda's back. Hilary glanced at Zelda's hips, which had spread out over the chair, the fabric in her skinny jeans strained at the seams.

"I hear we have wonderful catering on the set of The Zimmers? Would you recommend it?" Hilary looked directly at Zelda. The girl had begun to colour and a blush crept up her creamy white throat and tinged her cheeks.

"Oh, er, yes..." Zelda stammered. "He, er... they, are marvellous and really help me with all the prep for my recipes and things." Zelda dipped her head and fiddled with her Pandora bracelets. Her recently straightened hair fell forward and covered her face and shoulders.

"Well, that's good," Hilary said. "Heidi will make sure that Bon Appetite! is booked for the entire series, and the next," she added as Zelda looked up. "Should it get re-commissioned, and I'm sure it will..." Hilary smiled. She leaned forward and touched Zelda's hand. "You're doing a fabulous job, Zelda," she said quietly. "I'm thrilled with the way you are handling everything so diplomatically."

Zelda was wide-eyed. She stared into Hilary's green eyes and realised that Hilary knew about her relationship with Gary.

"I'm always here for you, Zelda," Hilary said softly; she'd lowered her voice so only Zelda could hear. "If ever you need me, no matter what – I'm here."

Zelda was speechless. This was a side of Hilary she'd never seen.

"Are your family here today?" Hilary sat back and reached for her coffee.

"Erm, yes, rather." Zelda composed herself and glanced around the room. "Mummy and Harry should be arriving at any time."

"Ah," Hilary said, "here they are now." She got to her feet and held out her arms as Madeleine bore down on them. Madeleine wore Versace jeans and a silk shirt and raised her talon-like hands out to greet Hilary. The two women embraced stiffly.

Harry hovered in the background and shook Bob's hand. Harry was dressed in wheat coloured cords and a red cashmere sweater with a checked cotton shirt. Zelda thought he looked like a clone of her father.

"Harry, you remember Hilary," Zelda said. She remained in her seat and turned as her fiancé pecked her on the cheek.

"By jingo, I most certainly do!" Harry grinned and pumped Hilary's hand.

"Have you eaten?" Hilary asked. "Bob will organise some pastries, you must be famished after your journey."

Zelda glanced up hopefully but winced as she caught Madeleine's withering glance.

"Gobble, gobble!" a loud voice rang out.

Hilary spun round to see Roger Romney race across the room.

"Hilary Hargreaves, we meet again and you look as lovely as ever!" Roger said and embraced Hilary fondly.

"Roger!" Hilary smiled, pleased to see him. Romney's Gold Turkeys were a regular exhibitor at the show and had a huge stand in the food hall.

"Oh look," Roger said, "Craig's making his way over." Craig Kelly headed in their direction, immaculate in a three-piece suit. Kelley's Kitchen Supplies also exhibited at the show and provided appliances in the cookery theatres.

Everyone was re-acquainted and introduced to Zelda and her family.

"Where's our investment?" Craig asked Hilary, referring to Lenny. "I hear he's got a demo today."

"I'm sure he'll be along shortly," Hilary replied. She hoped that Bob hadn't arranged a VIP pass for Lenny; he would be insufferable if let loose backstage.

The room filled up as chefs prepared for their shows and one by one, they made last minute checks with their sous chefs and were fitted with microphones then led to the various stages, where eager audiences waited patiently to see their TV heroes from the world of cookery and cuisine.

A flurry of activity rippled around the entrance to the room. Mickey Lloyd, surrounded by the crew from Fenums TV, had appeared and shook hands with the well-known presenter of Saturday Morning Cooks. Mickey had a guest slot and the show was to be transmitted live.

"Gosh, he's handsome," Zelda said as she followed everyone's gaze. All eyes alighted on a neatly turned out Mickey, complete with smart shirt and red bow tie.

"Isn't he just..." Madeleine licked her lips.

Harry looked perplexed as he glanced between Zelda, Madeleine and Mickey. Bob was on his feet and caught Mickey's attention and the crowd parted as Mickey headed over to their table.

Hilary watched her new signing. His charisma brought the room to life and everyone wanted to wish him well and acknowledge his return to the screen. *The knives are out...* Hilary thought, as she watched the performance. Celebrity chefs were fickle creatures and like many in media, their paranoia bubbled quietly under the surface, whilst their greed for fame engulfed and stamped on anyone who got in their way. But Mickey was a master; he'd travelled down this well-worn route before and, as he smiled and shook hands with his colleagues, Hilary knew that he could bring it all to the boil at the touch of his charm switch. He gave as good as he got and woe betides anyone who got in his way.

Mickey shook hands with Roger as Craig slapped him on the back. Heidi fussed round with coffee and Bob made sure that Mickey was familiar with the day's schedule. Zelda coloured again as she was introduced and Madeleine seemed reluctant to let go of Mickey's arm, she cooed coyly and batted her eyelashes. Harry sighed as he stood back and ran his hand through his mop of unruly hair.

Mickey pulled up a chair next to Hilary and despite being heavily involved in conversation with everyone around him, and newcomers who came over to say hello, he made sure that he looked at Hilary whilst he was talking and peppered his sentences with: "Ask my agent..." whereby Bob stepped in and handled the queries, making profuse notes in a moleskin notebook.

"Bleedin' hell, boys and girls! Thought I'd never find you!"

Everyone jumped back. Lenny had made his away across the room and pushed his way through the crowd. He wore a chef's jacket covered in logos and branding. The European World of Cookery was embroidered across his breast pocket, alongside his name: Lenny Crispin, Director of Cuisine. The jacket was tight and strained at the seams.

"He looks like a Christmas tree," Bob whispered to Hilary. "Where's he got all that branding from?"

"He's made it up," Hilary replied as she read the logos, which included a well-known German car manufacturer. "How's he got backstage?" she asked.

"God knows, he hasn't got a pass..." Bob replied.

Lenny looked hot and was sweating profusely. His little eyes darted nervously as Roger asked him about his demonstration. Roger wondered if Lenny would care to come and carve a few turkeys on the Romney stand.

Bob rubbed his hands together and gave Hilary a nudge. "Now we'll see what he's made of." Bob smiled as he anticipated Lenny's demo but was distracted as Mickey was called on stage. "Come on, let's grab a seat and watch the show," Bob said to anyone within earshot, and scuttled ahead.

Hilary watched Mickey. He seemed very relaxed, there had been no time to rehearse but Mickey was nonchalant. Cooking was his forte and with a huge repertoire of foodie tales on the tip of his tongue, he never dried up. If he did, he used his well-known trick of taking a slurp from a handy glass of wine, which was ever present when he was in front of a camera, and his audiences loved him for it.

Mickey winked at Hilary as he turned to leave and she wished him luck. He held Madeleine's arm and said, "Enchanted, dear lady. Do enjoy the show."

Madeleine stood sideways and ran her tongue teasingly over her glossy lips. She reminded Hilary of a zip fastener.

Lenny seemed at a loss. He glanced at his watch and realised that he needed to get over to his demonstration in the main hall pretty sharpish but he wanted to stay backstage. He'd had a hell of a job getting in and had managed to nick a VIP pass from the back pocket a chef who was busy on his mobile phone. Lenny's old skills as a pickpocket still came in handy. But as Mickey had disappeared to do his demo, so had everyone else, they were eager to watch Mickey's show.

Lenny was alone.

He looked around and saw a few unattended bags and tempting as it was to run his pudgy fingers through the contents, he felt sure there would be hidden CCTV. He yearned to bamboozle his way onto the stage and stand next to Mickey and do the live TV show with him as the cameras rolled, but there was heavy security surrounding the stage. Lenny was fed up with Mickey's popularity, everything the man touched seemed to turn to gold and Lenny knew that Mickey disliked him. Their hotel-share in London hadn't lasted long and Mickey had told Lenny in no uncertain terms that he couldn't continue to rent Fool's Landing. Lenny now had to stump up for hotel bills, but at least he had the sponsor's money and it wouldn't be long before he could make a sharp exit. He'd pushed the date back at Flatterley Manor and was due to take over the lease in January. The agent was pushing for a signature and deposit but Lenny could fob that off and prolong it, giving him time to get away. By January, he'd be soaking the sun up under a new alias; in fact, he was beginning to think he might go sooner.

He picked up a pastry and ate it in two mouthfuls then looked at his watch again. Prep had been done for his mackerel dish but Lenny's hands trembled as he thought about making a fresh tartar sauce and fennel mash potatoes with a puree of baby carrots. He was grateful that Hilary, Bob, Roger and Craig were watching Mickey; he doubted that they'd bother to come over to catch the end of his demonstration. He'd got away with it so far, but standing on a stage in front of a knowledgeable crowd made him feel physically sick. He wished he could do something to bugger up Mickey's return to fame, and glared as he watched Mickey come out of make-up, ignore him and head for the stage entrance. Lenny was seething! He picked up another pastry and as a loud round of applause and cheers rang out to welcome Mickey on stage, Lenny stuffed the cake in his mouth and made his way to the main exhibition hall.

26

The heavy traffic in Wardour Street had ground to a complete standstill and a frustrated cab driver wound his window down and yelled abuse at a delivery vehicle blocking the road outside the Pig and Whistle Pub.

Bob stood by the open window in his office and stared down at the mêlée below, the noise irritated him. He slammed the window shut to block it out and plonked himself down on the sill, then leaned forward and folded his arms tightly across his chest.

"It was a complete and utter disaster!" he said.

Lottie sat in his old leather chair and rocked up and down.

"Mickey had hardly been on stage for more than ten minutes," Bob went on. "I've never seen or heard anything like it, it was carnage!" He shook his head as he remembered the events of the previous day.

All had been going well. The crowd had roared as Mickey was introduced and cheered as he started his demo by toasting them with a large slurp of wine. He'd begun a jovial banter with the host and they were about to begin their dishes when a screeching sound rang out and brought the show to a complete standstill. All the fire alarms had simultaneously gone off in the main exhibition hall, causing panic throughout.

"We had to evacuate the building and the filming for the pilot was a complete waste of time," Bob continued. "They had to can it and now need more footage."

Lottie bit the end of her pencil and pulled a face. She spat out pieces of eraser. One landed on Bob's desk.

"Do you mind!" Bob said, and shooed Lottie out of the chair.

"What did the firemen say?" Lottie asked. She bounced across the room and perched on the edge of Bob's desk. Her pink playsuit gaped as she stretched her legs.

"Please…!" Bob rolled his eyes away from his bird's eye view of Lottie's flimsy underwear. He reached for his glasses and began to polish the lenses. "They said it was a systematic and deliberate act of vindictiveness." He placed the glasses on the bridge of his nose, then sat back and flexed his fingers, making a pyramid across his chest. "The alarms sounded like a tsunami warning. You've never seen such a stampede, evacuating the NEC is no joke."

Bob thought about the weekend events. The fire alarms had been set off in quick succession, as though a person or persons had raced around the building with malicious intent. The live filming of Saturday Morning Cooks had hastily switched over to an old episode of Celebrity Master-Chef, as everyone was ordered to leave the building. Mickey's return to the small screen had been short-lived, much to Bob's frustration and he thought it curious that all this had occurred as Lenny was also due to step on stage. Bob wondered if it was a mere coincidence; Lenny certainly had the motive. He'd like nothing more than to mess up Mickey's TV slot and perhaps he'd got cold feet at the thought of going on stage on his own? Bob wondered if he should say anything to Hilary but thought better of it. The cookery school was too lucrative for the agency and he didn't want to put a spoke in any of the wheels that would soon begin to turn.

"Did you have a roll call?" Lottie picked at the hem on her playsuit.

"What?" Bob dragged his attention back.

"When we practised fire drill at school, we had a roll call, on the tennis courts. The prefects would take your name and tick you off a list. I used to hide."

"Oh yes, of course we did…" Bob said sarcastically, "four thousand people, flung out into the freezing cold for three hours while the whole show came to a complete standstill…" He thought about the loss. Zelda hadn't done her demo or signed a book and Prunella took it as an excuse to leave and not come back, whilst all their chefs missed their various opportunities.

"Oh well," Lottie said, smiling, "as long as no one was hurt."

Bob stared at Lottie incredulously. Why couldn't his world be as simple as hers? "What's happened to Lenny's references?" he asked.

"I don't know, Hilary said she'd sort them out," Lottie replied and jumped off the desk. Cotton hung from her hem and began to unravel as she moved away.

"I hope you've got a change of clothes." Bob shook his head as he watched the thread forming a tail behind Lottie.

"Have a chant, chill out…" she called over her shoulder.

Bob watched Lottie disappear into reception. She was right – it wasn't the end of the world.

He'd managed to speak to the producer of Saturday Morning Cooks and they'd re-scheduled Mickey to film a pre-record, in the studio, later that week. They were still keen to have Mickey on the show. And Heidi was on her way to Leeds with Zelda – there were only two more episodes of Zelda and The Zimmers to film and things appeared to be going well. So far, Zelda was a hit with her recipes. Bob was surprised; he'd doubted Hilary at first but, according to the series producer, taking the Sloane Ranger to the provinces had somehow worked and they were delighted with filming to date, but she had Yorkshire and the East End to conquer, and Bob wondered if the ladies of Leeds and the Pearly Queen in the East End would fall so easily to her charms. Still, no doubt gorgeous Gary would be lending a hand.

Bob pondered for a moment. Zelda was treading dangerously deep in the relationship arena and if Hooray Harry found out, there would be tears before bedtime. Heaven knows what Madeleine would say about it all!

He reached for his prayer beads and leaned back in his chair, yawning as he put his feet up on the desk. A spring bounced up and struck his left buttock and Bob silently cursed as he wriggled to maneuver into a comfortable position, then closed his eyes and caressed the smooth droplets.

Bob thought about Anthony. Their relationship was blossoming and they really seemed to get on well. He visualised himself on a hill in Tibet with Anthony by his side, a gentle breeze carrying the prayers of a thousand searching souls caressed their sunburnt faces as they held hands and stared at the mysterious mountains underneath a clear blue sky. Bob sighed with pleasure and let his imagination carry him away.

The door to his office suddenly flew open.

"And you want to be a partner but you sleep all day?" Hilary said as she strode into Bob's office. She stood in front of his desk and watched as Bob kicked his legs off the desk and pushed his chair backwards. The action caused his chair to tilt and the ancient castors, unused to sudden movement, slid from under Bob's body and upturned the chair.

"Bollocks!" Bob yelled as he disappeared under the desk.

Hilary stifled a giggle and waited for Bob to compose himself.

Bob rose from the floor and in one swift movement, was back in his chair. With a tug, he pulled himself up to the desk and picked up his pen.

"Morning Hilary," he said, and drummed the pen on his blotter as he waited for her backlash. But Hilary was smiling and it unnerved him. She must be going soft... he thought with a puzzled expression.

"Have we found Prunella yet?" Hilary asked.

"Er, I was about to..."

"The phones are ringing with lots of disgruntled chefs, have you spoken to anyone?"

"I've got a list." Bob pulled a pad of paper towards him.

"Mickey's filming re-scheduled?"

"Thursday!" Bob beamed, satisfied that he'd got something right.

"Have you ordered paninis yet?"

"Er, I think Lottie's sorting that out…"

"Great, you seem to be on top of things," Hilary said, "or under them…" She nodded at the desk where Bob's prayer beads lay on the floor. "I'll have a tuna Panini; let's have lunch later." She smiled as she turned to leave and Bob looked at her in amazement. Monday morning and Hilary hadn't had a go at him? Perhaps he was partner material, after all! Bob grinned happily and reached for his phone.

∼

Hilary opened the window in her own office and stared at the street below. It was a cold November day and pedestrians, wrapped warmly in hats and scarves, battled against a chilly wind and hurried about their day-to-day business. She placed a cigarette in a holder and lit it, then exhaled and watched as the smoke slowly dispersed into the frosty air.

She'd received a phone call from Long Tom, late last night.

Hilary smiled as she smoked her cigarette. Long Tom was six thousand miles away in Barbados but at first, it seemed as though he was right next to her. She'd heard music in the background and asked where he was calling from.

"I'm doing a gig at this place in a couple of days," Long Tom had told her. "It's a great club called the Old Jamm Inn, with a big stadium at the back."

Hilary winced as she imagined Long Tom sitting at a bar, but he sounded stone cold sober.

"Best burgers in Barbados," Long Tom chuckled, "and the owner mixes a fine fruit punch."

Hilary sighed with relief.

"How are you?" Long Tom asked quietly.

"Oh, busy, you know…" Hilary had been sitting on a sofa in her apartment when she took the call. She nervously wriggled her toes in the fringe of an oriental rug.

"I called to apologise," he said. "Should've called before, but you know how I am with phones, babe..."

"You don't have to apologise," Hilary replied. She could hardly believe what she was hearing.

"I do. I was rude."

"You were kind; you looked after me after my fall."

"I was bad mannered when I dropped you off, babe, and you know it. Your fall saved me. God knows what I would have done if I'd drunk from that bottle."

"Well, as long as you're okay." Hilary had pulled her hair out of its pleat and was winding the curls around her fingers.

"Got your hair down?"

Hilary felt herself blush and pushed her hair back off her shoulders.

"Do you think we could meet up when I get back?" Long Tom said quietly.

Hilary closed her eyes and punched the air. She wanted to leap across the room and scream out in joy but instead, she composed herself and replied, "Erm, that would be nice."

"I'll be back at Christmas, it's not long. Might even get back in a studio for a while. Thank you for the notebook."

"You're welcome, I'm glad it arrived in time." The line began to crackle and Hilary could hear voices and music. "You're breaking up." She held the phone close to her ear.

"Gotta go, babe. Be good..."

The line had gone dead.

Hilary smiled as she remembered the conversation. She stubbed her cigarette out in an ashtray and closed the window. Christmas was only three weeks away and she'd not made any plans. Bob had asked everyone from the office to dine with him and Anthony on the day before Christmas Eve and Hilary had agreed, despite the thought of Bob's cooking – he'd mentioned a Tibetan banquet. She'd thought that she'd stay at home for the holidays and catch up on some reading and DVDs, but suddenly things looked different and Hilary felt a warm glow. Perhaps she'd take some extra time off over Christmas? She smiled to herself and flicked her laptop on, she better get some work done – her desk would need to be clear.

∽

Mickey wandered around the cottage at Fool's Landing. The place was tidy at last and restored to some sort of order. All traces of Lenny Crispin had been removed and sat in large black sacks by the road side, waiting for the refuse collectors. He intended to set up the spare room as an office. Fool's Landing was a good base and he must be organised, the year ahead was going to be busy.

Mickey had flown back to Ireland the morning after his appearance at the Good Food Show. There'd been a party on the Saturday night and, despite the day being ruined by the fire alarms, everyone was on good form and he'd spent half the night in the hotel bar with several chefs and suppliers. Hilary had struck a deal with Roger, whereby Mickey would endorse the Romney Gold Turkey Range, and they were planning to film for Roger's website, in time for Christmas. Roger had eagerly planned the campaign.

"Bob's got it all detailed," Roger had said. "We'll get you on YouTube with some seasonal recipes and we'll film a couple of TV commercials." The endorsement was lucrative and Mickey knew that Lenny would be put out. Lenny could gobble off! Mickey thought, and smiled smugly.

He sat down on the sofa and stared out at the estuary, where his cabin cruiser swayed, on the swell from a passing fishing boat, in the water. Gulls circled and cried overhead and Mickey sighed with pleasure, he never tired of this view and felt grateful that he was back where he belonged. The restaurant in Thailand still bore his name over the door and he was being paid a good fee. If Mickey's Far Eastern Odyssey came off, he'd get Bob to re-negotiate the deal – the restaurant would be packed from the power of TV and his value would double.

He rubbed the stubble on his chin and thought about Lenny. The local agent, who handled Lenny's tenancy at Fool's Landing, had confided to Mickey that they were struggling to get a deposit on Flatterley Manor. They were anxious to have the lease secured, as Lenny had plans to take over in January, but Mr Hendry didn't seem to want to push the matter. It had been decided that unless the monies were paid over by close of business on Friday, the deal was off. Mickey yawned and sat back, and wondered what the sponsors would think of that! He'd decided to tell Hilary when he was back in London on Thursday; she ought to know. Mickey also knew that Hilary hadn't signed Lenny. She'd had her doubts, and people like Roger and Craig stood to lose a lot if the little toerag didn't pull his weight, but at least Mickey was free of him.

Hilary had asked him out to dinner on Thursday, to celebrate his signing, and Mickey wondered if she'd softened. Dinner was certainly a good sign and with any luck they'd finish their celebrations back at Hilary's home or in his hotel. His phone buzzed and Mickey reached into his pocket. The screen flashed a text message from Louella. It was very suggestive and Mickey smiled as he read on – she wanted to know when he was back in London. Mickey decided to keep Louella on the back burner and replied that he'd let her know.

Mickey stood up and stretched – he needed a shower – and wandered across the hall to the bathroom. There was a large water mark on the wooden floor and the boards would need treating. Mickey shook his head with irritation and made a mental note to call a joiner.

***

THE FIRST CLASS carriage on the East Coast train service from London to Leeds was hardly occupied as it sped away from Kings Cross and began the early morning journey north. Zelda and Heidi made themselves comfortable in the quiet compartment.

"I'm starving!" Zelda declared and picked up a menu. Her muscles ached from the strenuous work-out she'd been made to participate in the previous day. Madeleine had arranged a personal trainer and instead of languishing in bed all Sunday morning, Zelda had been frog-marched into the gym and put through her paces.

"Me too," Heidi replied, and rummaged around in her briefcase for her notepad. She'd got a long list to work through with Zelda and wanted to complete it during the journey. Hilary had been making calls and Zelda's student starter-pack was due to be upgraded and re-launched with Zelda's Healthy Eating Tools, to coincide with the transmission of the TV series. The new pack would include a shaker for smoothies and fat-free dressings. They were also in talks to produce another cookery book, focusing on healthy family meals in minutes, and Hilary had approached a well-known industry brand and suggested that they design a range of female chef's jackets endorsed by Zelda. The "Zelda" would be tailored and chic and transform the image of female cooks nationwide.

Heidi spread the designs out on the table and stared at the sleek drawings. She'd thought that Zelda would look huge but, as Hilary had pointed out, with some careful airbrushing Zelda's beautiful face alone would have the jackets flying off the shelves. After all, how many female chefs were stick-thin? Heidi could see that Hilary had a point.

The train gathered speed and the suburbs of London flashed by. The girls ordered breakfast and sipped their coffee.

"How's the exercise regime going?" Heidi asked, putting designs away. She examined Zelda's outfit. The thin crepe blouse had a sweetheart bow at the neck and was tight across Zelda's chest, the capped sleeves pinched across the top of her arms.

"Not as well as I'd like," Zelda replied. She tugged at the blouse and flicked her long blonde hair to one side.

Heidi listened as Zelda told her about the workout and how hard it had been. Heidi wondered how much pain Madeleine intended to inflict on her daughter, by the sound of things it was severe and Heidi was surprised that the trainer wasn't accompanying them to Leeds. Zelda produced a printed exercise regime with strict instructions detailing her daily workout. The first fitting for her wedding dress was booked at Alexander McQueen the following week.

"Mummy wants me to look like Kate Middleton…" Zelda sighed.

Their breakfast arrived and Zelda tucked in ravenously. Heidi buttered a slice of toast and took a bite. As she munched on the doughy substance, she realised that she felt slightly sick. Heidi thought the motion of the train was probably causing it and pushed her toast to one side, no longer feeling hungry.

The journey progressed pleasantly and Heidi listened as Zelda told her about her weekend. Her demo and book signing had been cancelled at the Good Food Show and Zelda had arrived back from London earlier than expected on Saturday. When the alarms had gone off and the exhibition hall evacuated, Madeleine had refused to stand outside in the cold. She'd insisted that Harry fetch her Range Rover and take them all home. Madeleine had nagged throughout the two-hour drive. With a date now set for April, wedding plans had escalated and it seemed the Who's Who of Chelsea were being invited. Zelda explained her dismay as she had examined the guest list and knew that all eyes would be on her in her wedding dress.

"Zelda, you will look beautiful," Heidi said, imagining a TV series entitled My Big Fat Chelsea Wedding.

"Try telling my mother that," Zelda replied miserably.

"Is your ring ready yet?"

"It's due back next week. Harry keeps banging on about it, he can't wait to see me wearing it."

Zelda stared out of the window and contemplated her forthcoming marriage as the towns and suburbs flashed by. All her life, she'd dreamt of wearing a huge diamond and marrying well. She thought that she would have been thrilled to marry Harry, but her tryst with Gary was troubling her. Harry had been as amorous as ever over the weekend and Zelda felt guilty. She realised now that Harry hadn't a clue when it came to the bedroom and she wasn't sure that she could tolerate it much longer. She'd like to teach him some of her new found skills, in the hope that it would improve things a bit, but Harry might question her knowledge, and the way she felt right now, she wasn't sure that she'd be able to conceal things. She sighed heavily. At least she would be seeing Gary soon, perhaps he'd be at the station? Gary would say all the right things and be attentive and hopefully her confusion would lift.

Zelda forced herself to focus on work related issues as the journey progressed and before she realised it, the train had pulled into Leeds station. The girls gathered their belongings and hopped out onto the platform.

"Gosh, that went quickly," Zelda said to Heidi and looked around hopefully for Gary.

Heidi waved at a driver who held up a board with Zelda's name.

"Come on, it's this way," Heidi said, and helping Zelda with her luggage, guided her to the waiting people carrier that would whisk them off to Chappell Town, a suburb of Leeds. Heidi watched Zelda as she climbed into the back of the taxi. Zelda slumped into the seat and stared out of the window, her mood seemed to have plummeted.

"Cheer up!" Heidi said brightly. "We'll soon be having a lovely cappuccino and no doubt there'll be a warm brownie ready and waiting for you…"

Zelda sat up. Mention of the on-set catering seemed to have cheered her and Heidi smiled with relief as the taxi pulled away from the station and headed off to their next location.

∼

LONG TOM SAT in a large and comfortable rattan chair on the patio of his hotel room, on the west coast of the island, and stared out at the Caribbean Sea. The early morning air was humid and balmy and the scent of coconut oil drifted up from the sandy white beach below. Petals of jasmine fluttered across the tiles, their thick waxy leaves leaving an intoxicating scent that lingered in the breeze. Pretty bougainvillea ran along the edge of the balcony and edged up the walls. The heavy pink blooms reminded Long Tom of the climbing roses at Flatterley Manor, the stems thorny and discouraging to animals and trespassers alike. He reached for a glass of iced tea and, from his shaded retreat watched the hotel guests stroll along the edge of the surf. Two swimmers tackled the stretch from the shore to a platform floating a hundred yards away. The swimmers reached the steps and climbed up, their lithe bodies silhouetted in the golden sunshine.

Long Tom sipped his tea and contemplated the swell of waves as they gently rolled onto the beach, the pure white of the breaking spume a sharp contrast against the vivid turquoise of the warm sea under the hot rays of a constant sun.

A pretty girl, with a deep tan, wandered by in a pink bikini; the fabric was sparse and accentuated her shapely curves and Long Tom smiled as she sauntered confidently along the beach. It was high season in Barbados and a well-heeled clientele flocked to the west coast shores to lap up the luxurious lifestyle, afforded by a privileged mix of movers and shakers from around the world. His hotel was full of celebrities, all waited on hand and foot by liveried staff in crisp cotton uniforms with gold buttons.

He'd been rehearsing the previous day, in a studio in St John, a parish on the east coast. The studio had been created in part of an old plantation house, located high above the rugged Atlantic coastline. Pete had gathered the musicians together, and in the comfortable air-conditioned rooms they'd spent the day going over sets for the first gig. Long Tom had enjoyed being in the studio, he'd felt a ripple of anticipation as the words to his old songs flooded back and in the relaxed atmosphere, he'd soon become familiar with the new spin on his music.

The plantation house fascinated him. The owner, a Bajan musician, who'd had world-wide success, had been only too pleased to show him around the property where, in generations gone by, his ancestors had been slaves working in the sugar cane fields. He had taken Long Tom on a tour of the cellars, which had once stored yams and sweet potatoes and had a haunting smell of earthy vegetables, and then the gracious rooms with polished wooden floors and high ceilings that were filled with antique mahogany furniture – all recently acquired by the musician, who'd wanted to restore the house to its former glory. In the grounds, they'd wandered past a disused windmill which had been used to extract juice from the sugar cane and, to Long Tom's dismay, came across the remains of wooden stocks, with rusting chains, which stood on a hill overlooking the sea. The musician had explained that he kept it as a constant reminder of the emancipation of slaves. Long Tom had shuddered as he imagined the island's ghostly history, immortalised by the sinister structure.

Long Tom stood up. He raised his arms in an arc above his head and stretched lazily then wandered into his suite of rooms. Pale muslin drapes billowed as he padded across the cool tiled floors. Security in the hotel grounds was high and Long Tom had all the windows and doors open, he loathed air conditioning – it had been a long time since he'd ventured away from the damp climes of Ireland and he was enjoying the tropical weather. He glanced around the luxurious bedroom and found himself thinking about Hilary.

He envisaged her lying on the king-sized bed, her hair splayed out like a flash of amber lightning across the welcoming expanse, her soft, creamy skin blending sensuously into the cool, cotton sheets. She was temptation with a capital T. Long Tom yearned to pick up the phone and tell her to board the next available flight, but he doubted that she'd join him. Even if she did, he'd probably make a fool of himself. Making love still seemed impossible – a romantic destination was no guarantee of changing that – and Long Tom wasn't prepared to risk his pride. He'd take things slowly when he got back to London.

In the meantime, he had his gigs to focus on. He was going to wander down to the venue today, where he'd agreed to play. His first gig was tomorrow followed by another a few nights' later. The owner, Jimmy, a young English entrepreneur who'd been in the Caribbean for nearly a year, had been promoting the events with the local radio station and they were a complete sell-out.

Long Tom caught his reflection in the bedroom mirror, he wore khaki shorts and as he reached for a cotton shirt, he shook his head and sighed. The years could be cruel and although his body was lean, it wouldn't hurt get some sun on his pale flesh. Pete would be here later and they'd be heading back to the studio, he'd time to wander down to the beach and do some people watching, perhaps the girl in the pink bikini was still around? She would be easy on the eye from the comfort of a sun bed…

Long Tom buttoned his shirt and looked around for something to read. His gaze fell on the notebook. Pete had retrieved it on the plane and it now lay beside a Chinese vase on a wooden console table. Long Tom picked it up and turning a page, smiled as he read: Somewhere for your songs, Hilary x. He stroked the leather then tucked the book into a pocket and wandered through to the patio where he picked up a pair of Raybans and his Stetson. With a burst of energy, he hopped barefoot over the bougainvillea hedge and headed across the coral sands to the welcoming beach below.

27

Hilary slipped her feet into a pair of black patent court shoes and smoothed the skirt of her scarlet, sailor-style, circle dress. A gathered bow nipped her waist and accentuated the fitted bodice. She chose a pair of three-quarter length black gloves from a drawer in her dressing room and pulled the stretchy sateen gently over her fingers.

She was having dinner with Mickey. Earlier in the week she'd asked him where he wanted to go and he'd chosen a traditional British establishment. Rules was the oldest restaurant in London and one of the most celebrated in the world. Two hundred years ago, Thomas Rule had said goodbye to his wayward past and opened an oyster bar in Convent Garden. To the surprise and disbelief of his family, the enterprise proved to be not only successful but lasting, and contemporary writers, artists and actors had sung the praises of Rules's porter, pies and oysters ever since. It was perfectly suited to Mickey's choice and Hilary was looking forward to meeting him there.

The front door bell rang. Her taxi had arrived and Hilary grabbed a black astrakhan fur coat then slipped it over her shoulders. With a final look in a full-length mirror, she nodded approval to her reflection, turned off the lights and hurried down the hallway to step out into the cold dark night and waiting cab.

∼

MICKEY SMOOTHED aftershave balm into his skin and studied his face in the bathroom mirror. He'd had a very late night with Louella the previous evening but considering his lack of sleep, he thought he'd scrubbed up well.

He poured a shot of mouthwash and gargled for several moments, then spat the mixture into the porcelain sink and turning the tap to hot, carefully rinsed it away. He needed to be at his absolute best for the dinner and as he straightened up, he stood back and admired his reflection. Not bad, he thought, in fact, not bad at all!

Mickey was looking forward to the evening. He adored Rules; the restaurant was steeped in tradition and elegance, with immaculate and discreet service and food to match. It was a perfect setting to wine and dine Hilary. The evening wasn't about business, they'd already sealed that and he was well on his way to being a household name again. Tonight, Mickey intended to win back Hilary's affections. It was time to stop running around with twenty- and thirty-somethings, who only wanted a part of the fame game – he wanted someone with credibility on his arm, a beautiful sexy woman who he could settle down with, and Hilary ticked all the boxes. He wanted to rekindle their affair and make it more permanent and head into his middle years, and more, with stability and the love of a good woman. I must be getting old... Mickey thought, as he took a final look at the well-dressed man in an immaculate cashmere jacket and trousers, who stared back from the mirrored wardrobe in his hotel suite.

Pleased with his image and with a celebratory smile, Mickey reached for a switch and dimmed the lights. He took a last glance and, deciding that it was perfect for a romantic assignation later on, he gently closed the door and went in search of a taxi.

∼

COVENT GARDEN WAS BUZZING. Hilary stepped out of her cab and paid the driver, having decided to walk the short distance through the cobbled market area to collect her thoughts before she was bombarded with the Mickey Lloyd charm offensive.

She placed her heels carefully as she wandered past the evening buskers, who were out in full force to entertain the crowds on this freezing cold, November night. The atmosphere was jovial and people smiled as they milled about and took in the sights and sounds of this corner of historical London. Couples held onto each other as they headed to the ballet and theatre. Parties of tourists gasped and sighed as a street artist performed a daredevil feat with a flaming dagger, whilst suspended upside-down.

A huge Christmas tree stood on the western piazza and Hilary smiled as she watched a couple tentatively touch a branch of mistletoe. The mistletoe was electronically operated and as the couple kissed, the tree became illuminated with thousands of sparkling lights, which danced on the faces of the cheering onlookers. The couple stepped back and gasped, then laughed and kissed again. Oh to be in love... Hilary thought, as she gathered her coat around herself and headed to the welcoming warmth of Rules.

~

MICKEY STOOD in reception at Rules and shook the hand of the Maître d', then allowed himself to be guided across the soft pile of a blood-coloured carpet to an intimate section of the restaurant. He tucked himself into the red leather, U-shaped banquette and while he waited for Hilary, looked around the room with interest.

A smartly dressed couple sat within reasonable distance, and a group of arty types tucked into their main courses on a circular table in the corner. The vermillion walls were covered with gilt-framed paintings and celebrity photographs, and elaborate chandeliers and crystal wall lights gave a subdued and sensual atmosphere. A deer's head sat between two huge sets of antlers on the opposite wall and on the sloped ceiling above, Mickey studied a vast painting of Margaret Thatcher, all big-haired and blue-eyed, with the Falklands in the background. "The lady's not for turning...' Mickey heard her say, and as he saw Hilary approach, he hoped that it wasn't an omen.

Hilary looked stunning and all eyes in the room watched her. Mickey's jaw dropped and he gripped the table as he stood up to greet her.

"You look wonderful," Mickey whispered. He gazed at her hourglass figure in the hot red dress, and was drawn to her creamy white décolleté and off-the-shoulder neckline.

"Thank you," Hilary said, as Mickey stood back to let her slowly ease her body onto the banquette.

The Maître d' hovered and Mickey ordered champagne. Hilary pulled at the fabric covering her fingers and with great care, removed her gloves. Mickey was mesmerised as he watched her fold the gloves and place them neatly beside a black sateen clutch bag.

"Christ, I could eat you..." Mickey said as he raised a glass of Dom Perignon and toasted their future.

"I'm sure you'll find something much more interesting on the menu," Hilary replied and glanced at the leather-bound list.

Mickey looked more handsome than ever and Hilary felt butterflies in her stomach as she tried to regain some composure. She longed to reach out and touch his smooth, tanned skin and lace her fingers through his. His blue eyes seemed to dance seductively in the candlelight, the whites were bright and the irises sparkling reflections. Hilary feared that any resistance she'd battled to retain was quickly disappearing in the heady and romantic atmosphere.

"You choose," Hilary said and closed her menu. Her glasses were in her bag and there were no prices on her menu. She knew that Mickey would rise to the challenge of selecting their meal so Hilary sat back and sipped her drink as she watched him order her favourite foods. He still remembered, after all these years...

Their first course arrived: Devon rock oysters. Hilary felt her skin prickle with delight as the salty offerings slithered down her throat and for a moment, she was back on a beach beside a driftwood fire at sunset while Mickey cracked open oyster shells and toasted her health with cider.

"A bit better with champagne?" Mickey smiled and held up his glass. He'd broken her daydream and Hilary returned his knowing smile.

They talked about his contract with Romney Gold Turkeys. Mickey had managed to complete filming earlier in the week and a series of adverts would run on YouTube and TV in the weeks leading up to Christmas.

"Are you running courses at Flatterley Manor with the lovely Lenny this spring?" Hilary asked, as a waiter lifted the lid on a steaming tureen of lobster bisque and ladled the creamy soup into two bowls.

"Ah, don't mention the man's name…" Mickey shook his head. "I've only just managed to rid myself of him in the cottage. I have no intention of being in close proximity to his sweaty little body over a hot stove, surrounded by the next generation of master chefs and budding bakers…"

Hilary watched Mickey lean forward. He studied the chunks of lobster and rubbed his hands together in delighted anticipation.

"Heaven!" Mickey said. He tasted the soup and smacked his lips as a hint of brandy flooded his palette.

"I have grave doubts about Lenny," Hilary said, between mouthfuls. "There should be a report on my desk in the morning which could change the course of his cookery for the foreseeable future."

"I'm pleased you're checking him out," Mickey eyes wandered to Hilary's cleavage, "though I'd expect nothing less. I just hope the investors can get their money back if it goes tits up… pardon the expression." He looked up and grinned.

The next course arrived and Hilary tucked into scallops with braised pork cheeks, while Mickey set about a whole roast squab pigeon served with slow cooked peas, warm lettuce and mint.

"I couldn't eat another thing!" Hilary announced, as the waiter removed their plates and Mickey poured the last of a premier cru burgundy into her glass.

"You can manage a Rules brulee," Mickey said. "I seem to remember you liking my campervan version," he added nostalgically. "Oh to go back a few years, eh?"

"And watch you disappear into a Spanish sunset, again?" Hilary raised her eyebrows. "I don't think so, Mickey," she added quietly.

A crème brulee, in a rustic pottery dish, appeared before them. Mickey picked up a spoon and tapped at the caramalised topping, then scooped the creamy custard onto the spoon.

"This time it would be different," he said quietly, and held the spoon out. He watched Hilary lean forward and close her red lips around the silver spoon. She sucked the custard into her mouth and ran her tongue over the edges of her lips.

"Christ..." he whispered and reached for her.

Hilary was defenseless.

Years of frustration and pain seem to melt away and, as the delicious custard slid down her throat, she felt Mickey's strong arm wrap around her waist. He pulled her to him and cupped her face, then gently licked her lips.

"As sweet as the brulee..." Mickey mumbled and without hesitation, kissed her with a passion Hilary had never expected to feel again.

The world stopped. Hilary's heart seemed to sigh, then succumb and as she kissed Mickey back, she wondered what on earth had taken her so long.

Eventually, they edged apart. Hilary was conscious of the stares from guests on adjacent tables, who now recognised Mickey Lloyd and were intrigued by his antics.

"Coffee and brandy at mine?" Mickey asked.

His face was inches away and Hilary resisted the urge to reach for his shoulder and kiss him again. She didn't trust herself to speak and Mickey, sensing this, called for the bill and settled it hastily.

As they stepped out onto the lane, Mickey fastened Hilary's coat and raised the fur collar snugly around her neck. "Don't want you getting cold," he said, looking around for a taxi.

"No, wait," Hilary said, laughing. She reached for his hand and pulled him past the hordes of people tumbling out of theatres and pubs and led him over to the Christmas tree. "Here, take this." Hilary reached up for the mistletoe branch and held it out. Mickey watched her lean forward, then lift her face to kiss him, and as he took the branch, he closed his eyes and felt her lips brush his own.

A huge cheer erupted. Startled, Mickey opened his eyes. Thousands of twinkling lights flashed on the tree overhead. Hilary was laughing and clapping her hands and in that moment, with a hundred smiling faces cheering him on and blinded by the lights, Mickey was overcome with emotion and had the urge to race around the cobbles to tell the world how much he felt.

He stepped back and didn't see the taxi as it accelerated away from the kerb. As Mickey broke into a reckless run, the black cab screeched to avoid him but hit Mickey with a sickening smack, tossing his body high into the dark starry sky, before it fell like a rag doll onto the hard and unyielding cobbles below.

Hilary was paralised.

The crowd gasped and she heard a long, agonising cry as she stared at Mickey's body crumpled on the ground, unaware that it was her own voice piercing the night.

For the second time that evening, Hilary's world seemed to stop.

"Call an ambulance!" A man beside Hilary clutched his partner's arm and stared hopelessly at Mickey's body, while his partner took her mobile phone and with trembling fingers, pressed 999.

Hilary seemed to wake slowly and in a trance-like state, calmly moved forward and edged towards Mickey. The crowd stood back to allow her to pass and formed a circle as she knelt down and softly touched his ashen face. Blood trickled from a gash on his forehead. She gently traced his body through the soft cashmere, which was covered in dust and blood. Hilary removed her coat and placed it carefully over him. She tucked the warm fur around his neck and settled herself beside him, then leaned in and kissed his face. His skin was warm.

"Help's on its way, love," someone said.

Hilary heard another voice shout out to ask if there was a doctor anywhere.

The night was cold and Mickey's pulse was weak, but Hilary was oblivious to the commotion around her. Sirens sounded in the background and tyres screeched across the cobbles, followed by racing feet. As blood, from a gash on Mickey's leg, pooled beside her, it blended with the scarlet of her dress. Hilary dabbed at the wound with care and tried to staunch the bleed. She reached for Mickey's hand.

"Come on, Mickey," she whispered, "stay with me; I want to see Fool's Landing at Christmas and fish with you in the estuary…"

"We'll take over, sweetheart," a voice said softly.

Warm hands gripped her arms and lifted her to one side. She felt a blanket wrap round her shoulders and the sting of hot tears trickling down her cold cheeks.

The Christmas tree lights were dark as she watched the ambulance crew work on Mickey's inert body, and the vibrant air of Covent Garden stilled as he was strapped to a stretcher and carried to an emergency vehicle.

"Look after him…" Hilary whispered and gathering her blanket, made her way to his side.

28

Bob and Anthony lay side by side on the large futon in Bob's flat and listened to the whispered and haunting voice of Dechen Shak-Dagsay, a contemporary Tibetan singer, as she sang traditional and meaningful mantras against a backdrop of panpipes and soft chiming bells.

Anthony sighed; he would have preferred something a little gentler on the ear and longed for the calming notes of a piano recital by Debussy. He stared at the ceiling. It was lit with tiny lights and fluorescent stars and as Anthony watched them twinkle, he thought about Bob's music collection, which Bob described as an amalgamation of mystery, imagination, and healing power. In Anthony's opinion, it was possibly the worst CD collection in the world, and as Dechan peaked on a particularly piercing part of her chant, he braced himself, then sat up abruptly and reached for his wine.

"Enjoying it?" Bob asked dreamily, as he watched Anthony pour a glass of rosé.

Anthony wondered if Dechan modelled herself on a thousand brawling cats on heat, but smiled politely and offered Bob a top up.

"I might bring my iPod with me next time," Anthony suggested and crossed his fingers. He knew how sensitive Bob was, all things

Tibetan played a major part in Bob's life and the atmospheric karma had to tick all boxes before they could relax.

"Oh do, dear," Bob said sarcastically, and sat up too. "We can chant to Chopin and meditate with Mozart..." He swung his naked legs over the side of the futon and pulled a face.

Anthony sighed. Bob was having a strop, but Anthony wasn't in the mood for a lecture on the benefits of Buddhism and he decided to pacify Bob.

"Why don't we go out clubbing for a couple of hours?" Anthony suggested. "There's that new place in Vauxhall, or we could go into Soho?" Anthony didn't have to be at work till noon the next day and suddenly felt in the mood for a late night.

"Oh yes, why don't we!" Bob suddenly brightened and bounced off the soft cushions. "Let's go and find something scintillating to wear..." He reached for Anthony's hand and led him to the bedroom.

Anthony had got in the habit of leaving items from his wardrobe at Bob's flat and when he wasn't at the theatre in Chipping Hodbury, he spent at least two nights a week with Bob. It was only an hour's train ride back to his town house in the Cotswolds, where Bob joined him most weekends.

"What do you think of this?" Bob swept across the bedroom in a pale pink Vivienne Westwood shirt; the silk shimmered as he moved.

"Lovely, darling," Anthony replied and selected a similar shirt in black. It was carefully tailored and took pounds off his rotund waist.

"I'm in the mood for dancing," Bob sang as he glided round the room, dabbing his face with aftershave and smoothing his head with a tanning wipe. "Romancin', Ooh I'm givin' it all tonight..." He had a secret obsession with the Nolan sisters, but would never admit it to Anthony.

"Charming, dear." Anthony rolled his eyes back and shook his head as he held the door ajar. "Shall we go?"

"I'm all yours..." Bob blew Anthony a kiss and breezed into the hallway. He reached for his key, which lay on a side table beside his Blackberry. The phone rang suddenly and the shrill sound of panpipes on the ring tone startled Bob and he jumped back. He stared at the number then smiled as he recognised it. "Hilary reporting in..." he whispered to Anthony, and held the phone to his ear.

"Hello, boss. Did you play by the Rules tonight?" he nodded knowingly and winked at Anthony.

Anthony glanced at this watch. If they were going out, they needed to get going and find a cab, he hoped Bob wasn't about to engage in an hour's post-mortem on Hilary's dinner with Mickey.

"Jesus!" Bob uttered. He reached for the table and gripped it to steady himself. "I'll be there as soon as I can."

Bob had visibly paled and as Anthony reached out to support him, Bob placed the phone on the table and turned his head slowly.

"Mickey's had an accident. He's been hit by car," Bob said quietly.

"Is he alive?" Anthony gasped.

"Yes, he's in intensive care but he's not regained consciousness. It sounds serious."

"Darling, I'm coming with you." Anthony placed his arm around Bob's shoulders and guided him to the doorway. "Hilary needs you, and you need me."

The two men stared into each other's eyes and in that moment, a bond was made.

"I love you, Bob Puddicombe," Anthony said.

"And I love you, Anthony Merryweather," Bob replied.

"Shall we get married?" they said in unison and clung to each other as a wave of happiness flooded over both men, but it was short-lived as reality set in and as they pulled apart, they were reminded of the graveness of Mickey's situation.

Bob took Anthony's face with both hands and kissed him hard. "We must go!" he said and picked up his phone and key. Without a backward glance, he reached for Anthony's hand then slammed the door firmly and raced down the stairs to the street below, to search for a cab to take them to the hospital.

∽

Hilary sat in the stark waiting room and listened to the slow rhythm of the clock on the wall. The ticking felt like heartbeats and she prayed that Mickey's heart was keeping pace with the clock.

There was a dark stain on her dress. Mickey's blood had dried and hardened the fabric and as Hilary stared at it, she thought about his warm hands tucking the collar of her fur coat around her face only a short time ago. She closed her eyes and saw his face, illuminated under the Christmas tree – they'd been so happy and full of anticipation, but in a moment it had all been dashed, and now he was fighting for his life in intensive care, surrounded by a team of expert doctors and nurses.

Hilary remembered Mickey's ashen face in the ambulance as he lay unconscious during the journey. At the hospital, she'd raced alongside the ambulance crew as they hurried to A&E, where doctors suspected that not enough oxygen was getting to his brain and he might have internal bleeding. She'd winced as a tube was put down Mickey's throat to help him breathe, and had staggered back in a dream as she watched the medical team spring into action. A consultant, an anaesthetist, junior doctors and the registrar, supported by a team of nurses, busied themselves calmly and professionally as they worked on Mickey's motionless body. Hilary nodded in compliance as a kindly nurse suggested that she wait in a side room; they'd let her know as soon as they had some news.

The waiting room was stuffy and bright and Hilary shivered as she pulled her coat around her shocked body. She'd managed to phone Bob and knew that he would take over; she was too numb to do anything. A policeman had gone to get a cup of tea but would be returning in due course to get her statement.

Hilary closed her eyes. How she longed for Bob's calming chants and soft assuring voice, but most of all, she longed for Mickey to wake up. She wanted to see his blue eyes twinkle and hear his seductive Irish brogue tease her in his playful fashion. She wanted his warm, confident hand to stroke her own, as it had done so fondly in Rules, in what seemed like a lifetime ago...

"For the love of God, will you lift your head out of that computer and tell me how to get to the bedside of Mickey Lloyd..." Bob's normally calm persona had just blown a fuse and he angled his head through a night security screen and yelled again at the receptionist on the desk in the A&E department. The woman ignored him and continued to type.

"Darling, hysteria won't help," Anthony said calmly, and gently moved Bob to one side. With a few soft words and a plethora of thanks, Anthony established Mickey's whereabouts. He took Bob's arm and guided him through the sea of casualties waiting for medical attention in the busy foyer.

A man with a rusty nail protruding from his middle finger gesticulated angrily at the two men in matching shirts hastening past. "It's the Swingle Sisters getting special attention!" the man yelled as blood from his wound dripped onto the tiled floor. "Bloody poofs!" he added crossly.

"Less of the bloody..." Bob retorted and pulled a face as he skirted the offending protrusion.

They were admitted, via a locked door, to a corridor and hurriedly followed a nurse to the critical care area.

"You can wait in here," the nurse said, opening a door to a small side room.

Hilary stood up as they entered. Relief flooded her face and as Bob took her in his arms and soothed her trembling body, she began to sob, the fear and anxiety of the evening's events finally catching up.

"All's well, my darling," Bob whispered. "I'm here, and everything is going to be fine." He looked over Hilary's shoulder and nodded as Anthony gestured that he was going to find some tea.

"Come on now, let's sit you down." Bob gently led Hilary to a sofa and, keeping his arm firmly around her shoulders, sat alongside. He nodded gravely as Hilary explained, between sobs, what had happened and the extent of Mickey's injuries.

"He's made of strong stuff," Bob said. "If anyone can pull through, it's Mickey Lloyd. We mustn't think the worst. He's in very capable hands and I'm sure there will be news soon." He reached for his prayer beads and placed one end in Hilary's trembling hand, then closed his eyes and began to pray and chant.

For once, Hilary didn't mock him. She closed her eyes too and felt the comforting aura from the smooth warm stones and with a grateful sigh, let Bob's gentle words wash over her body.

∼

THE NIGHT SEEMED ENDLESS. Hilary, Bob and Anthony sat quietly huddled together on a low couch in the side room, their senses alerted with each passing footstep from the corridor outside. Anthony had dimmed the lights and found a couple of blankets, which he tucked carefully around Hilary's knees and shoulders. He was aware that she was suffering from shock and, with knowing glances and nods between himself and Bob, kept her plied with hot sweet tea and reassurance.

The policeman returned and took a statement from Hilary, he was satisfied that the incident was an unfortunate accident, and set off to inform the anxious taxi driver, who thankfully had suffered no personal injuries.

After what seemed like an eternity to the tightly-knit trio, a young doctor appeared and took a seat beside them. He looked tired and stifled a yawn. He held a clipboard in one hand and glanced at his notes before looking up and smiling at the anxious faces before him. They all sat forward and held hands as they waited for the doctor's words.

"Mr Lloyd has suffered considerable injury," the doctor began. "His left leg is broken and he's fractured several ribs. He has a severe concussion and we can't ascertain, at this stage, if there has been any lasting damage – his brain has gone into severe shock."

"But will he be all right?" Bob asked as he rubbed Hilary's cold hand.

"We're going to keep him sedated and assess him again later

today," the doctor replied. "You're welcome to stay here," he added, "but I think you would all benefit from a few hours' sleep at home. We'll let you know if there's any change." He stood up and ran his fingers through his closely cropped hair. "Try not to worry," he said as he looked at Hilary's fraught expression, "patients can make a full recovery from situations like this. Mr Lloyd is healthy and strong and no doubt a determined survivor, he just might not be behind the stove for a little while…"

Bob and Anthony simultaneously breathed a sigh of relief and fell back onto the couch. Hilary stood up. She took a deep breath, then held her hand out and shook the doctor's hand.

"Thank you so much," she said. "I know you'll all do your absolute best and it's a great comfort to us."

"Try and get some sleep," the doctor said, and with a boyish smile, he ambled out of the room.

"He makes me feel very old…" Anthony mumbled as the door closed.

"Never judge a book by its cover," Bob replied. "I'm sure he's more than competent, even if he does look like he's just come out of high school…"

"I think he's right," Hilary announced. She seemed to have regained some composure and looked thoughtful. "Mickey is in safe hands and if he's sedated, there's nothing we can do here." She looked down at her crumpled and stained dress. "I think I would like a bath and change of clothes. I'll come back in a few hours." She looked at Bob and Anthony and held out her hands. They both stood up and gripped her hard. "I don't know what I'd do without you," she said as she returned their grasp. "You're like my guardian angels." Tears began to trickle down her pale white face. "I can't thank you enough for being here with me," she said softly and smiled.

"Where else would we be…?" Bob dismissed her words and put an arm around her shoulders. "Now, let's get you in a nice warm bath with lots of lovely bubbles, you can't possibly stay here a moment longer looking like that." He glanced at Hilary's dress and frowned. "Anthony will call for a car. Come on, let's get you home."

Bob picked up Hilary's bag and slung it over his shoulder then reached for her arm and linked it into his own. Anthony went ahead and opened the door.

The bright light from the corridor illuminated the three figures as they stepped out and Hilary glanced over at the staff on the reception desk. Look after him… she willed the huddled figures of the medical team crouched over their notes and monitors.

"Sleep well, dear Mickey…" she whispered. Bob caught her words and with a reassuring hug, led her out of the hospital and into the breaking dawn of the cold November day.

29

Lenny lay back on the king-sized bed in a junior suite at the Hammersmith Court Hotel in West London and yawned as he stared at the moulded ceiling rose that surrounded a miniature chandelier. The light was subdued and complimented his mood. He sighed with contentment and rolled over onto his side. A plastic carton with debris from last night's half-eaten pizza lay on the pillow. He picked up a crust and began to chew. A piece of paper and a pen had fallen to the floor and Lenny reached down to retrieve them, scattering the remains of the pizza onto the carpet. He stared at his scribbled calculations. They showed that he'd far exceeded the amount that he'd hoped to pull in from the sponsors for the European World of Cookery and he grinned with satisfaction as he thought about their gullibility. Nothing felt so good as a very tidy sum with his name on it, especially when he hadn't had to do a thing to earn it!

The Irish scam had been a great deal of fun.

Lenny lay back and contemplated his skill in masterminding the fictitious cookery school opening. He'd pulled in some big names this time; it had to be his finest scam to date. Shame that the operations manager from Jet Set Air would in all inevitability lose his job for letting the Lear jet take off for Cork without pre-payment, but that wasn't Lenny's problem. David Hugo would deny all knowledge of guaranteeing the flight – Pillings were a powerful law firm and would close ranks. The letting agent in Kindale had been trying to reach Lenny all week and today was the final day for the deposit on Flatterley Manor. Lenny chuckled to himself – as if he was going to spend a chunk of change doing up that old pile of crumbling bricks and mortar! Let that ageing rock star live out his days amongst the decay and despair. Long Tom Hendry was only one step away from going off the rails again and Flatterley Manor was the perfect place to drink yourself to death.

Lenny scratched at the stubble around his unshaven face, thinking he'd have liked to have got a TV appearance though. He felt he was only a hair's breath away from securing something, but knew that Hilary was on his case and no doubt her radar had reached certain aspects of his life that he didn't want uncovering. The shit would hit the fan if he stayed around much longer.

Lenny wriggled into an upright position and grabbed the remote for the TV then idly flicked onto the news channel. He sat forward with interest as he heard the anchorman announce that a celebrity chef had been hurt in a car accident. A picture of Mickey Lloyd flashed up on the screen. Lenny's mouth fell open. He pressed the volume button and strained to hear. It appeared that Mickey had been knocked down in Covent Garden, after a night at a nearby restaurant, and had suffered several injuries including a broken leg. He was still under sedation and being carefully monitored.

Lenny punched the air. "Yes!"

He beamed from ear to ear, delighted that that jumped-up arrogant chef, who, in his opinion, was no more than a simple Irish fisherman who'd got lucky, was incapacitated to the extent that his newly found career may fall faster than a sinking soufflé. Mickey-bloody-Lloyd had ridden on the success of Lenny's plans, and had it not been for the cookery school and the events that followed, Mickey would still be stirring noodles around a wok in Thailand, with only a warm beer and jaded German tourists for company.

Lenny leapt off the bed with a renewed vigour. It was time to go and get himself some new threads and book his ticket to Spain. He'd also get some blond hair dye today, his beard was starting to grow and with a few simple changes, no one would recognise him in a day or so. He waddled over to the wardrobe and reached in to open the safe that sat on a shelf beside a row of shirts. He pudgy fingers pressed the combination and he picked up a handful of passports then studied the photographs, before selecting one with a blond-haired image of himself. The passport belonged to a Mr Tony Browne. Better get used to being a Tony... Lenny thought, and pocketing the passport, began to prepare for his last days in London.

∽

ZELDA BRUSHED a tendril of hair off her fraught brow and sighed as the director called "Cut!" She could feel the tension in the atmosphere at the Chappell Town Labour Club. It was the end of an excruciatingly long day and everything was going horribly wrong, and as Zelda stared miserably at the soggy mess in front of her, she silently declared that her dish-of-the-day was inedible. "Take ten, please..." the director announced wearily.

Zelda watched the crew scatter in the direction of the catering unit. They normally swarmed around her creations and gobbled it in moments but Zelda knew that her Yuppie Yorkshires were a hopeless failure, as was her Rhubarb Fluff.

Zelda's Leed's challenge had begun when the elderly cook from the working men's club produced a full roast dinner complete with roast potatoes, crisp Yorkshire pudding, creamy mash and several vegetables smothered in butter, alongside slabs of beef with a layer of thick white fat. The onion gravy that accompanied the dish was glutinous and gel-like, but when poured hot and steaming over the dinner, created an appetising and mouth-watering meal.

Zelda's lighter alternative combined a large Yorkshire pudding with a lean mince and vegetable sauce, but her pudding hadn't risen and the anaemic, watery looking sauce ran off the solid slab of batter.

A young girl, who'd been charged with shop-lifting and was working out her Community Service Order by assisting the elderly cook with the catering, had made a delicious rhubarb crumble and custard and Zelda had watched the crew's eyes light up, as the perfectly cooked pudding was dished up and thick creamy custard poured over. The "rhubarb triangle" – an area of nine square miles in Yorkshire that held a festival each year – produced some of the country's finest rhubarb, and, determined to use local produce, Zelda had created a lighter dessert using pureed rhubarb, gelatine, egg whites and sweetener – but the resulting Fluff had immediately collapsed into a pink acidic stew.

Zelda wiped her hands across her Jill Sander blouse and ignored Aisla's icy glare, as she rushed off the set and went in search of Heidi. It was a nightmare! Zelda knew that the director wanted the whole programme filmed in one day, and it was all made a hundred times worse because Gary had been inexplicably called away; his replacement hadn't been any help at all. Zelda knew that she had completely cocked-up her cooking and would receive a unanimous "No" when members of the working men's club tried all the dishes and voted for the traditional stodgy fare served up by the elderly cook and her young assistant.

Heidi met her en-route to the improvised changing room – a box-like space decorated in faded and peeling lime green paint.

Heidi studied Zelda's face and realised that the girl was about to have a total melt-down. "Fancy a coffee?" Heidi said.

"Only if it's got brandy in it!" Zelda flung herself down onto a wooden bench in the cluttered room. She reached for the clip holding her hair back and shook her head angrily. "God, these walls look like puke – nearly as bad as my food today," she muttered miserably and closed her eyes. What on earth had happened to Gary? She ached to see him and had been trying his mobile at every opportunity but it was switched off and he hadn't returned any of her calls.

"Oh, it wasn't that bad..." Heidi began. She placed a mug of weak looking coffee on the bench beside Zelda and sat down.

"It was terrible." Zelda said.

"Well, maybe that will make the series a bit more interesting," Heidi said brightly. "After all, if you won in each location, it would be pretty predictable."

"Nice try," Zelda snapped and picked up her coffee, "but I shall be the laughing stock of Yorkshire. And Chelsea…" An image of her mother's agonised face flashed before her eyes.

Heidi stifled a sigh and wondered what she could do to remedy her client's mood. Zelda would be called back on set in a few moments and needed to be upbeat and charming as she faced her first defeat. Heidi knew that the real problem was Gary and hoped that whatever troubles he was experiencing would soon be resolved, his absence was certainly affecting Zelda. They'd need to pull a rabbit out of a hat to maintain the momentum of the series; Zelda was plummeting into a slippery decline and would look terrible on camera unless something was done to lift her spirits.

Heidi looked anxiously at her phone. She was hoping to get a call from Bob, with an update on Mickey Lloyd. The news of his accident had been a real shock and Heidi wondered how Hilary was coping. Bob said that Hilary was back at the hospital today and would call when she heard anything.

"Five minutes!" Aisla bustled into the room. She held a damp cloth in her hand and motioned for Zelda to hold her arms up, so that she could wipe the stains away. "We canna have your sticky finger marks all over this lovely blouse."

"Oh, who the hell cares!" Zelda snapped and pushed Aisla's hand away.

"I do," Aisla said firmly, and ignoring Zelda's protests, began to work on the blouse. "You won't be cocking my career up just because your boyfriend has done a runner…"

Heidi gasped and Zelda turned so suddenly that she knocked her coffee off the bench and it splashed all over the wall.

"Agh!" Aisla yelled. "Watch your blouse! It's like a road accident in here!" She dabbed at fresh marks on Zelda's blouse.

An assistant poked her head round the door. "Wanted on set, please, Zelda."

"Is nothing sacred?" Zelda cried out. Her face had crumpled and Heidi realised that Zelda was about to burst into tears. Bang goes her make-up, Heidi thought and turned to Aisla, in an attempt to save the situation.

But it was too late. The frustrations and disappointments of the day had finally got to Zelda as she realised that the whole crew knew about her romance with Gary. She felt humiliated and unable to face the camera. Her shoulders slumped as her emotions took over and she held her hands to her face. Sobs began to rack her body.

Heidi rolled her eyes and shook her head as she reached out to comfort Zelda. There wasn't a prayer that Zelda would recover in time to finish the shoot, and that meant they would run over into another day and break the budget. Heads would roll on this one. Heidi knew that she had to remedy the situation soon or they may find that Zelda wasn't fit enough to continue in the morning.

Zelda's sobs were loud and rapid.

"She's hysterical," Aisla whispered. "Shall I give her a slap?"

"No, we're going to have to sit this one out," Heidi replied. "You take over here and I'll go and see the director." She gently unravelled her arm from Zelda's heaving shoulders.

Heidi opened the door and nearly knocked over the assistant, who was crouched against the keyhole.

"Excuse me!" Heidi said crossly and marched past. She wondered if Bob was free, he might have some useful advice; she couldn't possibly trouble Hilary and hoped that there might be better news from the hospital. Heidi reached into her pocket for her phone and began to tap in Bob's number.

"Drama, darling?" The director bore down on Heidi and from the look on his face, was in no mood for Zelda's tantrums.

"Erm, just a tiny hitch..." Heidi said. "Could we possibly have a quiet word?"

∽

LONG TOM WANDERED around the arena where he would be

performing later that night. Sound checks were complete and the stage was all set. A cool breeze blew across the enclosed space but Long Tom knew that, once full of people, it would be uncomfortably hot.

"Your room backstage has air-con," Jimmy, the owner, said. He was handsome and tanned and his vitality and youth made Long Tom feel very old.

"Thanks, Jimmy," Long Tom replied. "It's not important, I like the heat – just keep me supplied with your amazing fruit cocktails and plenty of water and I'll be a happy camper."

"You got it," Jimmy replied, "whatever you want…"

Jimmy led Long Tom out of the arena and through to the dim bar where it was cool as they crossed the wooden floors and pretty tiles, all restored from part of the original building. It was sunny and hot on the decking at the front and tall palm trees by the road swayed lazily in the balmy breeze. Long Tom eased himself onto a high stool overlooking the road below. Tourists in shorts and colourful sundresses strolled up and down the Gap, many stopping to read posters that announced the sell-out concert that evening.

"Cheese Royale with parmesan fries?" Jimmy placed a pink coloured cocktail on a coaster and pushed it towards Long Tom.

"You're the man!" Long Tom replied and took a sip of the strawberry and mint drink; it was ice cold and delicious. He removed his hat and pushed his sunglasses firmly into place, then closed his eyes and leaned back to let the warm rays caress his skin. Long Tom was enjoying Barbados.

Jimmy returned with cutlery and a napkin and set them down on the table. "Do you know a chef called Mickey Lloyd?" he asked. "Doesn't he have a place near you in Ireland?"

"Yeh, nice little pad down on the coast…" Long Tom replied. "Why d'you ask?"

"World News says he's been in an accident," Jimmy said, "alive but not conscious yet and with a few broken bones."

"That's too bad," Long Tom replied and considered the news. He wondered what Hilary made of it? He was aware that Mickey had feelings for Hilary and had witnessed his chase at the Gourmet Festival in Kindale. Long Tom had a feeling that she didn't much care for Mickey but he was a lucrative client for her agency and his accident would certainly affect the cookery school plans. If the cookery school was ever going to happen! Long Tom had a hunch that he'd get news from the letting agent later that day, that the loveable Lenny had disappeared without trace.

"Oh! There's Long Tom Hendry!" A group of tourists on the road below looked up towards the deck and pointed at the man enjoying a drink in the sunshine.

"I'll move them on," Jimmy said as he placed a large platter on the table.

"Nah, it's nice to have the attention," Long Tom replied, and began to tuck into what locals said was the best burger on the island, as warm cheese oozed out of the centre of the medium-rare grilled beef. He looked up and waved at the crowd as cameras clicked.

"Make sure you get the name of the bar in!" Long John pointed to the Golden Lion on the front of the building, above the bar's name, "The Old Jamm Inn – it's the place to be…" Long Tom smiled at the crowd.

He finished his meal and pushed the plate to one side, then looked around for Jimmy. "Can I use your phone for a moment?" he asked.

"Sure thing," Jimmy said, and reached for a mobile in the pocket of his khaki shorts. "Lost yours?"

"I don't do mobiles," Long Tom replied and tapped in Hilary's number. It rang for several seconds before switching to her message box.

Long Tom hesitated then took a deep breath and said quietly, "Just an old rocker, sitting in the sunshine – wishing you were right here, right now… with me." He paused then hung up and handed the phone back to Jimmy. Where had those words come from? He shook his head and stood up.

"Want a lift?" Jimmy asked, looking over the railings towards the crowd. Long Tom followed his gaze.

"I'd be mighty grateful," he replied.

"We'll go out the back," Jimmy said and nodded to his bar manager to monitor the steps and ensure that no one followed. He wasn't having his star turn harassed, it was a big gig tonight and Jimmy stood to make a considerable sum. They darted through the bar and Jimmy led Long Tom to a waiting vehicle at the back of the arena.

"Mathew will look after you," Jimmy said and nodded towards the smiling face at the wheel of the bar's courtesy car. "If you need anything at all – just call me..." he paused, then smiled. "Well, send me a message. Pete has everything covered, but if there's anything at all..." He shook Long Tom's outstretched hand.

"See you on stage!" Long Tom called out and climbed into the waiting vehicle.

30

Hilary sat at her desk and stared at the manila envelope in front of her. It was marked for her attention: Private & Confidential. She twiddled with the Mont Blanc pen in her fingers, then swivelled round in her chair and stood up. The street below was quiet. It was Saturday morning and the usual hustle and bustle of the busy working week was, for a while, diminished and the traffic light. Hilary stared out of the window and longed for a cigarette, but she refused to give into her craving – seeing Mickey on a machine that enabled him to breathe had been a shocking reality check – health was a precious commodity and she needed to make sure that she preserved her own.

Yesterday had seemed endless. She'd arrived back at the hospital not long after breakfast and had been allowed to sit at Mickey's bedside. Nurses fussed around all morning, checking monitors and tubes. At lunchtime a doctor had informed Hilary that he wanted to stop the sedation they'd been administering, to see if Mickey would wake up. Several hours later, in the late afternoon, Mickey stirred. He was confused and dazed at first and seemed astounded to find out that he was in hospital with a leg in plaster and his chest tightly bandaged. Movement made him wince in pain.

"You've broken your tibia," the doctor explained, "and fractured your ribs. You need at least six weeks' bed rest to recover." He checked Mickey's pulse and moved around the bed. "Your CT scan shows that you have a small swelling in your head," he continued, "but it's reducing; you need to take things very easy."

"How long will he be here?" Hilary asked the doctor.

"If he continues to progress, we'll transfer him to a ward tomorrow. He's going to be in hospital for quite a while."

"Not bloody likely..." Mickey whispered.

"You'll do as you're told," Hilary admonished, then thanked the doctor for all his help.

"Get me out of here as soon as you can," Mickey said woefully, as they watched the doctor move on to another patient.

"Only when you're good and ready," Hilary said gently and urged him to close his eyes and rest; she could sense that he was going to be a difficult patient.

She'd left the hospital quite late in the evening and as soon as she arrived home, she undressed wearily and fell into bed. She'd updated Bob on Mickey's condition and they agreed that he seemed to be making progress but would certainly need some time to recover.

"I've got things covered here," Bob had told her. "You take care of yourself and get your feet up, it's been a big shock for you too," he'd said kindly.

But Hilary was determined to get to the office and despite the day being a Saturday, she'd called for a car and arrived in Wardour Street by eight o'clock.

Hilary turned back to her desk; the manila envelope couldn't be avoided any longer. She sat down and reached for her glasses, which were on a gold chain around her neck, then opened the top drawer of her desk and found a letter opener with an ivory handle.

As she pulled a neat file out of the envelope, she read: Discreet Investigations/Reference Lenny Crispin. Her craving for a cigarette was stronger than ever but she ignored it and opened the first page. Several photographs appeared with various names neatly typed underneath, all of them, she realised, were of Lenny. In one, he had blond hair and a beard and bore the name Tony Browne. Hilary shook her head in disbelief as she turned the page and read on.

During the time that Lenny claimed to be working for a contract caterer he was, in reality, an inmate in Her Majesty's Prison, Wandsworth, serving three years for fraud. When he'd told Hilary that he'd worked in pubs and clubs and "some very fancy joints" he had, in fact, been running with a mob as a drug dealer and had again spent time behind bars. He was currently wanted by the Wiltshire police for investigations into a property scam involving a former prep school, whereby two investors had lost money on their credit cards, which had mysteriously disappeared after dealings with a "Frank Melody" – also featured on the opening page of the file. One of the investors had also lost his car – an Alfa Romeo Spider, which had never been found.

Hilary read on. The contents made gruesome reading. Lenny had been in and out of detention centres since he was a teenager before advancing to mainstream prison, but he was clearly getting more skilled at his scams as there were large gaps between sentences and nothing in recent years.

Hilary closed the file and picked up her phone. She doubted that he was still in the country; he'd been quiet all week. It was probably too late. First, she had to call the police, then she would place calls to anyone she knew who had invested money in the European World of Cookery, and also the letting agent in Ireland.

She had a long morning ahead.

As she began to dial, she realised that she'd missed an international call. Her phone had been switched to the silent tone in the hospital and she'd forgotten to turn it back on. She had one new message: "Just an old rocker, sitting in the sunshine – wishing you were right here, right now... with me..." Hilary was startled. It was so good to hear Long Tom's voice! She remembered that he'd had his first concert the previous night; she hoped that it had been a success and that Long Tom had found his confidence again, back in front of a large audience. His words stunned her and she played the message again. In any other circumstances she would have said he'd had too much to drink, but he sounded very sober and there was a new depth to his voice – it was endearing, almost as if he was appealing to her.

Hilary sighed, she was so confused! Mickey needed her more than ever and she simply couldn't turn her back on him, after all – she'd been only a short step away from going to bed with him forty-eight hours ago, but Long Tom pressed buttons that made her stomach lurch and her heart miss a beat and now he seemed keen to be with her. She longed to get on a plane and walk into his hotel suite, she was sure he'd be holed up at Sandy Lane with the sea at his doorstep and crickets chirruping long into the night – how good it would be to be with him!

She looked up Long Tom's number and began to dial; it rang for several moments then cut out. Of course… she thought – he "didn't do mobiles". There wasn't a chance that he would pick it up and it was probably just as well. Hilary sighed, raised her arms above her head and stretched towards the ceiling, then shook herself and focused on the file. She must put men out of her mind and concentrate on the job in hand. She had work to do!

∽

THERE WAS mayhem in Leeds as the morning began. Zelda was already late on set and Heidi had had an almighty job of getting her up and ready and back at the working men's club.

Heidi was exhausted. She watched with apprehension as the director shouted, "And, action!" and an extremely frazzled Zelda presented her dishes to the twenty or so regulars who dined every week at the club. Everyone had been called back to the set on Saturday morning, and Heidi shuddered at the thought of costs to the budget – no wonder the production manager looked suicidal.

Zelda, meanwhile, looked terrible. Her face was puffy and no amount of make-up had reduced the swelling around her eyes. She'd been crying for most of the night, and at one point Heidi had called Bob – she wondered if she ought to summon a doctor?

"It's stress," Bob had explained. "The Chelsea brigade are putting pressure on her over the wedding. Alexander McQueen doesn't do plus sizes and her newly found lover, who has clearly woken her up to sexual fulfilment never to be found with half-wit-Harry, has disappeared into the sunset without a backward glance." Heidi heard Bob sigh. "You've got to feel sorry for the poor cow," Bob continued. "Have a rummage around the Louis Vuitton, the maid is bound to have packed some calm-me-downs alongside the vitamins and laxatives. Get a handful into Zelda as soon as you can. You'll soon have her up and running," he'd added confidently.

It had been a gargantuan effort to get Zelda up and running, but she was now in situ and Heidi hoped for the best. The whole experience had made Heidi feel quite queasy and she wondered if she should slip off to the ladies.

"You're a white as a plate of tripe." Aisla appeared alongside Heidi and raised her eyebrows as she registered Heidi's pale complexion. The mention of the word tripe seemed to upset Heidi and she promptly disappeared, in the direction of the ladies' loo.

The director called, "Cut! Take five..." and everyone went in search of a coffee. Aisla went in search of Zelda and was pleased to see that her crisp pink shirt and Valentino jeans were immaculate, as was the pretty bibbed pinafore with a ruffled edge that hid strained fastenings on the shirt. Hilary's idea of adding a pinafore to Zelda's attire was genius and Aisla knew that Zelda now had an endorsement with the manufacturers. Lucky for some!

"Oh God, when will this ghastly filming be over," Zelda wailed and held one hand to her forehead. She was exhausted and had decided that she was going straight to Chipping Hodbury after the filming. She would hire a cab to get her there, sod the expense – she felt the need to be with her father and Brigitta and the comfort of their country home. London was simply too stressful at the moment, and with a few days off before she had to be in the East End for the final show, Zelda intended to get her head clear at Daddy's. Gary hadn't turned up again and still wasn't answering her calls and Zelda felt a fresh wave of misery threaten to engulf her as reality dawned when she realised that she'd probably never see or hear from him again.

"Where's Heidi?" Zelda asked Aisla. Perhaps Heidi could get the car organised and share most of the journey.

"Puking her guts up," Aisla replied abruptly. "You're not the only one round here who's stressed out. You've wasted everyone's time by making them work on their weekends. Do you think you could possibly wrap this up in the next take and let us all get off home to our loved ones?" Aisla re-tied the bow on Zelda's pinny and smoothed the sleeves of her shirt.

"Oh gosh, I never thought..." Zelda looked even more miserable as she glanced at the crew, who were, she realised, frosty to say the least.

"Places, please!" the director yelled and Zelda seemed to pull herself together.

"Crikey, I'm so sorry, Aisla," Zelda said. "I'm such a selfish beast... please try and forgive me." She leaned over and gave Aisla's tiny frame a hug, then turned and hurried back to the set.

Aisla was aghast. She never seen this side of Zelda and watched in amazement as Zelda turned on the charm and made light of her terrible dishes, laughing with the sea of critical diners as they tore her cooking to shreds. Zelda threw back her head and heartily agreed with them all and began to tell the elderly cook that she needed to take some lessons with her, and would the trainee be kind enough to let Zelda have the crumble recipe?

"Bloody hell..." Heidi had returned and stood beside Aisla. "What did you give her? Whatever it was, can I have some?"

"Och, just a wee telling off," Aisla replied. "You wouldna' be wantin' one of those..."

Heidi's jaw dropped as Zelda worked her magic. Her pretty blue eyes twinkled as she charmed the people of Chappell Town Labour Club and Heidi realised that this would make riveting viewing – after all, celebrity chefs never got it wrong, and the fact that Zelda had slipped up so badly but was humble and sweet in defeat, would endear her even more to her audience. Heidi couldn't wait to turn her phone on and call Bob.

~

BOB YAWNED as Anthony pulled up the blind and light flooded into Bob's minimalistic bedroom. They'd had a very late dinner at the Ivy, in the company of Prunella and the Vice President of PAP. Prunella, for once, had been on perfect behaviour.

"Do you think she's mellowing in old age?" Anthony asked as he slipped into a black silk kimono. A printed red dragon roared bright orange flames across the fabric.

"Not at all, she's up to something," Bob replied and frowned as he watched Anthony fasten the belt on the kimono, the dragon's flames strained across his paunch.

"You don't suppose she's got her eye on the VP, do you?" Anthony sat on the bed and turned to face Bob.

"Well, he makes good arm candy and could certainly lift her reputation up several notches, though I'm not sure that she'd be in line for a call from the palace in the immediate future. The only MBE Prunella knows is My Bottle's Empty…"

"I've heard he's got a place in the Hamptons and Bel Air," Anthony said.

"Oh dear, Prunella 'Ellie May Clampett', stake your claim!" Bob giggled. "There'll be PAP in them thar hills!"

Anthony smiled and stood up, he fancied a cooked breakfast. Bob only gave in to a fry-up on Sundays and would no doubt be serving natural yoghurt and dried fruit again today. Anthony baulked at the thought. He decided that if he slipped out to buy a newspaper, he could call in at the corner deli and have a bacon sandwich.

"I'm going to have a shower," Bob said. "I need to call Heidi back, although she seems to have pulled it off in Leeds and Zelda has finally finished the filming. Then I'll call Hilary." He slipped out of bed and wandered naked into the en-suite bathroom. "She's probably still at the hospital," he called over his shoulder. "I think this business with Mickey could have melted her frosty old heart and we might need to start thinking about engagement presents..."

"Never mind Hilary and Mickey," Anthony replied, looking longingly at Bob's taught behind, "what about our own impending nuptials? We need to make an announcement."

"I thought we'd do it at our Christmas soirée?" Bob called out over the noise from the powerful shower.

"Perfect!" Anthony said and clapped his hands together. "Just popping out for a paper..."

∼

Lenny wandered around the men's fashion department in Selfridges and chose a selection of short-sleeved shirts, knee-length shorts and several pairs of Speedos. No harm in letting the dog see the rabbit! He chuckled to himself as he selected the Speedos in a variety of bright colours. His sex life in Ireland had proved highly successful with the secretary of the Porthampton Friends of Kindale, even though he suspected that she'd slept with most of the festival goers – she was certainly quite a goer herself and had done his ego in that department no amount of good. He was confident that he would have wall-to-wall signoritas lined up in sunny Spain and maybe a few signoras too, as soon as he flashed the cash and twizzled his talent on the many esplanades and beaches that were waiting for his imminent arrival.

Lenny had decided to drive to Spain. He had an Alfa Romeo Spider in a lock-up in the East End, and with a set of false license plates to get him down to Portsmouth, he'd soon be sailing the high seas and setting off for his new life. He was looking forward to the drive from Bilbao to Marbella and had bought an international navigation aid to assist him on the journey. He'd thrown his mobile phone into the Thames that morning, it was a pay-as-you-go phone and no one could trace it – he'd get a new phone in Spain. His money was sitting in a case in the safe back at the hotel, he'd cleared most of the sponsor's funds now and would soon close his account down. The computer course in Wandsworth prison had come in handy and he was pleased that he'd mastered the knack of online banking; there'd be no CCTV footage for anyone to trawl through in the next few days, when it became apparent that Lenny had gone missing. He reckoned he'd need to be well on his way tomorrow; that would give him ample time to get ahead of any possible pursuers. But first, he had one last night on the razzle in London to look forward to.

"Will it be cash or card?" the bored sales assistant said as she wrapped Lenny's items in tissue paper.

"Cash, darlin'," Lenny replied, "lovely jubbly cash!"

～

BUT LENNY HADN'T RECKONED on Hilary's tenacity. She'd spent all day on the phone with sponsors and had a face-to-face interview with a sergeant from the Metropolitan Police Force. As she waited for a car to take her to see Mickey, she briefly updated Bob with her findings.

"O.M.G!" Bob exclaimed "You're our very own Miss Marple – how exciting!"

"We can't let the little toerag get away with it," Hilary said. "There's too much money at stake and people like Roger and Craig stand to lose a lot."

"Thank the Dalai Lama that we didn't put any money in it." Bob breathed an audible sigh of relief.

Hilary didn't think the Dalai Lama had much to do with it, but kept her thoughts to herself as she ended the call and locked the office. She felt drained and needed a shower but her first port of call was to see Mickey. She hoped that she'd find him in less pain.

As her car sped through the busy roads to the hospital in west London, she thought about her meeting with the sergeant. He hadn't held out much hope on catching up with Lenny, time was already running out and he was sure that Lenny would have skipped the country by now. He'd been in touch with the investigating officer in Wiltshire, where Lenny was wanted in connection with old offences, and promised Hilary that he would update her if he heard anything at all.

Hilary stared out at the bright lights of London as they approached Hammersmith and wondered where the hell Lenny Crispin was? She felt in her bones that he was probably somewhere quite close but realised that, in all probability, as the sergeant had said, Lenny Crispin was probably long gone.

31

The arena at the Old Jamm Inn had been packed, with standing room only on the floor in front of the stage. VIP booths around the arena were full of tourists and locals alike as they'd heartily and raucously welcomed Long Tom Hendry to his long-awaited return to the world of music.

Long Tom sat in the rattan chair on the patio of his hotel room and smiled contentedly as he thought about the previous evening. It was like the old days! His performance had been pitch-perfect and he loved every second of being on stage. If anything, it had been better than the past. He could remember every detail and see each smiling face so clearly – a far cry from the drunken days that rolled over into one seething mass of memory loss and hangovers. He never thought he'd stand in front of two thousand people then wake up the next day with a clear head and remember every detail.

It felt good. The old songs worked well in the new format and were perfect for the Caribbean. The crowd had gone wild and there was something quite magical about standing on a stage, on a hot balmy night, feeling the love and emotion wash over him.

Something was working. Now he needed to start writing some

new material. His notebook lay in his lap and he ran his fingers over the smooth leather and felt a sensation that he hadn't felt for years – a tune was going round in his head and as it did, he was fitting words to it.

The Caribbean was proving to be a very special experience for him, from the flight to the island of Barbados to the kindness and calm offered by the locals. Long Tom relaxed in his chair and stared at the vivid red sky. The sun was setting over the tranquil waters of the west coast sea, creating golden ripples like sparkling jewels. A cacophony of sound from tree frogs, crickets and hummingbirds drummed gently in the hot night air, and Long Tom felt a peace he hadn't experienced in years.

He thought of Hilary and smiled. He'd found his mobile on the table in the hallway and realised that he'd missed a call from her. She was returning his call! It was a start. Perhaps he hadn't screwed up after all? He wondered if she'd come out for a week or so. He had one more gig in two days' time, then Pete had suggested a few more days of relaxation before flying back to London to begin plans for a European tour next year. He'd call Hilary and ask her. Long Tom reached for the phone and dialed the number. Barbados was four hours behind London, it was late and the phone continued to ring. He thought she was probably asleep and so hung up. He'd try again tomorrow.

A calypso band was playing on the terrace near the restaurant and Long Tom tapped his fingers to the tinkling rhythm. He loved it here, it seemed to be giving him new life and a soporific feeling flooded through his bones. He felt better than he had in years and all this without the use of a single stimulant! He put his notebook down and stood up, then strolled across his patio. The night air was humid, and he sighed with pleasure as the warmth clung to his body. Fairy lights twinkled in the trees and the heady scent of frangipani and almond blossom was intoxicating to Long Tom as he hopped over the hedge and wandered down to the beach. He put his hands in his pockets and walked along the edge of the surf. The white sands were warm and as he stared out over the moonlit water he let his thoughts run freely. The sea and sand were so simple, it cost nothing to just walk like this and enjoy the moment.

Long Tom began to hum; a melody was running though his head. He remembered Pete's words on the plane as they'd looked out at the night sky... "You don't need a million pounds to appreciate a sight like that..."

Long Tom stopped. He closed his eyes and began to sing...

"You don't need a million dollars
   To wake up on a sun filled morning
   To feel my arms around you
   You're here
   Right here, right now, with me."

He opened his eyes and smiled. The song felt right.
   He was back!

~

Mickey's head was sore. His body ached all over and his ribs hurt like hell whenever he tried to sit up. He stared at the cast on his leg and watched his toes as he wriggled them for several moments – at least everything was working and it was only a matter of time before he'd be back in action.

He leaned back on his pillows and yawned. Hilary had visited at supper time and insisted that he have a separate room, now that he'd been transferred to a ward. She looked weary as she told Mickey about Lenny and, had Mickey been able to stand, he would have picked her up and swung her around – he'd always thought there was something dodgy about the loud mouthed chef. Mickey hoped that the police would catch up with the scumbag, but felt that it was probably too late.

Hilary hadn't stayed for long. She'd left grapes and magazines and ignored his request for malt whisky whilst assuring him that she'd be back the next day – it was Sunday and she'd bring the papers in, she could read him the news.

Mickey looked around, there was very little to stimulate his mind. The walls were stark and clinically white and the room held nothing other than a sink, a chair and a small wardrobe. He was bored. The drugs he'd been given alleviated all pain and the doctor said he must had the constitution of an ox, given the injuries sustained and the manner in which he was making a good recovery.

Mickey was keen to get out of the hospital and had begun to think about what his next step might be. He couldn't go back to Ireland just yet, the journey would be too painful, he needed a few days. Work was out of the question till his leg had healed but he could probably start penning the first part of his autobiography? Bob had recently told him that Hilary had a publisher lined up – that might give him something to do. He closed his eyes and thought of Hilary. Her luxurious flat in Kensington would be a perfect place to recuperate and it would also help their renewed relationship. He was sure that had the accident not happened, he would be home and dry and moving his things into Chez Hilary, his new London retreat.

He needed the accident to work in his favour.

A young nurse came into the room and checked his temperature and pulse. She smiled when she realised he was awake.

"Saw you on the TV last night," she said shyly. "I'm going to get one of those Romney's Gold Turkeys for Christmas, my family will love it."

Mickey smiled. "That's nice, sweetheart. Make sure I give you my gravy recipe – it's rich and strong and perfect with a bit of breast..." He winked at the nurse. "Bit like myself," he added.

The nurse giggled and blushed as she wrote on his chart. She pulled a phone out of her uniform pocket. "I got your phone charged, you can use it now," she said and handed Mickey the phone. "You've got a lot of missed calls and texts..."

Mickey watched the nurse leave the room, then pressed the phone and unlocked it. There were thirty-two missed calls from

Louella and as many texts. He smiled to himself and began to read them; a little bit of sex-text would certainly pass the evening away...

∼

LENNY CLIMBED into the Alfa Romeo Spider and revved the engine hard then reached for his seat belt and clicked it firmly into place. This is it, son! he told himself, and pulled away from the lock-up garage and out onto the main road.

He'd spent the afternoon in a lap-dancing club in the West End enjoying a few glasses of champagne and the attention of a voluptuous blonde wearing diamante high-heels and very little else. But as the day wore on Lenny began to feel a sense of paranoia, his eyes darted around the club nervously and he felt sure that he was being watched. He wondered if there had been something odd cut into the lines of coke he'd administered earlier, the feeling was definitely new and not one he liked. He'd decided to act on his instincts and leave the country a few hours earlier than planned and hurried back to his hotel, where he packed up all his things into two new suitcases and placed his money in a metal case. The case was now safely buried under the passenger seat beside him and the cases locked in the boot.

Lenny wanted to put his foot down but decided to take things steady, he didn't want to draw any attention to himself – the car was a bit showy after all, but he'd had it re-sprayed and knew that no one would look at it twice in Marbella. As he left London behind, he adhered closely to the speed limits and felt calmer as the miles slipped away. He decided that he'd get some supper at the harbour then get on the first available ferry – there'd be plenty at this time of year. He hadn't booked, there was no need, and he didn't want to leave a trail should anyone decide to come after him. Lenny felt considerably happier, he was glad he'd left London, it was time and now he was on his way!

∼

ZELDA SNUGGLED down on the comfy sofa in front of a roaring fire at her father's home in Chipping Hodbury as Rupert lay, upside down, beside her. The dog had placed his head on Zelda's lap and his large paws dangled as Zelda gently stroked his pink tummy and occasionally leaned forward to kiss his silky black head.

"Oh Roopie, what I am going to do?" she whispered as she stared into the flames. The dog turned his head and lovingly licked her hand.

Zelda had arrived early evening. She'd asked Heidi to organise a cab to take her to Chipping Hodbury, after filming had finished, and had offered to share with Heidi. But Heidi had declined and taken the train back to Kings Cross – it was quicker for her and she'd told Zelda that she wanted to get back to Stewie and spend what was left of the weekend with him.

A surprised Brigitta had welcomed Zelda. She immediately sensed that something was wrong and after applying female logic to the situation, Brigitta decided that Zelda needed cosseting and hoped that she'd talk about her problems when she felt ready.

Martin was away for the weekend. He'd decided at the last minute to pop over to Portugal for a few rounds of golf, and on the spur of the moment had asked Harry to accompany him. Zelda was massively relieved that she hadn't had to face Harry. She could hardly bear to talk to anyone. There was a pain in her heart that hurt like a knife wound and she was so confused. Her tummy hurt too and she felt sick, it was though she had a fever? What did it all mean? She longed for Gary to talk to her; it was agony not knowing what she'd done.

Zelda rubbed Rupert's head and buried her head in a cushion.

"Could you manage a little chicken soup?" Brigitta asked gently. She placed a wooden tray on the low table beside Zelda. It was covered with a pretty lace cloth underneath a small china tureen of home-made broth.

"I'm not hungry," Zelda replied and looked up miserably.

"Do you want to tell me what's happened?" Brigitta asked.

"You'll hate me if I do..."

"That said to a woman who went off with a married man?"

Brigitta raised an eyebrow. "Your father was married when we first met."

"Oh golly, of course." Zelda smiled wearily. She felt tired and confused and longed to confide in someone. She needed advice – she hadn't a clue how to handle things.

"Come here," Brigitta said and, lifting Rupert to one side, sat down beside Zelda and held her hand. "Talk to me, there's nothing that can't be mended. A trouble shared is a trouble halved..."

Zelda sighed and began to pour her troubles out to Brigitta. She told her how she'd discovered feelings she never knew she had and explained how she felt when she was with Gary, and how unbearable it was not to hear from him.

Brigitta considered the situation very carefully.

"Do you love him?" Brigitta asked.

"I don't know..." Zelda replied unhappily. "I just know that I've never felt like this before and I feel that I will die if I don't see him again."

"Then you have to go with your heart. My mother always told me that happiness is not with the one you love, but with the one you can't live without."

"But what about Harry?" Zelda asked.

"Can you live without Harry?"

"Easily!" Zelda replied too quickly and realised what she'd said. "Oh Lord! Mummy will have a fit, she's neck-deep in wedding plans."

"Martin will pay any cancellation charges and your mother will recover... This is about you."

"But Gary won't talk to me." Zelda looked imploringly at Brigitta.

"Give it time. You don't know what he's dealing with." Brigitta put her arm round Zelda and gently stroked her hair. "Throw yourself into your work, it can be very therapeutic, then see what happens. If it's meant to be – you'll be with him," Brigitta whispered. "After all, it was 'meant to be' for me..."

32

The alarm on Hilary's bedside table bleeped repeatedly, and as it continued, the irritating sound grew louder and woke Hilary. She threw an arm out from under her duvet and a waved a lame hand until she connected with the clock and silenced it.

Hilary opened her eyes and stared at the high ceiling in her bedroom. She didn't want to get up. It was warm and cosy in the soft billowing depths of her duck-down duvet and she was tempted to roll over and go back to sleep. She'd been dreaming of a sunny beach and warm sea and the dream was so real, she could almost feel the sand in her toes and sun on her skin. A heavenly escape from recent events, which had been exhausting and looked set to continue. Hilary yawned and pulled the duvet around her. She felt so tired – perhaps it wouldn't do any harm to have a few more moments? She snuggled down and closed her eyes and as sleep took over, she imagined herself back on the beach…

∼

MICKEY LAY against his pillows with a pile of Sunday papers piled up on his bedside table. He wasn't in the mood for reading and fidgeted with the counterpane covering his legs. His agitation lay with Louella, who'd appeared at breakfast time and somehow got past the nursing staff by pretending she was his sister. She'd told them that she'd recently returned from abroad and was so devastated by his accident that she had to see him immediately. It had worked and a nurse had even produced an extra breakfast for her.

Mickey wasn't thrilled to see Louella, even though she'd brought him all the Sunday newspapers and a bottle of his favourite malt whisky. He was conscious that Hilary might turn up at any moment, and if she caught sight of Louella swooning with sorrow, it might well scupper his plans. Fortunately, Louella hadn't been allowed to stay for long because Mickey needed a bed bath and was due a visit from the doctor. She'd left reluctantly after giving him a long lingering kiss and promised she'd back again the next day.

"Your sister's very affectionate," the nurse said, and hid a grin as she handed Mickey his morning medication.

"Erm... we've not seen each other for some time..." Mickey faltered.

"Obviously," the nurse replied and wrote on his chart.

Mickey sighed. He needed to get out of here.

He watched the nurse move around the room and wondered if he could enlist her help? He thought about Hilary. If she got wind of Louella, she would back right off and he didn't intend to spend the next few weeks recovering on a ward or some expensive rehab unit, his heart was set on Hilary's comfortable Kensington apartment in Marchant Gardens. It was a perfect retreat – somewhere to start writing his book whilst gently being administered to with comforting food and lots of Hilary's tender loving care. Christmas was just around the corner and with any luck he might make it home to Ireland. Imagine Christmas at Fool's Landing with Hilary by my side... The magic of an Irish Christmas! You never know, Mickey old man, he told himself, Christmas might just be the time to pop the question!

"How do you fancy a really big, Romney Gold Turkey in a lovely Christmas hamper?" Mickey asked the nurse and grinned as her eyes lit up. His plan was formulated – all he needed was a little help in carrying it out!

∼

ZELDA SAT at the breakfast bar in her father's house and pushed a slice of toast to one side. Her mobile sat on the granite counter beside her and bleeped persistently. Zelda had the phone on silent but could see that her mother's number flashed repeatedly.

"You're not hungry?" Brigitta asked. She placed a thin slice of cheese onto a crispbread and took a bite.

"Not really," Zelda said. She hopped off the stool and carried her plate to the sink. Rupert followed and thumped his tail gratefully as she handed him the uneaten toast.

"What are your plans?" Brigitta asked.

"I'm going to take your advice and focus on work. It will help take my mind off things." Zelda poured herself a cup of coffee from a jug on a hotplate. "I've got a couple of days to think about recipes, before filming begins in the East End." She put her cup down and wandered over to the kitchen's central island and ran her fingers over Brigitta's collection of cookery books, stacked neatly on a shelf.

"I can help you," Brigitta announced.

"Could you? Really?"

"I'd be pleased to. You need to make sure you go out on a high with the final programme."

"Oh, Brigitta, that would be such fun. And I don't need to think about Gary or Harry or even Mummy…" She glanced at her phone.

"No," Brigitta replied, "just concentrate on work for now." She stood up and reached for a pinafore. "Have you got your researcher's notes?"

"I certainly have, and a list of suggested dishes – I just need to give them my healthy twist." Zelda had come to life.

"Then let's get started," Brigitta said. "We'll be Cotswold Cockneys today, cooking in the country." She smiled. "Fancy a jellied eel?"

"Oh Lord, I don't even know what one is!" Zelda giggled. She reached for a pinafore too and fastening it firmly, began to work.

∽

Long Tom walked slowly through the sunny gardens of the plantation house in St John. A vehicle was waiting on the driveway and the driver held a rear door open.

"Come back soon, man," the Bajan musician called out and waved cheerily as Long Tom climbed into the car. "Preferably during the day!" the musician added with a smile and watched the car pull away.

Long Tom sat back on the smooth leather seats in the air-conditioned car and stared out at the cane fields surrounding the narrow road leading back to the highway on the west coast. He realised that he was hungry; it was six o'clock in the morning and he'd been working all night. It'd been a spur of the minute thing, to dash off to the recording studio again, but Long Tom had a song in his head when he sang on the beach and he simply had to lay the track down before he lost the impetus.

The musician hadn't been at all surprised to see him, late at night, on the doorstep and welcomed him back to his home.

"You're a high roller, man," the musician had said as he led Long Tom to the studio, "you gettin' the Caribbean in your soul." He'd chuckled and for the next few hours accompanied Long Tom on the recording.

The car pulled off the highway and headed past the security gates and into the private grounds of Long Tom's hotel. It pulled up alongside two large colonnades and stopped at low marble steps as a uniformed doorman came forward to open the door.

"Good morning, Mr Hendry," the doorman said. "Fine morning, sir."

"It's a beautiful day." Long Tom raised his hat and beamed as he handed the man a ten dollar bill.

He wandered through the hotel to the terrace restaurant and took a seat overlooking the beach. There were no early risers and Long Tom enjoyed a solitary breakfast of fresh fruit and an omelet with warm crusty rolls. He contemplated the day ahead and wondered if Pete fancied a game of tennis. Pete would be gobsmacked by Long Tom's nocturnal wanderings and keen to hear the new track. Long Tom yawned, he might just grab a few hours' sleep. He glanced at his watch – it was two thirty in the morning in London and he longed to hear Hilary's voice. He hesitated then sighed, it was far too late. He'd call her tomorrow; he couldn't wait to tell her his news!

~

"Breakfast is everything. The beginning, the first thing. It is the mouthful that is the commitment to a new day, a continuing life."

Anthony sat at a corner table in the Wolseley and grinned with happiness as he quoted the food critic, A.A. Gill. Anthony loved his breakfast and he adored the menu at famous restaurant in Piccadilly. He stared hungrily into a mixed basket of Viennoiserie and chose a mini Danish and croissant. Bob, meanwhile, was finishing a bowl of prunes with fresh ginger. To follow, Anthony had ordered "The English", and rubbed his hands together as a waiter removed the silver dome cover to reveal a breakfast of bacon, eggs, sausage, tomato, black pudding and baked beans. Bob's bowl was replaced with two boiled eggs in silver egg cups on a porcelain plate, with "soldiers" stacked high on the side.

"I don't know how you can eat all that stodge," Bob said as he neatly cracked the top of an egg.

"Watch and learn, my dear." Anthony ignored Bob's sarcasm and began to butter a slice of brown toast.

"We really should plan a menu for our Christmas soirée." Bob dipped a thin slice of toast into his perfectly cooked egg. The pale yellow yolk dribbled down the brown shell.

Anthony eyes slid sideways and he studied Bob's face. He crossed his fingers under the starched white cloth and prayed that Bob wasn't going to suggest a Tibetan feast.

"I thought we'd go traditional, as it's Christmas," Bob continued. "A festive buffet with a sliced ham and roast turkey and lots of lovely finger food. What do you think?"

"I think that would be wonderful, darling." Anthony breathed a sigh of relief and tucked into his breakfast. "I'll make some mulled wine."

They chatted happily about their planned party, and when the waiter had cleared their empty plates away, they settled back with a large latte each and picked up the Sunday papers.

"What a perfect way to spend a cold Sunday morning in December," Anthony said as he searched for the culture section in The Times. He shook the paper out and began to read.

"O.M.G!" Bob shouted.

"Darling, I do wish you wouldn't use that expression." Anthony put his paper down and stared at Bob. "Whatever have the red-tops got to say this morning?" He glanced at the paper spread out on the table before Bob and frowned as he noted Bob's astonished expression.

"Ready, Steady, Crook!" Bob exclaimed as a smile lit up his face. "Yes!" he shouted and punched the air, much to the consternation of diners at the next table, who'd observed Bob's reading matter and looked haughtily over their copies of The Guardian.

"They've got him!" Bob continued excitedly. He read aloud from the paper, "Lenny Crispin was arrested late last night attempting to board a ferry to Spain…"

"Bloody hell!" Anthony cried out and, throwing his paper to one side, leaned across the table to read the headlines. A photo showed a very disgruntled Lenny, clearly recognisable despite blond hair and a short beard, in handcuffs and being led to a waiting police vehicle.

"Really!" the man at the adjacent table said as Anthony's paper skimmed his breakfast.

"It's true!" Bob could hardly get his words out. "It says here that Lenny was travelling under the alias of Tony Browne, and driving an

Alfa Romeo Spider. Apparently, he was wanted by the police in Wiltshire for several counts of fraud."

"But what about all the money the investors stumped up for the cookery school? Has it been recovered?" Anthony asked.

"There isn't any more information." Bob sat back and clapped his hands.

"I think this calls for champagne," Anthony said and summoned the waiter.

"It most certainly does," Bob replied, "but we need to share it with Hilary. I wonder if she knows."

"Only one way to find out," Anthony smiled and asked for the bill.

"Taxi to Marchant Gardens?" Bob asked.

"Absolutely!" Anthony began to fold the newspaper. He tucked it under his arm and glared at the disgruntled diners. "I think that's mine," he said and reached to retrieve the culture section, then stood up and announced, "Post-haste, dear boy, post-haste!" Anthony took Bob's arm and they flounced out of the restaurant.

∽

The front door bell rang incessantly. Hilary stumbled out of her bed and through the hallway to reach the intercom.

"Yes," she snapped.

"Got the Sunday papers for yoooo..." Bob sang happily.

"Bugger off, Bob!"

"You're gonna like it..." Bob continued in a sing-song voice.

Hilary ran her fingers through her hair and glanced at the ormolu clock on the table. Eleven o'clock! She must have slept on for several hours! She pressed the street-level entry button and unlocked her front door to see Bob racing along the corridor with Anthony hot on his heels. He carried a bottle of champagne.

"My, oh my, someone had a late night..." Bob stared at Hilary with incredulity and looked her up and down. Her hair was tussled and she wore a black La Perla lace nightgown with spaghetti straps; it was crumpled and one strap fell off her shoulder.

"I must have overslept..." Hilary pushed the strap into place as Bob followed her into the sitting room.

"Well, we've got some news to wake you up!" he said and went to the windows to open the curtains. Anthony had disappeared into the kitchen and appeared with three crystal flutes. He popped the champagne cork and began to pour.

"Get your laughing gear round this," Bob said, as he spread the newspaper out on the coffee table and passed Hilary a glass.

Hilary wished she'd had time to comb her hair and brush her teeth, but she took the champagne and leaned over the paper. "I haven't got my glasses on; you'll have to tell me what it says..."

"Ready, Steady, Crook!" The men cried out and began to clap their hands as comprehension flooded Hilary's face.

"No!" Hilary gasped.

"Yes!" they both replied and picked up their champagne. "Cheers!"

"Cheers!" Hilary said and shook her head.

They sipped their drinks and Anthony topped the glasses up.

"There's very little information," Bob continued. "Hasn't your sergeant been on the blower to tell you what's happened?"

"I've had my phone off, I was really tired." Hilary went into her bedroom. She returned carrying her phone. "There are lots of missed calls and one message," she said and held the phone to her ear.

"Oh goody," Bob said and sat down on the sofa. He patted the cushion. "Let's make ourselves comfortable and you can fill us in on all the gory details."

Hilary picked up her message and nodded at Bob as she heard the sergeant begin to speak. His information was short and to the point.

"They found a case containing a large sum of money!" Hilary exclaimed as she put the phone down on the table.

"Hurrah!" Bob and Anthony cried.

"I've got to call the sergeant back and get all the facts but do you think we should have a little celebration?" Hilary asked tentatively.

"Not little. Large!" Bob and Anthony replied.

"There's more champagne in the fridge, help yourselves." Hilary sat back on a sofa. She picked up her glass and raised it. "To Lenny Crispin," she said "May he continue his long and illustrious career in the catering department at her Majesty's pleasure for many years to come!"

33

Lottie sat behind her desk and twiddled with a pair of earrings. She flicked a tiny switch and watched the miniature Christmas trees flash on and off. Perfect! she thought happily, and attached them to her ears. She wore a pair of red silk shorts trimmed with white fur, over thick wool tights, and completed the outfit with a ribbed sweater and pixie boots.

Lottie was looking forward to Christmas; it was her favourite season. She'd decorated the reception area with a pretty tree, which had been stored away from the previous year – complete with gold baubles and coloured lights. Festive garlands were draped across the ceiling and cards strung across a wall.

"Morning, sweetie," Bob called out brightly. He darted under a garland and removed his heavy overcoat. "Freezing out there but glowing in here. My, you have made it all look nice." He looked around the room and let his eyes rest on a Singing Santa ornament perched on the edge of Lottie's desk. The Santa wore a chef's apron over his red suit and held a wooden spoon.

"Love the Santa." Bob grinned and ran his fingers over Santa's thick white beard.

"Heidi got it for me at the Good Food Show," Lottie replied. "He sings, 'Last Christmas... I baked you a cake, but the very next day, you gave it away...'"

"Lovely, dear," Bob replied. "I'm sure, Wham, will re-release it..."

"Hilary's not coming in till later." Lottie ignored Bob's comment and began to paint her nails with scarlet lacquer.

"Oh, I thought she said she'd be in first thing?" Bob recalled a conversation with Hilary from the previous day; they'd all been quite merry as Hilary got ready to go to the hospital. Perhaps she had a hangover?

"Says she's got a guest and needs to make some arrangements..." Lottie leaned over her nails, her face hidden by her curly locks.

Bob was puzzled. Hilary hadn't mentioned any guest? Still, it wasn't up to him to question his boss's timetable, he had far more serious things to do – the Christmas soirée was only days away and then the office would close for the Christmas holidays and he had clients to attend to. December was racing away!

~

HILARY STOOD in her kitchen and examined the contents of her cupboards and fridge. She'd need to do some shopping, perhaps she'd have time to do it online from the office and have it delivered to her flat.

Hilary wasn't used to shopping for food. She rarely ate in and hardly entertained at home. She sighed, she was going to have to get used to it for the next few days.

She'd arrived at the hospital quite late the previous day, after celebrating with Bob and Anthony. They'd consumed two bottles of champagne and Hilary had felt quite merry, but she'd soon sobered up and stopped dead in her tracks as she entered Mickey's room.

Mickey sat in a wheelchair with his cast perched on a support. He wore a thick tartan dressing gown and red cashmere scarf. Dark blue velvet slippers covered his bare feet.

"Ah, my carriage awaits!" Mickey said as Hilary walked into the room. He waved a metal walking aid in greeting.

"What the hell do you think you're doing?" Hilary was gobsmacked. How on earth had he managed to get himself in this position?

"Time to go home... well back to Marchant Gardens," Mickey replied. "I can't sit around here all day doing nothing – I've a book to start and calls to make and Bob will want to plan my schedule for next year."

"Marchant Gardens?" Hilary was flummoxed.

"That's so kind of you, Hilary, I appreciate your gesture. It was a condition made by the doctors before they'd discharge me." He grinned cheekily. "Lots of lovely rest and TLC. Don't worry – I won't be any trouble."

Hilary thought that Mickey would be more trouble than she'd ever had in her life and she stared incredulously at him and shook her head as a young nurse came into the room.

"Here's my partner in crime!" Mickey smiled at the nurse and held out his hand. "What would we do without our nurses? These gals always go the extra mile..."

Hilary watched the nurse hand Mickey his credit card and belongings packaged up in a huge dark green carrier bag with Harrods embossed in gold letters on the sides.

"Enjoy your turkey!" he'd said to the nurse then took the card and placed it in his wallet. He'd no doubt she'd added a couple of personal extras to his shopping bill, but it was worth it. He felt quite cosy in his new dressing gown and scarf.

"Are we ready?" Mickey turned to Hilary and grinned again as the nurse took the brakes off his chair and began to push him out of the room.

"But... you're still recovering... It can't be safe to leave hospital so soon..." Hilary stumbled over her words.

"An Irish man is made of strong stuff, old girl. This will be the fastest recovery in history!" He'd waved the walking aid in the air and pointed to the corridor. "Tally Ho!"

Hilary gripped the wooden counter in her kitchen as she thought about the previous night. Somehow, her chauffeur had managed to maneuver Mickey's wheelchair, with her assistance, up the short flight of stairs to her flat. She'd had very little choice in the matter and seemed to be in a daze as she made up the bed in her spare room then fussed around Mickey as he'd insisted on staggering in, leaning heavily on the crutch. He really was remarkable! Only days before she'd thought he'd never recover and now here he was, ensconced in her flat; full of charm and wrapping her round his little finger.

But Hilary hadn't really wanted to put up a fight. She felt the accident was probably her fault – she should never have encouraged him under the Christmas tree in Covent Garden, and had he not been so ecstatic, he wouldn't have run in the path of the taxi. And, after all, hadn't she been about to jump into bed with him that night? Hilary felt confused but knew her duty lie in helping Mickey get better. She shook her head – she was getting soft in her old age, who'd have thought she'd be in this position?

"Don't worry about me, sweetheart!" Mickey called out from the lounge. He sat on the sofa with his leg resting on an upholstered mahogany footstool. His laptop lay on by his side. "You get off to the office, I have everything I need and we can have a takeaway later."

"You can't live on takeaways, you need nourishment," Hilary replied, racking her brain to think what to cook that evening.

"You're the only nourishment I need." Mickey winked at her and held out his hand.

Hilary walked over to the sofa and perched on the edge. She took his hand, it was warm and familiar.

"Perhaps we could go to Fool's Landing for Christmas?" Mickey said softly. "I'll be able to travel in a day or so and could go ahead and get things ready?"

Hilary looked into Mickey's blue eyes. They twinkled mischievously and she felt her heart being pulled into their intoxicating depths – he always seemed to cast a spell over her and it would be so easy to say yes…

The phone rang. Hilary turned sharply and the spell was broken. It was Bob calling to ask who her guest was.

"I'm on my way," Hilary said and hung up. She'd explain later. She looked at Mickey. "Is there anything else that you need?"

"Just a kiss and a cuddle," he replied and held out his arms.

Hilary held herself stiffly and leaned forward to peck him on each cheek, then withdrew quickly. She was in danger of wheeling him into her bedroom if she stayed any longer and she simply had to get to work.

"I'll see you later," she said and picked up her astrakhan coat and Birkin bag. "Call me if you need anything."

"Missing you already..." Mickey called out as Hilary disappeared through the door.

He leaned back on the cushions and sighed with satisfaction. Everything was going nicely... now to begin his book! He picked up his laptop and as he placed it on his knee he noticed that Hilary had left her phone on the arm of the chair. He shrugged; she'd probably come back for it. He turned the laptop on and contemplated his opening paragraph. He'd always wanted to see himself on posters in the windows at major booksellers and imagined his book signing tour. The book would be in international bestseller!

He picked up his laptop and began to type.

∼

Long Tom sat on the deck at the Old Jamm Inn and idly flicked through his notebook. He'd filled several pages now and as words came into his head, he noted them down. He was pleased with the song he'd recorded last night, it felt right. Pete and the boys from the band ordered burgers and beers and tucked in heartily when their food arrived. Long Tom bit into his favourite – the Cheese Royale – and licked his lips with pleasure. Even food tasted better these days.

They were having a last rehearsal before their final gig. It was hot in the arena at the back and it was pleasant to have a break on the cool deck at the front of the Old Jamm Inn, where a gentle breeze blew in from the beach across the road. Long Tom sipped his fruit cocktail and tipped his hat forward, he was getting a good tan but the sun was hot on his forehead and he welcomed the shade on his face.

"Everything okay, guys?" Jimmy asked as he checked their empty glasses. "Another round?"

The drummer, a large man named Stanley, who came from east London, held up his glass.

"Vodka and cran, Stan?" Jimmy smiled and took the glass. He nodded towards Long Tom's glass and raised an eyebrow. "Fruit punch?" he asked.

"Top her right up," Long Tom replied. "Could I use your phone for a moment?"

"You got it," Jimmy said and placed his mobile on the table.

Long Tom swung his legs over the wooden bench and picked up the phone. He punched Hilary's number in and strode into the cool, dimly lit bar. It was quiet in here and Long Tom looked around at the vintage travel posters and kitsch memorabilia that decorated the walls and ceilings. The phone began to ring and Long Tom smiled with anticipation, she would be sure to pick up at this time of day.

A man's voice answered. "Yes?"

Long Tom was puzzled? Perhaps it was her assistant, Bob.

"I'd like to speak to Hilary, please," Long Tom said politely.

"Who is this?" the man asked.

"Just a friend. Tell her it's Long Tom..."

There was a silence for several seconds and Long Tom could hear the man breathing.

"Long Tom, my old friend," the man said. "Mickey Lloyd here. How the hell are you?"

Long Tom was taken aback. Mickey Lloyd? Old friend? Why was he answering Hilary's phone?

"Heard you had an accident, Mickey," Long Tom spoke quietly.

"Buggered my leg up, but bouncing back," Mickey replied. "Obviously, I'm staying with Hilary in London. She's got quite a cosy little love-nest here – best recuperation a fellow could have!"

Long Tom walked out to the end of the deck and grabbed a wooden railing. "I'm glad you're getting better…"

"Oh, I'll be fine. A few days here, then back to Ireland for Christmas," Mickey continued. "I'm going to show Hilary a real Irish Christmas, can't wait to get her over to Fool's Landing. The old place always scrubs up well and it's a great place to get things on a more serious footing, if you know what I mean…?" Mickey laughed. "Was there any message I can give her?"

"No, nothing. It was just a social call." Long Tom stared out, oblivious to the busy road below.

"I'll tell her you called," Mickey said jovially. "Good to talk!"

The line went dead.

"Fruit punch?" Jimmy held Long Tom's drink out.

"I'm tempted to say stick a vodka in it," Long Tom said as he handed Jimmy the mobile and took the drink.

"Well, you know I wouldn't do that," Jimmy replied softly. "Bad news?"

Long Tom sighed. "You could say that."

"My mother always says, 'the time to be happy is now, let the universe take care of the how'," Jimmy offered.

"You mum is a wise lady, I should write that in a song." Long Tom took a sip of his drink. "Cheers," he said and with a heavy heart, wandered back to the band.

∼

MICKEY EASED his body off the sofa, and supporting himself with his walking aid, hopped over to Hilary's drinks cabinet. He reached for the malt whisky and poured a large measure into a heavy bottomed glass. So, Long Tom Hendry was hot on Hilary's heels? That explained a lot.

Mickey had always been mystified that Hilary had jumped onto the stage the night of Long John's concert in Kindale, and Bob had confided in Mickey and said that Hilary stayed at Flatterley Manor after her accident. The jigsaw fell into place. So Long Tom has got it into his alcohol soaked brain that he might just stand a chance with Hilary? Mickey took a swig of the whisky and laughed to himself. Well, one thing was for sure, there wasn't a chance that things would progress any further! Mickey had soon dispelled any thoughts Long Tom might have of hooking up with Hilary. The sooner Mickey got Hilary away from the distractions of her job and any possible dealings with Long Tom, the better.

He reached for his own phone and placed a call to the housekeeper in Ireland who looked after Fool's Landing in his absence. He told her to have the house thoroughly cleaned and prepared for Christmas, he was coming home.

And he wouldn't be alone...

∽

ZELDA SAT next to Heidi on a shabby, tartan covered banquette, in a dark corner of the Freemason's Arms, in the East End of London. They read through her call sheet for the day. Zelda fidgeted with a glass of sparkling water then placed it on the varnished wooden table, and listened attentively as the director brought her up to speed on the last two days of filming. She'd soon be meeting Joan Jolly, a local Pearly Queen, and a homeless lad named David, whom Joan had helped, through her charity work. Joan was going to cook a traditional Cockney meal of pie, mash and liquor and David would prepare a tapioca pudding.

Joan held a monthly "meet" at the pub and cooked traditional meals for the regulars – a mixture of old folk who lived in the locality and young people from the homeless shelter. The proceeds went to a charity fund for the local homeless people and Pearly Queen Joan was much respected in the area.

"Now, we simply have to get this tidied up in the next two days, Zelda," the director said, "and we can, if you work hard." He leaned across the table and raised an eyebrow. "Not going to have any more tantrums, are you?"

"Oh, absolutely not," Zelda replied, beaming. "I've been working hard all weekend, haven't I, Heidi," She turned to Heidi, who nodded enthusiastically. "I've even done all my own prep…" Zelda crossed her fingers under the table and thought about the endless plastic boxes of ingredients, all neatly chopped and weighed by Brigitta, who'd delivered them to the pub's kitchen from the safety of the cool box in her Land Cruiser.

"Perfect!" the director said. "As soon as Joan appears, we'll get cracking."

"Who's that at the cain 'n able?" a voice rang out from across the bar. It belonged to a stout woman dressed in a neat black skirt and jacket. She lifted the hatch on the bar and walked towards them.

"I think she means table," the director whispered to Zelda. "It's Joan and she's talking to you."

Zelda stared at the woman's suit. Thousands of pretty pearly sequins, sewn in the shape of anchors, covered the fabric and glowed as she moved.

"My, you've a pretty boat race," Joan roared, "and lovely barnet fair…" She pointed to Zelda's hair.

"Oh gosh, thank you," Zelda said and stood up to shake Joan's hand. "I love your suit, it's really spiffing."

"Oh, 'ark at her bubble 'n squeak!" Joan laughed. She grabbed Zelda's hand and pumped it.

"Can everyone take their places in the kitchen, please!" the director called out.

Heidi and Aisla hurried over to smooth Zelda's pinafore and straighten her pretty cream blouse.

"I love the buttons," Zelda whispered and smiled.

"Aye, well, we had to make a wee gesture." Aisla grinned and touched a mother-of-pearl button at the cuff of Zelda's blouse.

"All set?" Heidi asked.

Zelda looked anxiously around the room, ever hopeful that Gary would appear. She'd not heard a word from him and tried to remember Brigitta's words, "If it's meant to be…" It looked increasingly like it wasn't meant to be and Zelda felt a sharp, incessant pain in her heart that simply wouldn't go away. She had to go home after filming and Harry would be there, full of his golfing trip and keen to see his fiancé.

Then there was her mother to deal with. Zelda shuddered. Madeleine was going to have an absolute fit! But Zelda knew that she had to break the news, she simply couldn't marry Harry. She took a deep breath. She had to get it right today, it was the last episode in the series and she couldn't mess it up. But the competition was tough with Joan, the Pearly Queen, looking hell-bent on success amongst her regulars. If only Gary were here! Zelda thought to herself, he'd assure her and help with her recipes...

Heidi took Zelda's arm. "Come on, you can do this."

Zelda straightened her shoulders and thrust her head back. With a confidence she didn't feel, she forced herself forward towards kitchen.

"Yes, I can," Zelda said purposefully "You'd better Adam and Eve it!"

34

Hilary sat at her desk and worked diligently through a stack of paperwork, she had almost reached the end. It was quiet in the office, Bob had taken Prunella to the Ivy for lunch and Heidi was at a Christmas show, where the agency had several chefs appearing on the demonstration stage.

Hilary glanced down at the schedule that Bob had prepared for Mickey, for the coming year. Mickey aimed to be back on his feet from February, and looking at the detailed plan, Hilary thought that he'd need to be completely fit and well to carry out the massive amount of work that he'd landed since joining Hargreaves Promotions.

Hilary picked up another schedule and glanced over Heidi's proposals for Zelda. Zelda was turning out to be quite a star as well. Zelda and The Zimmers had received excellent pre-screening reviews and would air in the New Year. There would undoubtedly be another series, and her endorsements with various companies were set to turn over a considerable sum. Prunella, too, was successful. Sales of PAP were at an all-time high and her book was doing well in the bestseller lists at home and abroad.

Hilary pushed her chair away from her desk and spun round to face the window. Outside, the sky was grey, the clouds looked thick and heavy and she wondered if it was going to snow. It would be Christmas Eve in two days' time. The office would close today for the holidays, and everyone was looking forward to Bob and Anthony's soirée the following day – it would be a lovely event to mark the start of the festive season. Hilary crossed her legs and swung a mock-croc court shoe up and down; they were one of her favourite pair of shoes, with brown ribbons that fastened in a bow. She drummed her fingers on the wooden arms of her chair, it felt strange to not be lighting a cigarette and so far she hadn't given in to her cravings. But it hadn't been easy. Worrying about Mickey's injuries were more than enough to make her reach for a nicotine fix. He was on his way to Ireland now, to Fool's Landing, where she would be joining him on Christmas Eve.

She'd enjoyed having him at her flat. He hadn't been any trouble and even though she'd been working during the day, he'd managed to look after himself and was pleased to see her in the evening. It had been fun to cook and as he sat in the kitchen while she busied herself, he'd been unable to resist giving instructions and tips. They'd enjoyed a bottle of wine together and the evenings had passed very pleasantly. In the mornings, she left early. Mickey slept a lot and Hilary felt sure that the tranquility of her home had aided his recovery. Mickey's ribs were almost healed and the cast would be off his leg in the New Year, which gave him time to strengthen it before starting work again. He'd made a start on his book and seemed pleased with it.

Hilary thought back to the previous evening. She'd come home slightly earlier than planned and as she entered the flat, a smell of perfume drifted across the doorway. Mickey laughed it off and said it clearly belonged to the couple who lived next door; they must be out on the town. Hilary had assented, he was probably right, but the perfume had been spicy and strong and the memory niggled.

Mickey was being driven back to Ireland by a friend returning to Kindale for Christmas. They were booked on the early evening ferry and Mickey had been excited at the thought of going home. His excitement was infectious. Hilary knew that she was mellowing towards Mickey. The accident had shocked her and, so far, the emotions she'd felt during their evening at Rules hadn't been repeated. But she had a feeling that away from work and her busy life in London, she may well succumb. She also had a feeling that Mickey knew this too and couldn't wait for her to arrive at Fool's Landing, to fall under the spell and magic of an Irish Christmas.

Hilary stood up and walked over to the window. The office was stuffy so she opened the window and took a deep breath. The air was cold with a sharp nip of frost. Lights from the shops shone on the glassy surface of the road. It was beginning to feel like Christmas. Hilary leaned out and looked down on Wardour Street. A van had stopped beneath the window and the driver got out with a package to deliver to a neighbouring building. A song was playing on his radio and the strains of a familiar melody drifted up on the cold evening air.

Hilary froze.

It was a reggae version of No More War, Long Tom's revamped hit that was steadily climbing the charts. She closed her eyes and listened to the calypso ring of the chorus and felt a stab of pain in her heart. She wondered where he was. He'd never returned her calls and for a reason that she couldn't explain, she missed him, terribly.

She closed the window and moved back to her desk.

Why hadn't Long Tom called her? He'd seemed so keen and had asked if they could meet up when he got back to London. She knew that he was back from the Caribbean; there'd been a photo of him in the newspaper. He'd looked tanned and handsome as he strolled through the airport. The newspaper reported that he was working on a new album and a European tour was planned for next year. He'd obviously found his creative flow again and Hilary wondered if he was writing too. She sighed; he must have found love in the Caribbean – that would explain his silence.

She closed her eyes and remembered her time with Long Tom in Ireland – how easy it would be to fall in love with him; he'd been so warm and so kind. She'd felt his insecurities and had a notion that he doubted his ability as a man; it must be agony to be a recovering addict. Perhaps that was why he was cold towards her in London? Yet, he'd been different again when he called her and she really thought that their relationship had a chance.

The pain in her heart was like a toothache, insistent and unforgiving. She shook her head, men could be so unpredictable – did you ever really know where you stood with them? Was love, in the end, just a compromise? Would she compromise with Mickey?

Lottie stuck her head round the door.

"Is it all right if I get off now?" Lottie's curls bounced out from under the rim of a furry Santa hat.

"Of course, Lottie. Are you all packed up for Christmas?"

"The phones are dead and I've put away messages on everyone's emails and answerphones."

"Well, hurry off home," Hilary replied. "I'll see you at Bob's tomorrow."

"I can't wait!" Lottie called out. "Cheery-bye!"

Hilary smiled as Lottie disappeared. She had a great team around her and things looked very promising for the following year. The business was going to expand. She glanced at her watch; there was something she needed to pick up on her way home. Hilary turned off her computer and cleared her desk of paperwork, then placed her pens and general debris in her top drawer. She reached for her fur coat and buttoned it tightly. As she walked through reception, she turned off all the lights and locked the doors, then trotted down the stairs to the street. Hilary waved an arm and a taxi pulled over and as she settled into the back seat, she looked back at the glossy black sign above the office door. Gold letters announced Hargreaves Promotions. They glinted in the frosty night air and as Hilary read the letters, she smiled to herself.

～

HEIDI RAN into her flat in Muswell Hill and threw her bags onto a chair in the narrow hallway. She was exhausted after her day at the show and couldn't wait to get into a lovely hot bath to relax. Work was finished for the year and the holidays lay ahead – it was Christmas!

A pile of cards lay on the kitchen table and a note from Stewie: Popped out for some last minute shopping, see you later xx

She needed to pop out herself before the shops shut, but first she'd have a cup of tea and a bath. Bonky wrapped himself around Heidi's legs and purred with delight that his mistress was home. Heidi made her tea and sat down at the table. As she sipped the warm drink she opened the cards, smiling as she recognised relatives who appeared annually, sending love and best wishes for the festive season.

The last card was from Zelda. A photo, on the front cover, surrounded by holly, showed Harry and Zelda in matching cashmere sweaters, sitting by a roaring log fire with Rupert perched beside them. They smiled happily into the camera.

Heidi frowned and opened the card.

"Ha ha! Got you!" Zelda had written in black ink and had signed the card, "With love and thanks for all that you do… Zelda xx"

Heidi breathed a sigh of relief. So, Zelda hadn't gone back to Harry and the engagement was well and truly off! It seemed strange that Zelda should be using up last year's cards, but then nothing that Zelda did these days seemed straightforward.

Heidi thought back to the filming in the Freemason's Arms.

Joan Jolly looked set for runaway success with her pie, mash and liquor sauce – a traditional cockney meal much loved by the regulars despite the heavy pastry, thick mashed potatoes and creamy parsley sauce they called "liquor". David's tapioca was full of cream too, and he'd served it with a huge dollop of sugary jam. The diners had heartily tucked in and there wasn't an empty plate. Zelda had smiled as she watched Joan prepare the meal, she stood alongside and, with the director's prompting, asked lots of questions about the history of the Pearly Kings and Queens and the popular recipes that had traditionally been handed from one generation to the next.

The next day their roles were reversed and Joan stood by the stove as Zelda prepared her version of a "Ruby Murray".

"You'll never get them to favour a vegetable curry over pie and mash," Joan had scoffed, as she watched Zelda gently fry her ready-prepped onions and fresh spices, "they like meat on their dinner!"

Zelda smiled sweetly and continued with her recipe. To compete with David's tapioca, Zelda made a Knickerbocker Glory – a cockney favourite, but with a twist using a light yogurt sorbet, which Zelda carefully flavoured with vanilla then added fresh fruit and a raspberry puree sauce. The calories were halved in the low-fat version.

Joan scowled as the meal was presented and the diners began to tuck in.

Judging began.

Zelda held her breath as the diners were asked which dishes they preferred. She stood between Joan and David, in front of the cameras and stared anxiously at the faces of young and old before her. The crew gathered round and the room became still with tension.

"Well, it comes as no surprise to me..." the presenter began. Zelda felt her heart sink with disappointment. How did she possibly expect to win over traditional Cockney fare? She couldn't bear to look at the faces of the expectant diners and stared out towards to doors of the pub.

"That the winner on both counts, in a unanimous decision for the main course and dessert, is..."

The pub door suddenly opened and as Zelda turned her head a familiar form came into view.

"Zelda!" The presenter cried out to a rapturous round of applause from both the crew and diners.

But Zelda had hardly heard. Her eyes were like saucers and her mouth had fallen open. Her heart felt as though it was about to cartwheel out of her blouse and spin across the floor...

Gary stood in the doorway with a huge bunch of flowers in his hand.

The director zoomed in close on Zelda's face – it was a marvellous expression to capture for the closing scene, he'd no idea that she felt so strongly about the programme!

Zelda felt pats on her back and heard the crew calling out

congratulations as she went through the motions and finished the take. Her eyes never left Gary's and in moments she reached his side. He pulled her into the doorway and thrust the flowers into her hands.

"Zelda, can you ever forgive me?" Gary looked anxious.

"Oh, darling, are you back for good? I mean... are you...?" Zelda could hardly say the words.

"Yes, I'm free, if that's what you mean," Gary replied. "But are you?"

"Oh, absolutely. The fireworks went off a couple of days ago. Harry is livid and Mummy is threatening to top herself. She says I'll never find another double-barrel and I'll always be fat..."

"But you've lost weight." Gary put his hands on Zelda's waist.

Zelda hung her head. "Haven't had much appetite, old thing."

"But I love you however you are." Gary touched Zelda's chin and pushed her face up towards his own.

"But you left me."

"I had to." Gary stared into Zelda's eyes. "I had to sort things out at home and make a clean break, and if I'd spoken to you, I would have been confused. I didn't want to persuade you to do something you may regret."

"Oh, I've no regrets." Zelda began to smile. "I just wished I'd met you sooner."

"Does that mean you'll spend the rest of your life with me?"

"Oh, Gary, do you mean it?"

"We may have to live in the back of my catering truck to begin with..."

"Better make sure we never invite my mother..."

They stared into each other's eyes and felt their frustrations fall away, and as Zelda felt Gary's strong arms wrap tightly around her and his kisses on her face, she felt happier than she'd ever felt in her life.

Heidi smiled as she remembered Zelda's glowing expression when she returned to the pub carrying a huge bunch of flowers.

"Will those be for me?" Aisla had asked with a cheeky grin. "I think you should thank me for making you look so stylish."

"Oh, darling Aisla," Zelda had cried, "of course you can have the flowers! Whatever would I have done without you?" She embraced the astonished Scot.

Heidi put the card on the table and rested it against her Emma Bridgewater teapot. Bonky was mewing. Heidi opened a tin of food and spooned it into his dish. She glanced at her watch – she must hurry, the chemist shut soon and she needed to get there, she'd have her bath when she got back. Stewie would be back then too and she'd got lots to tell him...

35

Lenny was incarcerated. He stared glumly at the solid brick wall and winced as a plaintive voice from the next cell wailed out, "I'm dreamin' of a white Christmas..." Lenny closed his eyes and shook his head as he thought: I'd been dreamin' of a sunny one!

He sighed. It wasn't looking good.

A serious of outstanding charges from his last scam in Wiltshire had finally caught up with him and he'd no doubt that there would be a whole lot more from his dealings with the investors from the European School of Cookery. To top it all, the police had found his stash of cocaine, bundled up in a pair of pink speedos. They'd got plenty of charges to hold him on! It hadn't helped that he'd defrauded an investor in Wiltshire who had dealings with the press and, when alerted to Lenny's imminent arrest, had made sure a journalist was there to record it. His cover had been well and truly blown, the police must have been staking out the ports, knowing that Lenny's getaway would happen at any time.

Oh well, Lenny thought, as he yawned and lay back on the bench, perhaps a stretch wouldn't do him any harm, he could get lucky and work in the kitchens – a sure way to perfect his culinary techniques, after all – who knows? He may go to America when he got out, cookery was crazy out there and the American ladies would no doubt be accommodating. Lenny closed his eyes and folded his stubby hands on his paunch, then let himself drift off into what would inevitably be a very long sleep...

～

MICKEY SAT in a wing-backed chair by the window and stared out at the estuary. His leg was supported on a footstool and as he made himself comfortable, he adjusted the warm woollen blanket that covered his knees.

It was icy cold outside and a light frost covered the bushes and trees below. The winter sun danced off the water and sent shards of light spinning across the frozen garden. Fool's Landing was magical at this time of year.

Mickey reached for a glass on the table beside him and took a sip of malt whisky. He felt a glow as the silky liquid warmed his throat and aroused his taste buds with a hint of peat and heather. A fire roared in the grate and sent shadows dancing over the ancient walls of the cottage. Mickey's housekeeper had decorated a tall pine tree and it stood in one corner, while garlands of holly and ribbons hung in swags around the room. Pretty silver lights twinkled on the tree and reflected on the windows.

Mickey caught his reflection. He ran his fingers through his thick wavy hair and leaned forward to study his face. His skin was no longer pale, the bracing Irish winds had given colour to his cheeks and as he turned his head from side to side, he thought he looked quite handsome in his dark blue cashmere sweater and pale blue cotton shirt.

He couldn't wait to get the cast off his leg. With any luck he would be free of it in the New Year and soon back on his feet. Not that the injury seemed to have stinted the flow of his life. He was looking forward to Hilary's arrival, late tomorrow – she was here for Christmas and Mickey was delighted at the prospect. Finally, she would be under his roof, on his terms and in his home. He took another sip of his drink and sighed contentedly. It was time he tied the knot again and Hilary was definitely the woman he intended to have by his side for the next chapter of his life.

The latch on the bathroom door clicked and Mickey turned his head. A waft of heady, spicy perfume drifted across from the hallway as a bedroom door opened, then closed.

Mickey topped his glass up and smiled. Louella was a good sport and a man needed a few home comforts to help get him better. She'd be gone in the morning and no harm done. He held his glass up to the light and contemplated the rich amber nectar. Despite his accident, life wasn't too bad after all!

LONG TOM TUGGED on the lapels of an old quilted jacket and fastened it over the thick woollen scarf that wrapped snugly round his neck. It was cold in the garden at Flatterley Manor. He reached for a brightly coloured beanie hat from his pocket and pulled it over his head then tucked in his ponytail. He'd brought the hat back from the Caribbean, where someone had thrown it on stage at his final gig. He realised that he must look ridiculous in the bright reggae colours but didn't really care; there was no one but James to pass any comment.

He wandered over to the shed where the peacocks sheltered in the cold weather. They emerged expectantly as Long Tom approached. He reached into his pockets for some bread then broke it into small pieces as they milled around him and squawked with pleasure, dipping their heads and ruffling their magnificent feathers.

Long Tom smiled. It was good to be at Flatterley Manor.

He'd stopped over in London after his flight from Barbados. Pete had urged Long Tom to travel to Hertfordshire, where Pete and his family were spending Christmas, but Long Tom had felt the need to go back to Ireland.

Flatterley Manor suddenly felt like home. He'd abandoned plans of looking for a property in the Home Counties as soon as he'd heard that Lenny had done a runner, it was no surprise and Long Tom was quietly pleased that the cookery school wasn't going to happen. It was time to spend a bit of money on the old place.

He walked over to the lake, with the peacocks trailing his wake, and decided that he'd make a start here and have the water dredged and the banks repaired, then, no doubt, stock it with fish.

Long Tom felt at peace as he wandered around his property. The ground was frozen and firm underfoot; quite a contrast from the warmth and humidity he'd recently left behind. The last concert in Barbados had been another success and the arena at the Old Jamm Inn had pounded and vibrated with two thousand ecstatic fans cheering him on. He was back in business and next year would tour Europe as planned.

Long Tom wondered what Hilary was doing.

He thought that she was probably finishing up at work and preparing for her trip to Ireland, to stay with Mickey. He'd noticed coloured lights strung through the trees at Fool's Landing as he'd been driven past on his journey from the airport. Long Tom thought that Mickey was making a big effort and no doubt the cottage was decked out in a similar fashion.

He turned and stared up at the house. A Christmas tree stood in the bay window of the music room, and Long Tom noticed James moving around gracefully as he turned on table lamps and illuminated lanterns on the tree. The light cast dancing shadows on the frozen lawn and James became a mysterious silhouette as he readied the house for the evening ahead. Long Tom would have a solitary dinner before settling down in front of a roaring log fire, with a peppermint tea to comfort him. He might watch a movie.

He reached into his pockets and found a few raisins; they were sticky and bunched together, having been there for some time. Long Tom pulled the raisins apart then crouched down and held out his hand. The peacocks sidled over and gently took the proffered fruit, a favoured treat. They brayed with delight and fanned their feathers in a grand gesture. He smiled. Life should be simple – it was the small pleasures that counted. As he stood up and thrust his hands back into his pockets, he nodded to himself in affirmation. He'd come a hell of a long way in recent times and had a strange feeling that he'd soon come full circle. He remembered Jimmy's words, on the deck at the Old Jamm Inn: "The time to be happy is now, let the universe take care of the how…"

Long Tom shrugged and braced himself against the cold and, as daylight faded into dusk, he wandered back through the garden to the warmth of Flatterley Manor.

~

Zelda sat beside Gary in his catering truck as they rattled down the busy motorway. They held hands as Gary drove.

"Warm enough?" Gary asked, and fiddled around with the heating controls. An icy blast shot out of the vents, chilling their feet. Zelda giggled and tucked her Ugg boots up on the seat and wriggled her toes in the warm furry lining. She smiled happily to herself. They were making good time on their journey south, and with any luck they'd be back in London in plenty of time for Bob's Christmas soirée.

Zelda thought about the recent scene with Harry, when she'd broken the news. Madeleine, unfortunately, had chosen that moment to visit and promptly fainted when she realised that Zelda had broken off her engagement. Harry had waved a bottle of smelling salts under Madeleine's quivering nose and as she came round, stood back while she hurled insults at her daughter.

"I'll be the laughing stock of the Hurlingham Club!" Madeleine yelled. She gripped a chair and motioned for Harry to guide her rake-thin, fragile body safely into a sitting position. "Whatever will everyone say?"

"They might say that I'm a brave girl for facing up to the truth, so that Harry has a chance to find someone who really loves him and will make him very happy." Zelda gave Harry a wistful smile and looked imploringly at her mother.

But Madeleine ignored her daughter and lit a cigarette, then continued to rant and rave.

Zelda hadn't mentioned her relationship with Gary and knew that it was unfair not to bring the matter up. She tentatively began to explain that she'd met someone else, but before she'd time to finish, she reeled backwards from the hysterical outpouring of venom that Madeleine had summoned up.

"A caterer?" Madeleine hissed. "He drives a van and has a mobile catering company? What sort of life is that? How on earth do you expect him to support you?"

Madeleine droned on but Zelda ignored her. She knew that Gary's company had a very healthy turnover and, combined with her own earnings and her fee from Zelda and The Zimmers, they had more than enough to support themselves comfortably.

"A caterer!" Madeleine repeated. "You'll get even fatter!" She began to swoon again.

"I say, old girl, you could have aimed a bit higher," Harry said to Zelda. He looked miserable as he thrust his hands in the pockets of his wheat-coloured chords and stomped around the room. "A man has his pride, you know…"

Zelda sighed. Had she gone off with a wealthy city banker, she'd no doubt that Harry's ego would be intact and Madeleine would bless the union and immediately transfer the names on the church bands and invitations. But a caterer…!

Zelda stared out of the window as signs for the Borders, Carlisle and then Kendal, Lancaster and Preston receded behind them. She snuggled closer to Gary and remembered her earlier call to her father. Martin had taken the news calmly and offered them space in the Chipping Hodbury house, whilst they found their feet. Brigitta had obviously softened the matter, ahead of Zelda's call.

Harry had headed off in a frightful huff, to drown his sorrows at his parents' home, where he was staying for Christmas. Zelda knew he'd get over it quickly. He'd already booked flights for a skiing holiday in Courchevel for the New Year where, Zelda was sure, he'd be rubbing shoulders with most of the Royal Borough's upwardly young things, and in no time would hook an Anouska or Peridita to take his mind off his broken engagement.

"Shall we stop for a coffee?" Gary asked. "There's plenty of time." He pulled into the service area and leapt out of the truck to help Zelda. As he reached into the cab he tucked the fur hood of his Parka firmly round Zelda's chin. She wore the warm old jacket over several layers of t-shirts and a sweater.

"Hardly a designer number..." Gary put his arm around her shoulders as they strode past a coach party of shoppers on a pit-stop from the Trafford Centre in Manchester.

"I love it." Zelda shoved her mitten covered hands deep into the pockets of the Parka and smiled up at Gary.

"And I love you," he said and kissed her fondly on the forehead, then guided her across the foyer into the warmth of a Starbucks café.

∽

HILARY CHECKED HER BAGS. On one side of her bedroom there was an assortment of festive carrier bags, containing Christmas gifts for everyone at the office, whilst the other side of the room contained a suitcase alongside a large wicker hamper of luxurious Christmas fare, from Harrods, and more carrier bags. She stooped down to gather the gifts to take to Bob's soirée and tucked them neatly into two leather tote bags. The other bags were travelling with her to Ireland the next day.

Hilary walked through to her lounge. She'd decorated the flat with tasteful Christmas arrangements, despite the fact that she'd be away for the most of the holiday. Hilary loved Christmas. It was such a special time of year and with work out of the way for a while, everyone seemed to be happy and full of good cheer. She poured herself and gin and tonic and ran her fingers over a silver cigarette box – she hadn't succumbed, despite a few cravings and hoped that her battle with nicotine was won. Perhaps it would be a daily battle? Was that how it was for Long Tom with his addictive history? Hilary sipped her drink.

She was surprised that she was thinking about him. He'd never returned her calls and seemed to have disappeared from her life. His single had gone to number one in the charts and he looked set for success – she'd read that he was working on a new album and would be touring Europe next year. Hilary was pleased that he was doing well, the man she remembered from the garden and her time at Flatterley Manor had obviously come a long way. She sighed and shook her head. She must put him out of her mind; nothing was going to spoil her Christmas!

Hilary finished her drink and walked through to the hallway where she stopped and checked her reflection in the large gilt mirror. She wore her fringed, flapper-style cocktail dress with the long, 1920s' bead necklace, and reached for her thick wool swing coat with a leopard print collar that lay on a chair. Her car would be outside at any moment.

Hilary pouted and applied a dark red lipstick. Her hair was pulled back into a pleat and fastened with a brass-hinged tortoiseshell comb and she tucked a few loose strands into place. She was looking forward to Bob's soirée and to the time that lay ahead. It would be wonderful to unwind and relax in Ireland and forget about the office for a few days. Mickey had told her that Christmas lunch was all taken care of and he'd had a turkey sent over from the Romney's Gold range which was large enough to feed the whole of Kindale. Hilary imagined that there was a very good chance that the whole of Kindale would, at some point, appear – Mickey certainly loved to party and entertain. She smiled fondly as she remembered the Gourmet Food Festival and the characters she'd met. She never imagined that she'd be returning to Kindale, and so soon! It would be fun… Hilary told herself as the bell rang and her driver announced that he was outside. She fastened her coat and gathered her bags, and with a last look around in case she'd forgotten anything, Hilary carefully let herself out of the flat and ran down the stairs to the waiting car.

36

"Lights, camera, action!" Bob clapped his hands together and pressed a switch. He held up his camera and began to film. Anthony stood by an enormous Christmas tree as scores of tiny coloured lanterns lit up the room.

"It's like Santa's grotto," Bob exclaimed.

"Ho, ho, ho!" Anthony chortled. He wore a false white beard and red Santa suit, the wide leather belt strained across paunch.

"Darling, you look marvellous, Lottie will think you're real." Bob moved round the room, holding the camera steady as he recorded their preparations for the Christmas soirée.

"As long as she doesn't sit on my knee…" Anthony puffed from beneath the tickly beard. His suit was tight and he doubted that he'd be able to sit down.

Bob wandered around the room. He wore a short-sleeved kaftan in deep red silk and velvet slippers with gold embroidery. His arms were covered in an assortment of bracelets and plaited leather straps and his prayer beads hung loosely round his neck. The kaftan billowed as he moved across the room to a long table that ran the length of one wall, laden with food and drink. Red and white poinsettias decorated the table and Bob had scattered walnuts, chestnuts and star anise amongst bows of tartan ribbon over the starched linen cloth. Garlands of pine cones and red and gold baubles were hung around the room and cinnamon scented candles gave a festive atmosphere.

"Is your mulled wine ready, Santa?" Bob asked and placed his camera on the mantelpiece, behind a row of candles and cards.

"Warm, willing and about to cheer," Anthony replied and stirred his concoction in a vast silver tureen. He ladled the ruby red liquid into two glasses and handed one to Bob.

"Cheers!" they said in unison.

"Lovely and spicy." Bob grinned and licked his lips. "To us!"

"Happy Christmas, dear heart," Anthony replied. He tugged at the elastic on his beard and took a drink.

The doorbell rang.

"Oh, how exciting!" Bob said and placed his glass on the table. He clapped his hands together and said excitedly, "Christmas is about to begin!" He ran to open the door but stopped as he reached the hallway. He could hear singing from the corridor outside.

"Last Christmas I baked you a cake, but the very next day, you gave it away..."

Bob threw the door open and flung his arms out.

Lottie held the Santa chef statue in her arms and grinned from under the hood of a white fur cape as she joined in the chorus.

"Darling!" Bob cried and pulled her into the flat.

"I didn't have anyone to bring, so thought I'd bring Santa," Lottie said. She placed the gyrating toy on the hall table and slipped out of her cape. "But I can see you've already got one..."

Anthony appeared with a glass of mulled wine in one hand and began to sing along, wiggling his hips in time with singing Santa, and as the toy reached the chorus again, they all joined in.

The doorbell rang.

"Let the party begin!" Bob rushed forward to welcome more guests while Anthony guided Lottie to the lounge, where he poured them both a large glass of mulled wine.

"Love the threads!" Bob cried out to Hilary above the noise, as they danced to a selection of Christmas pop tunes under strobes of blue and orange light from a disco ball that hung in the centre of the room. "Reminds me of Ireland!" He took her hand and spun her around. Hilary laughed and wriggled her hips sending the fringed tassels into a frenzied whirl in the dimly lit room. Bob raised his arms in the air and tried to emulate her movements.

"Steady, dear, we don't want you displacing your ball and socket," Anthony called out as he shimmied past with Lottie. Lottie was dressed as an elf and wore red and green striped tights with a belted tunic and pixie boots.

"Nice to see Santa's got a little helper!" Bob retorted, pulling a face while Anthony tweaked his beard to one side and blew Bob a kiss.

The crowded party was in full swing. Bob and Anthony's friends mingled happily with the staff from Hargreaves Promotions and the lounge hummed with an animated flow of conversation. Martin and Brigitta arrived and shed their heavy outer layers in the hallway, then joined Heidi and Stewie at the buffet table, where a varied selection of drinks was laid out. They accepted glasses of mulled wine and as they thawed, they joined in a conversation with Prunella, who'd appeared, much to everyone's amazement, in a sober state with the Vice President of PAP on her arm.

Roger Romney carved an enormous roast turkey and told an animated audience that, following Mickey's endorsement, sales of the Romney Gold range had beaten all records for the time of year and he was looking forward to working with Mickey on Easter promotions, just as soon as Mickey was well enough. Craig Kelly chatted to Zelda about a new product – a remodelled steamer to cook healthy food; he hoped that she'd endorse it. The investors had been told that most of their money had been recovered from the European Cookery School debacle and Lenny looked set for a long stretch in prison. Roger and Craig were philosophical about the experience and considered their minor loss a small price to pay for the introduction to Hargreaves Promotions, and the increased turnover for their businesses that was being generated by Mickey and Zelda's respective involvement.

"After all," Roger said as he lovingly layered thick slices of succulent white turkey breast onto a serving platter, "we had a damn good time in Kindale and I wouldn't have missed it for the world!"

"Hear! Hear!" Craig agreed and poured everyone another mulled wine. He handed a glass to Hilary as she joined them.

"I hear that the operations manager from Jet Set Air has kept hold of his job," Hilary said. "The airline had bumper profits this year and Lenny's unpaid flight can go down as a tax loss." Hilary took a sip of her drink and thought of the lovely Lear Jet that had taken them all to Ireland. She remembered her flight home from Cork too, with Long Tom. She stifled a sigh and thought that he'd no doubt be celebrating at many exclusive parties in London this Christmas. The morning's papers had carried a photo of him wearing a multi-coloured beanie hat, at a record signing at a Leicester Square store. No More War was now topping the charts in its revamped form and had created a whole new generation of fans.

Aisla munched her way through a box of chocolate brownies, thoughtfully provided by Gary and wrapped in a Christmas box tied up with a satin bow. She chatted to Heidi about The Zimmers and both hoped that the series would be re-commissioned.

As the room filled up, guests flowed into the kitchen and balcony that overlooked the gardens below, where a tall Christmas tree, complete with fairy lights, lit up the frost covered branches of surrounding trees and bushes.

"It's a great party, Bob," Hilary said as she looked around at the familiar faces.

"It will set us all up for Christmas," Bob replied. He leaned forward and whispered in Hilary's ear. "Are you looking forward to Ireland?"

Hilary considered the question. "I think so…"

"Oh, pleeese…" Bob shook his head. "It's high time you had a man in your life and it's not as if you've just met Mickey!"

Hilary was about to reply but stopped as Anthony clapped his hands and asked the revellers to be quiet for a few moments.

"Ladies and gentlemen," Anthony began, "and elves..." He glanced at Lottie and everyone smiled. "Bob and I have an announcement to make." He walked slowly across the room and took Bob's hands. Someone turned the music off and the crowded room became hushed. The bank of pretty candles on the mantelpiece flickered as the two men looked lovingly at each other.

"We'd like you all to join us on Easter Saturday, next year..." Anthony looked at Bob, "to celebrate our wedding!"

Several people cheered and everyone began to clap – the noise could be heard in the garden below as Bob and Anthony hugged each other and graciously accepted congratulations from the delighted guests.

Hilary held up her arms and joined in with the clapping, she wasn't surprised by the announcement. She'd thought for some weeks that the two men were destined to settle down together. She turned and squeezed through the crowd then made her way to the Christmas tree, where she leaned down and picked up a long package that she'd placed there earlier.

"I think it might be an appropriate time to give you your Christmas present, Bob," she said.

"Oh my." Bob held his hands to his face. Anthony urged him forward and Bob took the gift that Hilary held out. "Gosh, it's heavy!" he exclaimed and began to remove the festive paper.

A long plaque appeared. The background was painted glossy black. The plaque had a narrow gold border and in large letters across the front read:

Hargreaves & Puddicombe Promotions

Bob gasped. Anthony's eyes were wide as he nudged his partner and urged him to say something.

"Oh, Hilary..." Bob faltered. "Does this mean...?"

Hilary held out her hand. "Congratulations – partner."

Hilary beamed as Bob shoved the sign into Anthony's arms and rushed forward to grab her hand.

A cheer went up.

"The paperwork is with our solicitor and will be ready for your signature in the New Year," Hilary told Bob. "It's just my way of saying thank you to the most loyal and kind person I've ever had the pleasure of working with." Hilary held Bob's hand. "I know we'll make a great team."

"Oh, I don't know what to say!" Bob's eyes were misty. "This is the best Christmas ever..." He hugged Hilary. "The business will grow and I promise I won't let you down. I'll be your eyes and ears and heart and soul and we'll have clients and chefs beating the door down to be on our books."

"Just be yourself, Bob," Hilary said softly. "You've always done a great job and you're a wonderful friend – you deserve to be a partner in the business." They stared at each other then embraced, while everyone milled round to offer congratulations.

"Erm..." a quiet voice tentatively called out. Zelda coughed and stepped forward. "I wonder if I might possibly be a pain and take a moment of your time to announce something too?" She'd removed Gary's Parka and was still dressed in jeans and t-shirt with a sweater draped over her shoulders, and as she grabbed Gary's hand, she led him to the centre of the room.

Bob flapped his hands and urged everyone to be quiet.

"Gary and I just want to let you all know," Zelda turned and stared lovingly at Gary, "that we got married at Gretna Green yesterday..."

Bob swooned and muttered that he wasn't sure if he could take any more announcements, but supported by Anthony, he moved forward to be the first to congratulate the ecstatic couple. Martin, who already knew about his daughter's nuptials, called for a toast.

"To my beautiful daughter," Martin began, "for having the courage and bravery to be true to herself." He raised his glass. "I wish you a life filled with love and happiness and know that Gary will make a splendid son-in-law."

"To Gary and Zelda!" everyone cried out.

Zelda held up her left hand. She wore a band of tiny coloured candies on her fourth finger.

"No!" Bob gasped. "Don't tell me the two carats have gone back to Hooray Harry and been traded in for an edible engagement ring..."

"Wow!" Lottie said and shook her head. "That's really cool."

"I wonder if we might have a few words..." Heidi had taken Stewie's arm and gripped his sleeve.

The room became silent again as everyone held their breath. Stewie coughed nervously and Bob called out that he simply had to hurry along with his announcement, Bob's nerves were shattered!

"Heidi and I," Stewie turned to Heidi and winked, "are thrilled to tell you all that we are expecting a baby in the spring."

"Oh, my goodness..." Hilary ran forward to throw her arms around Heidi. "What wonderful news!" She hugged them both.

"We'd like you to be godmother..." Heidi hesitated and looked anxiously at Hilary.

Hilary felt tears prick at the corner of her eyes. She was overwhelmed and nodded, not trusting herself to speak.

"I expect you'll both have 'him' or 'her' trained up by the time they are toddling," Anthony said to Bob and Hilary, then raised his glass. "To our brand new agent and the delighted parents!"

Guests moved forward to shake Gary's hand and congratulate Heidi, and as Bob and Anthony stood back, Bob nudged Anthony's arm,

"Brace yourself," Bob whispered. "The Queen of PAP looks set to join in the fun!" He nodded towards Prunella, who'd taken the VP's arm and moved forward too.

"We'd like to have your attention for a couple of moments," the VP said. Prunella gazed out from under her heavy fringe and fluttered her coal-black eyelashes.

"Oh Lord, let's hope Baby Jane's not pregnant too..." Bob whispered and gripped Anthony's arm.

"I just want to tell you folks that this little lady," the VP held Prunella's arm and stared lovingly down, "has not only helped make my business a market leader..." he said proudly, "but has done me the greatest honour by consenting to be my wife!"

"Oh Lord!" Bob staggered. "He wants to make an honest woman of her!"

"Hip, hip, hooray!" someone called out.

"Gobble, gobble!" Roger shouted above the cheers.

"This calls for champagne!" Anthony said, and hurried towards the kitchen.

"I don't think I can take any more surprises," Bob gripped Hilary's arm, "my knees are buckling..." He passed a hand across his forehead in a theatrical gesture.

"What an absolutely wonderful Christmas," Hilary said as she guided Bob to a chair and kissed him fondly on the cheek. "I'm going to help Anthony."

Hilary eased herself through the throng and caught up with Anthony in the kitchen. Lottie was reaching for more glasses from a tall cupboard ready for Anthony to fill with champagne.

Lottie turned as Hilary went to assist. She pulled at her tunic and fiddled with several bells that hung from the hem. "Can I have a promotion or something too?" Lottie asked as she watched Hilary place the full glasses on a tray. "Everyone seems to getting something really special for Christmas..."

"Absolutely, Lottie." Hilary said. She looked Lottie in the eye. "From January the first, you are officially Head of Reception for Hargreaves & Puddicombe Promotions. And I'll make sure you get a pay rise in the New Year."

Lottie began to jump up and down, her bells jingling and her curls bouncing. Anthony deftly removed the tray.

"More celebrations?" Bob asked. He scooped up a glass of champagne.

"Hilary's made me Head of Reception!" Lottie squealed and continued to race around the kitchen.

Bob rolled his eyes heavenward and as he took a large swig of his champagne. He glanced at Hilary. She winked back and grinned.

"Don't worry. From the New Year, all decisions will be made

together – with your full input," Hilary said.

"Good job you slid this one in now…" Bob shook his head and raised his glass for a top up. "Happy Christmas, Lottie, dear!"

～

Hilary wandered out onto the balcony. It was a wonderful party and she was overwhelmed and excited by everyone's news. She was to be a godmother too! Imagine having a precious child as part of her life; what an amazing start to next year.

She heard the distant strains of carol singers in the adjacent road and hummed gently as she leaned on the cold iron railings and stared out over the frozen gardens. She realised that she was humming the melody from No More War. She needed to get the song and Long Tom out of her mind! Long Tom had clearly moved on and this time tomorrow, she'd be with Mickey at Fool's Landing. They'd probably be sitting by the fire, staring into the flames as they enjoyed a glass of wine. Hilary knew that Mickey would have made plans for her time in Ireland and wondered how they would spend their days. It was going to be a very different Christmas.

She thought about the cashmere sweaters that she'd bought for Mickey and hoped that he'd like his Christmas gifts. She'd found a lovely antique fountain pen in a shop in Bond Street; it was twenty-two carat gold with a wide nib and was beautifully and discreetly engraved: From Hilary, with love. He may like to use it for book signings. She hoped that he'd like the hamper too, it contained some wonderful and unusual festive concoctions from Harrods food hall, and Hilary had been assured by the manager that it was a perfect gift for a chef.

Hilary rubbed her bare arms and moved away from the railings. She stared up at the stars as the tail lights from a plane blinked in the coal-black sky. Bob had been thrilled by her decision to make him a partner in the business, and Hilary was delighted. Onwards and upwards! she thought to herself, and with a final glance at the sky that she'd be crossing tomorrow, she went back in to the party.

37

Christmas Eve was one of the busiest days of the year at Heathrow airport and Hilary waited patiently in line as she checked in for her flight. Families with little ones stood in adjacent queues. Hilary marvelled at the adults' patience as the children impatiently pulled and tugged at their parents' arms and clothing, and ran around in circles. Hilary wondered what sex Heidi's baby would be. She looked forward to spoiling it and thought happily of future forays to her favourite vintage shops to search out the finest babywear.

Hilary smiled at the check-in girl as she placed her cases on the conveyor belt. They were way over the weight limit but Hilary didn't mind accepting the additional charges. She'd packed carefully and amply in preparation for any wild jaunts that Mickey might spring on her.

The flight was on time and as she began her journey to Ireland, she sat back and sipped a gin and tonic. It was her favourite – Bombay Sapphire – and Hilary stroked the miniature blue bottle fondly. The flight was noisy, most passengers were returning home to their loved ones for the holidays and were boisterous and high spirited, keeping the cabin staff busy with bar orders throughout the flight. The captain announced that they were about to begin their descent into Cork and if passengers chose to look out of the window on the left-hand side, they would have a clear view of the coastline. Hilary stared down at the dark grey waters below, where spumes of white surf bounced across waves that rolled confidently towards the shore. She strained to recognise hamlets and towns and finally found the estuary leading to Kindale. Somewhere along that lovely stretch, Mickey's boat bobbed about in the water. Hilary wondered if they would go out on it. She'd heard about Mickey's notorious boat trips, where he packed the galley with food and drink, and invited anyone who happened to be in the vicinity at the time.

The plane touched down smoothly, to a round of applause from the jovial passengers. Hilary found her cases with ease and as she pushed her trolley out to the taxi rank she buttoned her fur coat tightly. The weather felt at least ten degrees colder than London and Hilary shivered. She'd told Mickey that she would find her own way to Fool's Landing, as he was unable to drive and taxis were plentiful, it was only a twenty minute ride, after all.

She strolled across to join a queue, it was manically busy and she hoped that she wouldn't have to wait long. A vehicle pulled up a few feet away and a tall, shapely woman stepped out. Strands of long blonde hair tumbled out of the hood of her ski jacket and obscured her face as she placed an overnight bag on the ground beside her and dug into a purse, then handed the driver a note.

"Keep the change!" Hilary heard the blonde call out. The woman picked up her bag and then turned and headed toward the departure section of the airport. A waft of heady, spicy perfume drifted across on the icy cold breeze, the scent was unmistakable. As Hilary watched the woman walk away, she tried to remember where she'd smelt it before.

The taxi that had brought the blonde to the airport pulled up alongside Hilary. The driver wound down the passenger window and called out, "Will you be wantin' a ride?"

"Oh, yes. Thank you." Hilary was deep in thought as the driver stowed her numerous bags then settled his passenger comfortably into the back seat.

"Where are we off too?" he asked and looked at Hilary through the rear-view mirror.

"Do you know Fool's Landing?" Hilary asked.

The driver grinned and shook his head. "I most certainly do! Busy place!" He winked at Hilary then turned back to the wheel and starting the engine, pulled slowly away.

The journey was uneventful. The taxi driver made polite conversation; he seemed to know Mickey and repeatedly said what a fine fellow he was, and how pleased the local residents were to have Mickey back in the area. The countryside slipped by and Hilary gazed out of the windows at hills and fields that somehow felt familiar. They soon rounded the bend where Fool's Landing lay and the driver brought the car gently to a halt by the side of the road at the entrance of the cottage grounds. He leapt out and began to unload the bags. Hilary smelt a comforting aroma of sweet burning wood and glanced up at puffs of hazy ash smoke as it belched out of the cottage chimney.

The light was fading and the sun slowly setting over the estuary. Brightly lit lanterns were strung throughout the trees and twinkled on the frost covered branches. The air was still. Hilary watched the driver place the hamper and carrier bag containing Mickey's gifts, by the gate. He reached into the car for her suitcases.

Hilary heard her feet crunch over the frozen gravel and felt tense as she walked towards the cottage. A sudden vision of the woman at the airport swept across her mind.

Hilary stopped abruptly. She'd remembered where she'd smelt the perfume before.

Louella Kidd.

Hilary closed her eyes and let her head fall back. She smiled to herself and took a deep breath, then turned to the driver.

"Leave those things by the gate but put the luggage back in, please."

She took a pair of leather gloves out of her pocket and slowly pulled them over her fingers. She seemed deep in thought as she smoothed the soft hide over her cold hands.

"Will you be wantin' another destination?" the driver asked as he closed the boot of the car.

"Yes, I think I will," Hilary replied and sat down on the back seat. The driver shook his head and closed her door, then jumped back in the car and started the engine.

∿

MICKEY WAS asleep in front of the log fire. His housekeeper had recently left; having given the cottage a final clean and stocked-up for Christmas. Everywhere looked cosy and inviting. Mickey stirred and glanced at this watch. A car had pulled up and he realised that it was probably Hilary's taxi. She was due at any time.

He rubbed his hands together, then smoothed his hair and reached for his walking aid. Easing himself off the sofa, Mickey hopped across the room and out to the kitchen. He unlocked the stable door and leaned out into the cold evening air as he waited for Hilary to appear through the gate and walk towards him.

Several minutes ticked by. He heard the sound of tyres on the gravel beyond the gate and assumed that the taxi had pulled away. He smiled expectantly, then, opening the door fully, decided to go and meet Hilary. He struggled along the decking, expecting to see her at any moment. When he reached the end, he pulled an iron bolt and opened the gate towards him. He stared out and almost fell over a large hamper, and carrier bag filled with Christmas presents.

Mickey was puzzled.

"Hilary?" he called out, expecting her to appear at any moment. "Hilary, where are you?" he shouted into the deserted road. "Happy Christmas, darling!"

∿

HILARY SAT in the taxi in silence. The driver attempted conversation but receiving no reply, shook his head and made his way along the coastal road to Kindale. Night had closed in and the only light came from the car's headlights as they illuminated the tall hedgerows and narrow lanes. As the taxi headed down the incline that led to Kindale, Hilary spoke.

"Stop, please," she said. "Could you take this turning on the right."

The driver pulled off the main road and soon came to an electronic gate. He spoke into a speaker, placed on a post.

"I've a guest, I think…" he said, and watched the gate slowly swing open. He inched the car forward as he checked out his surroundings, then moved towards the silhouette of a large house, partially hidden by trees and thick vegetation.

"You can stop here," Hilary said, as they pulled up by the main door. She handed him two twenty-euro notes and told him to keep the change. His eyes lit up; he'd had a good evening! He gathered her bags and placed them on the steps.

"Will you be all right?" he asked.

"Yes, of course." Hilary smiled. The car disappeared into the dark of the night and gates closed behind it.

In truth, Hilary didn't have a clue whether she would be all right or not and her heart began to beat wildly. Her palms felt clammy and she shrugged off her gloves and put them in her pocket.

She turned to face the house and slowly climbed the steps. The pulse in her temple was pounding and she crossed her fingers as she reached out to press the brass bell. But the door opened ahead of her and a figure stepped out into the night.

"Good evening, Miss Hargreaves," James said. "What a great pleasure to see you again." He stood back and ushered her into the hallway. "Shall I take your coat?"

"Oh, okay…" Hilary faltered and loosened her coat.

"Mr Hendry is in the music room," James said. "Would you care to follow me?"

Hilary walked behind James across the parquet wood flooring. A tall decorated tree stood by the wide staircase and a roaring fire glowed in an Adam-style fireplace. The flames cast eerie shadows that danced over portraits of ancient occupants, long gone, who stared menacingly down at Hilary as she passed. The old house was as silent as the night outside, and her footsteps clicked intrusively as she traced James's soft steps along the corridor leading to the music room.

James stopped. He put his hand out to open the door and looked enquiringly at Hilary's anxious face.

"I'll leave you now," James said softly. He smiled and bowed his head then retreated into the shadows.

Hilary thought that she was going to be sick. Her stomach was doing somersaults and she wondered what on earth she was doing, turning up at Long Tom's home on Christmas Eve! Heaven knows what she would walk in to...

She reached for the door handle and slowly turned the knob, then gently began to push open the heavy oak door.

The most glorious sound of piano music greeted her. Hilary eyes were like saucers as she tentatively stepped into the room to witness a sight she never thought she'd see.

Long Tom sat at the piano. He leaned forward and moved his fingers deftly over the keys. His eyes were closed and he smiled as he softly sang along to the wonderful melody that filled the room. The perfect acoustics cast a spell over Hilary and she stood very still as the door closed gently behind her.

Long Tom seemed to be in a world of his own. His skin glowed and he looked calm, confident and handsome as he manipulated the keys and sang.

Hilary was rooted to the spot. It seemed as though her heart was being tugged out of her chest and pulled fiercely towards the man before her. She gripped her hands into a fist by her sides; her knuckles were white and she felt her nails bite into the skin. How she longed to run to him and wrap her arms around him! But she'd not heard from him for ages and her mind was in turmoil and she felt sure he'd turn her away.

Long Tom sang softly, he paused and played several bars before building to the chorus of his song...

You don't need a million dollars
To wake up on a sun filled morning
To feel my arms around you
You're here,
Right here, right now, with me ...

He turned to look at her and Hilary thought her heart would explode.

Long Tom stopped playing and stood up, then walked towards her. His hair was loose and fell onto the shoulders of his black t-shirt. He held out his arms and drew her into them.

"Happy Christmas, babe," he said, and kissed the top of her head.

Hilary looked up and searched his face. He smiled and softly stroked her cheek.

"I didn't hear from you..." she said.

"Blame Mickey Lloyd," Long Tom replied.

"But..."

Long Tom placed a finger on her lips and silenced her.

"A little while ago, someone told me 'the time to be happy is now, let the universe take care of the how'..." he said. He wrapped his arms around Hilary's body and held her tightly. "You feel so good." He nuzzled into her hair.

Hilary thought that an orchestra had entered the room and begun to play, she was so overcome with emotion and her legs felt weak as she gripped Long Tom for support.

He kissed her. It was long and passionate and filled with so much love that Hilary hoped it would never end.

All the nonsense with Mickey subsided and fell away. He was a great fellow but Hilary knew that she'd only been trying to rekindle a young girl's summer romance. Mickey would never change. As she felt the strength of the man in her arms she knew that she'd come home.

This was where she belonged.

She thought about her clients and her world in London and visualised the young hopefuls of the future, as they sat in Bob's office and he asked, 'So, you want to be a celebrity...Chef?'

It was another world, but one that could be combined with the one that lay before her.

Long Tom smiled. His fingers reached for the clip on her hair and he watched the chestnut locks tumble onto her shoulders.

He kissed her again.

A sharp cry pierced the night from beyond the windows, where Christmas lights illuminated the garden. The screeching continued and Long Tom grinned.

"The peacocks approve," he said. "Will you marry me, Hilary?"

Hilary couldn't speak. She nodded and reached out to cover his face with kisses, then settled happily into his arms as he held her and began to sing:

"YOU'RE HERE,
    Right here,
    Right now,
    With me..."

THANK YOU

Thank you for reading this book.

If you enjoyed it, please take a moment to review
on Amazon and/or GoodReads
or send Caroline a comment via her website

www.carolinejamesauthor.co.uk

* * *

FURTHER READING

Coffee Tea The Gypsy & Me

Coffee Tea The Caribbean & Me
#1 Amazon Best-Seller

Jungle Rock

Caroline's books are stand-alone reads but you might enjoy Coffee Tea The Gypsy & Me together with Coffee Tea The Caribbean & Me

Coming soon...

The Best Boomerville Hotel

CAROLINE JAMES

Caroline James was born in Cheshire and wanted to be a writer from an early age. She trained, however, in the catering trade and worked and travelled both at home and abroad. Caroline has owned and run many related businesses and cookery is a passion alongside her writing, combining the two with her love of the hospitality industry and romantic fiction. She is a member of the Romantic Novelist's Association and has numerous short stories published and as Feature Editor, writes a regular column for a lifestyle magazine. Caroline can generally be found with her nose in a book and her hand in a box of chocolates and when not doing either, she likes to write, climb mountains and contemplate life.

Printed in Great Britain
by Amazon